BATTLESTAR

Book One of the StarFight Series

T. Jackson King

Other King Novels

Mother Warm (forthcoming), Defeat The Aliens (2016), Fight The Aliens (2016), First Contact (2015), Escape From Aliens (2015), Aliens Vs. Humans (2015), Freedom Vs. Aliens (2015), Humans Vs. Aliens (2015), Earth Vs. Aliens (2014), Genecode Illegal (2014), The Memory Singer (2014), Alien Assassin (2014), Anarchate Vigilante (2014), Galactic Vigilante (2013), Nebula Vigilante (2013), Speaker To Aliens (2013), Galactic Avatar (2013), Stellar Assassin (2013), Retread Shop (2012, 1988), Star Vigilante (2012), The Gaean Enchantment (2012), Little Brother's World (2010), Judgment Day And Other Dreams (2009), Ancestor's World (1996).

Dedication

To my wife Sue, my son Keith and my dad Thomas, thank you all for your active duty service in defense of America.

Acknowledgments

First thanks go to scholar John Alcock and his book *Animal Behavior, An Evolutionary Approach* (1979). Second thanks go to the scholar Edward O. Wilson, whose book *Sociobiology: The New Synthesis* has guided me in my efforts to explore a future where humanity encounters life from other stars.

BATTLESTAR

© 2016 T. Jackson King

This is a work of fiction. All the characters and events portrayed in this novel are either fictitious or are used fictitiously. All rights reserved. No part of this book may be used or reproduced in any manner whatsoever without written permission except for brief quotations for review purposes only.

Cover design by T. Jackson King; cover image by Luca Oleastri via Dreamstime license; back image, courtesy of Hubble Space Telescope

Second Edition
Published by T. Jackson King, Santa Fe, NM 87507
http://www.tjacksonking.com/
ISBN 10: 1-53318-222-7
ISBN 13: 978-1-53318-222-1
Printed in the United States of America

CHAPTER ONE

Being in the Star Navy was not something Jacob Renselaer had ever wished for ... or wanted ... or needed. But as the son of Earth's only five-star admiral, that was his destiny from birth. The orders fell on him like an avalanche. Read naval warfare histories. Learn NATO tactical brevity codes. Study the India-Pakistan nuke war. Attend Binghampton High School in New York. Then attend the Stellar Academy at Colorado Springs. He'd graduated, barely. And then, as a fresh ensign, his father had called in a favor. He'd gone into space as the personal ensign to Rear Admiral Cornelius Johanson, presently in command of the Battlestar *Lepanto*, BBG-5 and its battle group of sister starships. Which were now in orbit above the fourth planet of Kepler 22.

It was a status that the admiral had ordered after the fleet exited from Alcubierre space-time transit, some forty-three hours ago. They'd detected an alien satellite out at the edge of the system's magnetosphere, which lay 45 AU distant from the system's yellow sun. The sat's broadcast signals had been a mystery. The ship's AI failed to decipher them. Same for the Science Deck's algorithm twisters. What wasn't a mystery was the presence of a dozen alien ships in orbit above the system's fourth planet. The admiral had been super excited. This was humanity's first encounter with spacegoing aliens. They had headed in at one-tenth lightspeed. Upon arrival near planet four, the *Lepanto's* AI had reported a visual signal from the aliens. The visual showed a simple graphic of people exiting the Earth ships to meet aliens leaving their ships, for a spot on the planet's equator. The other ship captains, their XOs, the *Lepanto's* admiral, captain and XO, and some ensigns had gone downplanet to meet with the aliens.

Jacob didn't care. Dealing with aliens was not a task for ensigns like him. Instead, he was doing the job he'd been assigned as the admiral's ensign. Which was to make the man's personal quarters look clean and well-kept. He thought briefly of putting a pad from a nearby beaver-tail cactus under the sheet just where the admiral's butt would rest, but he passed. He'd seen the *Lepanto's* brig during the

Stellar Academy's boarding orientation. It was a dump and smelled of urine, shit, sweat and sour milk.

His small quarters at the far end of the Command Deck hallway were luxurious by comparison. Looking around at the private bedroom, which opened onto a conference room that was the only exit to the hallway, he wrinkled his nose at the hand-blown glass miniatures that lined one wall shelf. They were of Earth critters. Not one was a horse, like the one he'd ridden with his mother.

At least the wall wasn't filled with antique paper books, like his father's study in Binghampton. That was the place where the man spent most of his time, leastwise since the death of his Mom. The thought filled his heart with sorrow and his mind with her image.

She had been a middle-aged woman with curly brown hair, a narrow chin, perky nose and amber eyes that glowed every time she saw him. Her love had been the only thing that had kept him from OD'ing on crystal meth at Binghampton High School. But she'd died three years before he graduated, leaving Jacob and his father alone in the brick and stone colonial that occupied two acres on Binghampton's west side.

To escape his father's hectoring and put downs of his anthropology studies, he'd enrolled at the Stellar Academy. Where he'd learned ship systems, basic stellar astronomy, space battle tactics and formations, the reasons for the Weapons Deck and the details of Earth's seven star colonies. Most of it bored him, but he'd learned what he had to learn in order to graduate.

Unlike other cadets, he'd never made friends with his two roommates or anyone else at the academy. While there had been plenty of young women in his graduating class, he'd avoided them. Jacob's high school prom disaster had cured any thoughts of romance. His month on the *Lepanto* since leaving Earth had brought him a few friends, mostly guys except for Lori on the Science Deck and Daisy, the admiral's personal pilot. He'd briefly thought of asking Daisy to join him for Dance Night, a weekly event on the Habitation Deck. But he'd held back. He'd come to know her since she always transported the admiral from the *Lepanto* to another ship, or downplanet, as pilot of her Landing Craft Assault. He admired her piloting skills, a field in which he'd gotten miserable grades. Her looks were also fine. Trim, pleasantly curvy and with blue-black hair that was full of tight curls, he'd been tempted to go beyond routine banter. The fact she was a mixed race woman, the offspring of an Anglo dad and a Black mother from Chicago, meant nothing to him. Or to their friends. Only the Marine boarding team had acted as if her racial mix was an issue. Which was silly beyond belief, considering that forty percent of the ship's crew were female, they came from twenty nations and represented all the ethnicities of Earth, even though the ship was an official member of the American Star Navy.

Jacob left the bedroom behind, entered the conference room and turned left for the Food Alcove and the fridge that occupied one corner. It held twenty types of craft beer, six bottles of white wine, cheese, sausages, lunch meats, fresh greens and the drink he was looking for. Ice tea. He could drink that while on duty. He opened the fridge door, pulled out the ice tea dispenser, and poured the golden brown liquid into a tall crystal goblet. There was no plastic in the admiral's chambers, a fact he'd discovered upon first arriving to perform upkeep in the chambers. He lifted the goblet and sipped slowly.

"Jacob? You in there?" called a female voice over the hallway announcer.

Daisy. Why was she back on ship, rather than downplanet waiting for the admiral and the top brass to finish their alien talk-talks? He put down the goblet, turned to face the gray metal door that opened onto the central hallway of Command Deck, checked his Navy dress blue uniform with a quick glance, then spoke.

"I'm here. Door, admit Ensign Daisy Stewart."

A hiss sounded as the titanium metal door plate slid sideways into the room's wall. The hallway's yellow light shone softly on Daisy, who was dressed in NWU Type I blue and gray camos. She wore them even though she was an ensign with the rank of O-1, just like Jacob. She must have put them on for the downplanet landing. Putting aside his musings, he spoke.

"What's up? And why are you up here, rather than downplanet with the admiral?"

She stepped inside, her arms swinging easily in the one gee artificial gravity produced by the ship's gravity plates. Her brown eyes glanced around the room, then fixed on him. Her manner was one of impatience.

"He sent me back up an hour ago, right after we landed," she said, her soft mezzo-soprano voice reminding him of the first time he'd met her, while they were still in low Earth orbit. She frowned. "Have you heard anything from him? My tablet is silent. And I can't get any signal from him. Which worries me. Every tablet—"

"Sends a constant carrier pulse to every other tablet on ship or downplanet," he finished. Then regretted interrupting her as he saw her expression move to irritation. Then back to worry. "No, I haven't gotten any text or audio signal from him since he left." Jacob pulled his palm-sized tablet from his jacket pocket, thumbed it on, then stared as a blinking red dot filled the app icon that automatically linked him to the admiral's personal tablet. He looked up. "Mine can't link up with him either. Could the meeting site be beyond our line of sight?"

Patience showed on her dark brown face. "Jacob, every ship in the battle group launched spysats and comsats the moment we moved into geosync orbit. The tablet signals are automatically routed through the comsats whenever the subject is beyond line of sight. Like on the far side of a planet." She frowned. "And the equatorial meeting location is indeed on this planet's far side." Daisy pulled out her tablet, glanced at it, then looked up to him. "Ensign, something isn't right here. Call Captain Miglotti and XO Anderson on your tablet. See if their signals link through."

Jacob did that, ignoring the cool lavender scent of Daisy as she stepped closer, stopping just a meter from him. His quick thumbing produced two more red dots on comlink icons. "Nothing. Same failure to link." He looked up. "Only time I recall that happening was during a solar flare, when our academy cohort was on the sun-facing side of the Moon. We got under cover quickly at the nearby Moon buggy hangar. We didn't regain comlinks until fifteen minutes later."

Daisy, nearly as tall as Jacob, pursed her dark brown lips. "I've been trying to reach the admiral for the last thirty minutes. While I was getting the LCA refueled and set for relaunch from the ship's Hangar Four. While I would never interrupt the admiral in a big confab like this, I always recheck my tablet link with him whenever we are apart. Now, I can't. I'm worried. What do we do?"

He felt shock. Then understood why she had come to him. The other Command Deck ensigns had gone down with Captain Miglotti, XO Anderson and Admiral Johanson. While there were a lieutenant commander, a lieutenant and a lieutenant JG running other decks, he was the only Command Deck officer still on the *Lepanto*. Which theoretically put him in command of the Bridge, a place he'd visited just three times, even though it lay at the front end of Command Deck. Those visits had been in company with the admiral. Daisy, while an ensign like him, was not part of the Command Deck chain of command. He was. Crap.

"Let me call Osashi at Communications on the Bridge," he said hurriedly. "Surely he's heard from the admiral or the captain or the XO." He tapped the ear-shaped app icon for the ship's comlink station. "Osashi? Jacob here. Daisy and I can't reach the admiral on our tablets. She's concerned. So am I. Are you in contact with our ground party?" He thumbed on the speaker function and looked at Daisy.

"No," grumbled the elderly Japanese-American chief warrant officer. "We've been out of touch for the last forty minutes. Cruiser *Hampton Roads* says her spysat sensors report an electrical storm above the meeting site. Or something with lots of electrical turbulence. We're waiting for it to clear."

Jacob's heart began thumping fast. "We're coming up. Daisy and I."

"If you insist," the man grumbled. The green dot of his icon went white on Jacob's tablet.

He stored the tablet, stepped past Daisy and headed for the room's exit. "Door, open," he said, briefly glad that the voice-activated functions of the *Lepanto* still worked normally. Touching a sensor plate to open a hatch, a door or a chamber had gone obsolete in 2071, when voice recognition circuits had become the standard on all American Star Navy ships. That had been twenty years ago. Back then, no one had expected some geek at the CERN lab to discover the means to generate an Alcubierre space-time bubble. But that had happened. In 2073 Earth had gone from a fusion pulse-powered exploration of the Solar system to being able to reach other stars. Now, eighteen years later, humanity had seven star colonies and was exploring distant systems known to have planets. Like Kepler 22. He stepped into the hallway and turned right.

"Jacob," Daisy murmured from close behind him. "Have you seen the holograms of the aliens at the meeting?"

"Nope."

"I did. Also in person. They're weird critters."

He had twenty more meters to go before they reached the Bridge entry hatch. "How so?"

"Well, from what I saw from the pilot bubble of my LCA, they look like giant wasps. Mostly yellow with black and red stripes on their bodies," she said quickly. "They walk on four limbs, two at the rear and two in the middle, with the front limbs acting like arms. Their head and thorax segments are upright, kind of the way a horse's front end is upright."

His mind filled with images of yellow jackets and mud wasps. He'd seen both types building nests under the eaves of the old wooden barn that lay at the back of his parents' property. Two horses had been stabled there, until his Mom died. His father had quickly sold the horses, removing one more memory of his mother. It had led him to spend hours alone in the barn during high school. It was a quiet place in which to use his school tablet for homework and for writing papers. And to research anthropology. He'd long wondered why other people acted the way they did. The discovery of cultural anthropology in his early teens had revealed some answers to the questions that had bugged him ever since second grade. That was when the bullies had discovered him to be an easy target. The bullying had only stopped in ninth grade, when he'd used his newly learned judo and karate lessons to drop three bullies. The broken arms they'd suffered had gotten him suspended for a week and caused his parents to pay their hospital bills. He hadn't cared. After that, everyone left him alone. The way he'd been alone ever since understanding how different his family was, compared to corporate exec families or the political types in gated exurbs. Unlike the urban ghetto folks, he'd always had plenty to eat. And his own bed, versus the street. The invention of fusion reactors in 2043 had reduced worldwide poverty, thanks to mostly free power. But castes still existed. And class levels were official now. Often ruled over by the super rich, which his family was not. But military it was. A fact that always set him apart from fellow students.

"Interesting," he finally responded to Daisy. "Kind of explains why we are meeting them on planet four rather than three."

He stopped before the eight foot high hatch that gave access to the Bridge. She stopped close behind him.

"How so? I just assumed since this world is Earth-warm with oceans and oxy-nitro air, that the aliens chose—"

"Gravity," he interrupted, recalling a high school biology lesson. "Large insects in Earth's ancient past happened only when there was lots of humidity and the oxygen level in the air was way higher than now. Some fossil insects reached two feet in length. To get bigger, the gravity has to be lower. Like the half gee on planet four. Planet three is close to two gees. That's because of their chitin-based limbs and exoskeletons," he said. "Hatch, open."

"Opening for Command Deck Ensign Jacob Renselaer," the hatch's response circuit replied. He put aside the reminder that only crew and officers registered as Command Deck personnel could enter their deck. It was standard on all Star Navy ships as a guard against invading boarding teams. Daisy had been added due to her piloting work for the admiral.

The hatch swung out toward him, then came to a stop in a whirring of gears. Bright yellow light shone from within the large circular room that lay at the front of the *Lepanto*, deep below its armored hull. He stepped through the open hatch and headed for the front half-circle of function posts. Automatically he inventoried those present. Women and men sat before the Power, Tactical, Weapons, Engines, Navigation, Communications, Gravity, Life Support and Science posts. Osashi was in the middle of the arc, facing the curving front wallscreen. Which was filled with the blue, green and purple colors of the planet below. One of the world's four continents lay below their geosynchronous orbit. The green of jungles, the blue of lakes and the purple of three mountain ranges showed. Ignoring the curious looks he got from half the folks on duty, he headed for Osashi. To get there he had to pass by the central elevated pedestal that contained three heavily padded seats with armrests that sparkled with embedded control patches and studs. The two lower seats were where the captain and XO always sat. Behind them was the admiral's seat, elevated slightly so anyone sitting there could look past the two in front. He stopped just behind the Communications chief. Who was staring at a holo that floated in front of his control pillar. The holo showed the far side of the planet as seen by the electro-optical scope on board the *Hampton Roads'* spysat. A purple-black thunderstorm filled the middle of the holo.

"Osashi, what does the phased array millimeter radar say about the landscape under that storm?" he asked as he peered at the thunderstorm that covered the mountain meadow that was the alien-chosen meeting place.

"Oh!" the man said as he jumped, clearly startled by Jacob's arrival. The fifty-year-old chief warrant officer swiveled his function seat around to look at him and Daisy. The man wore an NWU woodland camo uniform of shirt, pants and cap with visor. Ribbons filled the area above his left pocket, while his right pocket name tag read *A. Osashi*. Thin black eyebrows lifted.

"As I said . . . we're waiting for the storm below to clear," the man said, his tone exaggerated in its patience. "No need to radar ping them below. Might upset the aliens."

Jacob's peripheral vision told him all the people on the Bridge were now looking his way to see what the admiral's clean-up boy did when faced with defiance by a warrant officer. Who held the pay rank of CWO5, the last level before ensign. Daisy looked surprised by the man's attitude.

"Do as I just suggested. That's an order," Jacob said firmly, recalling his father's way of giving him orders morning, noon and night. "Or ask Tactical to work the spysat if you don't know how to change sensor settings."

The man's pale white lips opened in surprise, then muscles tightened in his face. "How dare you question—"

"This grants me the authority," he said, reaching up to tap the single brown bar of an ensign that filled the point of his collar. "I am the only Command Deck officer now present on the Bridge. Perform your duty."

Osashi was just five years short of full retirement. Perhaps the memory of that prompted the change in his manner. Which went from 'irritated by a child' to 'obeying as ordered'. He swiveled his padded seat around to face his control pillar. The man reached out both hands and tapped in a sequence on the left side of the pillar.

"Spysat retasked to scan landscape below," the CWO said succinctly, his tone now completely neutral.

Jacob looked at the holo in front of Osashi. The imagery changed from stormy mountain landscape to black and white pixels in the thousands. They beam painted the two nearby mountain peaks, a small lake lying two kilometers to the east of the meadow meeting spot, and the flat meadow area itself. Eleven oblong shapes showed in the millimeter wavelength radar return. Nine of them formed a half circle a few dozen meters out from the glass meeting dome he'd seen in a brief image of the meeting site just after they'd arrived in orbit. He had been with the admiral at the time. The dome location showed as a circular ring, which must be where its metal rim met the meadow soil. Glass was invisible to radar. The other two oblongs lay on the opposite side of the dome outline. Osashi looked back to him, expression very formal.

"There you are, Ensign Jacob Renselaer. All shuttles accounted for, including the alien craft."

Jacob nodded slowly. There were ten ships in the battle group led by *Lepanto*. The eleventh oblong had to be the weirdly shaped alien shuttle that had departed from the largest alien ship in the cluster that geosync orbited above the meeting site.

"Looks like they are still meeting," he murmured. "Any ideas on how to punch through that storm so we—"

"That's wrong," Daisy interrupted from the left of Jacob as she leaned forward a bit, a frown on her face. "My LCA is up here. There should only be *ten* shuttles down there. Our nine plus the single alien shuttle. When did number eleven arrive, Osashi?"

A chill ran down Jacob's neck. He should have realized what Daisy pointed out, before she spoke. But he hadn't, even though he'd been on the Bridge during their arrival in orbit, on the side of the world opposite from the twelve alien ships. He'd seen the spysat imaged meeting site, noted the clear glass meeting dome, seen an electro-optical image of the alien shuttle descending to the site, then had ignored the pending meeting as Johanson dismissed him from the Bridge. The last he'd known of the meeting events had been hearing Johanson order each fleet ship to send down a shuttle. Which was later joined by Daisy in her Landing Craft Assault. She and the LCA had been sent back to the *Lepanto* shortly after dropping off Johanson, Miglotti and Anderson. Which indeed meant there should only be ten shuttles showing in the radar return, not eleven. He looked away from the holo and met the black eyes of Osashi, who had looked their way with surprise.

"She's right. When did number eleven shuttle arrive?"

A brief grimace of irritation showed in the man's face, then he shrugged and turned back to face the black and white radar image. "Uh, about forty minutes ago. Just before the storm started up. It came from a smaller alien ship. Perhaps the aliens wanted language techs to help with setting up a common chat-chat lingo?"

Jacob took a deep breath and did his best to ignore the intense looks of the folks at the other function posts. He could not ignore Daisy, who stood just a few centimeters to his left. Her question had merit. The man who had decades of experience in communications had responded to her question. Still, Jacob felt uneasy. Why had the thunder and lightning storm begun just after the arrival of the eleventh shuttle? Was Osashi's speculation the answer? Or was something else going on down there? He looked left to the middle-aged Anglo woman who sat at Tactical.

"Chief Petty Officer O'Hara, do we have a Cloud Skimmer available to take a look at that site?"

The woman looked surprised, then thoughtful. She pushed back her red ponytail as she leaned forward to scan her control pillar's touchscreen surface. A milk white finger touched a spot on the pillar top. She looked his way, green eyes fixing on him.

"No, we do not. No battle group ship has launched one. We have six in inventory. Shall I launch one?"

"Do it," Jacob said, telling himself the winged drone could make it to the meeting site in less than twenty minutes, thanks to the speed it already had due to their ship's geosync orbital velocity of 7.4 kilometers per second. As it dropped lower it would gain speed.

Osashi slowly shook his head, as if disbelieving Jacob's sudden flurry of orders on the Bridge. He ignored the man and looked past Daisy to where the Tactical woman sat. She tapped her control pillar top, looked at the status holo floating in front of her pillar, then acted surprised.

"Armory Six refuses to launch the bird," she said, frowning. "It cites the ship status as Alert Orbital. Which prevents any release from the armories or the weapons banks." She looked his way. "The admiral ordered all ships of the group to assume Alert Orbital status once we entered orbit. I recall him saying something about not wanting to make the aliens nervous if their sensors picked up an accidental Weapons power-up."

A new chill ran down Jacob's back. The varied ship status conditions were intended to reduce human error or the action of a single crazed crewman. To change a ship status condition required the cooperation of the ship's AI.

"AI Melody, respond to me."

"Responding to Ensign Jacob Renselaer," the AI spoke from its ceiling speaker as his voice matched the AI's record of him in its voice recognition memory block.

"Change ship status condition to Alert Unknown Enemy," he said, working to keep his voice calmer than he felt.

"Provide ship status change code," the feminine voice of the AI said.

Despair filled Jacob. The ship status change code was known only to the admiral, the captain and the XO. Which was also the case on the other ships in the fleet, except just the captain and XO were in the change code loop on the other ships. Of course, the code was also present in the digitally locked safe in every captain's sleep room. But forcing open a safe to look at the piece of paper, or the thumb drive with the stored code, would take time. And . . . a sudden memory hit him. An image filled his mind. Two weeks ago, during Alcubierre transit, he'd been cleaning up the conference room while the admiral sat at his fold-down desk in the bedroom. The man had just opened his comp pad. But a call came over the room's loudspeaker from the XO. Anderson had asked the admiral to join him and Captain Miglotti on the Weapons Deck for some issue related to the Smart Rocks railguns. The man had stood up, pulled on his dress blue jacket and left the room in a hurry. Jacob, in keeping with his clean-up duties, had gone into the bedroom to close up the comp pad computer and return the work desk to standby mode. On the comp pad's screen he'd seen the twelve alphanumeric symbols that were the ship status change code. It had puzzled him until he recalled the admiral saying he wanted the ship crew to prepare for Alert System Entry status. The man had failed to shut down the comp pad before he'd left. Bringing the memory to the front of his mind, Jacob realized he was the only person on the *Lepanto* with knowledge of the vital code. He looked to Daisy.

"Uh, I happen to know the code. The admiral shared it with me. Do you think this silence really is—"

"Do it," Daisy said, her tone firm. Sudden sympathy showed on her dark brown face. "If something has happened to them, the *Lepanto* could be in danger. And so could the other ships in the fleet. We have to know our senior officers are all right."

Jacob knew that. He'd spoken only to delay the inevitable. He licked his lips. "I agree. We have to know, not guess or assume." Turning away from Osashi, he fixed on the three padded seats where the admiral, XO and the captain always sat whenever they were aboard the ship. Of course they rotated shifts so it was rare to see all three in the seats. But now, they were gone, the other Command Deck ensigns were gone, and none of the higher-ranked officers on the other decks knew what he knew. While he could order the AI to admit any ship person to the Command Deck, it would obey only Command Deck officers and personnel. Like Osashi and O'Hara and the other function post folks. None of whom were O-rank officers. With a sigh he kept mostly silent, Jacob walked toward the central group of seats. He stepped onto the low pedestal that held the XO and captain seats, then stepped up to the rear half that held the admiral's seat. He turned and sat in the wraparound seat. Looking ahead, he saw Daisy still standing beside Osashi. The two of them had joined the rest of the Bridge's warrant and petty officers in staring with surprise at him.

"Bridge, I am assuming temporary command of the Battlestar *Lepanto* as Acting Captain, until relieved by the XO, the captain or the admiral." He looked down at the touchscreen inset into the right armrest. A keypad lay just under it. He tapped in the ship status change code, then tapped Activate.

"Melody, have you received my ship status change code?"

"I have," the AI said, its melodious tone the reason for the name given it by Captain Miglotti, a man who loved his Italian operas.

"Change ship status to Alert Unknown Enemy. Confirm status change."

"Status change confirmed," the AI said quickly.

Above him yellow alert lights began blinking on the ceiling and on the walls that surrounded the Bridge. A low hooting sound filled the room. The sound and the yellow lights were now being repeated on every deck of the kilometer-long starship that was the *Lepanto*.

"Allow the launch of a Cloud Skimmer from Armory Six."

"Allowed. New ship status now permits full range of defensive movements, drone releases and Weapons Deck activation," the AI said redundantly, telling Jacob something he'd learned in class at the academy, but had never expected to occur by his own action.

He looked to O'Hara. "Tactical, launch the Cloud Skimmer. Send it into ground contour following mode right after atmosphere entry."

"Aye aye," the woman said quickly as she tapped on her control panel. A torpedo shape suddenly appeared in the true space image in the holo before her.

Jacob looked up front. "Daisy, come and sit in the XO's seat. I will need your support in whatever happens in the future." A thought struck him. His other friends might be of help in this situation. They knew tech stuff he didn't. "Melody, advise Ensign Carlos Mendoza, Ensign Lori Antonova and Spacer Quincy Blackbourne to report to the Bridge for consultation with me. Add them to the approved Command Deck personnel list."

"Directives sent. Personnel added," the AI said briefly.

Daisy stopped before the XO's chair and looked up at him. "Jacob, are we doing the right thing?"

What a question to ask in front of the other Bridge crew persons! Then again, she likely spoke what many of them were thinking. "I am acting on behalf of Rear Admiral Cornelius Johanson, who is out of comlink with this ship, as are the captain and the XO. A potential emergency exists. It is our duty to determine whether this comlink severing is due to natural weather events, or due to enemy action."

New sympathy filled her face. "Agreed." She turned and sat in the XO's seat, tapping the left armrest to bring up the holo of all ship decks and status reports for all ship systems.

That was one of the duties of an XO. It was something she, like Jacob, had learned at the academy. Which reminded him there was another duty that went with Alert Unknown Enemy ship status.

"Melody, send an encrypted neutrino signal to the other nine ships in our fleet that advises them to change their ship status to Alert Unknown Enemy." The other ships would wonder at the order from the fleet's flagship, but someone on their Bridge would go to their captain's quarters, force open the safe, read the code unique to their ship, and order their ship's AI to change ship status.

"Ship status change signal sent to each ship," the AI said quickly, her tone moving from routine to intense. Clearly there had been an algorithm change in the smart AI's interaction module. "Confirmation of signal received from ships *Chesapeake, Hampton*

Roads, Tsushima Strait, Salamis, Philippines Sea, St. Mihiel, Marianas, Britain and *Ofira*."

Jacob swallowed hard. He had moved beyond taking command of his ship's Bridge. He had sent new orders to the two cruisers, three destroyers and four frigates that made up the battle group. Briefly his mind rewound a lesson from the academy that described why some ships were named after famous naval battles and others were named after famous aerial fights. Shaking his head, he remembered a final academy lesson.

"All Bridge crew, put on your vacuum suits. Prepare for environment disruption. Melody, send my vacsuit order to all ship personnel and all decks."

"Complying," the AI said sharply.

A hiss from below his left armrest told Jacob a compartment had opened. It held his own vacsuit with flexible helmet. Its clear fabric would darken at any exposure to stellar radiation. He pulled it out, stood up and joined everyone on the Bridge in donning the precaution against sudden air pressure loss.

As he did so, he wondered what the leader of the wasp-like aliens was thinking. Surely the alien ships had detected the radar scan of the meeting site. Those ships had put out their own spysats before the fleet arrived. Those sats would soon report the *Lepanto's* launch of a Cloud Skimmer. What would the alien captain or leader or whatever passed for someone in charge now do?

CHAPTER TWO

Hunter One perched tensely on his control bench as his five eyes took in the behaviors of his Servants and Worker Leaders. Their Flight Chamber was large enough for a cohort of twenty Swarm members. Fewer than that worked at the instrument panels and watched the perception imagers that emitted pheromone signals for all to sense. Outside his Colony Nest was empty void, a cold, scent-less space that hated all life, even the lives of lowly Workers. At least his fellow flying nests were safe and warm and filled with life that yearned to occupy the inviting world below. The eleven Support Hunters who controlled the other mobile nests had been surprised by the arrival of other life in strangely shaped flying nests. Their world of Nest knew only the Swarm, a myriad of smaller, senseless hard-shelled life and the strange soft-skinned occupants of their world's skies, forests and oceans.

But three rest cycles ago the new flying nests had appeared at the edge of the local sky light's magnetic field. Their sudden appearance gave scent of movement by way of the alternate dimension the Swarm itself used to send Colony Nests to new worlds that winged about other sky lights. Clearly the ten new flying nests had come from elsewhere. Most seriously, the new nests had ignored the warnings against entry emitted by the Swarm's boundary globe. What kind of creatures could ignore the scents of repellent and territorial pheromones? One scent claimed this system for the Swarm. The other scent provided a noxious reminder to stay away. That was how other Swarm cohorts spoke to each other. And how the members of his ship cohort spoke among themselves. Even the Soft Skins on their world sensed the warning pheromones and stayed away from buried Swarm nests. But the flying nest intruders had ignored the globe's warning. They had moved close to the local sky light's warmth, aiming for the outermost fourth nest world that the Swarm had already claimed. Clearly they aimed to take the warm world for themselves.

His Servant who specialized in aberrant social behaviors had urged him to meet with the intruders before attacking their flying nests. Attack was the traditional means of defending one's territory. But as their world of Nest had grown more complex, as the castes of Swarmers had learned new scents and new results from studying the world about them, there had risen a need for Servants with specialized knowledge. Some Servants focused on mechanical devices. Some focused on invisible scent signals coming from the home sky light and other distant sky lights. And some Servants discovered ways for a cohort of Swarmers to fly further than their wings would normally convey them. Across the oceans. Out to the large moon of their world. Thence to other, colder sky nests that winged far beyond the warmth of their sky light's white-yellow glow. Then had come knowledge of alternate dimensions, and ways to travel to distant sky lights. His generation was the sixth to have control of such wondrous devices.

Now, it seemed other life had learned the same hard lessons. And it chose to invade their clearly marked territory. So he had proposed the meeting down on the world of Warmth. Defense of his home cohorts on Nest had taught him the wisdom of entrapping the Hunter leaders of opposing cohorts. The trap allowed the trap-maker to render the invading cohort members without leadership, without a Hunter, or useful Servants, or strong Fighters, maybe they even suffered the loss of their egg-laying Matron. A cohort without leaders and guidance became chaos. It then became a simple matter to impose his pheromones on the new arrivals and add them to his home nest. So he had invited the meeting, had created a nesting site, had sent down a small cohort of defective Servants, and then waited for the invaders to arrive. The memory of the perception images of the new beings had nearly emptied his inner gut. His breathing spiracles had become erratic in their pumping of air. Nausea had filled him as he realized the new arrivals were the worst type of Soft Skins. They were two-legged scavengers who resembled smaller soft skins on his world of Nest. Those tree-dwelling beings were known as crafty thieves. Clearly these larger Soft Skins, who had only four limbs rather than the normal six, intended to steal Warmth from the grasp of the Swarm.

The invaders had arrived. Transports from each of their ten flying nests had touched down on the empty meadow far below his ship. Close to four six-groups had walked in on just two legs. They had attempted to communicate with the defective Servants he had sent down. Those Servants knew their duty. They had pretended to cooperate. After one flying transport left the meeting site, giving him worry that some Soft Skin leaders might escape, he'd sent down a second transport. It carried the Storm Bringer floating globe. The globe, once deployed, rendered inoperable all signaling devices, whether pheromone or radiation-based. An added benefit came when the globe burst. The plasma created by its eruption incinerated all that lay below it even as the magnetic field created by the globe drew in local storm clouds. Those clouds covered the meeting site, making it invisible to normal perception imagers. While he could have destroyed the Soft Skin leaders with a particle disruption device, such weapons left behind deadly radiation residues that lasted for many lifetimes. He had no desire to sully the pure lands of Warmth. So the Storm Bringer globe had been deployed. And it had worked well.

"Hunter!" came an alarm pheromone from a Servant who occupied the bench which analyzed perception signals from the monitor globes they had dispersed in orbit above Warmth. "A Soft Skin monitor globe has cast a hard scent beam down on the meeting site! The beam will reveal our second transport."

Around him the other eleven Servants who operated the systems and devices that controlled the operation of his flying nest now flared their antennae. Their mandibles moved as if cutting through an enemy. Their spiracles pulsed in anticipation of his response pheromone.

"Have the Soft Skin flying nests changed their position above Warmth?" he scent cast, adding a food trail pheromone to entice quick response.

The Servant spread his wings. "They have not. The intruder flying nests remain in their cluster formation, acting like—"

"Alarm!" interrupted a releaser pheromone from a different Servant who monitored radiations from the cold of empty space. "The largest Soft Skin flying nest has released a small device. The device is a . . . a flying fabrication. It now enters the air of Warmth and flies toward the meeting site."

Hunter emitted a calming pheromone and spread it across the chamber by way of his wings. He followed it with an inhibitory pheromone to forestall hasty action by any Servant. "Servant," he scent cast to the one who had scent spoken. "Send a pheromone signal to the flying nests of our Support Hunters. Advise them of the monitor globe action and the flying device. Have them awaken their Fighter Leaders."

Sudden scent silence came from those about him. The Servant who had reported the Soft Skin flying nest behavior now emitted a releaser pheromone, signaling his intent to change his behavior. His front limbs touched the control panel that lay in front of his bench. "Signal pheromones sent. May I add perception images from our sensor devices?"

"You may do so," Hunter agreed with the release of a calming pheromone. He then followed the scent words with a brief territorial pheromone to remind the Servant that he, the Leader of all Swarmers aboard the Colony Nest, controlled their futures, their lives and their destinies. "Send an identical scent to the Fighter Leaders in our flying nest. It is time for the attack stations on this nest to become fully occupied. The moment of attack may come sooner than any hard shell expects."

"Sending," the Servant scented back to him with a strong aggregating pheromone as a signal of his loyalty.

Hunter settled down on his bench. It was elevated above the device boxes and tubes that ran along the chamber's floor and across the ceiling above. His flying nest was a poor imitation of his home shelter in a deep hole in a rock face that fronted a cool lake and meadow. Like every Swarmer in the twelve flying nests that made up their colonizing effort, he felt bereft of home. Such loss was a sensation that sent some Swarmers into chaotic behavior despite the pheromone scents of their leaders. Only Swarmers who could stand a long separation from the home nest, or home shelter, took duty aboard the flying nests that sought out new homes for the millions of new eggs produced by the Matron caste. Hunter was one of those who could handle such isolation from the familiar. But he did not pretend the loss did not affect him. Only the awareness of finding new home nests kept his inner gut at equilibrium.

Breathing deep through his spiracles, he focused his three simple eyes and two major eyes on all the perception imagers that filled his Flight Chamber. Unlike other hard shell groups on Nest, every Swarm member had trichromatic vision. They could see from the dark purple through blue, green, yellow and orange. Servants who studied distant sky lights said there were other colors beyond dark purple to orange, which their native Soft Skins could perceive. No matter. The Swarm's trichromatic vision had been a vital aid in defeating half-aware flying hard shells. Now, that vision told him much. Several imagers depicted the ten invading nests. Their shapes glowed in ultraviolet reflected from the local sky light. As did the many monitor devices dispersed by the invaders.

How would the Soft Skins on those nests react to the loss of their leaders, their guides, their givers of order and coherence? Chaos should fill those flying nests as the Workers, Fighters, Servants and Matrons left leaderless became confused and fearful. When the ten flying nests showed erratic movements, that would be the moment to strike hard. The twelve nests of the Swarm would fly in and englobe the Soft Skins, overwhelming any artificial stingers possessed by such strange lifeforms. A mass englobement had always been the method by which any Swarm cohort overcame an opposing Swarm cohort. Surely the same would now happen with the Soft Skins.

◆ ◆ ◆

Daisy scanned the ship deck and status holo as she waited for Jacob's friends to arrive. Her friend's order to change ship status made total sense to her in view of the failure to contact any senior officer from the battle group. Something strange was going on at the meeting site. They had to know what was happening. The Cloud Skimmer would bring them imagery and sensor data once it arrived at the site, in another twenty minutes. Until then, the *Lepanto* and the other ships had to prepare for possible conflict. Which meant she had to confirm every deck on the Battlestar was in combat alert status with people manning the vital stations involved in operating, fueling and fighting the giant warship. The holo drew her gaze.

She saw that the left and right side outrigger pods were now at Weapons operational status. The carbon dioxide lasers on the nose and tail of each pod were powered up and ready to unleash green hell against any target out to 10,000 kilometers. In the middle of each pod the proton lasers were up and aiming sideways, ready to cover any side-approaching enemy with their red beams. The proton range was the same as the lasers. On the spine and belly of the ship were the railgun launchers and the plasma batteries. They were equally powered and ready to defend the ship against enemies that got too close. The railgun mounts were aimed sideways, like the proton lasers, and fully covered the flanks of the *Lepanto*. The plasma batteries covered the top and bottom angles out to 400 klicks, which made them useful for taking out kinetic Smart Rocks, if the enemy possessed such. She looked at the ship's nose, the area directly above the Bridge on the ship's outer hull. The emitter node for the antimatter cannon showed Green Operational, and the particle accelerator tube that circled the body of the ship had accumulated a reservoir of negative antimatter sufficient for four shots. While the range of the black antimatter beam was just 4,000 kilometers, anything touched by the magnetically focused antimatter became instant energy. Similar to the yellow plasma balls shot by the plasma batteries. Finally, she confirmed the six armories at the rear of the ship and the four hangars at the ship's front were in fighting trim, ready to feed thermonuke missiles to the rear missile launch silos, Smart Rocks to the railguns, plasma canisters to the batteries, and laser artillery, rifles and pistols to the twenty person Marine boarding team. Which should already be at Silo Eight, ready to enter their Assault Darts if ordered to board an enemy ship. Finally, she noted the personnel count. There were 321 lives aboard the *Lepanto*, each one as vital to the ship as she and her friends.

Which made her wonder again at Jacob's order. Carlos was a programmer on Navigation Deck, Lori a biologist on Science Deck and Quincy a laser gunner's mate assigned to the front laser node on Weapons Deck's right outrigger pod. Which left out only Kenji. Course the man was a line cook in the Mess Hall, an important talent but not something they needed for a space battle. Would there be a battle? Or would some Lieutenant Commander on another ship or LC Bannerjee on *Lepanto* show up and order the battle group to leave the system? Retreat in the face of the loss of their captains, XOs and other ensigns did not sit well with her. They had to know more about these wasp-like aliens. Who were they? Where did they come from? Why were they in orbit above the system's outermost planet? Had they attacked the commanders of her fleet? If so, why? But answering such questions required a common language. A feat yet to be achieved. Maybe Lieutenant Branstead on Science Deck could figure out an algorithm that would—

"O'Hara," called Jacob from behind her. "What is the status of the Cloud Skimmer? How close is it to the meeting site?"

"The skimmer is twelve minutes out from the meeting site," O'Hara said, her Irish accent very pronounced. "It is now over the ocean that separates the meeting site landmass from the continent below us."

"What do our spysats say about the twelve alien ships?" Jacob asked.

Daisy looked ahead at the woman who had mentored her on space battle tactics. She liked Rosemary O'Hara. The woman reminded her of her mother. Who now worked on Pluto at the Wide Field Infrared Observatory on that small world. Her father, who'd divorced her Mom when Daisy was just nine, lived on Taiwan and worked at some kind of Chinese tech company. He had never sent her a birthday present, nor had he attended her graduation from the Stellar Academy. Her Mom had shown up. Which made her love the hard-working scientist even more than she already did. Thanks to her Mom, she had taken flying lessons at age 12, soloed at 13 and earned her jet pilot license at 16. That background, and help from the Illinois senator her Mom knew, had gained her admission to the academy. She had seen Jacob in some classes there, but had never spent time with him at the academy. Just before boarding she'd heard he was a loner, not sociable. Which did not fit his manner during the officers holo shoot at the orbital shipyard station. Or his manner on the *Lepanto*. While the man was shy, he had made Kenji feel welcome in the ensigns ward room, a place rarely visited by any enlisted Spacer. He'd done the same for Quincy, a Brit who came from a Royal Navy family. That reaching out had endeared Jacob to her. Which left her wondering why she had not taken the obvious step and invited him to join her at the weekly Dance Night. Surely he knew how to dance. While he was congenial to other women ensigns and enlisted, she had seen no sign he wanted close contact with women. Could she change that attitude?

"Acting Captain, the six spysats we have on that side of the world report every alien ship remains as they have been," O'Hara said softly. "There is a forward group of six ships arranged in a hexagonal pattern, and a following group of six ships arranged similarly."

Daisy blinked as a memory of her high school biology class filled her mind. She recalled a picture of a wasp nest hidden under the eave of an old wooden building. Each chamber built into the mix of plant fiber, mud and wasp secretions had six walls. They made for hexagonal chambers, similar to the honeycombs of bees. Larvae were born and fed in the hexagonal chambers until they became true wasps. The memory caused her to tap her right side armrest and bring up a holo image of the twelve alien ships. Yes! Each ship was long and had six sides faceting its shape. Tubular shapes stuck out from the front, middle and rear of each log-like ship. Were they lasers? Cannons? Missile launch silos? Something else?

"Thank you, Tactical," Jacob said. "Uh, CWO Osashi, those spysats uploaded continuous video of the meeting with the aliens, didn't they?"

"They did, sir," the man said, his tone formal but not amiable. She wondered at that.

Her left armrest's overhead image of the entire Bridge showed Jacob tapping his fingers on his armrest, clearly working at patience with the man who had challenged his right to issue any order. "Rerun on the front wallscreen the last three minutes of AV imagery. I assume the feed was cut off due to the lightning storm?"

"Sir, that is what happened," the elderly chief warrant officer said, sitting stiffly at his post. The man tapped the control pillar in front of him. "Last three minutes of imagery going up. Time stamps are in the lower right corner."

Daisy looked forward, trying to ignore the constant rasping of her vacsuit against her arms and legs. The suit was a bother but its wearing was in conformity with the new Alert status. At least the helmet-back position allowed her to breath normal ship air.

The wallscreen filled with a high density color image of the backs of the captains and XOs who sat on field stools facing a cluster of eighteen wasp-like aliens. Clearly the image came from the tablet of one of the ensigns who sat behind the senior officers. She saw the broad back of Admiral Johanson on the left side of the arc of officers. None of them wore vacsuits. All were dressed in woodland camo NWUs. In the middle of the room hovered a hologram that showed various Earth plants and animals. The imagery was controlled by some officer who was trying to establish a common language or terminology. A holo next to it was controlled by the aliens, one of whom held a silvery tablet in his upper arm pair. That holo showed color images of the fleet ships in orbit above the fourth planet. Behind the aliens was parked their shuttle, which like their ships had a hexagonal outer hull. Words were heard as the humans talked among themselves, while the only sound coming from the aliens were rare raspings of the top limbs against their thorax shell. She wondered if rasping their limbs against their chitin shells was how they talked.

"Does not look as if the two groups are understanding each other," Jacob said, sounding calm but determined.

"Maybe Lieutenant Branstead knows what is happening. I just watched on my seat's repeater screen, alert for any incoming signals," the Communications chief said, his tone indifferent.

Daisy respected Branstead. The woman had a Ph.D. in molecular synthesis of biological polymers and led a deck of 51 specialists in the natural and social sciences. Which included Jacob's friend Lori, a specialist in exobiology.

"I'm sure you were alert. That sparkle at the top! Is that the incoming eleventh shuttle?"

She fixed on what Jacob had noticed. The view from the back of the clear geodesic dome allowed a view of the landscape and sky in front of and above the dome. At the very top of the holo was a tubular image that shone silvery. As she watched, the tube quickly became an alien shuttle. In seconds it extruded six stick-like legs from its bottom hull, hovered on belly jets, then landed on the flame-fused brown soil of the meadow. It rested just ten meters to the side of the original alien shuttle.

"What's happening on its roof?" Jacob asked quickly.

Daisy, like everyone on the Bridge, was fixed on these last images of their senior officers. Who seemed intent on running through a series of numbers filling their holo, which might have been from a SETI common language program. None of them paid attention to the new arrival. Which, she now saw, was opening up its top. The alien shuttle's roof split open down the middle, then two hull flaps rose up vertically. In two seconds something round or . . . or globular, she now saw, lifted up slowly from the inside of the shuttle. She could not tell how big the globe was, other than by comparison to the shuttle itself. Daisy guessed the balloon-like globe was perhaps two meters wide. Which meant it was half as wide as the shuttle itself. The globe lifted up higher, then higher still, its rise steady. Was it a weather balloon? Something filled with helium or hydrogen? There were no jets or fans or propellers showing on the globe's exterior.

"That globe is rising from the inside of the new shuttle," Osashi said, answering Jacob's query.

"What *is* that thing?" Jacob asked sharply, his tone intense.

"Maybe a weather monitoring station?" Osashi said, sounding puzzled. "When I first saw it I wondered what it might be. Perhaps the aliens were concerned for a local weather change. Or something. I'm no meteorologist. Sir."

"Understood."

She watched the globe rise up and beyond the view angle of the tablet held by the ensign who was transmitting the meeting actions to the spysats above for retransmission to—

"Damn!"

A bright yellow-white light flashed down into the holo image. Then the image went dark.

"What the hell was that light flash?" Jacob said.

"I have no idea," Osashi said. "Maybe Chief Petty Officer Steinmetz can tell us. He's our science . . . expert."

She looked right to Willard Steinmetz, someone she knew only by name and rank and the fact he ran one of the Bridge function posts. The forty-something CPO gave a shrug, which made his large belly shake a bit.

"Acting Captain, I have no idea. Before this event, the air above the meeting site was calm, with a few scattered clouds and no sign of a storm or low pressure front approaching," the man said thoughtfully. "One of my jobs was monitoring the meet site for bad weather. Got a second undergrad degree in meteorology. This planet has normal weather. Equator is warmer than the poles. Primary winds come from the northwest. The meet site is distant from any ocean or sea. I saw no natural source for the light event."

"Nothing natural," murmured Jacob from behind her, his tone musing.

Behind Daisy the hatch that gave entry to the Bridge hissed as its pressure seal released. Those would be Jacob's friends. And hers too. She liked them and Kenji and also the four pilots who flew the Marine Darts. Piloting was a unique profession and every pilot on board the *Lepanto* knew every other pilot, no matter the deck or rank or gender. She left active the alien ship holo and her overhead screen image of the Bridge and the people on it, then looked left as the three friends came toward the command seats that filled the middle of the Bridge. What would Jacob ask of them?

♦ ♦ ♦

Jacob gave thanks the vacsuit's flexible helmet could be lifted up and hang against his upper back. It allowed him to breath ship air and hear every squeak, rustle or low word spoken by the nine Bridge crew who occupied the function posts in front of him and Daisy. Seeing him do that had resulted in the crew doing the same. Course, once they entered active combat, everyone would seal up. And cross their fingers that the outer hull's ablative coating and adaptive optics mirrors would deflect away or absorb the worst of any laser hit. Straight on laser hits would cut through the ablative coating that lay under the mirrors, but the two meters of titanium-nickel-steel armor that was the outer hull would resist any laser strike that did not stay focused for long minutes. Below the armor was a level of water, with the inner hull further below. Thousands of tons of water filled the space between the inner and outer hulls. The water gave them further shielding from stellar radiation that penetrated the outer hull. At the rear, the fuel tanks of tritium and deuterium isotopes gave further shielding to the crew folks working on Engines Deck, which filled the back half of Command Deck. Below the inner hull lay the seven decks stacked like a layer cake, with pressure hatches breaking every hallway and every gravlift shaft into spaces where air could be contained in case of a hull rupture. Course, if a beam or a deep penetrating missile hit the three fusion reactors that filled the central core of the ship, then life on the *Lepanto* would come to a quick end. The hiss of the Bridge entry hatch diverted him from the recorded imagery of the last moments at the meeting site. His friends had arrived. He looked left.

Lori led the group, followed by Carlos and Quincy. They faced him and saluted.

"Ensigns reporting as ordered," Lori said over her vacsuit's comlink. Seeing his helmet pushed back, she copied him. As did the two young men.

His three friends watched him carefully. Jacob sitting in the admiral's seat had quickly told them he was in command on the Bridge. But beyond that, and the ship status change, they knew nothing. He saluted them back.

"Thank you each for coming." Jacob gestured at the front wallscreen with its image of the opposite side of planet four. "We have lost contact with the admiral, our captain and our XO. The other ships have also lost contact with their captains and XOs. Using the ship status change code shared with me by the admiral, I changed our status to Alert Unknown Enemy." He pointed at the spysat image of the black lightning storm that still swirled above the meeting site. "A massive electrical storm happened forty minutes ago, right after the arrival of a second alien shuttle. I had Tactical launch a Cloud Skimmer to give us a direct eyes-on view of the meeting site." He focused back on his three friends. "The loss of tablet contact with everyone at the meeting site raises the chance this is due to enemy action. Presumably by the aliens on the far side of this world. We have radar painted the meeting site using a spysat, but it showed only the presence of eleven shuttles. Our nine and two alien. The enemy ships have not changed their geosync orbital attitude. I called you three here to get your thoughts." He fixed on black-haired Lori, who wore an NWU Type I uniform like Daisy. In fact, all of them wore the camo uniforms. No one wore dress blues unless ordered to do so. The Russian woman, a graduate of some exobiology institute in Moscow, peered intently at him. "Ensign Lori Antonova, you are a biologist with a specialty in exobiology lifeforms. You know what our colonists have found on Earth's seven colonies. You've seen the images of the wasp-like aliens. What do you deduce from the imagery of them and of their ships?"

    The slim woman adopted a parade rest stance. She glanced at the front wallscreen and at Osashi's holo that showed the alien ships, then back to him. "Acting Captain Renselaer, while the lifeforms on the colony planets show similar organization into mammal, avian, aquatic and insect-like lifeforms, with millions of exotic bacteria, the analogy to Earth animal life is risky. One world has lifeforms with tripodal leg arrangements. On another world, the animals resemble our radial pattern starfish. A third world has hopping as its primary locomotion mode. The presence of vertebrate life, predators and prey, scavengers and parasites, along with air and water-breathing lifeforms, is common to all seven worlds." She pursed her lips, glanced aside at Daisy, then sighed. "Yes, these aliens resemble giant yellow jacket wasps. The striking red and black bands on their yellow exoskeleton bodies suggest they are predators. Bright colors warn of danger. In biological science it is called aposematism. It also makes sense due to their presence off planet. Predators hunt for new territory." She paused, took a deep breath and continued. "But why they are here could be due to many factors. Exploration. Expansion of the home territory. Failure of the home world ecology. Or colonizing of suitable worlds. The fact the gravity on planet four is just a half gee suggests these insect aliens evolved on a world with low gravity, a high oxygen level, and perhaps dense plant life and ground life similar to what is found in Earth's jungles." She stopped.

Jacob nodded. "All of that makes sense. Assuming they have some analog with our wasps, what behavior do you expect of them?"

She grimaced. "They could behave in any manner. Fight, flight, freeze or negotiate. Or something stranger than Earth norms. My guess is this group of starships is led by at least one leader, maybe two, in view of the two six-groups of ships. The hexagonal hull shape of their ships suggests a tendency for the aliens to cluster tightly into social groups. That is, if we assume the hull shape indicates the structure of their nest building."

Jacob noted that Carlos was looking at Daisy's holo of local space, which carried the images of the twelve alien ships. That fit his Navigation work. Quincy, a Black guy he'd come to know as a happy go lucky beer drinker and lover of reggae music, looked bored. As you might expect from someone who was a Weapons Deck person. He fixed back on Lori.

"If they have a primary leader, would that leader be located on the bigger ship in the front group of six?"

She frowned, then shrugged. "He or she could. Our admiral was on the *Lepanto*, which is larger than any other Earth ship. The same may be true for the aliens."

"Are they eusocial?" Jacob asked.

She showed surprise. "Uh, taking E. O. Wilson's definition from the last century, you wonder if these alien insects have a division of labor, overlapping generations and cooperative care of the young? Like the ants, bees, wasps and termites on Earth. And we humans." She looked at Daisy's ship holo. "Oh yes, I am certain they have a eusocial society. Their behavior to date strongly supports that likelihood."

He nodded. "Are they inherently peaceful? Or quickly combative?"

"I have no idea," Lori said, her light brown lips pulling back from her white teeth.

Getting opinions from the woman was like pulling teeth. Or catching slippery rainbow trout. "Why did they invite our leaders to the meeting on the world below?"

Her blue eyes widened. "A good question. Perhaps to agree on a means to communicate. Perhaps to see us in person, versus imagery. Our only effective communication to date has been through an AV signal wavelength that we recognized. The electromagnetic signals from their outer system satellite did not correspond to any radio, radar or visual emission frequency. The signals were polarized, which says they conveyed something intentional. What, we have no idea."

"They are clearly insects," Jacob said, persisting in his effort to decipher the future behavior of an alien species. "How does one group of insects react when it encounters an opposing group of insects?"

"They attack one another. Immediately," Lori said, her Russian accent barely noticeable. "Or they avoid each other."

"How do they signal the decision to attack? Or to avoid?"

She squinted, then looked up at him. "Most insects use pheromones to signal a behavior change, or to provide info on something that matters, like food. Earth insects cannot see red or infrared, but they can see in the ultraviolet range. Plus, some insects like bees can detect polarized light, which helps them find their way back to the home nest." Her expression turned thoughtful. "A signal to attack us may be sent by pheromones, by ultraviolet signals or by polarized light emissions. Acoustic orders could also be sent by rasping of their hard shell bodies using arms or legs. The way grasshoppers make sounds."

"What about their technology," Jacob pressed. "How similar is it to ours? How different?"

Lori blinked, her expression going thoughtful. "Like us they use phased array aperture synthesis radar. And also pulsed Doppler radar. They emit complex encrypted radio signals between their ships. Their ships use fusion reactors, based on a neutrino signature that is identical to our reactors. And their normal space movement is by fusion pulse drives, based on the radioactives emissions from the rear of their ships. Unlike us, they have both compound and single lens eyes, similar to the eyes possessed by wasps, spiders, horseshoe crabs and other complex arthropods. Which means their video imagers will be different from ours." She fixed on him. "Acting Captain, these speculations are the most I can do based on analogy with Earth and other worlds' insect populations."

Jacob nodded, then focused on Quincy. "Spacer Quincy Blackbourne, you've seen the spysat imagery of the alien ships. Have you and your mates been able to detect signs of weaponry? Like lasers, cannons, missile launchers or other weaponry?"

The short, stocky man put both fists on his hips and frowned. "Acting Captain, it's been hard to tell. We've only been in orbit for a few hours. Our spysats and comsats have been in orbit for just that long." He pointed at Daisy's holo. "I've looked closely at expanded images of those ships. The rods at the front, middle and ends of each ship could be gas laser emitters, proton lasers, plasma tubes or Smart Rock launchers. The ships are maintaining their orbital position by use of attitude jets very similar to those our ships use. The rear of each ship shows exhaust funnels similar to our fusion pulse exhausts on the *Lepanto* and our battle group ships." His friend, who spoke with a London accent, shrugged his thick shoulders. "If we could move a spysat closer to one of those ships, I could make a more accurate guess on their weaponry. If they are similar to wasps, they surely have one or more stingers. I expect them to be dangerous opponents."

Jacob felt the same way. He focused on Carlos, a Latino from East Los Angeles who played soccer in the ship's Exercise Hall, loved tequila and played a mean classical guitar. Their group had always shown up for a guitar session hosted by Carlos. It was one of the things that had glued all of them, including Kenji, into a common friendship. Plus, Quincy and Kenji had been willing to join him, Lori, Daisy and Carlos in the ensigns ward room. That took some daring, which Jacob appreciated. His own quota of daring had peaked in his assumption of temporary command of the Bridge.

"Ensign Carlos Mendoza, you're a Navigator. If we have to run from these aliens, we will not head for Earth and Sol. What is the nearest star colony we can head for?"

The man jerked his head away from scoping out the looks of O'Hara, whose curvy shape showed well in her NWU camos. His brown eyes looked over Daisy, then fixed on him. "Well, Kepler 10 is just 65 light years away from this system. At our FTL speed of 25 light years a day, we could reach the system in two and a half days. Of course, Lieutenant Commander Bannerjee runs my Navigation

Deck. He could give you more star colony options. And Louise here at Navigation could have told you what I just shared."

Jacob knew that. A CWO named Oliver Diego y Silva was in charge of the Weapons post on the Bridge, while red-haired CPO Louise Slaughter headed the Navigation post. He didn't know them. Nor any of the other Bridge crew. He did know Carlos, Quincy and Lori. And Daisy. He was doing the best he could, recalling academy lessons and simulation scenarios that—

"Acting Captain," called O'Hara from Tactical. "The Cloud Skimmer is arriving at the meeting site. I'm putting its imagery up on the front wallscreen."

"Lori, Carlos and Quincy, take a seat in the observer row behind us," he said quickly. "Let's see what this shows."

At last. In a moment they would all know just what had happened at the meeting site nearly an hour ago. Jacob focused on the giant wallscreen that covered twenty meters of the curving front wall. The real time image of the dark storm vanished and was replaced with a scene that resembled Hell.

CHAPTER THREE

Jacob scanned the overhead view that showed a red-glowing crater where the glass dome had once been. As the skimmer began its automatic circling of the arrival point, he noticed the condition of the human shuttles. The front ends that faced toward the dome were melted into slag. The alien shuttle front ends were also melted. A glance at the spectroscope sensor readouts that filled one side of the skimmer's live video image showed the metal of the alien shuttles was the same mix of steel, titanium and nickel that made up the Earth shuttles. Beyond the melted shuttles, the green grass of the meadow had become withered brownness, while the red bark and green needle leaves of the alien trees were blackened on the sides facing the meeting site. Clearly something very hot and very violent had hit the meeting site. There were no survivors. No foot prints were visible in the dirt and ash that lay outside the central crater. The terrain looked overcast due to the storm clouds above. In the distance, yellow lightning bolts spiked down to touch the mountain wall that lay to one side of the site. As the skimmer continued its circling, more yellow bolts streaked down, hitting the nearby lake, some trees and then the mountain slope on the other side of the site. White steam still rose from the red-glowing crater.

"Fuck! What the hell hit them!" yelled Oliver from his Weapons post.

"So terrible," muttered Osashi.

"God, that's awful," called Rosemary from Tactical, her expression pained.

"Jacob," called Daisy from the XO seat below him, "there's nothing left. They're all gone. What could have done this?"

He gripped tight the ends of his seat's armrests. No more guessing now. It was a fact that all the senior officers of the battle group were dead and gone. Along with nearly twenty aliens. Was this enemy action? Would the wasp creatures kill their own people in order to kill the commanders of the ten Earth ships? If the wasps had killed his people, why were their ships not doing anything?

"AI Melody, transmit this imagery to every ship in the battle group. Maintain the transmission so long as the skimmer functions," he said.

"Transmitting imagery," the AI said, her tone sounding as tense as Jacob felt.

"Melody, activate our All Ship vidcom. Transmit this imagery over every ship vidscreen. Add my image."

"All Ship vidcom active. Transmitting imagery."

Jacob licked his lips, tried to sit straighter in his seat than he already did, and spoke.

"All personnel, you are now seeing imagery of the meeting site where Rear Admiral Johanson, Captain Miglotti and Executive Officer Anderson were meeting with the wasp-like aliens who invited our senior officers to meet with them," Jacob said, hoping his baritone did not sound shaky. "Whatever vaporized the meeting site did a complete job. The captains and XOs and ensigns from the fleet's other ships are also gone. The shuttles are half melted. Our Cloud Skimmer is circling the site. There is no sign of survivors." He paused. "Melody, move ship status to Alert Combat Ready."

Overhead the alert lights went to blinking red. The ceiling speakers gave out a high-pitched siren, which repeated three times. "People, it is possible the loss of our senior officers is due to enemy action by the wasp aliens. One of their shuttles released a floating globe just before we lost the tablet imagery of the meeting. I am suspicious that this is not a natural weather event. If the aliens did this, that is a hostile act. Therefore, all personnel are ordered to Battle Stations. All decks must prepare for possible enemy action. I will keep you informed of any change in the tactical situation. Acting Captain out."

He looked up at the ceiling. "Melody, prepare to transmit my words to each of the other nine ships in the battle group. Add my image."

"Encrypted audiovid neutrino signal established. Ready to transmit voice and image," the AI said quickly, a touch of curiosity now discernible in its human-like voice.

"Each ship, I am Acting Captain Jacob Renselaer, the only surviving Command Deck officer on the *Lepanto*. Earlier, I ordered a change in Alert status. I have now moved us to Alert Combat Ready status based on what you are now seeing. Whoever is in command on your ship, move to that alert stage. I require the cooperation of every ship, until we make contact with Earth or find a senior command officer in a human colonized star system." Jacob paused and drew a deep breath. "This destruction of the meeting site occurred after the aliens released a floating globe that rose above the site. That globe may have caused this destruction. If so, that is a hostile act. There is no change in wasp ship formation at the moment. There is no sign of a hostile act by any wasp ship. However, I judge we must be ready to move to Alert Hostile Enemy status whenever any wasp ship moves toward one of our ships. Advise me of your compliance and identify who is now commanding your ship."

    Silence filled the Bridge for long seconds. Then the AI spoke.
    "Incoming audiovid signals."
    "Display first signal to arrive," Jacob said. "Advise incoming signals they will link with me shortly."
    "Advising. First signal displayed."

A new image appeared at the top of the wallscreen's image of destruction. A middle aged woman dressed in woodland camo NWUs and showing the bronze oak leaf of a lieutenant commander on her collar tips filled the image. She was as black-skinned as Quincy.

"Acting Captain Renselaer, your live imagery from the meeting site is severely worrisome," the woman said, her tone sounding Midwestern America. "I am Lieutenant Commander Rebecca Swanson, now acting captain of the cruiser *Chesapeake*. We have moved to Alert Combat Ready. Since you showed the foresight to send a skimmer to inspect the meeting site after we lost tablet link with our captain and XO, I accept you, Jacob Renselaer, as acting leader of the battle group. Advise me of your further wishes."

Relief filled Jacob. Whatever deck this woman ran on the *Chesapeake*, she understood the necessity for unity in the face of an unknown and likely hostile enemy. Would the rest of them show the same spirit of cooperation and allegiance?

"Acting Captain Swanson, it is good to hear your words, coming as they do from the senior cruiser in our battle group," Jacob said, thinking fast. "Stand by. Monitor your spysats. Advise me of any sensor input that shows a change in behavior by any wasp ship. I am adding your image to my outgoing audiovid signal. Wait a moment as I accept calls from the other ships."

The woman just nodded. He noticed a younger man sat in the XO seat next to her. He looked Slavic, maybe a Russian like Lori. Jacob looked up at the ceiling.

"Melody, put through the next in line response. Display the signal beside that from the *Chesapeake*."

"Signal displayed."

The older man who appeared on the wallscreen was someone Jacob recognized. He ran the Navigation Deck on the other cruiser. The man was a friend of his father's, a fact that had caused him to personally welcome Jacob upon his arrival at the orbital shipyard station where the *Lepanto* and the other battle group ships had been docked. He blinked dark eyes.

"Young Renselaer, I am Lieutenant George Wilcox of the cruiser *Hampton Roads*. As you know. I broke into our captain's safe and used the ship status change code to change our alert condition. And to become this ship's acting captain." The man, who was bald on top but still had black hair above his ears, turned intense. "We too have moved to Alert Combat Ready. And I agree with Swanson. Your initiative tells me you will do well as the battle group leader until we contact higher command. What can I and my people do for you?"

An electric tingle swept down Jacob's arms to his fingers. This man was the second, more mature officer to accept his leadership. And to understand what Jacob knew had to be done. "Acting Captain Wilcox, thank you. This has been a surprise to me and to my entire Bridge. And surely to the other deck leaders on the *Lepanto*. My orders to you are simple. Be alert. Be ready to repel any enemy attack. Monitor your spysats. Report anything done by the wasp ships. And hold your position at the front of our orbital group. With the *Chesapeake* at our rear and you at the front, we are best positioned to respond to any attacking ship."

"Will do," Wilcox said quickly, gesturing to the woman who occupied the XO seat next to him. "Lieutenant JG Wakanabi is our new XO. I assume you are filling slots over there as quickly as you can?"

"I am," Jacob said. "My new XO is Ensign Daisy Stewart. While I sit in the admiral's seat, I am acting captain of the *Lepanto*. As you may have heard earlier, I am the sole surviving Command Deck officer. I am relying on fellow officers on the other decks to bring this ship to its full capabilities."

"Your ship is very powerful," Wilcox said. "The 210 people on the *Hampton Roads* will do as you order."

"Good. Please monitor this conversation I am holding with all battle group ships," Jacob said. "We all need to be aware of what is happening on every other ship. And we need to work together in case of an attack from the wasps."

"Monitoring," the man said bluntly.

"Melody, display the third signal. Put the imagery next to the two captains now on the wallscreen."

"Displaying."

A middle-aged man with white hair, Asian face and black eyes now appeared. Like the cruiser captains, he sat in one of the two central command seats on his ship's Bridge. A younger man who looked Hindu dark sat beside him. The white-haired man spoke.

"Acting Captain Jacob Renselaer, I am Lieutenant Douglas Zhang, now acting captain of the destroyer *Tsushima Strait*," he said, his tone firm and confident. "Fully agree with the points made by Wilcox and Swanson. My ship is at Alert Combat Ready. The 113 people on board this ship will fight any enemy and act in concert with the rest of the battle group."

Jacob felt new encouragement. The man led one of the three destroyers in the battle group. While smaller in size than the cruisers or the *Lepanto*, still, his ship had formidable weapons and swift maneuverability. Three down, six more to go.

"Acting Captain Zhang, thank you for your response and your loyalty to our continuing mission of exploration. Which may soon change to active combat," Jacob said. "Maintain your ship's position on the outer right flank of the *Lepanto*. Do your missiles carry x-ray laser thermonukes?"

"They do," Zhang said, his expression intense and focused. "But we only carry nine missiles, much less than the forty on the *Lepanto*."

"Still, your ship is a vital component of our battle group," Jacob said, offering his best effort at showing his appreciation for the man's loyalty to him despite the sudden change in circumstances. "Stand by and monitor my discussions. Once I have heard from all battle group ships, we will discuss tactical options."

"Standing by," the man said with a quick nod of his head.

"Melody?"

"Displaying fourth incoming signal."

A dark-skinned, black-haired, Hindu-looking man now appeared as part of the wallscreen lineup of other ship captains. An Asian woman sat to his left in the XO seat. The man spoke.

"Acting Captain Renselaer, I am Lieutenant Commander Chatur Mehta, now acting captain of the destroyer *Salamis*." The man paused, licked his lips, then frowned. "I cannot accept the authority of a former ensign to lead this battle group. While I agree our senior officers are now dead, perhaps due to enemy action, I judge it my duty to leave this system and report these events to Earth Command. My ship is now leaving orbit."

Shock filled Jacob. "Mehta! We need every ship! We are outnumbered 12 to 10 by the wasps! Are you refusing a direct order?"

"I dispute your authority to issue me a direct order," the man said. Beside him the woman looked unhappy. "You are an ensign. I am a lieutenant commander, formerly in charge of the Science Deck on the *Salamis*. I have obtained the ship status change code and now assert my right to command this destroyer due to being the most senior officer now present on this ship. My rank exceeds your rank. I wish you luck in whatever happens here." The man reached to a control spot on his right armrest.

"Wait!" yelled Jacob, knowing he sounded like a pleading child to anyone listening. "If you must leave, go to Kepler 10. That is the nearest colony star. Alert the Star Navy base there to these events. Whatever you do, do *not* set your vector track for Sol! These aliens cannot ever know the direction to Earth!"

The man raised black eyebrows. "As you wish. The *Salamis* now departs for the edge of this system's magnetosphere. I will set vector for Kepler 10. Good day."

♦ ♦ ♦

Daisy felt shock at the Hindu man's rejection of Jacob. She thought he looked frightened under the shell of defiance. She felt for the Asian woman who was acting as his XO. Breaking the chain of command and the cohesion of the battle group was clearly upsetting her. She looked back and up at Jacob.

Her friend blinked, then his clean-shaven face became tight-muscled. His gray eyes became more intense than when she'd first seen as he sat in the admiral's seat, thereby signaling to everyone on the Bridge that he was not only claiming acting captain status, but was also claiming the right to command of the battle group. Her shock at his daring had eased as he fell into a calm, orderly and professional manner with the Bridge crew and with the other ship leaders. What would he do now?

"Melody, display the next in line signal," Jacob said, his tone calm, almost at ease.

"Displaying next signal," the AI said in a swift response.

A blond-haired young woman who wore woodland camos, sat in a central Bridge seat and looked as calm as Jacob's voice, now joined the vid images of Swanson, Wilcox and Zhang.

"Acting Captain Renselaer, I am Lieutenant Joy Jefferson, formerly chief of our Weapons Deck on the destroyer *Philippines Sea*," she said succinctly. "Mehta is an asshole. He retreats in the face of enemy action. A fact which I will report to Earth Command. My ship and crew are at Alert Combat Ready. How may I assist you and the rest of the battle group?"

She smiled at the woman's blunt statement. Jefferson looked barely 30 years old, but must be years beyond that in order to have reached the rank of Lieutenant. And her former work as chief of her ship's Weapons Deck said she must also be a deadly opponent. Daisy looked away from the wallscreen image and up to Jacob.

"Your support and allegiance to our battle group is very welcome," Jacob said, his tone and manner nonchalant, as if Mehta's defiance had never happened. "Keep watch on the enemy ships by way of your spysats. Report any behavior change to me. And move to the left flank of the *Lepanto* to cover the spot left open by the departure of *Salamis*. Monitor the remainder of my discussions with the other ships."

The woman spoke a few words to her XO, then nodded, her blue eyes bright. "The *Philippines Sea* is moving to your left flank. We stand ready to launch missiles and fire gas and proton lasers upon your orders." Jefferson sat back, crossed gloved hands over her vacsuit and changed her mood. "Frankly, I don't give a damn what your old rank was! You found the status code, changed the *Lepanto's* status to Alert Hostile Enemy and actually *did* something when we lost all contact with our senior officers. Your launch of the Cloud

Skimmer told us facts, versus useless speculation. I will always follow and support any officer who dares to act!"

Jacob smiled briefly. Then his expression became sober serious. "Thank you, Acting Captain Jefferson. I rely upon the assistance of the *Philippines Sea* and her 113 personnel of all ranks. Working together, this battle group can present a deadly response to any enemy attack. Stand by and monitor."

"Monitoring."

Daisy sat back, feeling amazement at Jacob's calmness in the face of defiance from one ship's new captain. Was this an ability he had learned from his five star admiral father? She knew of his famous family heritage, even though he had never mentioned it. It was clear early on that Jacob was doing his best to earn respect by doing his ensign job to the best of his ability. The man had never asked Admiral Johanson for any special favors, nor sought to use his father's name to influence others on board the *Lepanto*. That manner, joined with his welcoming of two enlisteds to the ensigns ward room, now made her even more determined to remain as his friend, his ally and, perhaps in the future, something more.

In minutes the acting captains of the group's four frigates had called in, had pledged their allegiance to Jacob's leadership and had joined the images of the captains of the group's two cruisers and two remaining destroyers. Counting the *Lepanto*, that gave them a battle group of nine ships versus the 12 enemy ships. Would they win a battle with the wasps? What secret weapons did the wasps possess that were unknown to the battle group?

"O'Hara," Jacob called firmly. "We have six spysats over there keeping an eye on the meeting site and the aliens at geosync. Move one of our spysats up orbit to a close pass-by of the largest alien ship. Let's see what that ship looks like, close up."

"Changing vector of spysat A4," O'Hara said quickly.

Daisy fixed back on her holo of the enemy ships. But her armrest screen image of Jacob showed him leaning forward.

"Power, Engines, Gravity, Life Support and Science, feed me your current status reports," he called to the Bridge crew who had not been involved in any of the events of the last hour or so.

"Science transmits status data," called a man she recognized from her study of Command Deck staff. It was Willard Steinmetz. His deep booming voice echoed off the Bridge walls.

"All fusion reactors are at full power output," called Maggie Lowenstein from Power.

"Fusion pulse engines are hot," responded Akira M'Bala at Engines.

Daisy listened as the other posts sent Jacob their status reports. It was, in a way, a means of distracting everyone from the uncertainty of the next few moments when the spysat would approach the enemy's flagship. What would happen? Would a weapon fire on it? How would the wasps react to the departure of the *Salamis*? And how would the officers in charge of other decks on the *Lepanto* react to the sight of the destroyed meeting location, Jacob's orders to the battle group and the defiance of one ship captain? She hoped the *Lepanto's* officers would follow the manner of the cruiser captains. Now was not a time for disunity.

◆ ◆ ◆

"Alarm!" came the pheromone signal from a Servant at the control panel that monitored external space. "Soft Skin flying nest is changing position. It is leaving its perch above Warmth."

Many pheromones now filled the Flight Chamber. Hunter drew in the varied scents through his spiracles, focused his two major eyes on the perception imager that depicted the Soft Skin flying nest, and saw with his three minor eyes the spreading of wings among his Servants. The time for waiting had drawn to a close.

"Prepare for attack flight against the Soft Skin flying nests," he sent by way of a releaser pheromone mixed with a territorial pheromone to remind his fellow Swarmers of the need to defend their new home territory.

"Propulsive devices are reaching peak heat," said an older Servant with long experience in handling the devices that moved their nest by use of particle fusion events. The Servant's compliance pheromone carried an overlay of aggregating pheromone.

Hunter liked the creature's emission of loyalty. The scent now spread among all Servants who worked in the Flight Chamber. "Speaker To All," he scent cast to the young male Servant who managed the device that sent pheromone-laden words to the other flying nests in his two six-groups of mobile nests. "Advise the other

Support Hunters to do as we do. Prepare to leave our high flight for an englobing attack on the Soft Skins."

"Scent transmitted by low sound signaler," the Servant replied by way of a primer pheromone that signaled a change in behavior was now ordered for all Swarm members and cohorts.

"Hunter!" called the first Servant. "A Soft Skin monitor globe moves up toward us. It is unknown if it carries a stinger."

"Allow the globe to approach us," Hunter said by way of a sharp releaser pheromone. "Advise the Fighter Leader in charge of our sky bolt weapons to prepare his Fighters."

"Signal sent," rasped the Servant in charge of between chambers communication. "What of our fellow flying nests?" she said by way of an aggregator pheromone mixed with a trail pheromone.

Loyalty shown deserved confidence given by him. "Our fellow flying nests aggregate with us," he scent cast. "Be not alarmed. Attend to scents on our nest levels and advise me of any alarm among our Workers."

The within nest communicator Servant flared her elderly wings. "Attending to the scents of other chambers!"

Hunter watched the approach of the monitor globe. Let it come. They would meet it with a sky bolt. That would bring fear and chaos to the invaders. Already one Soft Skin nest had flown away in fright. More might do the same. While his two six-groups of ships could fatally sting all the Soft Skin nests, he welcomed the arrival of disunity among the Soft Skins. Their chaos gave him time and opportunity for imposing his command over the world of Warmth. Which reminded him of a last duty before they winged to the attack.

"Matron," he scent cast to the large female who occupied a bowl at the rear of his Flight Chamber. "Signal to your fellow Matrons on our other nests it is time to release the Pods! Send down our eggs with the Servants and Workers needed to raise them to adulthood. We must finish colonizing this new home nest before we fight the Soft Skins!"

Rasping came from behind him, followed by a strong scent of primer pheromones.

"Pods release is being sent to my fellow Matrons," called the Swarmer who occupied the second most important post on any Swarm flying nest. His acoustic membranes heard her tapping on a pheromone signal device that allowed her independent communication with the other flying nests. "Scent has been sent to my Servants and Workers on this nest who will ride the Pods down to the new nest of Warmth!"

Hunter's four foot pads felt the floor of the chamber vibrate as twelve six-groups of Pods flew out of his flying nest the way some plants on Nest shot forth their own seeds. Similar vibrations would be felt by the Support Hunters on the other flying nests of the Swarm. One more new nest was now being colonized. The Soft Skin and Hard Shell life below them would be rich food sources for the newborn larvae of the many Pods now raining down on Warmth. The Servants and Workers would sting any large creature, paralyze it and bring it back to a Pod to serve as food for the new lives. Such was the way it had been on Nest for long generations. Such was the way it would be on Warmth, the ninth world colonized by the Swarm. Briefly, he wondered if the two-legged Soft Skins who flew about in their own flying nests would understand the meaning of the Pods descent. No matter. The Pods would reach the warm soil of Warmth well before the Swarm came within stinger range of the intruding Soft Skins. Perhaps some Soft Skins would survive the attack of the Swarm. Any that did would be added to the paralyzed food that would nourish the first generation of Swarmers on the world of Warmth.

♦ ♦ ♦

Support Hunter Seven inhaled the scent of the Pods release order from Hunter One's Matron. It was the only good scent news he had sensed in many rest cycles. At last, Hunter One was doing what they had been sent to do. Colonize the nest world below them. That effort had been interrupted by the arrival of diseased Soft Skins. Rather than attack immediately as was Swarm tradition, Hunter One had arranged the deception of the meeting site. He gave brief credit to the colonizing leader. The deception had allowed for the killing of Soft Skin leaders. And a Soft Skin flying nest had already departed in an early sign of chaos and confusion. Soon, their two six-groups of flying nests would attack the intruding Soft Skins. Perhaps in the attack, Hunter One would be injured or killed. He hoped so. However, he guarded his feelings least he emit any sign of disloyalty. Pheromones were the natural way of speech. Thought gave way to pheromones which conveyed one's feelings, one's emotions and one's words to anyone close enough to smell them. The invention of remote pheromone signaling devices meant he smelled every pheromone released on the nest of Hunter One, just as that leader smelled every scent released on his ship. With an effort he released an aggregation pheromone, signaling loyalty to the orders of Hunter One.

"Matron, release our Pods," he scent cast to the female resting behind him in his Flight Chamber.

"Release scent emitted," rasped the older female.

There was only a single Matron on each flying nest of the Swarm's colonizing flight. Which made them both unique and valuable. Eventually his Matron would join the Matrons on other Swarmer nests in descending to the world of Warmth, there to give guidance to the new generation of Swarmers. That was for later. Now, it was time for the attack.

"Servant," he called to the Swarmer in charge of directing Fighter Leaders and Fighters. "Tell our Fighters to move to their sky bolt devices. Also send some Fighters to our sky light weapons. Make sure our mindless particle disruption seeds are ready for launch. And warn the defender Fighters to prepare for Soft Skin attack on our outer hard shell."

Alarm and releaser pheromones filled the Flight Chamber.

Inside, in his mind, Support Hunter Seven planned for the day when he would lead the other flying nests. Hunter One could not make perfect scent casts all the time. A moment of error would come. When that happened, he would lead his flying nest to take control of the colonizing effort. Being in charge of what mattered was a long tradition in the cohort of Hunters.

◆ ◆ ◆

Aarhant Bannerjee listened with anger and frustration as the young whelp Renselaer took command of the *Lepanto* and the battle group. He was alone in his office on Navigation Deck. Up to an hour ago, he had been asleep in his personal quarters. That period of rest had stolen from him the opportunity to appear on the Command Deck, announce he was taking command of the *Lepanto* as the most senior officer still alive on the ship, and then be the one ordering the Cloud Skimmer launch and garnering the allegiance of the other ships in the group. At least his culture mate Mehta had had the sense to defy the young ensign who had seized command. No doubt Renselaer's presence on the *Lepanto* had come about so he could seize control of one of Earth's Battlestars for the glory of his father. Well, his people had a long history of battling invaders. American he might be by birth, but Hindu he was by the grace of the Lord Shiva and by the influence of his parents, who occupied high posts in Earth Command. Surely they would support his elevation to command of the *Lepanto*, once the battle group left this accursed system and made contact with the Star Navy base in Kepler 10. Gritting his teeth he wished for the miracle of FTL communications with Earth. Such did not exist. Orders came from Earth only by way of a traveling starship. News came to Earth the same way. Well, the sly French had a word for what he planned to achieve. It was called *fait accompli*.

But for the moment he must pretend allegiance to the young whelp. If the wasp aliens really did attack, the only way he would survive was for the *Lepanto* to survive. He would work to ensure that. And to ensure they soon made their way to Kepler 10. That was the single comment he'd heard Renselaer make which made sense in view of the disaster at the meeting site. Maybe the officers on site had insulted the aliens. Maybe a lowly ensign had shown disrespect, as was common among the American lower classes. Perhaps the aliens had a right to this world. Although humans could live well on a world with a half gee gravity, it was healthier living on an Earth-like world with stronger gravity. Sadly, planet three was twice the size of Earth, had nearly twice its gravity, and the inner two worlds were analogues of Venus and Mercury. Which meant humans either took control of planet four, or they left for another star system.

"Lieutenant Commander," spoke his tablet as it lay on the surface of his fold-down desk. "This is CPO Louise Slaughter on the Bridge. Have you been following the surprises here?"

He tapped the tablet to voice active. "I have. Provide Acting Captain Renselaer with the coordinates and vector track for Kepler 10. We can only hope we can depart this system before we are attacked."

"Sir?" the woman said, her tone puzzled. "The aliens attacked our captains and XOs and ensigns. That is an act of war. Why should we retreat?"

Louise, Louise, how blind you are to class reality. "It is not a retreat to warn Earth of the presence of deadly and dangerous aliens.

They are the first space-going aliens we have met." What should he say to sound properly loyal? "Our first duty is to warn Earth. Which we can do by heading for Kepler 10. On our arrival there we can send a frigate to Earth with word of these aliens. The frigate can leave before the aliens arrive, if they are able to plot our vector track and deduce the star we are headed for. Understood?"

"Understood, sir. I will provide Acting Captain Renselaer with the coordinates and vector track to Kepler 10. Sir, do you plan to visit the Bridge?"

Ah. A sneaky fem this woman is. Has she already slept with the Renselaer youth? "There is no need for my presence on the Bridge. I will monitor the All Ship transmissions from the Bridge in case my assistance is needed. Carry out your duties."

"Thank you, lieutenant commander," Slaughter said, her tone sounding relieved. "Good day sir."

"Good day to you, Chief Petty Officer Slaughter."

The tablet went silent. The image of Slaughter disappeared.

Well, that should keep the bitch out of his hair. Meanwhile, he must sound out the other officers, CPOs and CWOs who ran the other decks. Were any of them as bothered by the arrogance of Ensign Renselaer as he was?

♦ ♦ ♦

Jacob watched the holo in front of him that depicted the twelve wasp ships. They were arranged in two groups of six. Holding a fixed orbit above the meeting site, none of the ships had done anything since the lightning storm, the end of tablet contact, his launch of the Cloud Skimmer and his assumption of command of the *Lepanto* and the battle group. The spysat that O'Hara had sent up toward those ships now passed within 10,000 kilometers of the largest wasp ship. Nothing happened. Surely they were aware of the spysat's approach. What did the lack of action mean?

"Acting Captain," O'Hara called from her function post. "Spysat imagery in normal light, ultraviolet, infrared and radio waves now going up on the wallscreen."

He watched as a series of different colored views of the 12 ships took shape alongside the images of the wasp ships. The local star's white-yellow light was strong at 1.1 AU out. It gave the wasp ships a silvery look, leastwise on the sides that faced the star. Being at geosync meant the wasp ships were out of the shadow cast by the planet below. His battle group ships lay on the opposite side of the world, with the star behind them as they viewed the daylight side of the world below. Their geosync orbit had allowed them to maintain position directly opposite the alien ships.

"Captain!" called Oliver from his Weapons post. "The wasp ships are ejecting little pods! Dozens of them. Each ship is ejecting them. Uh, the pods appear to be on a freefall trajectory down toward the planet."

His heart slowed its fast beating. This was not an attack on the spysat, but something else. What? These pods were half the size of the transports that had landed at the meeting site. Which meant they could only carry ten or so wasp people. Surely the wasps were not bombarding the planet. Were these colonizing ships? Earth's shuttles that carried down colonists were the size of frigates. Seventy people could fit inside one of those colonizing shuttles. But who said the wasps had to send down colonists the way humans did it?

"Chief Warrant Officer Diego y Silva, thank you for that information. I do not see any cause for alarm in these pods." He looked over to O'Hara at Tactical. The woman controlled all sensors on the spysats and comsats that orbited on the far side of the world below. "Chief Petty Officer O'Hara, what do your sensors say about those pods?"

The woman looked down at her control pillar, then up at her tactical graphic hologram that depicted their ships, the planet below, the wasp ships on the far side, every spysat and comsat launched by humans or wasps, and nearby space out to a hundred thousand kilometers. "Acting Captain, infrared says each pod is warm. Warm enough for people to be inside. Ultraviolet says there are chemical rockets on the nose of the pods. Maybe for attitude control. Each pod resembles a metal cone with its rounded base aimed toward the planet. The bases may be re-entry heat shields. There are radio emissions passing among the pods. They are not visual imagery signals. Uh, I would guess there are wasp people inside the pods and that the pods plan on landing on the continent below them."

Jacob nodded, thinking hard. "Weapons, can you tell anything about those tubes on the wasp ships from the multi-spectral imagery coming in from the spysat?"

"Very little," the man said, his Brazilian accent almost non-existent. "They show warm in infrared. There are ultraviolent glows about them. Energy emissions are localized at the base of each tube. They are—"

Bright yellow light filled the true space holo that showed the ship nearest the spysat. The crooked light beam came straight at the imager eye of the spysat. Then the image went blank. Other spysats watching from a lower orbit showed an expanding yellow glow where the spysat had once been.

"Spysat destroyed," O'Hara said sharply.

Jacob knew that. The imagery was clear about what had happened. "Tactical, Weapons, do either of you have any idea what kind of weapon that yellow bolt was?"

"A lightning bolt," muttered Osashi from his Communications post, surprising Jacob.

Ignoring the sudden comment from the warrant officer, he looked to O'Hara and Diego y Silva.

"Sir," called the Weapons chief, "it does indeed resemble a lightning bolt. My sensors report an extremely powerful electrical emission from the tube that emitted the bolt."

"Same data from my spysat sensors," O'Hara said quickly.

He looked to the Navigation post. "CPO Slaughter, what was the distance from the spysat to the ship that blasted it?"

The Navigation chief jumped in her seat at his words, then bent forward to check her control pillar. "My nav sensors compute the distance as being just shy of 4,000 kilometers."

"Thank you."

Jacob thought that was a hell of a range for a non-coherent beam weapon. Then again, their antimatter beam reached that far out, thanks to magnetic lensing of the emitted antimatter. Maybe a similar electromag lens had controlled the lightning bolt beam.

"Weapons, share your data with the Weapons stations on our other ships. Tactical, do the same for your sensor feeds with other ship Tactical posts," he said, racking his mind for what else he should do or say or realize.

"Captain!" cried Slaughter at Navigation. "The wasp ships are moving!"

He saw now what the Nav chief reported. His separate holo that depicted the twelve wasp ships now showed yellow-orange flares coming from the rear of each ship. Sensor datafiles said they were fusion pulse exhausts. The same as the normal space drives possessed by every battle group ship. As best he could tell from the spysat imagery, the twelve ships were angling down toward the planet, but aiming for its north pole. His academy courses in astrophysics and orbital mechanics told him what was happening.

"Melody, activate the All Ship vidcom. And transmit what I say and my image to all other ships."

"Activating. Transmitting."

"All personnel. The alien wasp ships are leaving geosync orbit," Jacob said, doing his best to make his tone sound firm, determined and confident. "They are moving to a lower orbit and aiming for the planet's north pole. Which will give them an increase in speed. That means they will arrive on our side of the world within 40 minutes. Or less if they keep thrusting. Prepare for combat. Melody, change ship status to Alert Hostile Enemy."

"Ship status changed to Alert Hostile Enemy," the AI said, her tone a mix of excitement and worry.

Jacob reached up and pulled his helmet down over his head. It sealed with a snap-click. The vacsuit's enviro controls started up with a blast of oxy-nitrogen. Telltale status lights appeared in a chin-up position just below his nose. His seat vibrated as automatic straps moved out and over his chest in an x-pattern. Pairs of straps went over his legs. The straps were a backup to the inertial damper field that covered the entire ship. Above, purple lights blinked from the ceiling and a whirring siren that sounded like an old-style fire engine filled the Bridge and echoed over his helmet's comlink speaker.

"Crew, prepare for combat. Battle group, crosslink your Weapons Deck targeting with the targeting sensors of other ships." He paused, then realized what else he needed to say. "We will prevail!"

CHAPTER FOUR

Thirty-three minutes later, the wasp ships were rising up to Jacob's geosync orbit. Electro-optical scope imagery on the front wallscreen showed the enemy still maintaining its two six-ship clusters as yellow-orange fusion flames pushed them toward Jacob and his battle group. Carlos and Lori were still seated in the observer seats behind him. Quincy had left for his combat post at the right pod laser node. Daisy sat in the XO seat below him. Filling the seat formerly occupied by the ship's captain, at Daisy's right, was the man he had called up to the Bridge right after the declaration of Alert Hostile Enemy. The timer on his left armrest said the enemy would reach the range of their CO_2 and proton lasers within nine minutes. Time enough.

"Chief Warrant Officer Richard O'Connor, what do you make of the enemy formation?"

The man in command of the twenty Marine boarders on the *Lepanto* wore a vacsuit and helmet and was strapped in just like Jacob, Daisy and everyone else. Keeping his attention on the front wallscreen, with its sensor listings on the right and left sides of the true space image, the man spoke.

"I think their maintenance of the two six-ship formation means their commander is wedded to traditional attack formations," the man said, his deep bass voice sounding thoughtful. "Which means our fleet movements may surprise him. Or her. Or it."

Jacob almost smiled. He didn't. Everything that now happened on the Bridge and on every other deck of the *Lepanto* was being recorded by the ship's AI. It would be subject to review by Earth Command. And perhaps by the captain in charge of the Star Base at Kepler 10. He was not about to show amusement when lives were at stake. The reality of his first combat had been the reason he had called O'Connor up to the Bridge. The man was the only officer on the *Lepanto* with true experience at deadly combat. He'd led a Marine battalion in the invasion of the island Mauritius after its elected leaders were overthrown by a Muslim jihadist group. While the Islamic State was dead and old history, the extreme fringes of Islam still tried to recreate the caliphate of ancient times. America and other nations had moved to end the newest safe haven for religious fanatics. O'Connor's battalion, assisted by Darts and F-37 jets, had reduced the jihadist stronghold in the island's capital. Then had come the ground attack. The fighting had been bloody, without mercy, and the man carried a scar on his left cheek from that fighting. That had been twelve years ago. His presence on the *Lepanto* showed his superiors had confidence in his judgment. Which was a second reason Jacob had called him to the Bridge. The man might understand enemy actions that Jacob didn't.

"Good," he replied. He looked up. "Melody, activate our neutrino audiovid link with the other ships."

"Encrypted link activated."

Jacob stared straight ahead, but his mind was already visualizing three dimensional maneuvers. "All battle group ships, change your orbital orientation by 90 degrees. Point your noses downplanet and toward the oncoming enemy."

Compliance responses came from the two cruisers, two destroyers and four frigates that surrounded the *Lepanto*.

"All ships, move to the Alpha Ring formation," he said, giving thanks he had paid attention to the academy class that covered standard spaceship battle formations. "Cruiser *Chesapeake*, move to directly above the *Lepanto*. Cruiser *Hampton Roads*, move to directly below the *Lepanto*. Destroyer *Tsushima Strait*, move to the right side of us. Destroyer *Philippines Sea*, move to the left of us. Frigates *St. Mihiel, Marianas, Britain* and *Ofira*, move to the 45 degree spots between the four majors."

"Moving," called Swanson.

"Dropping," said Wilcox.

"Going to your right," responded Zhang.

"Going left," Jefferson said tightly.

The frigate captains each responded and moved to their positions between the heavier ships.

"Battle group, move your ships out from the *Lepanto* to a distance of one thousand kilometers. Maintain the same separation between nearby ships."

Jacob watched as yellow-orange flares spit out from the rear of each ship in the battle group, followed by purple flares from attitude control thrusters.

The end result satisfied him. The *Lepanto* lay at the center of the circle of eight ships. There was enough space between each ship so the plasma batteries could be set on automatic against any incoming Smart Rocks or missiles. The 400 kilometer range of each ship's plasma battery, or batteries for the five larger ships, would cover the space between each ship, with no blue-on-blue accidental damage.

"You like wheels, don't you?" O'Connor muttered.

Was the man challenging him? Or just making small talk until the real fighting began?

"I do. In Binghamton where I grew up, the kids in our exurb played the Wheel Game with metal hoops. It was fun." Jacob paused, knowing the nine crew at the front function posts, plus Daisy, Carlos and Lori, were hearing everything he said thanks to their helmet comlinks. "More importantly, this formation is suited to an attack coming from a linear direction. It allows maximum beam energy weapons use while minimizing accidental cross-fire."

The middle-aged man, whose white hair was crewcut with sidewalls in the traditional Marine look, chuckled. "It's fine, young Renselaer. I would be doing the same. Though I do like attack probes from unexpected directions."

Jacob licked his lips, his tension rising as the enemy fleet neared their orbit. "I do too. The frigates may try sniping runs after the first exchange."

"Good," O'Connor said.

Jacob felt his heart beating faster. His fingertips, which hovered just above his armrest control patches, trembled slightly. He took a deep breath, told himself that the officers in charge on the other decks had all pledged their allegiance to him, and the Darts did not need O'Connor's presence to launch on boarding attacks. Or to launch and defend against wasp efforts to board the *Lepanto* or other battle group ships. For a moment, he felt calm.

"All ships, wait to fire upon my command. Cross-link your fire control targeting with that of every other ship."

♦ ♦ ♦

"Alarm!" scent cast the Servant who monitored external space events. "Soft Skin flying nests have changed formation. They are assuming . . . a defense pattern."

Hunter could both see and sense what the Servant was reporting. The evidence of coherent behavior by the flying nests was a disappointment. He had thought the loss of their leaders would render the Soft Skins confused and fearful. Instead, it appeared some Fighter Leaders had survived on the mobile nests.

"Soft Skin nests are moving with controlled propulsion," scent cast another Servant tasked with monitoring the individual flying nests of the Soft Skins. The signal pheromones emitted by the elderly female Servant were calm and helpful.

Hunter responded to the surprise by emitting a mix of aggregation, primer and territorial pheromones. Each Swarmer in the Flight Chamber was being called to defend their new home nest, while being reminded that an englobing attack by the Swarm required complete loyalty and group coordination. His scent mix was also being sent to every other Swarmer mobile nest.

"Speaker To All," he said to the young male Servant who managed the device that sent pheromone-laden words to the other flying nests. "Scent cast to our Support Hunters it is time to move our mobile nests into a half-globe. Make the outer edge of our globe larger than the major eye width of the Soft Skin nests."

"Casting your scent orders," the Servant replied by way of a releaser pheromone.

Hunter breathed deep the mixed pheromones of the Swarmers in the Flight Chamber, then the cooler scents emitted from each flying nest that held Swarmers. The feelings from other nests were excited, eager and ready to sting. His own stinger twitched in automatic response to the scent sense of other Swarmers. Moving as a cloud to envelop the enemy had always worked for the Swarm when battling other cohorts. Surely it would work even better in the attack on the Soft Skins.

◆ ◆ ◆

Daisy's peripheral vision noted the calm, relaxed manner of O'Connor the Marine. She had been surprised by the man's arrival. Then she had realized she, Carlos, Quincy and Lori were only the beginnings of the brain trust that Jacob was bringing to the Bridge. It impressed her that her friend had had the guts to call to the Bridge a man with deep experience fighting deadly battles. It made sense of course. Neither Jacob, nor herself, nor any of their friends had ever been in a true battle against an enemy who sought to kill you. Digital and video simulations at the academy were useful training. But you always knew you would come out of the simulator in one piece. At least until the warrant officer in charge showed up to harangue you on what you had done wrong. Now, they were indeed entering battle. It was an experience new to most enlisteds and officers on the *Lepanto* and on the other battle group ships. The last true spaceship-on-spaceship battle had been the Callisto Conflict of twenty years ago. After the discovery of faster than light star travel, every group of humans had focused on putting together the funds and resources to send off a colonizing group. Routine arguments had withered in face of the wonders of star travel. Now, that innocence had ended.

"XO," called Jacob. "Are the Weapons Deck and our weapons systems at Battle Condition One?"

She glanced at the ship deck layout holo, which hovered to the left of the holo that showed a true space image of the approaching wasp ships. "They are, acting captain. Our antimatter cannon has a reservoir of four shots."

"Good." Her armrest screen image of him and everyone else on the Bridge showed him sitting back in his seat. "Weapons chief Diego y Silva, advise the petty officer in charge of the AM cannon to not fire until I give the order."

She saw the Brazilian reach out and tap his control pillar. "Directive sent, acting captain."

The wasp ship hologram drew her attention.

"Captain!" Daisy called quickly. "Wasp ships are changing formation. They are moving to a half globe shape. Their primary ship is at the center and rear of the new formation. Approach speed is slowed to 900 kilometers per minute."

"Sir," called Rosemary from Tactical. "That is also what my sensors show. Like us, they are moving on fusion pulse and attitude exhausts. Uh, my EMF sensors report the forward tube groups on each wasp ship are energizing. Power emissions are spiking."

Did that mean the enemy was about to fire on them? Daisy glanced at the range tracker that showed the kilometers to each wasp ship. The range showed as a number icon next to the Wasp number applied by Rosemary as a means of referencing a particular enemy ship. Briefly she recalled that Rosemary's icon designation was being shared with the Bridges and Weapons Decks of other battle group ships. Those signals went by neutrino transmission through an alternate dimension. It meant each ship could coordinate with other ships even in the midst of a thermonuclear blast that disrupted normal EMF emissions.

"All ships," called Jacob. "Multiple hostile bandits approaching. You are cleared hot. Kill is authorized. *Philippines Sea, St. Mihiel, Chesapeake* and *Marianas*, coordinate your laser and proton fire at single targets in sequence. *Tsushima Strait, Britain, Hampton Roads* and *Ofira*, do the same. The *Lepanto* will fire on targets of opportunity."

Daisy's mind filled with the tactical imagery of the coming battle. The wasp ships were a bowl approaching the flat plate of their formation. Jacob had just ordered the other ships to link their laser and proton fire on a single target, the better to achieve punch through. His ship naming made for two groups of four ships that would fire on a single target. Which meant two wasp ships would be hit at first, along with whatever the *Lepanto* fired. Then two more, followed by two more. The beam energy firing would rotate among the oncoming ships. The firing of Smart Rocks by the *Lepanto's* four railguns and the launching of thermonuke missiles from their tail launch silos would happen later as the enemy grew closer than the outer 10,000 klick reach of their CO_2 and proton lasers.

"Acting captain," called Rosemary from Tactical. "What target for our gunners?"

"The enemy's formation is six ships in the outer and closer rim of the half globe," Jacob grunted. "The other ships are scattered further back, with the largest wasp ship at the center and rear of the half globe. Target the wasp ship at 10 o'clock radial track, bandit W9."

"Targeting," Rosemary said, tapping her control panel to send the selected wasp ship coordinates to the carbon dioxide laser gunners at the front ends of the right and left outrigger pods.

Daisy saw those stations go Red Active on her ship deck holo. Everyone else was at Orange Ready status. The proton lasers were aimed sideways at a 90 degree angle off of their head-on aim. The rear pair of lasers and the missile silos waited for an enemy to enter their targeting zone. And the railguns and plasma batteries waited for close-in targets like self-guided missiles and Smart Rocks. She felt her heart beat faster and her skin felt sweaty under the vacsuit fabric. Cool air in her helmet did nothing to relieve the tenseness of her body.

♦ ♦ ♦

Hunter rose off his control bench. His five eyes took in all the perception images and scent trails emitted by the Servants in front of and to either side of him. What did the shape of the Soft Skin formation mean? They had not moved into a half globe for enveloping of his Swarm mobile nests, as another Swarmer would try to do. Nor had they run away on propulsive emissions as a small Swarm group would do when faced with a larger Swarm group moving to attack. On his world of Nest the rule was simple. Fight and defend your territory. Fly away and lose the territory. Or surrender to the new Hunter by offering the sacrifice of their failed Hunter. The last option was how the Swarm had come to control all parts of their home of Nest. No creature, whether of air, water or ground, challenged the Swarm. All other creatures sought to survive. These Soft Skins chose to fight even though they had fewer flying nests than the Swarm. Nine against twelve was an obvious flight path to defeat and death. So be it.

"Stinger Servant!" he scent cast with a strong primer pheromone. "Are the Soft Skin nests within attack range?"

"Not yet," the young female replied. "Within seventy beats of our wings they will be. Very soon."

He inhaled her mix of pheromones. And those of Stinger Servants on the other Swarm flying nests. All were ready. All were eager to attack and kill the enemy that sought to claim their new home nest. "Support Hunters, sting and move as you desire," he said in a mix of aggregation, primer and signal pheromones. "Maintain the shape of our formation, but sting the way your ancestors stung!"

"Range achieved!" signaled the Stinger Servant.

"Sting them!" he scent cast with a massive flow of signal pheromones.

His four foot pads felt the floor humming as the front group of stinger tubes unleashed sky bolts and sky light strikes. His hearing membranes heard the rasping of forearms against hard shells as everyone in the Flight Chamber joined in the attack excitement.

♦ ♦ ♦

Jacob felt shock as yellow lightning bolts and green laser beams shot out from the front group of six wasp ships. The enemy was still 11,000 kilometers distant. Beyond the range of their own CO_2 and proton lasers. But not beyond the enemy's range.

"Spinning ship!" yelled Slaughter at Navigation.

His eyes saw the red dots of laser and bolt strikes as they struck parts of the *Lepanto* cross-section that floated to his right in one of the four holos before him. Four hits. Two laser strikes on the lower hull just below the Bridge and two lightning bolt hits on the upper hull, just ahead of the right front railgun launcher. He blinked, then realized the adaptive optics and ablative hull coatings had deflected most of the incoming energy. What did penetrate was stopped by the ship's thick armor.

"All ships, accelerate forward!" he yelled over his helmet comlink that linked him with both his Bridge crew and with the other ships by way of the constant neutrino signals that passed among all their ships. "Break orbit and approach enemy at 900 klicks per minute!"

"Our three main fusion thrusters are firing!" called Akira M'Bala from her Engines post.

Everyone was doing their job. Slaughter had activated the attitude jets to spin the ship about its long axis, thereby reducing the time of impact of enemy beams on any part of the *Lepanto's* outer hull. M'Bala had kept the ship's three main fusion pulse drives hot and ready for further use. The *Lepanto* and the eight other ships of the formation now moved forward toward the enemy, no longer holding a stationary geosync position. That joint movement made it harder for the enemy gunners to target any Earth ship and brought the nine of them within range of their own weapons sooner. They needed to fire, now that it was apparent the wasp ships had a slightly greater range for their lasers and lightning bolt weapons than the range of human beam energy weapons.

"Steinmetz!" he yelled. "Analyze enemy weapons. How can they have greater range than our weapons?"

The portly man reached out one hand and touched his Science control pillar. "Sensors report the front ring of tubes on each enemy ship contains both lightning bolt and laser emitters. No idea how the bolt weapon can reach us. The laser beams that impacted had weak power. Clearly they were operating at the extreme end of their weapon's focusing power."

Which told him something but nothing of real use. "Tactical! Fire! All ships, fire on enemy hostiles!"

"Firing!" called O'Hara.

Jacob watched as the left and right front laser nodes shot out two green beams at wasp ship W9. The two side proton lasers had to wait until wasp ships were to the left and right of the *Lepanto*. As would the proton lasers on the top and belly of the ship. The Battlestar had incredible weaponry. Two laser nodes on the front ends of the two outrigger pods, two at the rear of the pods, plasma batteries on the spine and belly, eight missile launch silos that circled the ship's three main exhaust funnels, two front and two rear railguns on the top half of the hull along with four on the bottom half of the hull. Plus their *coup de main* was the antimatter cannon at the front nose of the ship. Its emitter portal had little directional mobility. It could only fire straight ahead, at whatever the ship's nose was pointed at. Which right now was the largest enemy wasp ship. It lay well beyond the weapon's 4,000 kilometer range given the enemy's placement at the rear of the wasp formation.

"Hits on W9!" cried O'Hara.

He saw that in the true space holo that hovered to the right of his seat. There was the silvery sparkle of hull fragments and white puffs of something that must be air. Leastwise, that was what his ship's topside electro-optical scope showed in the telescopic view of the enemy. The left side holo with its sensor glows for each enemy ship showed three red infrared spots on the forward hull of the enemy ship. Damaged it was, but not destroyed.

"Hits on two other wasp ships!" called Daisy from her XO seat.

Jacob's eyes drank it all in. Wasp ships W2 and W5 had been hit and damaged by the lasers fired by the cruisers, destroyers and frigates of his formation. Mentally he visualized the weaponry placement of each ship. The cruisers were nearly as powerful as the *Lepanto*. They had dual lasers at the nose and tail, proton lasers on the right and left sides of the ship, plasma batteries at top and bottom, a single railgun launcher on the front nose and four missile launch silos at the rear. The destroyers were smaller but just as deadly. Each one had a single proton laser at the nose, two CO_2 laser nodes at the tail, plasma batteries at top and bottom, and two missile launch silos at the rear. The frigates were swift and mobile but lacked proton lasers. They carried CO_2 lasers at the nose and tail, a single plasma battery and a single missile launch silo at the rear.

"*Britain* reports damage to its topside plasma battery," Daisy called out, adding words to what Jacob saw in his left side holo that showed sensor images of the battle group's eight ships. "*Philippines Sea* reports glancing strike on one of its two nose lasers. Both ships remain combat operational."

Three enemy ships hit in return for hits on three battle group ships, including the *Lepanto*. Jacob did not like equal exchanges. "Slaughter! Shift our forward angle by twenty degrees. Bring us within target aim for W9!"

"Adjusting ship's vector track," the woman said hurriedly. "But W9 and all the wasp ships are now jinking erratically. Looks like a random walk formation. Or something like that."

Jacob saw the enemy ship movements in his right side true space holo. Which now showed the six nearest enemy ships again firing green lasers and yellow lightning bolts at the battle fleet ships. In the same instant his left side holo showed the two groups of his ships firing lasers at two new wasp ships. That made for twelve lasers aimed at two ships. Surely punch through would happen—

"W8 shows an explosion on the middle of its hull!" cried O'Hara from Tactical. "Ship's jinking has stopped. Motive power is disrupted."

"*Ofira* and *Hampton Roads* each report laser and bolt hits on their front ends," Daisy called over their shared comlink. "Both ships are still combat operational."

Impatience filled Jacob. The range to the front group of six enemy ships was now down to 4,875 kilometers, thanks to the continuing fusion pulse acceleration of the *Lepanto* and the battle group. The enemy was rushing toward them and they were rushing toward the enemy. Which gave both groups a rapidly increasing closure speed.

"Navigation, shift *Lepanto's* swing to focus on W8." He licked his lips and told his nerves to get the hell out of his mind. "Tactical, link me with the chief petty officer in charge of the antimatter cannon," he said.

"Linking," called O'Hara.

"CPO Jim Linkletter reporting," came the voice of a young man over Jacob's helmet comlink. "Acting captain, you have orders for me?"

"I do. Prepare to target wasp ship W8. It's wounded and not jinking. Advise me when it enters the impact zone of the cannon's beam."

Seconds passed. A third volley of laser and lightning bolt fire passed between the wasp ships and the battle group. Ships in both groups were jinking sideways using attitude thrusts and sometimes main drive flares so as to avoid presenting a simple fixed target to enemy gunners. Ships in both groups reported new hits. The frigate *Britain* reported a punch through to its midbody cargohold. Three dead. The ship was still operational and firing back with its nose laser.

"Target within reach!" called Linkletter.

At last. "Fire antimatter cannon!"

A black beam of magnetically confined negative antimatter shot out from the front of the *Lepanto* and impacted on the middle of the W8 wasp ship.

A small sun replaced the matter and living bodies of the wasp ship.

The expanding yellow-white globe of total matter-to-energy conversion grew and grew, then gradually began to fade as the absolute coldness of empty space drained the plasma ball of its coherence and energy. Eventually only a pale red shell of energetic particles marked the spot where an enemy ship had once lived.

"Linkletter!" Jacob yelled. "Fire at any wasp ship that comes within the impact zone of the AM cannon! Slaughter, shift our nose aim toward whatever enemy ship is closest to where W8 used to be."

"Shifting!" the woman responded.

"Ready to fire," Linkletter replied.

Jacob hoped the wasp ships and their leaders would be shocked into brief immobility by the total destruction of one of their ships. Moments were all he needed to gain a lock-on against another wasp ship. Would he have them?

CHAPTER FIVE

Shock filled Hunter's inner gut. The intruding Soft Skins possessed a black beam unlike anything known to the Swarm. What the beam hit instantly became a globe of plasma. No fragments remained. All aboard the flying nest he knew by its name of *Soft Nest* were gone. Vanished.

"Stinger Servant!" he alarm scent cast. "What kind of stinger is that?"

"Unknown," the young female scent cast in confused alarm pheromones. "The result resembles what happens in our propulsive devices that fly us through cold space. Or something hit by a flying seed. But particle disruption seeds leave fragments behind. This was not such a stinger."

"Hunter One," scent cast the Servant who monitored the cold radiations from space. "The weapon's impact resembles the few times we have seen distant sky lights explode and die. Perhaps the weapon captures whatever causes such sky death."

Hunter's shell hairs stood out as a chill filled the three sections of his hard shell body. Did these Soft Skin intruders possess a weapon capable of killing a sky light? Breathing fast through his spiracles, Hunter realized that only one Soft Skin flying nest had fired the deadly black beam. Which must mean other intruding flying nests lacked this terrible stinger. And the weapon's range was half or less than that of their sky bolt and sky light stingers. He scent cast a triple level of aggregation pheromones crossed with releaser pheromones.

"Support Hunters! Move your mobile nests outward! Move beyond the stinging range of this new weapon." What else must he scent cast? "Fighter Leaders, continue your attacks with our sky bolt and sky light stingers! Keep buzzing swiftly to avoid Soft Skin stingers! We have damaged four of their flying nests. A visit with the Matron goes to the stinger Servant who kills a Soft Skin flying nest!"

Sex always motivated every Swarmer. That was something Hunter knew as deeply as he breathed. The millions of eggs birthed each year by the thousands of Matrons on Nest were the cause of their search for new nest homes about distant sky lights. Giving the male stinger Servants an extra motivation for defending their flying nest could not hurt and might help. A new pheromone scent of *fertilization welcome* came to Hunter from the Matron behind him. Good. She agreed with his offer. Now, how soon before a Soft Skin flying nest died?

♦ ♦ ♦

Jacob watched as the wasp ship formation grew closer. The remaining five ships in the front wasp group were now within 3,987 kilometers of his ships. Less than a minute had passed since the antimatter beam firing. A fourth round of laser and sky bolt firings had occurred, with strikes on ships in both fleets. His eight allies were still whole and fighting. The *Lepanto's* right and left front laser nodes now joined a group of four ships firing at target W3, one of the five remaining front line wasp ships. But the inner group of wasp ships were at 4,312 kilometers out, including the giant wasp ship at the center of their half globe formation.

"Wasp ship W4 is now head-on to us," Slaughter called from Navigation.

"Ready to fire!" called Linkletter.

"Fire antimatter cannon at W4!" yelled Jacob.

A black beam speared out to the wasp ship that lay straight ahead but was jinking sideways, up and down in short, sharp movements.

It didn't matter. The meter-wide beam grew in width the further out it traveled.

A second star bloomed yellow-white against the darkness of space.

The plasma fireball's glow cast light on the dark terminator line of the planet below them.

"Yes!" yelled O'Connor from the seat to the right of Daisy. "Two enemy gone. That makes it ten enemy to our nine ships. Better and better."

Jacob agreed but stayed quiet. His father the admiral nearly always beat him at chess, ending up with the comment "Don't count your chickens before they hatch, young man." The early results of this first engagement were encouraging. But surely this enemy possessed more weapons than the laser and lightning bolt beams. He just hoped the wasps did not possess antimatter cannons. If they did, his ships could die just as easily as the two wasp ships had died.

A new star flare surprised him.

"W3 is gone!" cried O'Hara from Tactical.

How had this happened? His memory of images from the four holos in front gave him the answer. Their two groups of four ships had joined their twelve laser beams on a single wasp ship. The green lasers fired by Quincy's laser node and the *Lepanto's* left side node had joined in. Punch through had happened in three places, according to infrared emissions. One of the punch throughs must have hit the wasp ship's fusion reactor. Or something equally volatile. A yellow-orange fireball now consumed the wasp ship, the fireball spreading from the middle out to the nose and tail of the wasp ship. In seconds only small fragments were left, flying off in all directions.

"Outstanding!" Jacob said, knowing he had to join his Bridge crew's happy celebrating. "Watch out for—"

"Enemy ships are flying outward!" cried Slaughter at Navigation.

"They are!" called Daisy from her XO seat. "Their sterns are firing fusion pulse blasts. The remaining eight ships are speeding up. Moving away at 2,000 klicks per minute and increasing rapidly. Acting Captain, do you think they are fleeing?"

Jacob gulped. Amidst the good news of enemy retreat even as both groups exchanged a fifth round of laser and bolt beams, the ninth ship stayed on its heading aimed directly at the *Lepanto*. The mother ship. Or lead ship. Or whatever the aliens called it. That ship, which was twice as large as the other wasp ships, stayed on a course aimed at the *Lepanto*. Well, in moments it would arrive within the AM beam's 4,000 kilometer range. Then would come—

"Incoming enemy fire!" O'Hara called from Tactical. "All their ships are firing just on us! Uh, the fire is concentrated on the front top of the *Lepanto*. They—"

"They're aiming for the antimatter emitter node!" yelled O'Connor.

Jacob saw that. There was only one answer to preserve the ship's most powerful weapon.

"Slaughter! Fire our nose jets! Move us up so our belly armor plates take the incoming fire!"

♦ ♦ ♦

Support Hunter Seven could hardly believe the perception images that filled his five eyes. Three Swarmer flying nests had just died. Two disappeared in stupendous blasts of plasma that left nothing but glowing rings of ultraviolet and orange light, while the third had died from the impact of Soft Skin lasers that cut through to the nest's central energy unit. That was where particles were joined just as they were combined to produce propulsive power. But the black beam that had killed two Swarmer nests was something he'd never seen. Was this the moment to challenge Hunter One?

"Hunter Seven!" cried the Servant who studied distant sky lights and radiations from the cold darkness of space. "That black beam kills the way some distant sky lights die!"

New pheromones filled the Flight Chamber as signals arrived from Hunter One's flying nest. They spoke of aggregation and release and a new direction for all Swarmer nests to fly.

"Propulsive Servant, move our nest upward and away from the largest Soft Skin flying nest," he ordered in a mix of release and trail pheromones. "Join our other nests in flying beyond the reach of this new stinger. Stinger Servant, focus your sky light and sky bolt weapons on the front end of the large Soft Skin nest. Destroy the spot that emits this new beam!"

Eager pheromones of aggregation and compliance came to him from the seven Servants in front of him. Like most Swarmer castes, they responded well when given direction by a Hunter or senior caste leader.

He would put off challenging Hunter One. This moment of immense danger put his own flying nest at risk. Already the hard shell of his nest had been struck three times by sky light beams from the Soft Skin nests. Only the thickness and density of the minerals used to build Swarmer flying nest shell skins had prevented the beams from hurting those inside. Waiting was hard for any Hunter. But it was the flight path of wisdom and survival for now. He chose to fly that path, hoping for a later chance to show the superiority of his leadership.

♦ ♦ ♦

Hunter felt surprise at the death of two more Swarmer flying nests, then intense anger. He had begun this attack certain of their victory over the Soft Skins. But now, somehow, the Soft Skins had found enough Fighter Leaders to fight back, even to advance on the Swarm! Such could not be permitted. His three small eyes fixed on a perception imager that gave distances between the flying nests. His remaining eight nests were approaching the sky line at which they would be safe from the black beam of total annihilation. And his nest would soon come within its range. Which, he was pleased to see, was motivating his Stinger Servant to order the sky light and sky bolt Fighters in other chambers of his nest to focus their beams on the front end of the largest Soft Skin nest. The beam had come from a spot on the upper head of the enemy. A spot that would lie just above the three small eyes that lay between the two major eyes of every Swarmer. The Stinger Servants on his other flying nests saw what his Fighters were doing and now joined in. In less than four wing beats every Swarmer flying nest was firing at the same spot on the Soft Skin flying nest, even as eight of them fled outward.

"Alarm!" scent cast the elderly female Servant who monitored external space and the actions of the Soft Skin flying nests. "The largest Soft Skin flying nest is lifting its head! It presents the hard shell of its abdomen to the flames of our sky lights and sky bolts!"

"Stinger Servant," Hunter scent cast to the young female in charge of sending orders to the Fighter Leaders and Fighters in other chambers of his nest. "Concentrate our sky light and sky bolt weapons on the next largest Soft Skin nest!" What else must he scent? "Speaker To All, signal to our Support Hunters that each nest must fire at the same Soft Skin nest. That was how the Soft Skins killed the nest *Bright Day*. Let us do the same and claim a Soft Skin nest!"

Those two Servants did as he ordered. A pheromone of approval came from the Matron behind him. The older male Servant who handled the propulsive devices that moved his flying nest also sent aggregation and trail pheromones as a sign all Servants should follow the leadership of Hunter One.

The elder's helpful scent reminded him of his nest's final attack option. The device was rarely used due to the danger it posed to other Swarmer nests that came too close. But his support nests were now beyond the range of the device. Which left his ship as the single Swarmer nest to confront the terrible Soft Skin nest with the black beam. Other Soft Skin nests fired sky light beams at his nest and at his supporting nests, but the hard shell skins of his allies withstood those beams. It was time.

"Servant of the Pull Down device, let your device take wing against the largest Soft Skin nest," he scent cast in a mix of signal, primer and territorial pheromones, reminding the Servant of his duty to protect the home nest.

"The device takes wing," the elder male scent cast in response. "Recall it will take nine hundred wing beats before it fully replaces our hard shell segments."

Hunter felt inner satisfaction. "We have the time. The largest Soft Skin nest is coming within the device's range. And it cannot fire its black beam at us due to its changed flight angle."

His five eyes watched as the dark cold space between his flying nest and the terrible Soft Skin nest grew smaller. It was fitting that his nest would deliver the final sting to this enemy. Once it was dead, he would lead the other Support Hunter nests against the remaining Soft Skins. Which reminded him of a needed order.

"Speaker To All, tell our fellow flying nests to swing around to the rear of the Soft Skin flying nests. Tell them to continue their sky light and sky bolt attacks as they move behind the Soft Skins," he scent cast in a strong dose of releaser and signal pheromones.

There. That would further shield his fellow Swarmers from the effects of the Pull Down device, while allowing them to do what came naturally to every Swarmer. Attack the opponent who endangers your nest. Satisfaction briefly filled him. How would the Soft Skins feel when they realized they were held in the grip of the Pull Down device?

◆ ◆ ◆

"Captain," called O'Connor from his seat below Jacob. "The wasps are moving to mount a pincer attack on us."

Jacob saw that in the true space holo that showed the dispersed wasp ships, now well beyond the range of his antimatter cannon and curving around to the rear of his ring plate formation. Worse, the wasp ships were concentrating their laser and lightning bolt beams on the hull of the *Chesapeake*, which still maintained her position a thousand kilometers above the *Lepanto*.

"Acting captain," called O'Hara from Tactical. "The giant wasp ship is still oncoming. It is firing its lasers and lightning bolt beams at our belly. Our belly proton laser is firing back. It . . . it seems to be damaging the front end of the wasp ship."

"Confirmed," said Daisy from her XO seat. "Infrared and ultraviolet sensors report enemy hull is melting at proton laser impact point. How thick *is* that damned hull!"

Jacob had wondered that about the wasp ships. Single or even triple laser hits on a single spot had not penetrated. Punch through only came when six or more lasers hit the same spot on an enemy hull. Which his ships were now doing as they focused on ship W2. But the change in enemy formation required a change in the battle group's formation.

"Osashi, establish a neutrino comlink to the battle group," he said over his helmet comlink.

"Encrypted signal link established," the older Asian said quickly.

"All ships, move to Alpha Anvil formation behind us. Prepare to repel oncoming enemy," Jacob said.

"Good choice," O'Connor muttered.

Jacob scanned the sensor holo to his far left that showed the heat shapes of the wasp ships. Now scattered into a rough circle larger than his attack circle, the wasps were using their fusion pulse thrusters to come to the rear of Jacob's ship group. Which was why he had ordered the new formation. The two cruisers would move backward and become the point of the anvil, with the destroyers being the next layer and the four frigates being the final base of the anvil. That put the frigates closest to the *Lepanto*. Which he had earlier ordered to stop forward thrusting when it became clear the enemy was accelerating toward them. Perhaps it was time to give the anvil ships some room.

"All ships, reverse thrust. Move out and away from the *Lepanto*. Combine your weapons firing to take down individual ships," he said, feeling thankful again for his study of ancient sea battles and the academy's history of space battles. History and anthropology were two subjects he had loved ever since entering high school. His father the admiral had dismissed them, saying what mattered was gaining his Star Navy commission and becoming a senior officer. He'd done as ordered. But he had not enjoyed his time at the academy. Strange that the lessons he had studied so reluctantly were now vital to their survival.

"Acting captain!" called Swanson from the *Chesapeake*, her image appearing to one side of the front wallscreen. Her black curls looked sweat-laden despite the cool air of her helmet. The woman gave no sign of the pressure she must feel as the thick hull of her cruiser absorbed more than a dozen laser and lightning bolt strikes. "Our flank proton lasers are hitting the wasp ships as they pass by us. Should we launch missiles and Smart Rocks?"

"Yes!" Jacob said quickly, wishing he had thought to order it earlier as the wasp ships came close enough to be reached by the solid fuel powered missiles. "Launch your missiles tipped with x-ray laser thermonukes first. Maybe the x-rays can penetrate those damn hulls better than our lasers!"

"Launching missiles," Swanson said as she looked to one side and gave a thumbs-up gesture to a Bridge crewperson who was not in her image. The middle-aged woman looked back, her dark brown eyes fixing on him. "Acting captain, I don't like how that giant wasp ship is advancing on you. Its hull is holding up, even against your proton laser. It's planning something. Maybe a boarding attempt."

Jacob had been thinking the same thing. Why was the giant wasp ship advancing and taking severe punishment from his battle group ships, and now his proton laser on the *Lepanto's* belly? At least the two proton lasers on his ship's right and left flanks were now able to target the passing wasp ships. The proton laser had the same reach as the carbon dioxide lasers. Whatever.

"Agreed. We are alert to any boarding attempt. Our Darts are ready to launch and our railguns will riddle any approaching craft with Smart Rocks," Jacob said, knowing he was stating the obvious to a woman with more space command experience than him. Actually, the new captains on the other battle group ships all had more experience than he did. But he was the one with the vital ship status change code and he had dared to take action when tablet linkage was lost with their senior officers. No other ship in the group had done what he had done. And they were following his orders. What else should he—

"Captain!" called O'Hara from Tactical. "The big wasp ship is changing! Its hull plates are . . . they are pulling inside. New plates are coming out. Is this a response to our proton laser hits?"

"Daisy?" Jacob called, hoping the sharp savvy pilot had some idea.

"No clue," she said quickly, her soft soprano sounding puzzled.

"Weapons?" he called.

"No idea," Diego y Silva said.

"Willard?"

The portly man at the Science post shrugged, his wide shoulders stretching the fabric of his vacsuit. "Maybe they are adding more armor?"

"Captain," called Lori from behind him, reminding Jacob that she and Carlos were still back there. Had been there during the whole first engagement time. "Scan the new hull plates with our sensor array. That might tell us something."

Giving thanks for his friend's help, he looked to the right of the Bridge. "Science, focus our stern sensor array at the enemy ship. It's still functioning."

"Focusing," Steinmetz replied, his hands tapping the top of his control pillar. A new image of the big wasp ship now took shape to the right side of the front wallscreen, which showed the daytime surface of the planet in the lower right corner of the screen, and the enemy ship's normal light appearance in the middle of the wallscreen.

Jacob scanned the new sensor image. Multiple ship images showed, each one representing a distinct EMF frequency. X-ray, gamma ray, ultraviolet, infrared and far infrared images took shape in the sensor display. Briefly his attention was distracted by his left side holo that showed the eight ships of the battle group all launching thermonuke-tipped missiles at the wasp ships as they crossed the sides of the battle group, even as the twelve CO_2 and four proton lasers speared into two wasp ships. Those ships showed bright infrared glows on the middle of their hulls, but they continued under power.

"It's disappeared!" cried Osashi.

Jacob jerked his attention back to the wallscreen. The true daylight image of the approaching wasp ship was now gone. The dark space where the ship had been looked a bit blurred. And his ship's proton laser beam was . . . it was bending!

"Proton beam fails to strike," called O'Hara from Tactical.

"Science!" Jacob said sharply.

"The ship's emissions in other EMF frequencies have also vanished," the man said, his tone frustrated. Then he looked back to Jacob, surprise and shock filling his florid face. "Captain! I'm picking up gravitons and gravity waves coming from where the ship used to be!"

Sudden fear hit Jacob's spine. A chill swept down his arms. The hairs on his neck rose up. "What does that mean? Gravity waves hit us all the time from distant stellar events," he said, recalling a cosmology class lesson from the academy. "What is—"

"Jacob!" yelled Lori from behind him. "Move the *Lepanto* away! Put the engines on full power thrust!"

What the? "Why move away? And where the hell is that ship?"

His ship jerked.

Jacob felt the jerk in the seat of his vacsuit as he sat in the admiral's command seat. The slight movements of the crew at their posts showed they felt it too.

"Gravity," he called to the woman petty officer who operated the post that managed every gravity plate on every deck of the *Lepanto*. "Why did we feel whatever that was? I thought our inertial dampers prevented us feeling any accel change."

"They do, acting captain," called the woman whose name was Cassandra Pilotti. "All ship gravity systems are functioning normally. This came from outside."

"Jacob!" yelled Lori over his helmet comlink.

Deep unease filled him. "Navigation, flip us fully over so our fusion pulse thrusters face the spot where the enemy ship was. Do it now! Then hit full emergency fusion thrust!"

"Flipping," responded Louise.

The wallscreen's true space image changed. The partial planet image disappeared. The spot where the enemy ship had once been swung toward the bottom of the screen. Before it passed out of view, he saw three green laser beams, fired by other group ships, hit the blurred space spot. They joined the red proton beam. But all four beams bent sideways as they came close to the wasp ship's former position. Then a strange thing happened. The red and green beams became a circle. The beams were not just being deflected. They were being captured and made to circle the spot in space where the enemy ship had been.

"Science?" he called. "What the hell is happening to those beams?"

"Gravity," the man said, his tone amazed. "They are being gravitationally warped."

His seat vibrated as the *Lepanto's* three fusion pulse thrusters now fired streams of raw energy out through the exhaust funnels that, eventually, would give the ship a normal space speed of one-tenth of lightspeed. The fusion pulse thrusters were what had allowed them to move into this system within 40 or so hours, from the distant magnetosphere boundary that marked the edge of the local star's magnetic field.

"Captain," called Lori, her tone breathless. "It's an event horizon. Like what forms around a black hole. Those beams are becoming what is called an accretion disk. It happens when outside matter and energy hit a black hole's event horizon. They are forced to orbit the black hole, never to escape!"

Dismay filled him. "Navigation! Are we moving away?"

Louise shook her head. "No, acting captain. Or maybe a few meters. Something is holding us back."

"Gravity," said Steinmetz. "We are within the gravitational pull of that ship's black hole weapon."

Jacob swallowed hard. Were they to die now? Was the *Lepanto* going to become riptide shattered metal fragments that would orbit the invisible wasp ship?

"Weapons, fire every stern missile silo. Let's see if x-ray lasers from our thermonuke warheads can pierce that field and hit the wasps inside that ship!"

"Launching eight missiles," Diego y Silva said.

His left side holo that showed sensor imagery of where the wasp ship had been now glowed only with the ultraviolet and infrared glows of distant stars. An orange spot in the middle of the holo was new to him. A glance at the text panel at the bottom told him its identity. Orange indicated intense gravity. How could anyone produce an artificial gravity field that equaled the strength of a black hole? Gravity plate theory was something he had flunked in the academy. But clearly, the wasps had gone beyond producing the usual range of gee levels, which on the *Lepanto* could range from zero gee up to ten gees.

Eight yellow-white stars suddenly filled the true space holo that imaged the enemy ship's position. Bright yellow globes of plasma spread out. Invisible x-rays sleeted down toward the gravity-warped spot where the green and red laser beams still circled in endless orbit. Would the intense gravity of the artificial black hole capture the x-rays? Or would they punch through the thick metal hull of the wasp ship?

"Negative entry," Steinmetz murmured. "Our sensor array reports the eight x-ray beams bent sideways. They are becoming part of the accretion disk."

Despair filled Jacob.

This was the unknown enemy weapon he had feared. But he had worried about an enemy with an antimatter cannon. Never in his wildest nightmares had he ever thought of being captured by a black hole. He wanted to escape. Fear filled him. He didn't want to die.

"Jacob, you're the captain," called Daisy. "What do we do now?"

He shook himself. She was right. It was up to him to find a way out of certain death. But what was the answer to a gravity field that held them in an invisible lasso?

CHAPTER SIX

"Alarm!" scent cast the elder female Servant who monitored the perception imagers that tracked Soft Skin nests. "A new stinger beam hits the top of our head! It comes from the abdomen of the large Soft Skin nest. It cuts deep."

Hunter felt irritation. "What kind of stinger is this?"

"Unknown," the female Servant scent cast in pheromones of alarm.

His three small eyes fixed on the Servant who monitored radiations from cold space. "Servant," he scent cast to that Swarmer alone. "Do your devices tell us a scent story about this new stinger?"

The male Servant, who was a member of Hunter's personal cohort, tapped his control panel with a manipulator pad. "They do, Hunter One. The particles striking our hard shell exterior are one of two particles that make up the basic unit of all substances. They are denser than the sky light beams sent by the Soft Skins. That is why they bite deeper."

"Pull Down Servant, is this new stinger harming our device shells?"

"Not yet," the elder male scent cast to him in a mix of aggregation, releaser and primer pheromones that were as complex as the Servant's thinking. "The Pull Down shells have not yet reached the head of our flying nest. The mineral hard shells are what is being harmed."

He could not allow the Pull Down shell units to be damaged. "Servant for propulsion, move our head upward so the new stinger beam hits the dead tip of our nest."

"Flying upward," the Servant scent cast.

Hunter felt satisfaction as his nest rose up, leaving the red stinger beam to strike only the dead hard shell that caped the tip of his nest. The Pull Down shells replaced nearly all the outer hard shell plates, except those at the tip of their nest's head and those which surrounded the rear propulsion units. And once the Pull Down device activated, no harm could—

"Device activated," scent cast the elder male Servant. "Soft Skin flying nest now faces away from us. It attempts to escape our bite."

The perception imagers that showed external events now all went dark. That was normal when the Pull Down device activated. None of his five eyes, nor those artificial eyes that his nest used to wing through cold dark space, now saw anything. Which also meant no weapon could penetrate to the outer shell of his nest.

"Speaker To All, what do our Support Hunter allies scent cast? Are they attacking the other Soft Skin nests?" he said to the young male Swarmer who occupied a bench to the left side of the Flight Chamber.

"Each Support Hunter reports they are attacking a single Soft Skin nest as earlier ordered," the energetic Swarmer scent cast. "Support Hunter Seven reports the large Soft Skin flying nest is being left behind by the other Soft Skin nests. It shoots out flames but cannot escape the bite of our Pull Down device!" The youth changed his pheromones to a releaser scent. "The scent signal from our allies comes by way of another shade of reality. Do you wish to view what Support Hunter Seven now views?"

"Servant, display on our front perception imager the particle signal from Support Hunter Seven."

Hunter felt satisfaction as he saw the largest Soft Skin ship become locked in the claws of the Pull Down device. It had turned away and pointed its propulsive end at his nest. Yellow-white flame now spat out from three locations, reflecting the primeval energies that happened when special particles joined together. He knew little of the outside radiations that filled cold dark space. He just knew that those energies moved his flying nest and gave power to his nest for normal pull down and light and warmth. While his particle disruption seeds created energy-filled plasma blasts useful for destroying a flying nest, a rock moving through space or excavating the land hole for a new Swarmer nest of millions, they were of small power when compared to the Pull Down device. The creation of it had been the surprise achievement of those Servants who studied radiations from space and distant sky lights. They had discovered sky lights whose pull down strength made them invisible. Then, two generations ago, those Servants had learned how to create the Pull Down device. It was the ultimate stinger.

"Stinger Servant, have any of our nest allies destroyed a Soft Skin nest?" he said by way of a primer pheromone mixed with a sex pheromone to remind all Swarmers of his promised reward.

"Not yet," the young female scent cast. "They are concentrating on one of the smallest Soft Skin flying nests. It has fewer stingers with which to bite back. They express optimism."

Such emotion was good to scent. After the loss of three Swarmer flying nests, all Swarmers needed to scent the good news of a strike pheromone. The Pull Down capture of the largest Soft Skin nest was part of that good news. The death of a Soft Skin flying nest, which would reduce the Soft Skin nest numbers to one less than those of the Swarm, was a much desired second news scent. Hunter settled down on his bench, attempting patience. Being patient was not normal to any Swarmer. Either one attacked, fled, mated or made something new from the combined efforts of one's cohort in work with another cohort. Action, not patience, had gained the Swarm nine new nest homes around distant sky lights. Their presence at the world of Warmth, which was welcoming despite being illuminated by a weaker yellow sky light, made this the tenth success of the Swarm. That success would be complete when they destroyed all flying nests of the invading Soft Skins. Taking a deep breath through his spiracles, he told himself that soon his five eyes would perceive the breakup of the largest Soft Skin nest into thousands of pieces once it came close to the Pull Down field. That would be a welcome perception!

◆ ◆ ◆

Jacob realized they faced death. It could come at the invisible hands of the wasp ship. Or it could come by the choice of him and his crew. Their ship might explode if it did what he had in mind. But it would surely die when it closed with the invisible wasp ship and its gravity riptides tore apart every seam, every wall, every person inside the *Lepanto*.

"Power," he called to Maggie. "Move our three fusion reactors beyond their rated output. Feed ten percent more power to the fusion pulse thrusters." He looked to another strong woman on the Bridge. "Engines," he called to Akira. "Increase the flow of tritium and deuterium isotopes to the three engines. Increase the containment magfields using the extra power from Maggie's reactors. Let us see if we can achieve 12 percent lightspeed thrust."

Sudden silence filled the room.

Below him, Daisy gave him a thumbs-up. To her right, O'Connor raised his right hand in a fist of approval.

"Increasing reactor power output," Maggie said, her tone calm over his helmet comlink.

"Fusion isotopes flow increased," Akira said quickly, her black hands moving over her control pillar. "I'm increasing the thruster magfield containment power. It may be enough to control the fusion reaction of the pellets. If it does, our thrust will increase and the ship's max speed will hit . . . " She looked at the holo in front of her. "The three fusion thrusters will hit 12.3 percent of lightspeed."

Relief filled him. Then new fear. How long would the thrusters hold up under the increased plasma energies that were like small stars going off inside each thruster reaction chamber?

"Thruster integrity is holding," Akira called from Engines.

He looked to the redhead. "Navigation? Are we pulling away?"

Louise gave a long sigh. "We are, slowly. We are a kilometer further away from the enemy ship. At this rate it will take a day or more to get beyond the weapon's reach. Which I calculate is 3,917 kilometers. That was the enemy ship's distance when it disappeared from view."

They needed more power and more thrust.

"Power, increase reactor yield by five more percent."

"Sir!" Maggie cried. "That will put the reactors at 15 percent beyond their maximum safe rating!"

"Yes it will. Do it." What could he do to increase the power flow to the thrusters. "Gravity," he called to Cassandra. "Cut power to all gravity plates not involved in the operation of the fusion reactors, fuel feed and thruster operation. Warn all decks, but cut power. That will reduce the load on the fusion reactors and increase power flow to the thrusters."

"All decks," the woman called over the shipwide comlink. "Null gravity coming." She reached out and tapped her control pillar. "All gravity plates shut down. Sir."

He looked ahead to Akira. "Engines, increase thruster output as much as you can with the increased fuel flow and power feed."

The young woman nodded, her black curls floating out from her head as the Bridge gravity plates shut down. "Increasing thruster power. Moving up to 12.9, 13.1 . . . 14 percent of lightspeed! That is the max the thruster magfields can produce!"

The ship jerked.

"We're free!" yelled Louise.

"Navigation, vector us to join the anvil formation ahead."

"Changing ship's vector track," Louise said, sounding relieved.

"Captains Swanson, Wilcox, Zhang, Jefferson, Lorenz, Metz, Wilson and Mansour!" Jacob called over the ship's neutrino comlink. "Follow our lead. Shift your vector track upward and north of the planetary ecliptic. The giant wasp ship has a black hole weapon that we barely escaped. None of you could escape it. We are heading out of this system, fighting as we go." His left side holo showed the four frigates and two destroyers of his battle group moving sideways. The cruisers *Chesapeake* and *Hampton Roads* also moved sideways, allowing the *Lepanto* to take the nose of the anvil position. "All ships, maintain Alpha Anvil formation. Fire at the enemy, combining your beams! Do it in groups of four ships. And tell your Engines people to increase speed to eleven percent of lightspeed. Power can give you what you need. My people are sending you their settings for Power and Engines. We will slow down to that speed once we reach the nose of the anvil."

"Amazing," called Carlos from behind him. "Acting captain, my tablet has sent the coordinates for Kepler 10 to Chief Petty Officer Slaughter."

"Thank you," Jacob said. "Engines, reduce thrust to eleven percent of lightspeed. Gravity, restore grav plate functioning. Power, reduce reactor output to five percent above rated levels. Send your settings to each battle group ship."

"Reducing thrust," Akira called, relief in her voice. "Transmitting new settings."

"Cutting power flow," called out Maggie.

"Gravity restored," said Cassandra.

"Acting captain," called Louise. "This new vector is not aligned with the position of Kepler 10."

"You are correct," Jacob said, the fast beating of his heart slowing as the fact of their escape from certain death swept over him.

"Once we are further out, we will turn as a group and follow the vector track of the *Salamis*."

"Captain," called Andrew Osashi from Communications. "What if the wasp ships follow us out to the magnetosphere? They may compute the star we head for."

Jacob wondered at the sudden chattiness of the man. Was he adjusted to the fact of an ensign being acting captain and leader of a battle group? Or was he simply voicing what some on the Bridge might be wondering?

"CWO Osashi, if the enemy follows us to the magnetosphere, well, so be it," Jacob said bluntly, hoping his answer would be acceptable to the captains of the other ships. "We will get to Kepler 10 before they do. It will take the wasps a few hours to exactly compute the vector track. Then they have to decide which star along that track we are heading for. That gives us time to set up a Smart Rocks minefield at their likely emergence spot. And to ask the Star Navy base for help."

"Thank you, sir," the man said as he bent over his control pillar.

Jacob looked right to the middle-aged Latino man who managed the ship's Life Support post. What was his name? He'd just finished memorizing the names of the four frigate acting captains. His Bridge crew were just as vital. And . . . Joaquin Garcia it was. "Life Support, are things back to normal on all the decks?"

"Most decks report normal functioning," Joaquin reported, his black crew cut hair shiny with perspiration. "The hydroponics room went into automatic drain closure at the loss of gravity. The system will restore itself within a half hour. The pond in the Forest Room is now falling as rain. Supplies Deck is sorting loose boxes that broke open upon gravity renewal."

"Good."

Below him, O'Connor turned in his seat and looked up at Jacob. The man's white eyebrows lifted. His thin lips showed a slight smile. "You earned your captain's eagles with that escape thrust decision. Got some in my cabin."

Jacob did not smile. He just nodded, then sat back. Everything he did and said now, everything he had done during this first battle, was being broadcast to all the ships of the battle group and to all decks of the *Lepanto*. And to the destroyer *Salamis*, which was now four AU distant and headed outward. Plus the ship's AI had recorded it as part of the official record. That was normal on any Star Navy ship. What was not normal was for a fresh ensign to take command of a Battlestar, fight it, destroy three enemy ships and then order the battle group into a tactical retreat.

A bright star suddenly glowed in his left side holo. The one that held the images of all battle group ships. Sadness filled him.

"The *Britain* is gone, sir," called O'Hara. "The wasp ships concentrated their beams on the frigate. She rotated but there was still punch through."

Seventy-three lives gone.

He had never wanted to feel what he now felt.

♦ ♦ ♦

Hunter felt intense dismay that was only slightly improved by word of the death of a Soft Skin flying nest. How could any nest escape the teeth of the Pull Down device? How! Then he recalled his feeling of impatience at the loss of three Swarmer nests. In reaction to that he had ordered the activation of the Pull Down device just after the Soft Skin nest came within the device's reach. Perhaps if he had waited and allowed the large nest to be closer when he activated, it would not have escaped. Briefly he recalled the elder Servant who managed the device telling him that the Pull Down bite of the device increased twice for each unit of distance a target came closer to their nest. That meant the device's bite was far weaker than if it had become active when the Soft Skin was well inside its bite range. Well, sometimes a target escaped the bite of a Swarmer. But escape could not last forever.

"Pull Down Servant, deactivate the device. It is time for us to add our stingers to the efforts of other Swarmers," he scent cast in a strong primer pheromone.

"Deactivating device," said the elder male in a mix of signal and releaser pheromones.

The perception imagers on the walls of the Flight Chamber suddenly came alive, filling with the images of cold dark space, distant sky lights and the varied appearances of the Soft Skin nests as their radiations betrayed them to the scent sensors on the hard shell of their nest.

"Alarm!" signaled the elder female Servant who monitored external space. "The eight Soft Skin nests are moving up and away from Warmth. They move at speed. Perhaps they seek to escape the final bite," she said in a rush of territorial pheromones.

Hunter saw the change in Soft Skin formation. The largest nest now led the group of seven remaining nests. Each Soft Skin nest fired green sky light beams and red stinger beams at the surrounding nests of his Swarmer allies. Many of the Soft Skin nests had also shot out particle disruption seeds, nearly all of which were destroyed by Swarmer sky light beams. The few that exploded sent a strange radiation at nearby Swarmer nests.

"Servant!" he signaled to the male who monitored radiations from cold space. "What are the strange radiations cast by the Soft Skin seeds?"

The male Swarmer flared his two wings. "The radiations are similar to those emitted by sky lights and by our own particle disruption seeds. But these radiations are tightly bound, like our sky light beams. They pose harm to any Stinger who suffers their touch," the Servant cast in a mix of alarm and signal pheromones.

"Be strong!" Hunter scent cast with a mix of aggregation and territorial pheromones. "The hard shells of our flying nests protect us against external radiations. Is that not true?"

"They do," the Servant signal replied. "However, these radiations could make sick any Swarmer who is touched by them."

More strange stingers from the Soft Skins. It was bad enough that their particle seeds used the combination process to create energy blasts versus the disruption process used by Swarmer seeds. But it seemed the Soft Skins had found a way to cause such radiations to all fly in a single direction. Aware of how his worry might smell to his cohort and to Swarmers on other nests, he emitted a strong victory pheromone that reminded all Swarmers of larvae newly hatched from eggs. Recalling the words of the Pull Down Servant, he realized there was an answer to this new threat.

"Flight Servant, signal our fellow nests to move away from the Soft Skin nests," he said by way of a sharp primer pheromone. "Let them increase the distance to the outer edge of the range of our sky light and sky bolt weapons."

"Signaling fellow Flight Servants," the male Swarmer scent cast in a strong mix of territorial and aggregation pheromones.

Hunter cast all five eyes on the older Servant who monitored their propulsion units. "Servant," he scent cast just to that Swarmer. "Increase our propulsion to match the flight speed of the Soft Skins. We must stay close to them in order to sting."

The Servant looked back to Hunter, his red and black-striped head swiveling so all five eyes met Hunter's. "Leader, increasing the radiation emissions of our propulsive devices to match the Soft Skin flight speed is dangerous. It goes beyond their normal range."

Was this defiance? "Obey!" he said, using the strongest aggregation pheromone he knew how to emit. "We are Swarmers! No attacker ever escapes us. We always pursue and destroy any who invade our lands and our nests!"

The Servant's two black antennae pulled back. The older male lowered his head to touch the upper end of his thorax. "Apologies, Hunter One. I obey."

Brief satisfaction filled Hunter. Then he dismissed the emotion. No other group of Colony Nests had ever lost so many flying nests. Would he face a challenge from one of the Support Hunters? Perhaps not while they still fought and stung, but perhaps later, when they returned to the world of Warmth? He must stay alert to the low scents emitted by other flying nests. Hiding one's true feelings was nearly impossible for any Swarmer, no matter the caste or cohort. While those born to each caste were fated to perform the duties of Hunter, Servant, Fighter, Fighter Leader, Worker, Worker Leader and Matron, still, the emotions among each Swarmer were not identical even if their caste design was the same. He had become Hunter One of this colonizing group by pretending loyalty to the Swarmer Hunter who had assembled the flying nests into their group of twelve. He had deposed that Hunter before their departure from Nest. Any of the remaining Support Hunters might attempt to do the same to him, in view of Swarmer nest losses. Well, victory in attack was the cure for any hidden rebellion. Turning his attention to the perception imagers that displayed the Soft Skin flying nests, he gave deep thought to how he could destroy them, either in this sky light system or at another. He was a true Swarmer. He never gave up an attack until the opponent was dead or added to his cohort. For these Soft Skins, only death would do.

♦ ♦ ♦

Aarhant Bannerjee sat among his two co-leaders of the Navigation Deck, their presence in the deck's control center a normal event during combat. It was a Star Navy regulation that every chief of a deck be alert and present in that chief's control center for their deck, the better to respond to orders given by the Command Deck. Soon enough, once they reached the edge of this system's magnetosphere, he would confirm the vector track coordinates for Kepler 10. Those numbers had been given to his Bridge representative by young Carlos Mendoza. The man was a talented programmer, able to conjure unique algorithms suitable to unusual stellar events. But escaping from an artificial black hole was not a normal stellar event. He felt amazement the young whelp Renselaer had had the guts to risk explosion of the fusion reactors or the loss of magfield containment in the three primary thrusters. Both groups of complex devices had maintained their integrity. That further amazed him. The quick loyalty of the other battle group captains displeased him. The whelp was building links with the new captains on the other ships. He had even brought forward the Marine in charge of their boarding team, seating him in a spot on the Bridge. That was unheard of. Just as bad was the disinterest of the chiefs of the other six decks when he had complained about the ensign's bypassing of him, the most senior officer still alive on the *Lepanto*. The Science Deck woman had even scolded him for raising the issue! Well, he could be patient. Eventually he would claim control of the Battlestar, either here or in Kepler 10.

♦ ♦ ♦

Daisy scanned the holo that depicted her ship's various decks and weapons stations, then shifted to the situational holo that depicted the nine wasp ships, their positions relative to battle group ships, the nearby planet and the thermonuke carrying missiles that the destroyers, frigates and cruisers were firing at the wasp ships. Most missiles were killed by wasp lasers and lightning bolts. Four managed to disperse their warheads, which exploded and sent x-ray laser beams at wasp ships W2 and W5. They had been damaged earlier. Four of their ships now combined their CO_2 and proton fire, hitting W2. Four other ships, including the *Lepanto*, fired at W5. The wasp ships were jinking as madly as a bee defending its honeycomb, but the Weapons chiefs on their eight ships were very good. Their beam energy strikes mostly stayed on target. This coordination happened even as the nine enemy ships now concentrated their beams on the *Hampton Roads*. Who would be the first to die?

"Navigation, move us to between the *Hampton Roads* and most of the incoming enemy beams," Jacob said from behind Daisy.

"Shifting vector track," Louise said quickly, her red hair long and stringy within her helmet. "We are both at eleven percent of lightspeed. We are nearing the range of *Hampton's* plasma batteries. Sir?"

"Understood. Communications, open a signal to that ship."

"Signal sent. Response incoming," the older Japanese-American said tightly.

Daisy looked up to the front wallscreen. The middle of the screen carried the true space images of the wasp ships, green, red and yellow beams from both groups of ships crisscrossing black space, and the silvery sparkle of ships reflecting the yellow light of the local star. At the top of the wallscreen there appeared the face and shoulders of George Wilcox. The man's bald head had a sheen of sweat under his helmet. Worry showed on his face.

"Renselaer! What now?"

"Captain, I will not allow you to absorb all the enemy beams," Jacob said firmly. "We are moving in front of you. Our hull can handle those beams. It's thicker than your hull. Disable the auto function on your plasma batteries."

"Disabled!" Wilcox said, quick relief showing on his shaven face. The man's blue eyes looked at them. "Captain of the battle group, your ship also has damage. Is this wise?"

"It is most wise," Jacob said. "Continue your beam strikes on wasp ships W2 and W5. Maybe if we kill another one of them, these bastards will back off."

"We can hope. Thank you, and Wilcox out."

Her ship deck holo began showing red spots indicating hits on their outer hull. Her feet felt a small vibration as the topside railguns shot out Smart Rocks to the right and left of the *Lepanto*, their onboard sensors picking up the IFF signals of the battle group ships and ignoring them as tiny jets on the rocks shifted their trajectory toward wasp ships. All of which now lay at 9,987 kilometers out. The enemy ships had moved outward after the x-ray lasers had hit W2 and W5. Had the x-rays hurt anyone on those ships?

"Acting captain, W2 is barely jinking!" called Rosemary from Tactical.

"Same for W5," called Oliver from Weapons.

Her armrest screen that showed Jacob and the other Bridge crew had him leaning forward, his gloved hands gripping the ends of his armrests. "Pour on the proton laser fire! Aim for that midbody spot on W2 where the lasers are hitting. That's the same spot where we had punch through on the last wasp ship that died."

Daisy bit her lip as she did her XO duty of monitoring incoming laser and lightning bolt strikes on the lower hull of the *Lepanto*, even as the ship's belly proton laser fired again at W2. In the holo of the ship decks, red glows on the hull became blue alerts of water loss as three spots lost two meters of metal to the ferocious wasp strikes. The inner hull integrity was still good. But they would have to start spinning soon if they were to continue blocking strikes at the *Hampton Roads*. Which, she now saw in the other holo, was venting air and water from near its rear thrusters. But the cruiser was maintaining full maneuverability from its two thrusters. Like the other battle group ships, it was making eleven percent of lightspeed. Which the wasp ships had matched after a brief delay. No ship was accelerating, but stern flares showed as ships maneuvered.

A star flare grew yellow-white in the situational holo.

"Yes!" cried Rosemary. "W2 is going up. Punch through at its midbody. The fusion plasma is spreading to its tail and nose."

"Captain," Daisy called over her helmet comlink. "We have hull penetrations at three spots. We are venting water. Time to spin."

The image of the man frowned, then nodded quickly. "Louise! Spin us."

She felt brief surprise at his use of the woman's first name. Jacob had always given orders by using each person's function post title or their last name. Maybe he was feeling the strain of this running battle. Or maybe he was finally relaxing enough to see the Bridge crew as his friends. And his allies.

"Spinning," the chief petty officer said.

Another star light flared.

"That was W5," Rosemary said from her Tactical station. Looking up front, Daisy saw the woman look back to Jacob and give him a V-for-victory sign.

She looked back also. Jacob's young face was tight, tense and intent on watching multiple holos that glowed in front of him. It was now seven wasp ships against their eight. Would the enemy commander do anything different? The large wasp ship was at the bottom of a half-globe of wasp ships, at a range of nearly 11,000 kilometers. It was firing green lasers and yellow lightning bolts from nodes on its front end. Then she noticed something different. The big ship's beams had shifted sideways to focus on one of the frigates, which lay at the base of their anvil formation. The remaining six wasp ships now did the same firing shift.

"Acting captain," she called, "the enemy ships are concentrating on the *Marianas*."

"I see it," Jacob said, his expression moving to one of worry. "Navigation, hit our belly nose jets. Flip us so we face back toward the enemy ships. Engines, hit full thrust. Slow us down. I want the tip of the anvil to be reversed, with us and the cruisers taking point."

"Flipping ship," Louise said, her tone calm.

"Reverse thrust happens once the flip is completed," called Akira from up front.

Daisy understood Jacob's aim. Their momentum would remain at eleven percent of lightspeed. In fact, all the battle group ships had ceased active acceleration thrust once the new vector track away from the planetary ecliptic had been achieved. Inertia and momentum would keep them moving up and eventually out of the star system. Until they changed vector to follow after the *Salamis*.

"We are joining you at the anvil tip," called the voice of Swanson on the *Chesapeake*.

"We're following also. Flipping over," Wilcox said over the audio comlink from the *Hampton Roads*.

In seconds their Alpha Anvil formation reversed. The *Lepanto* and the two cruisers now formed the anvil tip that was pointed at the following wasp ships. Behind them were the destroyers *Tsushima Strait* and *Philippines Sea*. Behind those were the three remaining frigates *St. Mihiel*, *Marianas* and *Ofira*. No longer were the smaller ships taking the bulk of incoming laser and lightning fire. She watched as all eight ships concentrated their green lasers and red proton beams on two of the nearest wasp ships. Those ships jinked and jiggled, working hard to avoid a long-term impact on any part of their remarkable hulls. Those hulls had stood up better than the frigate hulls. But they could die. As she had seen happen five times.

"Captain!" called Rosemary. "The wasp ships are falling back."

Daisy saw each wasp ship now applying reverse thrust even as they still fired beams at the *Lepanto* and the two cruisers. But the effort was half-hearted. It was clear some wasp commander had ordered the enemy ships to move out of range. Her situational holo had a distance counter in one corner. The wasp ships hit 10,000 kilometers distance, then 10,700, then finally 11,000. But they continued deceleration, not stopping the reverse thrust until they were 12,000 kilometers away. That was beyond the range of even the wasp lasers and bolts. Firing ceased. But the enemy followed after them at a momentum of eleven percent of lightspeed.

"Hostiles have ceased attacking," said Rosemary, sounding surprised.

"Tactical, thank you," Jacob said, relief clear in is voice. "All ships, remain at Alert Hostile Enemy status. Cease firing. Assess damages. Perform repairs as possible. However, do not allow EVA repairs. The enemy can reach us within a few minutes or less if it chooses to do so."

"As you command," said Swanson from the *Chesapeake*.

"Glad to work on our wounds," called Wilcox from the *Hampton Roads*.

"Good news," spoke Zhang from the *Tsushima Strait*. "Our plasma battery needs repairs."

"Damn!" called Jefferson from the *Philippines Sea*. "Was hoping to get another one of those bastards!"

Daisy smiled at the fight hunger of the woman in charge on the destroyer. Then listened as the acting captains on the three frigates called in their acknowledgments. Was this the end of the battle?

"Navigation, plot a vector track to take us sideways and after the *Salamis*," Jacob said, surprising her.

"New vector track plotted," Louise said.

"Transmit new vector track to all battle group ships."

"Transmitted."

"All ships, we are turning to follow the *Salamis*. At the edge of the magnetosphere we will aim for Kepler 10," Jacob said over Daisy's helmet comlink. "This is a fighting retreat! Stay on full combat alert. Maintain weapons at Battle Condition One. Maintain velocity at eleven percent of lightspeed. However, you may rotate relief breaks among your Bridge and Deck crews. No more than ten percent of any crew is to be out of their vacsuits, doing their business. We will take meal breaks later, if this end of hostile fire persists. Acting captain out."

Relief filled Daisy. She and Carlos and Quincy and Lori and Jacob and Kenji had all survived their first live fire battle. As had Jacob. Those who had sought their deaths had suffered the loss of five ships, to their single ship loss. The *Britain's* death touched her deeply. She had known Jane Wilson from trips conveying the admiral to her frigate, while they had still been in Earth orbit. The Brit woman always made her feel welcome, even when it was clear the admiral was the center of everyone's attention. She would miss the woman's big smile and friendly hug. At least she had a holo cube of Jane. It had been taken when all the officers of the battle group had gathered for a going away dinner at the orbital shipyard where their ten ships had gathered, before heading out.

Erratic contact with her seat's armrest drew her attention. Her right hand was trembling, causing her fingers to tap, then pull away from the armrest. Taking a deep breath, she clenched the fingers of her right fist and told herself to stop being afraid. Or at least, to stop showing it. Fear was normal in a battle. Showing it where battlemates could see was not done.

CHAPTER SEVEN

Hunter tasted deep anger. He had lost two more Swarmer nests in his effort to close on the Soft Skins and end their lives. The Soft Skins had fought better than his fellow Swarmers. Their sky light weapons and hard radiation beams had deeply wounded the last two nests, causing the Support Hunters and Servants on those two nests to become erratic and incoherent. Then, just as the combined Swarmer sky light and sky bolt attacks were promising to kill one of the larger Soft Skin nests, the largest nest had moved to block most of those beams. Like his nest, its hard shell was thick and dense and tough. But it could be hurt. When he had seen the water signature of hard shell bite through, the creature had begun to spin, thereby reducing the effect of their beams. It had continued to fire the red heavy particle beams at his fellow nests despite such movement. Then had come the tiny rocks that moved intentionally toward his fellow nests. Those rocks rarely penetrated deep, but their impact disturbed the stinger Servants on each nest. So he had ordered the attack flight to pull back beyond the reach of those terrible weapons. He knew he must attack again, before the Soft Skins reached the outer edge of the local sky light's magnetic field. Either attack or face defiance from one or more Support Hunters. Now, as his fellow nests attended to tears in their wings and repaired what could be repaired, he must come up with something that would forestall a challenge.

"Servant," he scent cast a signal pheromone to the Swarmer who studied aberrant social behavior. "How can these Soft Skins still fight as if their leaders still lived? A normal Swarmer cohort that lost its Hunter, Matron and Fighter Leaders would either accept my rule or fly away to a distant land."

The older male had done little during the swarming stings of this stretched out sky battle. It had simply fixed its five eyes on two perception imagers that were part of his control panel. His posture on his bench bespoke of lassitude, not the eagerness to bite that was common among nearly all Swarmers. The Servant lifted his two antennae, then shifted position so his thorax and head faced Hunter.

The white-yellow light of the Flight Chamber revealed the aged look of his body's yellow hairs. But the dark eyes seemed intent and alert.

"Hunter One, it is strange how these Soft Skins maintain their cohesion as if there were a central leader still living," the Servant said in a mix of releaser, signal and primer pheromones. "Our flight of seven nests attacks eagerly because of our shared pheromones. This aiming of our stingers at a single Soft Skin flying nest is new to us. But it seems to be normal for these Soft Skins." The Servant paused, picked up a water bulb and sipped liquid through his mandibles. His complex major eyes seemed brighter. "On our home of Nest, we have similar shaped Soft Skins who infest the trees of the cooler parts of Nest. Those tree dwellers have one or several nest leaders. But in my study of these non-aware creatures, I noticed that their young males often form groups that wander, seek new territory and cooperate among themselves even though they lack a single Hunter leader. Perhaps small group cooperation is normal for these new Soft Skins. Some of their stingers are new to us. It seems reasonable their social behaviors will be new to us."

Hunter inhaled the mixed pheromones that flowed from his twelve fellow Swarmers. Both sexes, young and old, they gave off the scent of intense frustration. Even the Matron behind him gave scent to frustration. What to do?

"It would seem that these Soft Skins can cooperate even when they lack senior leaders," Hunter said in a mix of trail, aggregation and signal pheromones. His two wings spread his mix broadly, until it dominated the air of the Flight Chamber. The transmitters to other flying nests would be conveying his scent mix to those Swarmers, who no doubt were also feeling frustrated. "It is a small event. We are Swarmers! We rule on Nest! We have colonized the new world of Warmth! No kind of life can defeat us. Let us study these new stingers of the Soft Skins, how their nests move in cooperation, then I will cast the scent for a new attack!"

The wing pairs on every Swarmer in the chamber now fluttered quickly. The pheromone scents changed to a mix of territorial crossed with trail. They were willing to be led. He would accommodate them. "All Swarmers!" he scent cast strongly with a forelimb gesture to Speaker To All to alert him to the duty to share this new scent mix with every flying nest. "We are seven to their wounded eight. We can prevail! We will prevail! Attend to your wounded ones, repair your nests, and in a single rest cycle we will attack again!"

Rasping came from nearly every Swarmer in the chamber. The scent broadcasters that conveyed the smell of the other flying nests now let loose a wave of similar scent responses. His fellow flying nests were still loyal, though there was a suspicious low scent coming from the craft led by Support Hunter Seven. He bore watching. Meanwhile, Hunter would study the imager records of the recent sky battle, seeking out the hidden crevices by which future success could be attained. He led. All would follow him.

◆ ◆ ◆

Support Hunter Seven inhaled the scent words coming from Hunter One and marveled at how the older Swarmer put the polish of success on the hard shell of disaster. Their colonizing group had arrived with twelve flying nests. Five had been lost in confusing sky battles with the Soft Skins. Now they were seven, including his nest. He had no doubt Hunter One would attack once more, before the Soft Skins could flee from the grasp of the Swarm. But whether he would find success, or more frustration, was a matter of speculation. One did not count the fruits on a tree until they were fruited. And had drawn small hard shells to their nectar. Thus giving the Swarm targets for their englobing attacks. These Soft Skins were far from defenseless. He must study the actions of each Soft Skin flying nest. Perhaps a focus on one of the smaller flying nests would yield success and the death of such a nest. One success was all he needed to make challenge to Hunter One. And success required a healthy nest.

"Stinger Servant," he scent cast to the Swarmer who led the Fighter Leaders in the operation of his nest's many stingers. "See to the repair of your stingers. And search out a means for killing those flying seeds that cast forth hard sky light!"

The red and black-streaked Swarmer, younger than Seven, rose up on his bench. His two forearms reached out and tapped his control panel. "Sending orders now!" the Servant scent cast. "Studying now methods of killing the Soft Skin flying seeds!"

Hunter Seven inhaled the mixed pheromones of aggregation, signal and trail as the stinger Swarmer and other Servants bent to their duties. None of them wished to show evidence of fear or worry or defeat. That way lay the bite of death, at his grip or at the grip of a fellow Swarmer. The surprise of a strong enemy must never give way to the scent of defeat!

♦ ♦ ♦

Jacob sat back in his seat, then flipped back his helmet. It was a small luxury, but one he needed. At his action, the Bridge crew did the same, as did Daisy, O'Connor and, behind him, Lori and Carlos. Which reminded Jacob the time of rest was not a time of indolence. His study of the history of war said brief moments of non-war were best used to prepare for the next phase of battle.

"Ensign Antonova, come forward. Ensign Mendoza, follow her," he called over the comlink shared by everyone on the Bridge. Should he shut down the All Ship vidcom comlink so he could have a private talk? Yes. There was no sign the wasps were moving back to attack and the acting captains on the other ships did not need the distraction of his chatter. "AI Melody, discontinue comlinks with other ships. Chief Warrant Officer Osashi, discontinue All Ship transmission of our Bridge conversations."

"Linkage to other Star Navy ships discontinued," the AI said, her tone less tense than during the deadly battles.

"All Ship transmission shut off," Osashi said from up front. Like everyone else the older man had pushed back his helmet and was enjoying a sense of non-confinement.

The white streaks in the man's black hair reminded him of his CWO5 seniority. "Osashi, coordinate with your fellow Bridge crewmates on relief break rotations," Jacob said. "Keep it to one person a time."

"Yes sir, acting captain!" the man said, sounding pleased.

From below, O'Connor looked up to Jacob, gave a quick nod, then looked interested as Lori and Carlos stopped in front of him and Daisy. The two saluted him.

"Ensign Antonova reporting!" called Lori, her Russian-accented English strong and measured. The woman's blue eyes fixed on Jacob.

"Ensign Mendoza reporting," said Carlos, his stance one of ease.

Jacob saluted them back. He noticed Daisy had looked up at the arrival of their two friends, then had focused back on the situational holo that showed the positions of the wasp ships, their ships, the retreating form of planet four, and the small moon that orbited planet four. As the battle group's speed took them away from the four worlds that made up the planetary parts of Kepler 22, the scale of the holo enlarged and the distances between ships grew smaller. Eventually they would pass through a thin asteroid belt that lay at 10 AU, then a Kuiper Belt-like spread of icy comets that circled the system at 39 AU. Beyond the comets was the system's magnetosphere boundary at 42 AU. Which was now 40 hours away. Plenty of time for new surprises, more battles and more death to happen. Inside, he promised himself he would do all in his power and mind to prevent the loss of any more ships. That began with these two.

"Antonova, thank you for the black hole gravity warning. That is a field beyond your biology specialization. When we get to Kepler 10, I will recommend a commendation be entered into your permanent record. You are a credit to the Science Deck," he said.

Lori lifted one black eyebrow, looked surprised, then pleased. "Thank you, acting captain. Gravity plates and gravitational fields are my secondary field of study. My teachers at the institute insisted we be diverse in our knowledge."

That was pleasant news. Who else knew stuff he didn't? Jacob fixed on Carlos, who stood at parade rest stance. "Mendoza, thank you for the quick sharing of the Kepler 10 coordinates with CPO Slaughter. You too are a credit to Navigation Deck."

His fellow chess player grinned. "No sweat. The system lies on nearly the same right ascension and declination track as this system does. And at 564 light years out from Earth, it was the closest colony to us. Leastwise in terms of short travel time."

Jacob understood that. Earlier he had tapped the Library patch on his seat's left armrest and scanned the images and data on the system. There were seven planets circling the system's yellow star, most of them small. It had a single gas giant. Most importantly, it had a small Star Navy base, as was the case for every colony system. There should be at least a frigate in parking orbit next to the orbiting Star Base. Plus a captain in command at the base. Those details were in the future. Right now, he had to plan their survival for the next 42 hours.

"Antonova, give me your read on the cultural patterns and behaviors of the wasp aliens," he said, looking back to her. "Why did they keep attacking after the loss of two ships? Why do they still follow us even after planting some kind of colony on planet four? Surely they can see we are leaving the system to them."

She frowned, then put gloved hands on her hips. "Analogy with the insect societies on colony planets and on Earth to these wasp-like aliens is both helpful, and dangerous," she said.

"How dangerous?" Jacob asked.

She blinked. "Because we will think we understand them better than we do," she said quickly. "Based on their behavior to date, it is clear these insect aliens are highly intelligent, possess an advanced technology, communicate between their ships as seen in their later adoption of combined laser firing at a single ship, they are aggressive and the presence of stingers on the butt ends of every alien we saw in the tablet images says they are predators." Lori paused. Jacob noticed that several of his Bridge crew had swung their seats around and were listening closely. Among the listeners were Maggie, Rosemary, Oliver and Willard. His friend licked her pale brown lips. "The dropping of pods from every wasp ship before they attacked us says they were here to establish a colony. That confirms these aliens are a eusocial species with cooperative brood care, overlapping generations and a division of labor."

"Fine," Jacob said. "But why did they behave the way they did? Why attack our senior officers? Why attack us? Why keep attacking even after five ship losses?"

She shrugged. "I'm guessing. But early this century a bio study by Dr. Sean O'Donnell documented something strange. Unlike mammals and other animals, he found that the brains of social wasp members were less developed than the brains in solitary wasp species. In short, he argued for what he called distributed cognition. That means there is less need for individual smarts when the group's cooperation provides most of what you need."

Surprise filled Jacob. He'd never heard of such a thing. His anthro studies documented that human brains got larger the more humans worked together and hung about in clans and large families. He recalled one prof saying that individual competition for food, shelter and mates was the cause of increasing human smartness. But on Earth, among the social wasps, Lori said the opposite had been documented. Or at least proposed. Weird.

"Well, these alien insects think well enough to create an artificial black hole, something we humans have yet to do," Jacob said, working to make his voice sound thoughtful versus dismissive. "And the tablet images showed 20-something individuals. Not all of them behaved the same way. So how does this Earth pattern apply to these wasp-like people?"

Lori took a deep breath. "Predatory social insects like wasps show lots of individual initiative. These aliens resemble the yellow jackets of family *Vespidae*. If this Earth wasp study has any meaning for aliens, it may mean the wasp aliens are more willing to be led as a group. And to respond as a group. That does fit what we know about ants, bees, wasps and termites, the main eusocial insect groups on Earth."

Jacob nodded slowly. "So, this means the wasps will act as a group, both in attacking and in falling back, like they just did?"

"Yes," Lori said. She frowned. "Again using Earth wasps and alien colony insects as examples, it means each wasp spaceship has at least one primary leader who determines what everyone else does. Kind of the way a captain runs her ship." She blinked, looked back, saw her audience of Bridge crew, then looked back to him. "One thing about Earth wasps. When they fight off invaders, or when they found a new wasp colony, they swarm. That means they all gather together and act to achieve a single objective."

"Which means," Daisy said from below. "That their killing of our admiral and the captains and XOs was meant to make us vulnerable to their later attack."

Lori nodded, then focused on Jacob. Her expression was intense. "Acting captain, my guess is these alien insects intended to attack us from the beginning. The meeting on the planet was just a ruse to gather our leaders together for a chance to kill them all. Their pursuit of us now is the function of their leadership leading a swarm against an invader."

"But we weren't invading!" Carlos said, sounding angry. "We were just exploring this system cause we knew it had planets in its liquid water habitable zone."

Lori shook her head. "Our purpose in coming here is irrelevant. What matters to these wasp-like insects is how we *appear* to them. They see us as an invader coming to take over the site of their new colony, their new nest site. They swarmed to its defense. Recall how early on each of their ships fired at whomever they could target? Those are the actions of a swarm of angry wasps going on the offensive."

"Then later," Daisy murmured, "they began combining their laser and lightning bolt fire against singleton ships. Guess that means there is an overall coordinator of this attack. An alien admiral, you think?"

"I do," Lori said.

Jacob felt deep worry. There had been no real attempt at communication with the wasps, or by them with humans. His battle group's mere presence branded them as an enemy. So the wasps had attacked.

"Antonova, will the alien insects keep attacking us?"

"Yes," she said briefly. "They will keep attacking us until we leave this star system."

"What about later?" interrupted Rosemary from her Tactical post.

Jacob wondered how a real captain would handle such an interruption. Then again, it was a question he too had been thinking. "Antonova, what will they do when we go into Alcubierre space-time?"

The slim, young woman lifted both hands in a Who Knows? gesture. "They could ignore us. They might follow us, figuring we are heading for a system with a habitable planet. A planet they could take away from us for their own use."

He grit his teeth. "Antonova, you make these aliens sound like unthinking insects who react completely by instinct. But they are not unthinking people. They have tech, they have starships, they plant colonies like us, they do more than just follow their instincts."

She gave him a grim look. "Have we not reacted instinctively? They attacked, we defended. We counter-attacked. For good cause, yes. Of course these aliens act on more than instinct. But in social insects, instinct *is* very powerful. My guess is these alien insects, with their compound eyes, warning colors of red, black and yellow, and their three body sections will indeed react much like predatory Earth insects. But they have tech. So think of yellow jackets from hell."

"But what do we do when they next attack?" Daisy asked. "What do we do if they follow us to Kepler 10?"

Those were exactly the questions he had had at the beginning of this brain picking. "What else is different about these aliens when compared to us humans? Anything else that might help us defend ourselves? Defend a colony world?"

Lori closed her eyes. She looked tired and worn. Which was exactly how Jacob felt. With a sigh, she opened her sky blue eyes. "Acting captain, most social insects on Earth, and the insects on five of the seven colony worlds, communicate by way of pheromones. These are hormone-like scents that convey distinct messages. As in, this is our territory, this is the action you must take, this is the way to food, and so forth." She looked aside to watchful Daisy, over to a thoughtful O'Connor, next to pensive Carlos, then up to Jacob. "Communication by pheromones can make a group very cohesive in their actions. Which means we should prepare for a very coordinated future attack. Our bigger ships will need to do as you did. Move in front of any ship that is being hit by all the enemy beams in order to prevent punch through of that ship's hull. Our cruisers and the Battlestar are best-suited for that defensive role."

Jacob nodded. "Fine for defense. What about offense? What could most discourage these alien wasps?"

Her eyes fixed on him in a way that went beyond friendship. Was she seeing him as their leader? As the leader of the entire battle group? "Acting Captain Renselaer, our best weapon is the antimatter cannon, which only this ship possesses. The enemy knows its range is 4,000 kilometers. They will likely stay well beyond that range when attacking. You need to . . . we need to find a way to get close to the big mother ship and either kill it with antimatter, or wound it badly. The loss of single ships has not made them pull back. If their chief leader is located on their biggest ship, attacking it by any means available will be the only way to discourage future attack."

Jacob sat back in his seat, his stomach feeling uneasy and unsettled. Food might settle it. Something not spicy. But could he take a break from the Bridge?

"Acting captain," spoke O'Connor from below. "I agree with Ensign Antonova. We have to attack their giant ship. My Darts are able to penetrate a thick hull. That's why they have solid titanium nose cones. If you give us covering fire, I'm willing to lead them."

Jacob felt surprise, then deep appreciation that the single person with repeated deadly combat experience was willing to sacrifice himself and his Marines for the benefit of the battle group. Could he do any less?

"Chief Warrant Officer O'Connor, thank you for that offer. I will consider it." He looked beyond Lori and Carlos to those watching from their function stations. "Weapons, we did well with combined fire targeting by groups of four ships. Next time, let's have *all* our ships combine their fire! Eight on one, that one being the giant wasp ship, might make a difference." A memory hit him. "When our proton beam hit the top of that ship's nose, it lifted up a bit to prevent penetration. That was just before they replaced their hull plates with gravity plates and went black hole. We have five ships with proton lasers. The *Lepanto*, the two cruisers and the two destroyers. I think it will be useful for us five to combine our proton beams on that giant ship, while everyone's lasers hit a second spot on the ship. Maybe we can punch through in two spots!"

Oliver looked thoughtful, then gave him a thumbs-up. "Acting captain, that is an outstanding idea! Our proton beams hit with greater penetrating force than our gas lasers. And our imagery did show the spot we hit was melting into a deep hole. Whatever that metal is, we can cut through it."

Willard raised his hand from Science. "Acting captain, my spectroscope sensor readings from that last battle say the hull of the giant wasp ship is extra resistant to heat. Besides the titanium, nickel and steel we knew made up the hulls of the wasp shuttles at the meeting site, my sensors report the presence of iridium, chrome, tungsten and molybdenum in that ship's hull. And also in the hulls of the other wasp ships."

"So it will take multiple beams to make a penetration?" Jacob asked.

"It will," Willard said firmly.

Milky-skinned Rosemary stood up. Her red hair was pulled back in a ponytail. She wore her vacsuit as if it were normal dress. Her green eyes fixed on him. "Acting captain, may I suggest that during the next attack, when you take the Battlestar close to the giant wasp ship, the rest of the battle group should assume an outer post above the enemy ships? That will allow the cruisers and destroyers to shield the three frigates, while combining their beams in a single attack on the wasp mother ship."

Jacob thought fast. She was proposing a variation on the formation known as Alpha Squeeze, which was a basic pincer movement. "Tactical, that is a very good suggestion. I will consider your proposal, and the idea of CWO O'Connor."

"Captain!" called Louise from Navigation. "My system plot shows the *Salamis* is turning back! They are reversing course and heading for us."

That was a surprise. "Melody, establish a neutrino comlink with Captain Mehta on the *Salamis*. Share the incoming signal and my responses with our other ships and with all decks."

"Link established. Imagery shared on All Ship vidcom and with seven other ships," the AI said, now sounding moody.

Interesting. One could never tell what an AI's algorithms would come up with to match the current behavior of humans. He looked to the front wallscreen that was filled with stars, black space and distant galaxies. A swirling spot at the top of the wallscreen became a round image. Filling it was the long black hair, dark brown skin and brooding eyes of Chatur Mehta.

"Captain Mehta, you have reversed course. What do you intend?"

The man sat in the captain's seat on the smaller bridge of the destroyer. Behind him were a line of empty observer seats. None of his crew were visible. And the XO seat next to him was empty. His expression was sour.

"My XO reminded me that whenever any member of Star Navy is being attacked, all nearby Star Navy ships must respond to aid that ship. I am responding. We have a full load of missiles. My observation of the first battles with the wasp aliens indicates we could be of help to you. Some of your ships are damaged."

Would wonders never cease? "I agree. Thank you, Captain Mehta." He looked aside at his situational holo. "It appears you will rendezvous with us in two hours, maybe less."

The man blinked black eyes. "Less. My Engines chief received the fusion pulse magfield settings you broadcast to the other ships. We are heading your way at eleven percent of lightspeed."

"I thank you," Jacob said. What else was needed? Here was a rebel who had turned back and proposed to lend his firepower to the next battle. "I will have my Tactical station send you our future formation details after I consult with the other ship captains. I'm also sending you the last few minutes of alien behavior analysis and future attack options presented to me by my staff. Perhaps the data will interest you."

"Perhaps," the man said, his tone still sour. "In accordance with Star Navy regulations, the destroyer *Salamis* is coming to your aid. Further contact will happen once we are in range to assist."

Ahhh. The rebel captain was concerned how his recorded actions and statements might appear to Earth Command now that human ships had been attacked. He had left when there had been no ship-to-ship fighting, just the absence of senior officers. Clearly, Mehta was concerned for his future career. Well, Jacob was not about to turn down the chance to have nine ships face off against seven alien ships.

"Understood. Thank you Captain Mehta. Link out."

The man's image vanished. But in Jacob's situational holo, the green icon of the destroyer now appeared at the top end of the holo, which marked the outer end of the vector track they were now on. Below, Daisy looked up to Jacob. Her brown eyes were bright, though her expression was neutral.

"Our chances have just improved," she said. "I like that his XO had the guts to remind him of his duty."

"Me too," Jacob said. "Which is exactly what I expect of you, and of every crew person on the Bridge. And also from the chiefs of each deck. I may have the ship status change code, but I do not have all the answers."

She smiled, then turned back to focus on her holos.

Jacob released his seat straps and stood up. "Now, I am heading aft to my quarters for a necessities break and to get a snack. I suspect we have more fighting to do in future hours." He stepped down to the lower level of the command pedestal, then further down to the deck's floor. He turned and faced Daisy.

"Executive Officer Stewart, I relinquish command to you until my return."

She released her straps, stood up quickly and saluted him. "Change of command accepted."

Jacob saluted her, then turned away and headed aft for the exit hatch. There would be no one present in the Command Deck hallway, a fact that pleased him. Maintaining his formal command appearance was a strain that he needed a break from. The reality of commanding a spaceship with 321 people onboard, each as real and vital and hopeful of life as himself, was far different than anything he had studied at the Stellar Academy. Knowing that hundreds more on eight other ships also relied on him for their survival, for guidance, for a clear sense of what they should do, well, that was just the boulder on top of the mountain that sat atop his shoulders. Escape he must. But for no more than an hour. He could not allow himself more than that when everyone else was on combat alert, ready to defend his ship with their best efforts. And with their lives. He had seventy-one ghosts riding him already. More he did not need. Briefly he wondered how many ghosts rode on his father, the five star admiral. The man had led the defeat of the rebel miners during the Callisto Conflict. People and ships had died then. Was that why his father always focused first on what Jacob should do, versus how he should feel?

CHAPTER EIGHT

Jacob's quarters were small but adequate. They consisted of the entry slidedoor, a long room that served as an office with a fold-down sleep rack on one wall, his fold-down comp desk on the other wall, then the entry to the toilet and shower space. Two rooms. It was enough. The hard wall felt good as he sat on his bed rack, his vacsuit pulled off, his hands on his lap, his legs in the aisle that ran down the room's middle. He stared at the images that were hidden by his desk when it was folded up against the opposite wall. Now, it was lowered.

His Mom's flat photo showed her smiling at him from within their home's partly automated kitchen. She wore a flowered spring dress of green and yellow, with a white cook's smock hanging from her neck. She loved to bake fresh bread. He loved to eat it. He remembered that day, back when he'd been 14 and had just started attending Binghampton high. After a day spent ignoring the hall bullies, then defending his tablet from a nasty classmate who had chosen him for her target of the day, he had walked home after being dropped off by the school's airbus. When he'd walked into the house and headed for the kitchen, he'd seen her there. His tablet still in his hands, he lifted it up and snapped the photo.

Beside her image was a flat pic of the old barn in the back of their property. A brown gelding horse was standing in front of the barn, his reins tied to a lonely post. The horse had been the first large animal he had ever seen or spent time with. The gelding had seemed to like him. And it had not insisted on changing from a trot to a fast run. Riding a horse while it ran fast over the land was something he had felt only once. It had scared him. That had happened while he rode with his mom on her Arabian stallion, Butch.

Below the images was the fold-down metal desk plate. His comp pad sat on it, closed for the moment. Sitting atop the comp pad was a holo cube. It showed him just as he posed for his father, right after his graduation from the academy. Two admirals, a captain and two Army colonels stood near Jacob. They were friends of his father. The man had shown him off to them. He had kept the holo cube because of the green forested Rocky Mountains that rose in the background of the graduation field. That day had been Southwest blue sky touched with puffy white clouds. He'd always loved being in nature, and the Rockies near to Colorado Springs were a totally different kind of nature from what he'd seen near Binghampton. Now, inside his quarters, he felt alone, distant from what mattered to him. The fact he had five friends on the *Lepanto*, friends who had accepted his choice to take command, friends who had stood with him in the face of death, that felt good. He should remember that whenever he sat in the admiral's seat under the vidcom eye of the ship's AI. A series of bings came from above his slidedoor.

"Jacob, you in there?" called Kenji's voice. "Can I come in?"

What was he doing here now? Jacob glanced at his finger watch. It said the time was noon. His friend should be back in the Mess Hall, providing hot food to the ten percent of the crew who were now able to take a quick break before heading back to their posts so another ten percent could eat. Or whatever they needed to do.

"Sure. Door, admit Kenji Watanabe."

The slidedoor swished open.

Kenji stood there, dressed in a vacsuit with helmet pushed onto his back, both hands supporting a food tray. On it, uncovered, were plates with brown croissants, jam, three link sausages, some green grapes, a slab of cheddar cheese and a glass, real glass, that held brown liquid. Likely the ice tea his friend knew he liked. His stomach rumbled.

"Hey," Kenji said as he strode in. "Looked for you at the admiral's quarters, then the captain's place, then the XO's. No reply at any place. So I tried here." The tall, slim, black-haired young man pushed the holo cube to one side and put down the tray on top of his comp pad. Then he stood back and eyed him. "Jacob, you gotta eat. Can't be any good to the rest of us if you starve yourself. Low blood sugar and all that, remember?"

Jacob recalled the story his friend had told of how his mother had had diabetes for 30 years and how she had to eat frequent small meals to keep up her blood sugar. He'd met the woman in the orbiting shipyard when she had come up to stay goodbye as her son the line cook headed off into deep space. The woman had treated Jacob as if he were just another young ensign whom her son had befriended. It was a good memory. He smiled, then gestured at the tray.

"Yeah, I remember. And thanks for the food. I was feeling a bit famished. How are things in the Mess Hall?"

"Busy," Kenji said, standing there as he looked around Jacob's small quarters. His friend looked up. His attention fixed on the hologram of the Milky Way galaxy that Jacob had told the room's stupid AI to always create just below the room's ceiling. It provided the same light that could be had from the light strips that illuminated every room on the Battlestar, and anyway, it was fun to look at in the dark, before he dropped off. "Neat holo. I like."

Jacob gestured at the swing out plank that served for a sit down place before his desk. "Have a seat."

"Thanks." Kenji sat and faced him, his pale white face showing little expression beyond normal alertness. His friend hated the old 'Asian inscrutability' term, but did nothing to be boisterous the way Daisy did. He nodded aside at the tray. "You gonna eat?"

"Soon." Jacob gave his friend a thumbs-up. "Really, thanks for looking me up and bringing me the tray. I just needed time here to cope with all that's happened in the last three hours. You know."

Kenji squinted. "Actually, I don't know. You're the officer. You and Lori and Daisy and Carlos. Me and Quincy are the honorary jokesters."

"Wrong!" Jacob sat up and leaned forward, putting just two feet between him and Kenji. "You and Quincy are Spacers. You are just as valuable to the *Lepanto* as me or anyone else. What's the chatter in the Mess Hall? About the death of the top brass and what I've done to protect us?"

Kenji's expression grew thoughtful. "Everyone was shocked at the Cloud Skimmer images. Some of us wondered why we had not heard back from the ensigns who'd gone down with them. You weren't the only ensign to hang with Spacers. Though you are the nicest," his friend said quickly. Jacob nodded, encouraging him. "When you took command, there was surprise. Then when we saw over the All Ship vidcom that the wasp ships were coming our way, plenty of folks got scared. You being up there, with the Bridge crew and our friends, that helped a lot of them cope with it. When the ship status changed to Alert Combat Ready, folks ran out to their posts. We in the kitchen shut down the flammables, locked the food storage, then took our fire-fighting posts on Habitation Deck." His friend paused. "Was really good being able to see and hear over the All Ship vidcom just what was happening, what you folks were doing, what the other ships were doing. Me, it gave me the sense we had a chance."

Jacob felt relief. Then appreciation. Kenji, though a Japanese national, had always treated Jacob and their other friends as if Kenji had grown up with them, rather than in Yokohama. Where he'd attended an American base school in order to learn English. His friend said his time on base had convinced him to join the Star Navy. "Good to hear. But it's not over. We've got nearly two days time before we get to the magnetosphere and make tracks for Kepler 10. I expect the aliens to attack us again."

Kenji shrugged, then stood up. "So, we'll fight them again. Maybe kill another ship of theirs. And I'll head for my fire-fighting station once we get the word from the Bridge to head to combat stations."

"I know you will." Jacob stood up. Kenji stepped back toward the slidedoor. He grabbed his friend's vacsuited arm. Kenji stopped, his look puzzled. "Kenji, thanks for bringing the food. I'll eat it soon. Then it's back up on the Bridge for the duration. Take your Awake pill when your chief hands them out. We all may have to stay awake until we go Alcubierre."

"Will do. Guess I can sleep during Alcubierre. We'll be safe there."

"Yes, we will be," Jacob said, letting go his friend's arm. "Maybe I'll bring our friends down to the Mess Hall for a round of beer and dried seaweed once we enter Alcubierre. Sound okay?"

Kenji smiled big. "Very okay! Later."

"Later," Jacob said to his friend's back as the man exited through the slidedoor.

The hiss of its closing told him it was time to eat, then to head back to the Bridge. The image of him sitting in the admiral's seat, in command, was clearly an image the *Lepanto's* crew needed to see. And likely, an image the new captains on the other ships needed to see. Sitting down, his mind swirling with images of a close run against the giant wasp ship, he took a bite of a cold sausage link. Spicy it was, but Italian in flavor. Just what he liked.

♦ ♦ ♦

Hunter returned from sucking in liquefied fliers in the Nourishment Chamber of his flying nest. He saw that all twelve of his Servants were present, seated on their benches, their attention focused on the wall perception imagers and the colors flowing across their control panels. He moved his abdomen over his bench, lowered until his four footpads could lift from the chamber's cold surface, then inhaled deep the aromas of the chamber.

Aggregation pheromones dominated, along with a strong flow of territorial, trail and signal scents. They were what he expected. And what his Servants knew they should emit if they were to survive his displeasure. "Speaker To All, send the Attack Ready pheromone to all other flying nests. In six hundred wing beats we will attack the Soft Skins!"

Excitement and curiosity pheromones now joined the chamber's air mixture. Those pheromones would be transmitted to the other flying nests, just as he would scent the responding pheromones from those nests.

"Attack Ready pheromone sent," the young male scent cast to him.

Hunter swung his head, fixing all five eyes on the young female who managed their stinger weapons. "Stinger Servant, are all our stinger tubes ready to kill the invaders?"

"They are ready," she scent cast back to him. "Repairs were made. The hole in the forward head shell has been filled with quick hardening nest liquid."

"All Servants," he scent cast, knowing his scent orders would be inhaled on the other flying nests. "Prepare to attack the Soft Skins. Our flying nest will lead the way. The nests of Support Hunter Seven and Support Hunter Nine will come close to our nest, the better to hide them from the perception of the Soft Skins." Excitement scents now dominated. "We move to the attack. While most of us will stay beyond the reach of the black sky light carried by the largest Soft Skin nest, the two nests closest to us will suddenly dart forward and attempt a killing sting against the largest Soft Skin nest. That is where their best Fighter Leader must now hover. When we kill that nest, we kill the other nests ability to fight us. It will then be simple to sting them all to death!"

The responding pheromones from the other six flying nests were uniformly excited and eager to attack. Even the scent from

Support Hunter Seven, whom he suspected of planning a Challenge, came through loaded with aggregation pheromones. So. The youth would wait until the Swarm completed the destruction of the Soft Skins before mounting his challenge. Well, Hunter would await his arrival with sharp mandibles and deadly sting!

♦ ♦ ♦

"Captain!" called Rosemary from Tactical. "The enemy is coming!"

Jacob reached back, pulled his helmet over his head and spoke. "Melody, change ship status to Alert Hostile Enemy. All decks, prepare for combat. All ships, move to the positions we discussed." He scanned the several holos in front of him. One showed an overhead view of the Bridge. Lori and Carlos were at their seats in the rear, making their vacsuits air-tight. Below him Daisy and O'Connor were doing the same. Up front, his nine Bridge crew were either pulling helmets shut, or had done so and were now leaning forward to scan their control pillars and status holos. In front of him was the situational holo that was a copy of the one Daisy always kept in front of her. "Tactical, report disposition and range."

Rosemary tapped her control pillar. The red enemy ship icons in his holo now gained additional text, along with arrows indicating the vector angles.

"The largest wasp ship is in the lead, sir. Flanking it are four other ships. Which makes five." She paused, looked up at her holo, then back down to her Tactical pillar readouts. "That's five ships. There were seven survivors. I do not see the other two in either radar, infrared, ultraviolet or by our ship scope. As for range, the ships are at 11,432 kilometers and closing. Their approach speed is 900 kilometers per minute."

He checked the holo. It showed the *Lepanto* at the base of their formation, with the other seven ships arranged in two tiers above him, which put them slightly further away from the oncoming aliens. A separate green icon was the *Salamis*. It was coming in fast. It might arrive before the wasps began firing. Or soon after.

"Science, can your sensors tell us where those two missing enemy ships are?" He looked right to the man at the far right of the front line of function stations.

Willard, who wore a Flower Child decorated vacsuit, was strapped in, like everyone on the Bridge. Still, he leaned forward to scan his control pillar and its sensor readouts.

"Uh, acting captain, a moment. I'm switching settings on the forward sensor array settings." Silence came. "Yes! The two missing ships are below, close to and out of direct sensor image pickup. That's according to my moving neutrino sensor. The giant ship's location is the source of three moving neutrino sources, not one." He paused, tapped his right armrest, and scanned a new holo. "Plus, I've got an electro-optical view of the three ships now. It's from one of the monitor sats we put in fourth planet orbit. Since the enemy fleet is between us and the planet, it has a great view of the enemy's rear. So to speak."

Jacob smiled at Willard's talkative manner. The portly man was in his late thirties, older than many crew on the ship, and had few friends. But he was an accomplished chess player. After Carlos beat Jacob once, Willard had taken on the young Latino and beaten him handily. Which told Jacob he should never bet in any gambling game where Willard was present. What mattered now was the man's decisive knowledge of physics, astronomy, orbital mechanics, biology, sociology and the many other disciplines on the Science Deck. While Lori had better chops in gravity and bio-cultural stuff, the man had earned his way to the Bridge the honest way. By being smart, creative and willing to think outside of the box. Or so said his personnel file, which Jacob had scanned during his personal quarters break. In fact, he'd scanned the personnel files of every Bridge crew member, right after Kenji had left. He looked to the Brazilian who sat just to the right of Rosemary.

"Weapons, we are nose down and facing the oncoming enemy. Can you depress the spine or belly or flank proton laser nodes enough to shoot ahead?"

"Acting captain, that is not physically possible," replied Oliver Diego y Silva. The swarthy man tapped his pillar. An external hull image of the *Lepanto* now showed in the middle of the front wallscreen. The imagery rotated, top to bottom, then back to top. "Our four proton lasers are intended to protect the ship's flanks. Which means they fire at a ninety degree angle from the ship's central axis. The proton nodes can tilt by 20 degrees off vertical, but that's it."

Which meant for the *Lepanto* to put one of its proton lasers on target on the giant wasp ship meant his ship had to dip its nose by seventy degrees. Thereby exposing a long stretch of its hull to any enemy lying ahead of them. Right now, all eight ships of the battle group had their noses facing the enemy. Behind the *Lepanto* were the two cruisers, lying just to the right and left of his ship's vector track. Behind them were the two destroyers. They occupied the top and bottom slots along his vector. Behind the four heavy ships were the three frigates, which were clustered directly behind the *Lepanto* in order to reduce their exposure to combined enemy laser fire. In short their current formation was a four layered tube. That would change once the *Lepanto* made its leap ahead against the giant wasp ship.

"Weapons, thank you. Tactical, put up both the true space starlight imagery of the enemy fleet and the situational holo sensor imagery."

"Displaying."

In seconds the image of his Battlestar disappeared. In its place, overlapping where stars had once been, were a telescopic true space image of the enemy ships on the left side of the wallscreen, and the situational holo imagery on the right side. The width of both images was about 100,000 kilometers and getting smaller as the enemy got closer. His duplicate of the oncoming wasp ships holo said they were nearly at 11,000 kilometers. Which was the maximum range for their laser and lightning bolt weapons.

"Communications, is everything on this Bridge going out on the All Ship vidcom? And out to the other ships?"

"It is, acting captain," Osashi said quickly.

"All personnel, combat is imminent. Gunners, you are cleared hot. Kill any enemy target that is within your weapon's range. Coordinate your fire with the Weapons chiefs on the other ships," he said quickly. "Remember, every ship fires its carbon dioxide lasers at one spot on the giant wasp ship, while the proton lasers fire together at another spot. Target spots will be designated by the first hits by the *Lepanto*. Everyone join in!"

Below him, O'Connor looked up. "Acting captain, I accept your decision to go with Tactical's attack formation Alpha Squeeze, and your close-in run as proposed by Ensign Antonova. What about my Darts? We could penetrate the giant's hull, plant nuke mines, then pull out before they detonate."

"CWO O'Connor, I am sure your Marines could do just as you propose," Jacob said, his eyes watching the range countdown on the situational holo. "*If* they could reach the enemy ship. But the middle and rear hulls of your Darts are thin. Two hits by a lightning bolt and a Dart is gone. Plus, I prefer to reserve your Darts for the defense of Kepler 10, after we get there."

"Accepted, acting captain."

His peripheral vision told him the white-haired Marine had turned back to watch the two images on the wallscreen. The man had been patient earlier, after he'd come back to the Bridge, contacted the captains on the other seven ships, discussed Rosemary's formation idea with those captains, then passed the data on to Mehta. He had not challenged Jacob during those discussions with the battle group captains. Which Jacob appreciated. However, the man believed deeply in the value of his Darts for taking down prime targets. Jacob did too. Just not in this battle.

"Enemy is firing," called Oliver from Weapons, beating the same words from Rosemary by two seconds.

Green laser beams streaked past the *Lepanto*, heading deeper into space. Yellow lightning bolts came crackling out from the five wasp ships that shielded the two hidden ships. What did the enemy commander plan by hiding those ships?

"Nose impact by bolt," called Joaquin from Life Support.

The red dot of the impact showed on Jacob's cross section holo of the *Lepanto*. The holo confirmed that all decks were locked down and air-tight. All staff were at combat stations. And the chiefs of each deck were in their control centers, ready to respond to any emergency on their deck.

"The *Chesapeake* is hit," Rosemary said quickly. "On its upper hull, just ahead of its plasma battery."

"*Tsushima Strait* hit by bolt," called Osashi, surprising Jacob that the Communications chief would choose to talk about other ships. Course he was in charge of other ship com linkages, especially the FTL neutrino comlink that allowed real time talk between every Earth ship. Still . . .

The wasp ships hit the 10,000 kilometer distance mark.

"All ships, fire CO_2 lasers at the stern of the giant ship!" Jacob yelled. "Cruisers and destroyers, fire your proton lasers at the top front of the ship. Weapons, fire!"

"Firing," responded Oliver.

The *Lepanto's* two front lasers fired from the right and left side outrigger pods. Their green streaks blazed ahead and hit the top rear of the giant ship's stern. Laser fire from seven other ships joined the Battlestar's fire. That made for nine green beams hitting within meters of each other.

The true light image of the enemy ships jiggled as the *Lepanto* jinked sideways, then up, to avoid incoming bolt and laser fire. The other battle group ships were doing the same, relying on attitude jets to move the heavy inertia of their ship off the direct line-of-sight that beam energy gunners were limited to.

Six red beams streaked past the Battlestar, zeroing in on the front end of the giant wasp ship. That was the maximum that could be fired by the cruisers and destroyers. While the cruisers had dual flank side proton lasers, the destroyers had only a single proton laser node at their nose. The proton laser positions on all four ships were aimed in a way that allowed them to fire directly ahead. Well, the *Lepanto's* turn would come, but not right now.

"Power, increase reactor output! Engines, take us up to twelve percent of lightspeed!"

"Reactor output increasing by ten percent," responded Maggie.

"Ship's three thrusters are taking increased isotope flow," called black-skinned Akira. "Magfield confinement of fusion implosions is holding. Speed increasing. To 11.5, 11.7 . . . and now at twelve percent!"

Jacob felt a thrill run down his back. Both fleets were paralleling each other at twelve percent of lightspeed, but closing on each other at far slower speeds of a thousand klicks per minute. Whatever the giant enemy ship commander was planning by hiding two of his ships, the *Lepanto* was about to spring its own surprise. Everyone had agreed the enemy ships would all stay outside the 4,000 kilometer range of the Battlestar's antimatter cannon. And no battle group ship would get within the 3,917 kilometer range of the giant wasp ship's black hole weapon. But that gave Jacob eighty kilometers in which to get close enough for him to fire the AM cannon at the enemy ship. Running up the ship's speed so suddenly was not good on the microelectronic matrices of the reactors and the thruster magfields. But it was the only way he knew of covering the distance faster than the enemy could move out of range.

"Range to giant enemy ship is now 5,143 kilometers," called Rosemary from Tactical.

"Carbon dioxide lasers are firing a third burst at the enemy," called Oliver from Weapons. "So are the proton lasers."

"Reactor stability is holding," called Maggie.

Briefly Jacob eyed the middle-aged chief warrant officer who managed the ship's three fusion reactors. Maggie's file said she was born in the Bronx, had attended MIT and had designed small fusion reactors like the ones that provided power to science bases on Pluto, Europa, Mars and elsewhere. She was also a lesbian with a partner, two boys and four cats at home in the Bronx. The Jewish woman had held up well during the emergency escape from the black hole weapon. The strain on her reactors was less now, but still beyond the safe ratings. Her attention to detail, noted in her file, was now on display.

"Weapons, launch four missiles from our stern silos," Jacob called. "As we discussed, set them to precede us by five hundred klicks. Set their thermonuke warheads for proximity detonation. And for remote det."

"Launching missiles," Oliver called over the helmet comlink. The man's gloved fingers tapped his control pillar. "Detonation options input. At twelve warheads per missile, we will have 48 nuke-busters flying ahead of us!"

Jacob knew that. He also knew that many of the warheads would be zapped by the enemy's lasers and lightning bolts. But he only needed a half dozen or so for what he planned. Briefly he wondered what the enemy commander thought of the *Lepanto's* sudden rush toward the wasp ship, which was also moving toward the battle group. The combined accelerations of both ship groups was rapidly reducing the distance between them. Which made the enemy's counterfire even more accurate.

"Our nose plasma battery is gone!" called Rosemary.

Soon. Soon they would be in range.

CHAPTER NINE

Surprise filled Hunter's gut. The Soft Skin flying nests had turned to point their heads toward his Swarm. His group had just begun to fly faster when the enemy shifted nest orientation. It was as if their Fighter Leader wished to enter a swirling mix of the two groups of flying nests. Strange. It was not what a Swarmer would do. Then again, as his elderly Servant had said, different lifeforms meant different ways of organizing themselves. No matter.

"Stinger Servant, bite that largest Soft Skin nest with our head ring of stingers!"

"Biting," the young female scent cast to him in a mix of aggregation, release and food pheromones.

Clearly she wished to eat of the enemy's flesh. "Support Hunter Seven, Support Hunter Nine," he scent cast over the scent talker that linked all Swarm ships. "Are you ready to fly out and sting the large Soft Skin nest?"

"Seven hungers to bite the Soft Skins," scent cast the young male Hunter who led that flying nest. The youth's pheromones were full of excitement scents mixed with territorial and trail scents.

"Nine is ready to buzz quickly to the attack," scent cast the older female Hunter who led that nest.

Hunter knew her. She came from a predecessor cohort, one of the cohorts that had led the consolidation of all Swarmers into the Nest-wide cooperative that now guided their world and every Swarmer on it. She had declared her Hunter eagerness while still a young larva, biting the forelimbs of the Workers feeding her fresh caught meat. That aggressive biting had followed her through five levels of study, until she moved from a land nest to the flying nest that circled their world in the cold of dark space. Once there she had claimed the right to lead one of the nests being gathered together for the colony trip to the yellow sky light that now lay behind his group of nests. She was someone he could rely on.

"Bide your eagerness," he scent cast to them in a mix of aggregation and trail pheromones.

A change in the oncoming Soft Skin nests drew his attention. They were stinging back against the Swarm with their sky light and heavy sky light stingers. But now the largest nest sent out flying seeds that came forward, sniffing for the scent of his Swarmers. The seeds moved slowly, but they moved fast enough to draw ahead of the cluster of Soft Skin nests. Which, he now saw, had moved to an unusual formation.

"Servant for external space, what do you make of the Soft Skin nest formation?" he scent cast to the older female seated on the bench ahead of him.

The red and black streaks on her well-shaped body shone brightly against the yellow of her undercoat. Her antennae leaned forward. "The perception imagers take in many colors from these strange nests," she scent cast in a strong signal pheromone. "It appears the larger flying nests seek to shelter the smaller nests from the concentrated bite of all our nests."

He could see that, in detail with his two major eyes and in broad sweeps of ultraviolet through his three small eyes. The largest nest was in the lead of this formation, just as he was in the lead of all the Swarmer nests. That meant his decision to attack the largest Soft Skin nest was correct. Clearly it held the chief Fighter Leader of the Soft Skins. Though, he now noticed, the Soft Skin nest that had flown away from Warmth when the Soft Skin device had discovered the death of Soft Skin leaders, that nest now returned. It was winging toward the other Soft Skins with a fast wingbeat. Good. This battle would lead to the death of all the Soft Skins.

"Hunter!" scent cast the older male Servant in charge of his nest's propulsive devices. "The Soft Skin sky light weapons are all striking the shell above my devices! There could be a deep bite soon."

Now was the time for his guidance to all the Servants and all the Swarmer nests. "Patience, elder. Our hard shell is thick and resistant to the heat of concentrated sky light."

"Our head skin melts!" scent cast the elderly female Servant in charge of pheromone signals to the other chambers of his nest. "The heavy sky lights hit hard and deep! The bite goes deeper than before!"

The Servant's ragged alarm pheromones were afloat on the air of the Flight Chamber. He could not allow her to make fearful the other Servants, let along the nests of Hunters Seven and Nine. He flapped his two wings rapidly, rising up from his bench and going forward the few body lengths that separated him from the female. Before she could scent cast more defeat, he flew down, landed on the top of her abdomen and then bit her life cord at the spot where her head joined her thorax. Her head came loose. It hit the bottom of the chamber with a loud swish of fluids.

"Servants! We attack! We defeat the Soft Skins! No Soft Skin can oppose us! Bite now and hard!"

The shock of his action, combined with the overwhelming scent of his pheromones, pushed each Servant to a rapid wing fluttering even as they each emitted intense aggregation pheromones.

"Biting harder!" scent cast the young female Servant in charge of their stingers.

"Aiming our head exactly at the oncoming Soft Skins!" scent yelled the Flight Servant in charge of their nest's movement through cold dark space.

"Look!" cried the old male Servant who studied aberrant social behavior. "The largest Soft Skin nest jumps toward us! It flies faster than any Swarmer!"

Dismay hit him hard. No sooner had he killed the defeatist Servant than the ancient Servant who knew not how to bite or fight or do anything but hum and buzz, he too emitted a scent of confusion and alarm.

"All Swarmers! Our target comes to us! Rejoice!" he scent cast in strong waves of signal pheromones. "Join your stingers against the large nest's approach! Support Leaders Seven and Nine, launch your nests now! Swing out to either side of this Soft Skin nest and bite from the sides as we bite its head!"

The swirl of confused pheromones now cleared as each Swarmer understood their purpose and bent to it. The scents echoing back from the two nests he had hidden under his wings were filled with aggregation loyalty, trail determination and anger hunger. Flapping his wings, he spread those new pheromones among the Swarmers in the Flight Chamber, thence out to other chambers in the depths of his nest. They might suffer wounds to the outer hard shell. But the essential parts of his nest were hidden deep. They could fly and bite even with half their hard shell bitten away. Inhaling deep, he brought to mind images of the Soft Skins from the meeting site, before the Storm Bringer had ended their lives. Would the best way to kill a survivor be to bite its neck, the way he had done to the disloyal female? Or should he first sting its middle, the place where his deep color vision said the most heat resided on a Soft Skin? All that mattered was that there be some survivors on which to try all stinger options!

♦ ♦ ♦

Support Hunter Seven sent out the attack pheromone to all the Servants in his nest's Flight Chamber. Each fluttered wings, bent antennae forward and activated their parts of his flying nest. A vibration that he felt through the bench he sat on told him the nest's propulsive devices were moving his nest outward and away from the shelter of Hunter One's massive nest. It was twice the size of any other Swarmer nest, and the leader's plan to deceive the Soft Skins made sense to him. It was a variation of the historical Swarm attack whereby the strongest Hunter led the swarm forward, his form being the first to be sighted by the major eyes of an enemy cohort. The enemy would think there were fewer nests coming to bite, when in the glow of the day's sky light there were more!

"Stinger Servant, hold your sting until we are closer to the large Soft Skin nest," he scent cast in a mix of signal, trail and aggregation pheromones.

"Holding our bite," the young male scent cast back in a strong odor of hunter pheromones, signaling he wished to eat of the enemy's flesh.

As did he. Killing the large nest would do much to increase his standing among all Swarmers. He was not the one who had lost five nests to the leaderless Soft Skins. Hunter One was. Once the Soft Skins were dead and gone, he would call for a meeting of all Hunters from all seven flying nests. While Hunter One surely expected him to Challenge, the older leader did not know two nests had already pledged loyalty to him.

"Support Hunter," called the Servant in charge of monitoring radiations from cold space. "A new Soft Skin nest now flies back to the eight nests that now face us. But it is still distant, even though its wings fly swiftly."

He inhaled the trail signal emitted by the older female. The Servant spoke truth. But his five eyes judged the speed of the oncoming flying skin to be inadequate to join the battle that now loomed as both nest groups flew toward each other at a large part of the speed of sky light radiation.

"Stay alert," he said by way of primer and releaser pheromones, mixed with a touch of aggregation to remind her of her loyalty to him. "Soon we will reach the proper flight angle at which to sting hard the disgusting Soft Skins!"

Revulsion pheromones peaked briefly as all Swarmers in his Flight Chamber viewed the perception images of the Soft Skin nests, none of which possessed the orderly outer hard shell that marked a safe nest. Then excitement pheromones became dominant as his fellow Swarmers felt eagerness to attack, that scent enlarged by his release of a releaser pheromone that reminded them all that soon there would be a change in their duties. Soon, their nest would bite hard the head of the large Soft Skin nest, just as Support Hunter Nine's nest bit hard from the opposite side. Surely no Soft Skin nest could survive bites from both sides and against its head!

♦ ♦ ♦

"Bannerjee, I don't give a damn what you think about what you deserve! And we're now in combat!" yelled Alicia Branstead over the between decks comlink.

Aarhant winced. The image of the Australian woman on his tablet showed a brown-haired, middle-aged, stocky Anglo woman dressed in a vacsuit, sitting beside her two principal assistants, in the control center on Science Deck. His own assistants sat behind him in the Navigation Deck control center. He hoped her assistants were not hearing what she was saying.

"I know that," he replied, his attention partly focused on the situational holo that floated in the middle of the room filled with navigation panels, Library databases, algorithm crunching comp blocks and antique paper files in case a stellar flare wiped all the digital electronic data. "But you are an O-3 Lieutenant, ranking just below me. Surely you must agree that as a lieutenant commander, I am the highest ranking officer still alive on the Battlestar!"

Her frown went to a grimace of distaste. "So what? You know as well as I do that Star Navy regulations prevent an officer from one deck taking over operations on another deck, without an encrypted approval code from Earth Command! Or approval by the ship's captain. The rules say the Command Deck chain of authority runs from the ensigns up to the admiral or captain. We are *not* in their chain of command. Not until Earth Command says otherwise!" She looked aside at some holo. "Let me go! We are getting close to the attack on the giant wasp ship!"

"As you wish," he muttered. "Good day."

Shutting down his tablet link that conveyed images and voice and data only to his helmet's comlink, Aarhant felt intense frustration. Whatever the Star Navy regulations were, he should be in command! If he had been, the entire battle group would have left the system before the wasp aliens could attack! The image of the vaporized and melted ruins of the meeting site said clearly the First Contact encounter had come up a failure. Every ship should have accepted his leadership. Instead, while he slept, the whelp had entered the ship status change code, assumed command, and then fought a battle that had resulted in the loss of a frigate! Why, a fresh ensign like Renselaer would not even be in command of a frigate, leastwise not until he made the lieutenant JG grade. But the reality was there were only three commissioned officers still alive on the *Lepanto*. Himself, Branstead and Lieutenant JG Jane Yamamoto, who ran Life Support Deck. Everyone else was a Spacer, a warrant officer or a petty officer, none of whom possessed an O-ranking. Even James Alvarez, who was technically in charge of routine Command Deck operations, was just a senior chief petty officer. Who was outranked by any ensign! With a sigh, he told himself to be patient. Once they arrived in Kepler 10, he would talk directly to the captain in charge of the Star Navy orbital base. Surely the man, he hoped it was a man, would agree with him assuming command!

♦ ♦ ♦

"Range to giant enemy ship is now 4,212 kilometers," called Rosemary from Tactical.

Jacob's heart beat fast. "Navigation, keep us jinking from side to side, up and down and spiral and any mode that reduces weapons impact!"

"Maneuvering," replied Louise, her gloved fingers tapping the touch controls on the top of her control pillar.

Briefly he gave thanks for the woman's expertise. Like Daisy she had been a pilot before earning a Ph. D. in celestial mechanics from Princeton. Her file said she was married to a man who was a mechanical engineer involved in building small dams on lesser streams in the Rockies and the Cascades. They had no children. But the woman had piloted every type of spacecraft in the inventory of the Star Navy, including small LCAs, cargo tubes and sensor blooms. She was the perfect person to be at Navigation. Her deck's boss, Aarhant Bannerjee, had impressed Jacob as a bureaucrat too focused on his personal image and advancement. Thank the Goddess he was not now on the Bridge!

"Carbon dioxide lasers are firing a seventh burst at the enemy," called Oliver from Weapons. "So are the battle group's proton lasers."

That reminded him. It was time. "Navigation, lift our nose up seventy degrees so our belly proton laser can fire on the giant enemy ship."

"Lifting. Fourteen seconds to proton engagement," she said over his helmet comlink.

Looking down at his two armrests, Jacob scanned the readouts and control patches that lined half of each armrest.

"Reactor stability is maintaining balance," called Maggie.

That was good news. He could see from his armrests that the three fusion pulse thrusters were maintaining an outward acceleration of twelve percent of lightspeed. They were angling closer to the enemy, that was also headed outward at twelve percent. Their closure speed was 900 kilometers per minute. Soon, the two groups would pass each other, with some intermingling of ships, or one or both ship groups would swing away to the side to avoid close passage. He knew what the *Lepanto* was going to do. And he knew the orders he had given to the two cruisers, two destroyers and three frigates following behind him. He looked up and scanned the situational holo. The *Salamis* was now 40,000 kilometers out and closing on the other ships, but it would play no role in the early fighting. Maybe the running fight.

"Belly proton laser firing," called Oliver, his voice excited as he brought into play one of the Battlestar's most destructive weapons.

Soon the man would be able to launch Smart Rocks from the four topside and four belly railgun launchers. While the self-directed rocks would be launched at Earth's escape velocity of eleven plus kilometers per second, they would continue forward even as they spread out to either side of the Battlestar. They were more of a miss than hit weapon, but still, they had seemed to bother the wasp ships in the first battle. Any distraction he could add to this battle, in addition to the thermonuke warheads, was welcome. Distraction improved survival. And survival allowed them the chance to kill the giant wasp ship.

"We are taking damage to our belly hull," Rosemary called from Tactical. "The five wasp ships are all firing at one area. Punch through!"

Jacob saw that on his ship cross-section holo. A large red spot glowed on the forward part of the belly hull. Blinking yellow lights reported the loss of water. Well, the water shield was compartmentalized. Only a portion of their water rad shielding would be lost.

"How close?"

"We are at 4,009 kilometers. Shortly we will be within antimatter range," Rosemary said quickly, her manner distracted as she monitored the hits being taken on the battle group's seven other ships, the firing of lasers from the right and left outrigger pods, and the flow of new missiles to the stern launch silos. Among a dozen other things happening that related to the tactical situation.

"We can take it," muttered O'Connor from below.

"The frigates are avoiding incoming laser fire," reported Daisy, as his new XO closely monitored the other ships in the battle group. "Lightning bolt hits on *Philippines Sea, Hampton Roads* and *Chesapeake*. No punch through. All ships are spinning."

The true space image holo of those ships showed seven mirror-like tubes. Only a few showed black streaks where enemy lasers had cut through the adaptive optics lenses that coated the hull. Below the lenses was a black ablative layer based on re-entry nose cones from last century, then armor. Below the armor was a shell of water, followed by the thin metal of the inner hull. At least the vapor from a fountain of water served to dilute following laser strikes. On the other ships, the armor was less thick than on the *Lepanto*. It had two meters of hardened armor, the cruisers one meter, the destroyers a half meter and the frigates just ten centimeters of armor. Which was why the *Britain* had died so quickly. While every ship had the adaptive optics and ablative hull coating, none of the frigates could withstand eight or ten simultaneous laser strikes. The lightning bolts were even worse when they hit a hull. Their charge spread out sideways and cooked more optic lenses that those killed in the initial impact.

"Captain!" cried Rosemary. "The two hidden wasp ships have launched out sideways from the giant ship. No firing from them yet."

"AI Melody, analyze enemy ship formation and tactics," he said, running what he saw through his memory of academy classes, vids and real space maneuvers he'd seen while on the Moon field trip.

"Enemy appears to be focused on the *Lepanto*," the AI said tensely, her speech quick and sharp. "Most lasers and bolts are aimed at us. Few at other battle group ships. Two new enemy ships appear aimed for an attack on our flanks."

It was time. "All ships! Swing right as briefed! Maintain minimum of 4,000 kilometers range between enemy and your ships. Maintain laser and proton fire on the giant ship!"

"Swinging right," called Swanson from *Chesapeake*. "Losing proton laser lock-on. Tail lasers firing."

"Turning right," rumbled Wilcox from the *Hampton Roads*. "Same for us."

"Swinging," said Zhang. "*Tsushima Strait* is unharmed. Losing nose-on lock for proton fire. Tail lasers now firing at enemy,"

"Launching missiles from our tail," called Jefferson from the *Philippines Sea*. "Adding our tail lasers to the mix."

Acting captains Lorenz, Metz and Mansour said the same from the frigates *St. Mihiel, Marianas* and *Ofira*, though they were limited to lasers.

Offensive fire continued even during the turn. The cruisers had CO_2 lasers at their nose and tail. Plus proton lasers on each flank. The destroyers had a proton laser at the nose and two gas lasers at the tail, plus missiles. The frigates had lasers at their nose and tails, and some missiles.

The *Lepanto* was turning with the battle group ships. But it had rear-pointing lasers on the aft ends of the outrigger pods. Plus proton lasers on top, belly and both flanks. That left the *Lepanto* able to add a proton laser to the battle group's mix of attacking beams. Which its belly proton laser was now doing, the red beam shooting rearward at the gaping hole in the giant wasp ship's nose. Water and air were shooting out from the punch through but there had been no change in the wasp ship's vector track or in its steady flight toward the *Lepanto*.

Jacob knew this was the time of maximum vulnerability for all battle group ships. In order to swing right and off their forward vector track, every ship had to point its thrusters at a right angle to the *Lepanto's* axis of attack. That reduced the group's offensive fire. Well, he could help with that.

"Weapons, fire all Smart Rock launchers!"

"Firing," Oliver said, sounding quite eager.

Jacob knew there was no wasp target to their right or left. Not yet. But as they closed on the *Lepanto*, the two flanking wasp ships would fly into the Smart Rock clusters. The rocks would hit at a right angle to the forward vector track of each flanking wasp ship. And perhaps some rocks would hit on the tight cluster of wasp ships that surrounded the giant enemy ship. When the *Lepanto* flipped back to a nose-on position, its thrust momentum would keep the ship on the right turn vector track. But it meant the Battlestar would trail behind the other seven ships of the battle group. Just as Jacob had planned.

"Captain!" called Louise. "The flanking wasp ships are angling their track toward our right side turn. So are all the wasp ships! They are following us!"

Damn. That made things complicated. Most of the Smart Rocks would miss any target.

"Weapons, detonate the surviving thermonuke warheads. They are still between us and the enemy."

"Detonating seven warheads," Oliver said, his tone breathless.

Behind them, behind the white-orange flare of their three thrusters, which were now pushing the *Lepanto* into sideways flight at twelve percent of the speed of light, there now bloomed seven small stars.

The first burst of energy from a thermonuke detonation was a shell of x-rays and gamma rays. That was followed by a shell of neutrons. Next came the visible plasma ball of yellow-white fusion as the embedded atomic warhead compressed the deuterium and tritium globe of the hydrogen warhead into superdense implosion. It was a lesson learned not long after the end of World War II. To create what was then called the super-bomb required a normal atomic fission reaction to induce a fusion of the two hydrogen isotopes. The result was a blast equal to a small sun visiting the air or land. In space, the result was the same except the plasma ball was a perfect globe that expanded outward, shell after shell as nearby warheads did the same. The radiation output of seven thermonuke warheads created an electromagnetic storm unlike any known to humans, short of a coronal mass ejection from the Sun.

"That should screw their targeting," O'Connor said from below.

Jacob grinned. "Just so. Engines, shut off the main thrusters."

"Primary thrusters shut down," Akira said.

"Navigation, flip our nose upward. Stop the flip once the antimatter node is aligned with the targeting box for the giant ship," he said calmly, hoping everyone else on the other decks of the *Lepanto* heard him as they saw the battle group maneuver away from the wasp ship cluster. Building crew confidence was just as important as preserving their primary weapons.

"Flipping upward," Louise responded.

Soon, once the thermonuke plasma haze cleared, the *Lepanto* would have a clear shot at the giant wasp ship. And at any wasp ship within twenty degrees of their target. They had four AM loads ready to launch. The black streaks would travel at the speed of light. Surely one of them would hit something vital.

CHAPTER TEN

Hunter's five eyes felt blinded by the perception image of seven small sky lights blossoming between his nest and the Soft Skin nests. He looked away. The blinding glare lessened. His three simple eyes were the first to recover. He perceived what he needed to perceive.

"Soft Skin nests are turning away! Flight Servant! Turn us to follow them!" he said in a rush of signal, primer and trail pheromones.

"Turning our nest to follow," the Servant said in a strong aggregation pheromone.

"Speaker To All, send the same scent to the other Swarm nests! Make sure Support Hunter Seven and Support Hunter Nine take the new flight angle!"

"Pheromones sent," the young male scent cast.

"Stinger Servant, continue biting the largest Soft Skin nest!" he said with a flap of his wings as his two major eyes saw the sky light and sky bolt stingers stopping.

The young female hunched low on her bench. "My fellow stinger Servants have lost the scent track of the large nest," she said in a signal pheromone loaded with fear. "The star light bursts make blind our hard shell tools."

Clearly she worried he would fly over and bite her neck. That he would not do. She was too useful. And she might yet become a Matron with heredity markers that would improve all of Nest.

"How soon will the bursts clear?" he scent cast in a peremptory mix of primer and territorial pheromones.

"In two hundred and three wing beats," she replied, her strong black antennae lifting as she realized she would live beyond his displeasure.

The older male Servant who had taken over the between chambers signal duty of the dead female now hunched low on his bench. What else was dropping out of the sky?

"Servant!" he scent cast to that male alone. "Report your findings!"

"The deep hole in the head of our flying nest has cut deeper. The energy unit for the front ring of stinger tubes has shut down to prevent its explosion," the old male said in a frail scent cast of signal pheromones. "Three six-groups of Swarmers are gone. Their chambers lost all air."

The heavy sky light beams from the Soft Skins had indeed hurt his nest. But there were many flight lengths not touched, despite the green sky light beams that had cut a hole above the nest's propulsive section. The Swarm's return sky beams had damaged the large Soft Skin nest's abdomen and nose. Water had shot out from the abdomen of the nest. Surely it would die before his nest became flight erratic.

"Hunter!" hailed the elder female Servant who monitored Soft Skin nest formations and external space. "The sky light haze is gone! The Soft Skins are fleeing us!"

He saw that with all five eyes. But he also saw something that worried him. The largest sky nest was flipping its cold tail downward. Its deadly nose with the black sky light beam would soon aim his way. *No!*

"Stinger Servant, bite the largest Soft Skin nest! All nests, bite at the same spot as we do!" he pheromone cast, relying on Speaker To All to transmit his pheromones to the six other nests. What else might help? "Support Hunters Seven and Nine, fire your sky lights and sky bolts at the sides of the largest nest! Bite them. Hurt the Soft Skins!"

The perception imager that showed the beams of his sky lights, sky bolts and those of other nests in a colorful mix of bite tracks showed those two nests doing as he directed. They were joined by the four nests close to his nest. Three spots on the large Soft Skin nest glowed darkly in ultraviolet. More water spurted from the belly of the enemy leader's nest.

"Hunter!" cried his Stinger Servant. "The large Soft Skin nest is now within flight range to use its black beam! Do we go to our Pull Down field?"

He would. Except the deep head wound of his nest had killed the forward energy producer. That meant a third of his normal weapons and a third of the Pull Down plates would not operate. While he knew little of the high scents involved in fabricating the Pull Down device, he knew well its limitations. He could order the older male Servant in charge of the device to activate it. It would comply. But the device would fail to produce the fully enveloping field that was required for the hidden sky light weapon to work. There was only one thing to do.

"Servant!" he scent cast to the young female who managed the control panel for the particle disruption seeds. "Launch five six-groups of seeds ahead of us! We can create our own sky light haze! Surely that will block the black beam's track!"

"Tossing out seeds!" the female scent cast back in a mix of aggregation and trail pheromones.

He watched as the seeds shot ahead of his nest, propelled by solid scents that blazed brightly. Soon the star light haze would blossom before his nest. Would it protect him? At least the Soft Skin leader did not know his Pull Down device could not work.

The largest sky nest completed its turnover. Its nose aimed his way. Sky light beams and sky bolt arcs hit it from three sides. But still it hovered there, just within the flight distance for its weapon to work.

The appearance of two red beams shooting out from the sides of the Soft Skin nest shocked him. They were heavy sky light identical to the multiple sky light beams that had cut the deep hole in the head of his nest. The red beams reached out.

Support Hunter Seven's ship was hit on the side. Support Hunter Nine's ship was also hit, though it was rolling to one side even as it fired its front ring and side ring of stingers at the Soft Skin nest. Would his allies complete their enveloping attack before they died?

♦ ♦ ♦

Jacob felt his seat vibrate under him as explosions happened on the belly and sides of the *Lepanto*. The flanking wasp ships had let loose with all their weapons. Yellow lightning bolts and green laser streaks all hit a single spot on his right flank. The other wasp ship did the same on his left flank. Meanwhile, the four wasp ships directly ahead concentrated their laser and bolt fire on the nose of the *Lepanto*. Which now added its water shell to the diffuse cloud of water coming from the belly hole cut by earlier combined wasp fire. But there was no fire coming at him from the giant wasp ship. Its front ring of tubes were silent. Why?

"Range is 3,933 kilometers," called Rosemary.

"Weapons, activate the antimatter emitter node," he said, looking forward to the death of the giant wasp ship. And with that death, perhaps an end to the danger to his people, his ship and the other battle group ships.

"Activating," Oliver called from up front. "Twelve seconds to firing release."

"Captain!" called Louise from Navigation. "The right side wasp ship that is flanking us, it's moving closer!"

Jacob saw that. The *Lepanto* and the battle group were in a curving turn to the right. The wasp ships, both the flanking ships and the five core ships, were also turning in a curve to their left. Theoretically the two vector track curves would end up paralleling each other as both groups of ships headed out and away from the system's ecliptic plane of planets. Both groups were moving at 12 percent of lightspeed, in parallel with each other. As was the *Salamis*, which now curved to join their outward track. The destroyer's proton laser now added its fire to the attack on the giant wasp ship. He noticed the eight battle group ships were pulling away from his ship as they continued their fusion pulse thrusting, while the *Lepanto's* thrusters were silent. For the moment.

"Weapons, fire our right and left side proton lasers at those ships!"

Oliver tapped his control pillar. "Firing. Impacts on both ships. No change in vector tracks."

"Rosemary . . . uh, Tactical," he corrected himself. "What the hell is that right side wasp ship doing? Moving closer to our axis of travel means it will lose lock-on to our right flank."

The Irish woman tapped her control pillar, then looked back his way. Her jade green eyes looked at Daisy, then up to him. Her expression was puzzled. "No idea, sir. Uh, acting captain. It does not make any tactical sense." She turned back and gestured at the front wallscreen, which was filled with true light and multispectral sensor images of the seven wasp ships. "The giant ship's hiding of the two ships was meant to allow it to get close enough to launch those two ships on a flanking attack, while the other wasp ships hit us head on. That is what is now happening. The *Lepanto* is damaged, water is leaking from our nose and belly, but most weapons systems are operational. The rest of the battle group is firing as they head outward. There is no counterfire against the other battle group ships. It does not make sense to me," she said.

"Three seconds," called Oliver.

"Acting captain!" called Louise. "The right flank wasp ship is speeding up! It's closing on us! It's moving closer to the zone of other wasp ship fire."

It made no sense to him. And if the right flank ship came closer, it would make for a good second antimatter target. It already was within twenty degrees of the direct line of sight targeting box for the giant wasp ship.

"Fire the antimatter cannon!"

A black beam of negative matter shot out into the coldness of mostly empty space.

A new sun blazed where once a wasp ship had lived.

♦ ♦ ♦

Daisy could not believe what she saw in her situational holo. Nor in the multispectral sensor feeds. The star-like antimatter explosion had briefly caught her attention, then she had refocused on her XO duties of monitoring internal ship status, the worry of two spots with punch through holes that were leaking water into space, the melting of hull armor on the sides of the ship and the low bing-binging from her seat that signaled hull breaches. But the sensor feed reclaimed her attention. She shook her head. Could it be real?

"Acting captain, the giant wasp ship is still alive! The beam hit the right flank wasp ship! It moved into the path of our beam."

Gasps came from the crew up front and from Lori and Carlos in the back, where they were watching this third battle play out its deadly, deadly dance.

"Tactical, verify the XO's report," Jacob called from behind her.

Brief irritation hit her. Then approval. A good captain always sought verification of a splash down event.

"The XO is correct," Rosemary said, her voice wondering. "The giant wasp ship is intact."

What would happen next?

♦ ♦ ♦

Hunter felt shock at the death of Support Hunter Nine's nest. The female Hunter leading that nest had been among his most fervent supporters. Now she was gone, along with thirty six-groups of Swarmers. The death of her nest meant the Swarm now controlled just six flying nests, while the Soft Skins still had eight, with a ninth newly added. Which now fired its heavy sky light beam on his nest. Well, sometimes the Swarm must change its flight path.

"Stinger Servant, explode the particle disruption seeds!"

Surprise pheromones came from the young male. Then aggregation followed quickly. "Exploding nine seeds! Those are the ones that survived the Soft Skin sky light and heavy sky light beams."

Hunter knew that. "Flight Servant, bend our flight path away from the Soft Skins," he scent cast to the male Servant. They must move their nest out of the black beam's range. He emitted a new pheromone aimed at a different Servant. "Propulsion Servant, reverse our propulsive device push. Aim your propulsion against the Soft Skins!"

Shock pheromones came from every Servant in the Flight Chamber. Then a new scent of confusion rose up as his Swarmers wondered why they were pulling away from the Soft Skins.

"Stinger Servant, continuing firing sky lights and sky bolts against the other Soft Skin nests," he scent cast in a mix of aggregation, primer and signal pheromones. Their new sky light haze prevented any attack on the largest nest. "Speaker To All, tell our other nests to change their stinger beams to bite on the other Soft Skin nests. We attack now!"

Those orders went out, both on his nest and on the other Swarmer nests. A hint of confusion still floated through the air of the Flight Chamber. Which scent must surely invite a challenge to his leadership. Briefly he felt sadness that the dead nest was not the one led by Support Hunter Seven. That Hunter would surely declare a Challenge at the sight and smell of Swarmers pulling back from an attack. Well, he was ready for that challenge. The challenged Hunter always had the right, by tradition, to set the place and terms of the resulting fight. And he had not survived to lead this colony group by failing to plan ahead.

♦ ♦ ♦

Nine new stars filled the space between the *Lepanto* and the giant wasp ship.

"Acting captain, we have lost lock-on from the AM emitter," called Oliver. "Same for our forward lasers. Your orders?"

"Concentrate your laser fire on the left flank wasp ship," Jacob said quickly, realizing the plasma haze created by nine atomic blasts now hid the five central wasp ships from target lock-on. "Communications, give the same order to all battle group ships."

"Transmitting order," Osashi said quickly.

"Enemy is now outside the range of the antimatter cannon," Oliver said, disappointment clear in his voice. "No evidence of black hole field. Largest wasp ship is now firing at our battle group ships. Which are continuing to fire back."

Jacob saw that in his situational holo. While they could not fire on the central five wasp ships due to the plasma haze, the same applied to the enemy. Which gave him time to think beyond simple attack and response, so he could look ahead.

"Life Support! Send damage control and firefighting teams to the punch through hull breaches on the nose and belly of the *Lepanto*," he ordered . . . Joaquin Garcia it was, he recalled.

"Sending orders," the American Latino said, his voice gruff.

"Acting captain," called Louise. "The five enemy ships are moving further out. So is the left side wasp ship, which is diving to join the main group. They are at 8,432 kilometers. Range is increasing. They are paralleling us at 12 psol."

That news from Navigation drew his attention back to the situational holo. The giant wasp ship was leaking water from its massive nose hull breach and its front ring of tubes were silent. But its middle and rear rings of laser and bolt tubes were now spitting out deadliness at the other ships of the battle group. As were the other wasp ships. Except the attacking beams were not concentrated on a single ship, thank the Goddess! He noticed that *Chesapeake* and *Hampton Roads* had adjusted their vector track to intercept most of those incoming beams, acting to shelter the three destroyers and three frigates. But their thick armor could only take so many direct hits from yellow lightning bolts and green laser beams.

"Navigation! Flip us so our nose is aimed at the battle group. Engines, fire all three primary thrusters at maximum yield. Bring us up to a thousand klicks per minute on intercept," Jacob said firmly. He looked at his situational holo, then over to Rosemary. "Tactical, how soon before the *Lepanto* can intercept those beams hitting the two cruisers?"

"A few minutes or less," she said quickly, her gloved hands tapping her control pillar's touchscreen. "The battle group was not that far ahead of us. And we all shared the same sideways vector track. The enemy is shooting along the hypotenuse of the triangle formed by the group at top, us at bottom angle and the wasps at the left end of the right triangle," she said.

Her words matched the picture in Jacob's mind and the images on the situational holo. Clearly the enemy was aiming to get beyond the reach of human proton and CO_2 lasers. Could they do more? His mind picture told him that as soon as their vector track toward the hypotenuse line passed beyond the plasma haze, their left side proton laser could fire on any wasp ship. Which might be a wise thing to do. He could not use the ship's belly hull to block more incoming beams thanks to the deep hole already cut in the middle of the hull, just ahead of the belly plasma battery. Nor could he angle the top hull toward the enemy, or he would lose the AM node. Which left exposing one side or both sides to enemy beams in order to reduce the damage to the cruisers, destroyers and frigates. Which were all firing at the enemy. But like the wasps, the battle group's counterfire was dispersed. Well, time to fix that.

"Weapons, fire our left side proton laser at the giant wasp ship," Jacob ordered, noticing they were just clearing the haze. "And signal to your fellow Weapons chiefs on the other ships to join their laser and proton fire on the giant ship. Maybe we can make the enemy move further out if big mama starts hurting more than she is already hurt!"

"Firing left side proton laser at ship's rear," Oliver said hurriedly. "Sending co-targeting orders to other battle group ships. Yes! We have punch through on the rear of the giant ship, back where the CO_2 lasers had been hitting its engine area!"

The news pleased him. But they were still in danger, even from a retreating enemy. He looked down. "CWO O'Connor, what do you make of the enemy's movements?"

The white-haired Marine leaned forward a bit as he concentrated on several holos that faced his captain's seat. "They aren't giving up on attacking us," he said. "But the loss of another ship has made them pull back. That and seeing the impact of our antimatter beam. They are now six ships to our nine. Some battle group ships have hull breaches. But all have operational weapons and full thrust capability. My guess is the enemy commander is assessing his or her options. While still hitting at us. Attacking us is likely the wasp way of pretending they are not retreating."

That sounded familiar. Very human familiar. "We will continue to fire on the wasp ships so long as they are in range," Jacob said. "Any suggestions?"

The older man looked up at Jacob. His gray eyes fixed on him. Thin lips opened. "Recommend that all ships reduce fusion pulse thrust to normal ten psol, sir. No need to risk sudden failure when the enemy is not closing on us."

A good idea. One he should have seen earlier. "Engines! Reduce thrust to ten percent lightspeed. Communications, pass on my order to other battle group ships to reduce speed to standard fusion pulse thrust."

"Reducing thrust," Akira said, her black-skinned forehead shiny from sweat.

"Passing on your orders to the battle group," Osashi said quickly and professionally.

Interesting. "Andrew," he called to the senior crewman. "How are you feeling?"

The Japanese-American jerked his head to the side, looking directly at Jacob. He seemed shocked by Jacob's use of his first name. Then his face relaxed. An amiable look now filled his high-cheeked face. "I'm feeling fine, acting captain. Ready to stay at this for another 30 hours!"

Which they just might have to do in order to reach the magnetosphere boundary and the safety of Alcubierre space-time travel. An image in the situational holo drew his attention. "Navigation, we are coming up on the direct line of beam attack on the battle group. When we hit that line, turn our nose so we are following the rest of the battle group. Also, tilt the ship's nose down a bit so the incoming beams hit the rear of the ship's bottom."

Louise frowned, nodded and touched her control pillar's touchscreen. "Adjusting ship's vector track. Top hull thrusters are pushing the nose down by ten degrees."

He looked back to Oliver. "Weapons, fire missiles from the rear missile silos. Create a thermonuke warhead spread behind us at about 80 kilometers. Shortly we will do a plasma haze event by touching off those warheads."

Oliver grinned. "Firing eight missiles from our stern, vector track to the rear. Will advise you when they are 80 klicks behind us."

Jacob nodded. "Engines, add our fusion pulse exhaust to that plasma haze."

Akira looked back his way. Her dark brown eyes were bright. "Three primary thrusters are down to ten percent lightspeed acceleration. Our fusion flame tail reaches out 60 klicks to our rear, acting captain."

That was something he had not known. Like anyone in space who had watched spaceships maneuver in the black vacuum, he knew every ship's thruster engine produced a plume of plasma from the implosion of pellets of deuterium and tritium isotopes. But the giant tail produced by the Battlestar was new to him.

"Taking laser and lightning bolt hits," called Rosemary from Tactical. "Rear belly taking the hits. Adaptive optics deflecting much of the incoming energy. We are not yet down to the ablative skin. The lightning bolts, though have ruined our rear sensor array."

So be it.

"Warheads are at 80 klicks out," Oliver called.

"Weapons, detonate all surviving warheads," he said, his voice echoing in his helmet.

"Detonating twelve warheads," Oliver said softly.

The front wallscreen that showed the view of the enemy wasp ships now filled with twelve yellow-white stars. The plasma balls quickly spread out and joined each other, forming an oblong haze that drank in the incoming laser and bolt beams.

"Hits on the hull have stopped," called Joaquin from Life Support.

"Most hits on battle group ships have stopped," Rosemary said, sounding pleased.

He had bought them some time. Jacob checked the distance counter in the situational holo.

"Enemy is now beyond 11,000 kilometers," called Louise from Navigation.

He looked up. "Melody, do you project any further enemy attacks on us?"

"None projected. The enemy ships are moving close to each other. They are assuming the six-sided formation from before they attacked the battle group," the AI said, her tone sounding pleased and surprised.

Jacob was not surprised. He'd spent plenty of time watching wasps swarm about their hexagon-chambered nests under the eaves of the barn on his home's property in Binghampton. These aliens were close enough to Earth wasps for him to understand some of how and why they behaved, as a group, the way they did. Still, at home, no wasp colony had ever left its eave home unless the nest was knocked down by water or burned out with fire. Clearly this star system was a home nest to the aliens. Would they follow his nine ships out to the magnetosphere? If they did, would they follow them to Kepler 10? They were two questions he needed to pose to Lori and to Science Deck chief Alicia Branstead.

"All ships, change ship status from Alert Hostile Enemy to Alert Combat Ready. All decks on the *Lepanto*, change to Alert Combat Ready. Crew are allowed breaks in groups no larger than ten percent of each deck. No break lasts longer than one hour," Jacob said.

The overhead alert lights went to blinking red. The ceiling speakers gave out a high-pitched siren. Jacob heard acknowledgments from the command centers for each deck. Seven people replied for the ship's seven decks. The voices sounded relieved, worried, busy and routine. Should he go there? Or have Branstead come here? Maybe the better spot would be the conference room in the admiral's quarters. Where this had all started. He scanned his armrest. It showed the All Ship vidcom was still active.

"Science Deck chief Lieutenant Alicia Branstead, please join me in the admiral's conference room. I have need of your advice."

"Acting captain, I'm heading your way," came the Aussie-accented voice of the woman.

"Acting captain," called Daisy. "May I join you? I have ship issues that need discussion with Lieutenant Branstead."

Her request did not surprise him. His friend was a forward thinker. That was why she had asked about the sudden silence from the meeting site in the first place. There were some others he should have there too.

"Ensign Antonova, Ensign Mendoza, join me at the admiral's conference room. All Ship, acting captain orders Spacer Blackbourne to join him at the admiral's conference room on Command Deck. Acknowledge."

Acknowledgements came.

He unsnapped his seat straps, took a last look at the situational holo, and noted the wasp ship cluster was now 15,000 kilometers out to one side and receding even as they matched the battle group's vector track out to the boundary of the magnetosphere. They had also slowed to ten percent of lightspeed. The wasp ship thrusters now stopped accelerating, just as the battle group thrusters had stopped once the new vector track had been set. Both groups held outward momentum at 10 psol. Stepping down, he nodded to O'Connor, then faced forward.

"Chief Warrant Officer Osashi, will you accept command of the Bridge in my absence?"

The man's vacsuited form turned his way. His black eyes fixed on Jacob. The man stood and saluted him. "Change of command accepted, acting captain."

Jacob saluted him back. "Good. You know where I will be. Allow Bridge crew to take breaks, one at a time, as before. Command transferred."

Jacob turned, gathered up Daisy with his eyes, then headed for the exit door, where Carlos and Lori were already awaiting him. Briefly he gave thanks for friends who stood by him. Then he felt the chill of being responsible for their lives. It was a new feeling. But a welcome one.

CHAPTER ELEVEN

Support Hunter Seven felt satisfaction as his nest settled into the standard Swarmer defense formation. His flying nest was the sixth to come close to Hunter One's larger nest. Then again, his nest had had further to fly to reach the other five nests. Looking ahead at the perception imager that displayed images of the other nests, he felt deep surprise at the massive hole on the head of Hunter One's nest. The hole was nearly as wide as his nest and clearly the Soft Skin heavy sky light beams had cut deep. The lack of stinger fire from the front ring of tubes now made sense. Energy to power the front ring was clearly dead. But why had Hunter One not used his Pull Down device to shield his ship from the Soft Skin black beam?

"Hunter Seven, the Soft Skin flying nests slow the pace of their flight," scent cast the Servant who handled the nest's propulsive devices.

"Then let us slow to match their flight speed," he scent cast in a mix of signal, primer and territorial pheromones, reminding the Servant and all in the Flight Chamber that he was the Swarmer who led their flight.

"Obeying," the servant scent cast back in a mix of primer and aggregation pheromones.

His three small eyes noticed a change of colors on the control panel before the Servant who was Speaker To All other nests. "What scent arrives?" he scent cast strongly.

The older male's two antennae bent forward. "Hunter One accepts your Challenge. He sets the encounter site as being in the Practice Chamber of his nest. He requires you to arrive with only your natural weapons."

Seven flapped his two wings, sending forth a strong scent of trail pheromones. It was his way of saying his path was set. "Respond to Hunter One that I will arrive within nine hundred wing beats."

"Responding," the Servant said, lowering his aged abdomen to his bench. Though his four leg limbs shook.

It was clear the Servant had feared his response to the news from Hunter One. Good. Fear in one's Servants guaranteed maximum stinging effort and full loyalty. He stood up from his bench. He scent cast to the Matron at the back of his chamber. "Mistress, lead these newly hatched ones until my return," he said with strong trail and signal pheromones.

"Until you return as prime leader," she scent cast to him, her aggregation scent distinct in its aroma.

She was fully loyal. That was why he had chosen her to be the Matron of his flying nest. Now, soon, he would meet his other ally, Support Hunter Four, whose air bubble was even now leaving his nest. Seven moved past the Matron, then through the chamber's opening that split apart the way two flaps of soft shell opened on a Soft Skin's eye. Entering the round tube, he flapped his wings and flew toward the chamber which housed the air bubbles used to move Swarmers and dead matter between nests. As he flew, his mind considered many possible attack angles for forcing his stinger into the head of Hunter One.

♦ ♦ ♦

Daisy sat at the long table in the admiral's conference room, with Lori on her left and Carlos on her right. Jacob sat at one end of the table, with his back to the Food Alcove. This was the room where, hours earlier, she had shared her concerns with Jacob about the loss of tablet comlink with Admiral Johanson and the other officers of the battle group. It felt strange to be here, a place she had only seen briefly when arriving to meet the admiral for a trip somewhere in her Landing Craft Assault transport. Now, she and her friends had survived two space battles, she was the ship's new XO and Jacob had shown a side to him that she had never before seen.

Watching him as they all waited for the arrival of Quincy and Lieutenant Branstead, she noted he was focused on his personal tablet. What was he reading? Or seeing? Messages from the other acting captains? An image of his mother, who was the only family he ever mentioned during the times they all shared a beer in the Mess Hall or met for games of chess? Did he possess an image of his father, Earth's only five star admiral and the hero, to some, of the Callisto Conflict? Whatever Jacob thought of his father, it was now clear to her that the young, shy man she'd come to like had inherited the daring genes of his father. And maybe the ruthlessness the man was reputed to have shown to some mining rebels who tossed Star Navy captives out of an airlock without a vacsuit. In violation of the updated Geneva Conventions. At the academy, while the Callisto Conflict space battles were required study, no professor discussed the admiral's handling of rebel captives. Rumors floating through Colorado Springs said the admiral had similarly ejected the rebel ship captain and four men who had killed the Star Navy captives. Watching Jacob over the hours since they had gone to the Bridge, she could believe her friend had inherited both the daring and the ruthlessness of his father.

"Acting Captain Renselaer, Spacer Blackbourne requests admission," came her British friend's deep voice from the speaker patch over the slidedoor that gave access to the Command Deck's hallway.

Jacob looked up, his face still as serious as when he'd sat down. His gray eyes fixed on the slidedoor. "Door, admit Spacer Blackbourne."

The slidedoor slid into the wall. Quincy scanned them all quickly, nodded and stepped inside. The short, stocky East Londoner, whose ancestry traced back to Kenya, saluted. "Spacer Quincy Blackbourne, laser gunner's mate, right side outrigger pod, reports as ordered."

Daisy and her two friends sat on one side of the antique walnut table, with Quincy standing to the right and Jacob seated to the left. Jacob now saluted Quincy with his right hand as his left held the tablet he'd been studying. "Spacer, take a seat where you wish. When Lieutenant Branstead arrives, I'll begin this discussion."

Quincy looked startled by Jacob's serious expression and short words. "Sir, thank you," he said, his bass voice filling the room.

Lori waved to him. "Quincy, sit here with me. Gotta let the lieutenant have the other side of the table all to herself."

Quincy grinned, raised curly black eyebrows as he looked to Jacob for a reaction, then shrugged his thick shoulders when their friend looked back at the tablet in his hand. "Thanks, gal, coming your way."

As Quincy sat beside Lori, Daisy looked past a thoughtful Carlos to the slidedoor. It had closed right after Quincy stepped in. She looked back and studied her programmer friend. Was Carlos jealous of Quincy being next to his girlfriend? He shouldn't. They were all friends first. Romance happened however it happened. Should she bring out her own tablet and study it? She'd downloaded the *Lepanto's* deck layout, cross-section, weapons emplacements and the last holo image of the enemy ship cluster. Which now lay 30,000 kilometers out, but still paralleled the battle group as their nine ships headed north of the ecliptic along the track previously taken by the *Salamis*. The destroyer's captain had said little since arriving with multiple blasts from his CO_2 and proton lasers. His ship had fallen into formation with the other destroyers. Did the man now accept Jacob's authority? Or was he just covering his butt against any future Star Navy inquiry? Politics. It was a topic she had spent much effort to avoid ever since gaining admission to the academy. Pilots should pilot, not engage in—

"Acting Captain Renselaer, Lieutenant Branstead requests admission," came the soprano voice of the Science Deck chief, a woman who hailed from Melbourne and the Sorbonne in Paris.

Jacob laid down his tablet. He looked up. His expression changed to thoughtful. "Door, admit Lieutenant Branstead."

The slidedoor hissed open.

The woman, dressed in a clear vacsuit over her officer's dress blues jacket and pants, stepped into the room. She saluted Jacob. "Lieutenant Alicia Branstead reporting as requested."

"Thank you for coming," Jacob said, his baritone sounding firm and determined. He saluted her back. "Please have a seat wherever you wish."

Without another word Branstead, who carried her personal tablet in one hand, strode over to the opposite side of the table and sat down on the wooden seat that was fixed to a support pedestal. Like the old Navy ships that traveled the seas, most furniture on the *Lepanto* was permanently attached to something. The advent of inertial dampers had not changed that tradition. The lightly tanned woman nodded to Lori, a member of her deck staff, then her amber eyes scanned Daisy, and next moved on to Carlos and Quincy, before finally meeting the intense gaze of Jacob.

"How can I help?" she said, her voice firm, her manner that of a manager of people who did not care for wasting time on minor chatter.

Jacob's gaze fixed on her. His clean-shaven face, now exposed thanks to his helmet being pushed back, grew a small smile. That quickly disappeared. "Lieutenant, your Bridge representative CPO Willard Steinmetz and Ensign Lori Antonova of your deck have been of vital help to me as we coped with two attacks from the wasp-like aliens. Earlier I told Ensign Antonova I would put her in for a commendation for her warning about the black hole weapon of the aliens. You have very good staff. Thank you for the loan of them."

Branstead blinked. She nodded. "Thank you. Glad they could be of help in these unique circumstances. How can I help?"

Jacob laid both hands on the table and leaned forward, his expression almost fierce. "You can help by sharing with me, and with my brain trust people, your impressions and analyses of the wasp-like aliens who killed our senior officers and have now attacked us two times."

Branstead's serious expression did not change. Her brown eyebrows lifted. "From the imagery and words shared over the All Ship vidcom, I gather that Ensign Antonova has already made some basic analyses about these insect-like aliens. I support what she has said," Branstead said, nodding to Lori. "I would add these insect aliens are remarkably similar to the yellow jacket wasps of Earth. Similar to our wasps, these aliens have hard shell bodies adorned with red and black stripes on a yellow exoskeleton. They have both compound and simple eyes, again like our wasps and spiders. The aliens may see well in ultraviolet, unlike us humans. They have mandibles and antennae, but unlike our wasps the midbody or thorax of these aliens is upright. That allows their upper limb pair to work as arms and hands do on us. Since they are planting a colony, they are likely to have perennial life patterns like the *vespula squamata* species in the south of the wasp range on Earth. There is no way an alien wasp species could develop high tech with every generation dying each winter, like some wasp species do on Earth." The woman sat back, though her posture remained stiffly upright and almost formal. "What issues matter most to you?"

"My issues are four," Jacob said quickly. "Will these wasps follow us all the way out to the magnetosphere? Will they follow us to Kepler 10? Will they attack us again? And can you suggest any means for communicating with them?"

Branstead pursed her lips, her oval face going thoughtful. "As Antonova said earlier, these aliens are predators, the bright colors of their body indicate an aposematic warning to other lifeforms to stay away, they are eusocial and it is highly likely they communicate using pheromones," she said, her light tone sounding almost musical to Daisy. "They have chosen to fight us, they have at least one primary leader, along with leaders on each starship, and they are in this system to plant a colony on planet four. All of those characteristics are background to my estimate of their intentions."

She licked her lips. "As for your questions, the wasps are now following us out to the magnetosphere. Their behavior to date shows a consistent purpose. Which is to attack and defeat us. So yes, I believe they will follow us out to the magnetosphere. I suspect they will follow us to Kepler 10, if only out of curiosity, which they must have in order to have developed spaceships, beam energy weapons and the remarkable black hole weapon. As for attacking us again, yes, I think that will happen. But not soon. Losing half their attacking force while we lost only a single ship has clearly caused their prime leader to pull back and assess her or his options. It is likely they are trying to figure *us* out, much as we are trying to figure them out."

Jacob nodded slowly. "How do we communicate with them?"

Branstead frowned. "By using the image frequency which they used to propose the meeting of our two peoples down at the meeting site. My people, despite applying the Topol linguistic analysis algorithms, have been unable to make sense of whatever signal was being sent by the satellite we encountered upon first arrival. The signal contained polarized emissions. Beyond that, we know nothing."

"I had hoped you might think of some other means to communicate," Jacob said, sounding distracted. "Lieutenant, will you please use your top people to develop a cartoon-like video that depicts the six wasp ships turning back to planet four, landing, being greeted by wasps on the planet, while our nine ships travel to the magnetosphere edge, then disappear, with some kind of dotted path or arrow or whatever indicating we are leaving this system, never to return?"

"I can do that," the woman said. "What's our timeline?"

"Get it done well before we reach the magnetosphere," Jacob said. "We are 29 hours out from reaching it. I am concerned the wasp aliens may attack us again right at the boundary. And do you really think the wasps can figure out which star we are jumping to?"

Branstead chuckled dryly. "Acting captain, people who figured out how to create an artificial black hole can surely figure out what star we are heading for. At a minimum, with their six ships spread out, they can perform triangulation sensor analyses to get our exact heading. Since they know we came here, to a yellow G-type star, they will look for all G-type stars along that outbound track. Kepler 10 is the closest such G-type star. They will follow us."

"I was afraid of that," Jacob said, sounding tired to Daisy. "Lieutenant, what do these aliens care about? Losing two ships, then three, then a final one has not stopped them from pursuing us. How can we dissuade them from attacking us? And will this First Contact disaster lead to perennial interstellar war between our two species?"

"That question frustrates me," Branstead said, her tone giving life to that feeling. "The fact they planted a colony using dozens of landing pods says they care for their young. Whether larvae or hatched from eggs or even live births like with mammals, their children matter to them. The reason they attacked us may be as simple as their effort to protect their young from an invading species. It's what we would do. It is what we *will* do in order to protect the colonists at Kepler 10."

"And my second point?"

She blinked, muscles tightening on the high cheeks of her face. "I hope to hell we do not get into perennial war with a species we know almost nothing about! How many wasps are there in the galaxy? How many colonies do they have? Where is their home star? Do they have starships more powerful than this Battlestar? While we have won the equivalent of the Battle of Trafalgar, where the British faced a larger French and Spanish fleet, we have no assurance future battles will work out as well." She fixed on Jacob. "Acting captain, I am amazed that the battle group has done so well. With new acting captains, with most crews never having seen true battles in space, and facing an unknown enemy possessed of ships as powerful as our destroyers and cruisers, we survived, we prevailed and you have saved the lives of more than a thousand people. Your choices of battle formation, the mix of weapons and your use of the cruisers and the *Lepanto* to shield our more vulnerable ships from concentrated beam attack, those actions were inspired. I'm glad I was not in your place."

Jacob's eyes grew large. His somber mood seemed to lift for a moment. He let out a deep sigh. "Lieutenant, thank you. Nothing in my academy studies prepared me for today's events." He waved toward Daisy and the others. "I had a lot of help. Good help from folks who are my friends and who are good at what they do." Jacob licked his lips. "I thank you and the other deck chiefs for showing loyalty to me, to my XO Acting Lieutenant Stewart and to the other people on the Bridge."

What! She was now a lieutenant? That was a normal rank for an XO. But still . . .

Branstead shrugged. "You had the initiative to change the ship status, to declare the Alert Unknown Enemy condition and then send the Cloud Skimmer to give us facts about the silence from our officers. No one on any other ship did that. To me, those actions earned you the right to lead us. The battles since then have justified my belief."

Daisy could tell Jacob was trying hard not to smile. Which would be normal for a person as young as him, her or any of the other folks in the room. Even Branstead, with a Ph. D. in molecular synthesis of biological polymers, looked as if she was trying hard to be command proper. She was the leader of a deck with 51 staff, but she was also the mom of three girls, the keeper of two Chihuahuas and the wife of American fighter pilot. Or so Daisy had heard from Lori, during one of their beer and pretzel breaks on the trip out to Kepler 22. It sounded as if Branstead was fully on Jacob's side as the leader of their ship. But how did the other deck chiefs feel about a new ensign taking over the *Lepanto*?

"Thank you," Jacob said, his voice measured. "Please advise me of anything your deck needs for your people to do their jobs. And let me know the moment the wasp cartoon project is done. I want to send it ASAP and maybe save lives on the wasp side and on our side."

"Sounds reasonable," Branstead said, seeming to relax in her seat. But her gaze grew intense. "Acting captain, when we get to Kepler 10 you will make a neutrino report to the Star Base captain about these aliens, what happened, why you took control of the Battlestar and so forth. The base captain is a Star Navy Command rank captain. He could order you to give up control of the *Lepanto* to him, to one of his officers or to someone on this ship." She slapped her chest. "For myself, I plan to send a signal to the base captain saying I strongly support your continued captaincy of the *Lepanto* and your leadership of the battle group. So long as these aliens follow us, they may attack us. You are the only person who has demonstrated the ability to withstand those attacks, then lead us to victory."

Daisy looked to Jacob. How would he react to the woman's blunt assessment of future options? She had known things could change once they got to Kepler 10. But if the wasps attack right after following the fleet to the nearby star, a change in command would be disastrous. Disastrous for the *Lepanto* and for the other eight ships in the battle group.

Her friend, who now acted years older than his 24 years chrono age, lifted black eyebrows. "Lieutenant, thank you for that endorsement. I appreciate it, more than you can know." He paused, looked over to her, Carlos, Lori and Quincy, then back to Branstead. The muscles in his face stiffened. "My first duty is to preserve this ship and the battle group and the lives of the people on our ships. To that end, I will fight any enemy, alien or domestic. As for the Star Navy base captain, yes, he might theoretically outrank me. But it will take 52 hours to travel the 45 AU from the system's magnetosphere inward to the planet the base orbits. Until we all arrive at the base, I plan to be in command."

Branstead looked relieved. "Good. But be alert for politics and game-playing by Lieutenant Commander Bannerjee. He has twice complained to me that he should have been the one to take command of the *Lepanto*, since he is the senior surviving officer on the ship."

Jacob did not look surprised. She wondered if his matter-of-fact manner was also something he'd inherited from his father. "Understood. But you are the next senior officer by rank, followed by Lieutenant JG Jane Yamamoto of Life Support Deck. With the support of you two, and of the warrant and petty officers in command on the other decks, I am confident Bannerjee will remain where he is now. As chief of the Navigation Deck. No more."

"Agreed." Branstead waved at the pitcher of water in the middle of the table. "I'm a bit thirsty. May I?"

"Of course!" Jacob said quickly. "Help yourself."

"Acting captain," Daisy said quickly. "I recall there are some cans of beer in the fridge behind you. Perhaps the lieutenant would prefer a beer?"

Surprise showed briefly, then an almost relaxed smile filled Jacob's face. "Excellent idea. And from this group's past history, I suspect none of you would turn down a beer. Right?" he said, looking from Daisy to Lori, Carlos and Quincy.

"Sounds fine to me," Lori said, her soprano sounding cautious.

"Right-o with me," Carlos said, his manner turning relaxed as the formality of Jacob's talk with Branstead moved to a relaxed mood.

"Exactly a fine idea," Quincy said, his deep voice filling the space between them all. The man stood up. "I'll get us six cans."

"Thank you . . . Quincy," Jacob said.

Daisy liked that Jacob seemed to be relaxing a bit from the worry load of nasty aliens and the surprise of having to become the ship's acting captain. His use of Quincy's first name now, versus his Spacer title, said a lot to her. She gave Quincy a smile as she took the beer her Brit friend offered, then she focused back on Jacob. Would there be any time for the two of them to . . . to get more personal? At the academy she had learned quickly one did not date the instructors, and most of the young men cadets were alpha types who always treated women as an afterthought. Not Jacob. While intensely focused on his studies, Jacob had always given her the impression of someone who looked beyond himself. That was why she had taken the time to visit with him at the orbital station when they all gathered for the group photo of *Lepanto* officers, then later on the long cruise out to Kepler 22. Now, seeing the new command side of him, along with his humility in inviting to the Bridge the Marine boss Richard O'Connor, she wanted to spend personal time with him. Group time was fine. But personal one-on-one time was the only way to get to really know someone. Would Jacob like the red and white carp fish she kept in her quarters? Would he understand what it had been like to grow up in a single parent family? Did he even understand the idea of a tight family budget, in view of his father's family fortune and fine retirement income from the Star Navy? And what were Jacob's personal joys, the things he did for fun, versus work? Or duty? She wanted to know the answers.

Jacob met her gaze, gave her a wink, then he looked to their beer distributor. Who had just sat down beside Lori. "Quincy, what was the mood like on your post? What did your buddies think of the alien counterfire using laser and lightning bolt strikes? How did your right front laser node hold up to the enemy strikes?"

The young black dude put down the beer he'd been sipping. "Well, we were all focused on getting as many repeat laser strikes going out from our node as we could. Plus, my CWO was always adjusting the node's angle to bring as many wasp targets into our hit zone as possible. Until we joined with other ships on a single target." Quincy paused, looked around, and saw Daisy, Branstead, Lori and Carlos all watching him. Being the center of attention seemed to surprise him. Her friend looked back to Jacob. "Uh, our mood was good. And when our laser fire joined with the lasers of other ships to strike a single wasp ship, we really felt good! It was clear they had tough hulls. But putting multiple laser beams on a single wasp ship meant we cut deep into their hulls. Or so my CWO told me as he monitored the electro-optical scope at our node." Her friend paused, took a sip of beer, then shrugged. "Some wasp lasers hit the upper end of the right outrigger pod. The adaptive optics lenses and the ablative hull coating reflected or absorbed most of the incoming energy. We had no punch throughs on our hull, unlike the nose and belly of this ship."

Jacob nodded slowly. "What did you think of the lightning bolt strikes?"

"Weirded me out!" Quincy said. "I recall lightning strikes from when my parents took me out to the countryside south of London. Saw bolts then during thunderstorms. Never expected to see 10,000 kilometer long lightning strikes in space!" He paused, noticed Branstead was watching him closely, then continued. "The enemy bolts did take out several hundred square meters of adaptive-optics lenses on our outrigger, though."

Branstead nodded and looked to Jacob. "Acting captain, the damage to the right side outrigger pod, to the ship's nose and to its belly and the belly plasma battery are things we need to repair. As best we can."

Jacob set down his can of beer. "Agreed. But we can't allow folks out in EVA right now. Not with the enemy still close to us. Can we repair the deep hull breaches on the nose and belly? The ones that caused us to lose the water between the outer and inner hulls in those spots? I know we have spare water. But can we seal up those breaches so we can inject water into those hull segments?"

Branstead frowned, then reached up to push brown bangs out of her eyes. "Well, we do have good repair robots that can handle vacuum. And the Engines Deck has some fine teleoperator engineers. Put the engineers to work managing the repair bots, along with some hull plates, and we should be able to cover those two breaches. But the ship will need the services of a full spacedock to restore the outer hull to its two meters of armor."

Jacob winced, then nodded. "No spacedock at Kepler 10. Guess we will have to wait for that until we get back to Earth, or to a colony with a spacedock." He fixed on the Science Deck chief. "Lieutenant Branstead, will you work with the Engines Deck chief on those repairs? I've only met Chief Warrant Officer Billy Chang once, during the boarding tour for new crew. You've served with him for years."

Branstead gave a quick smile. "You are learning too many of the tricks of a good manager. Combine a delegation of work with a compliment. Yes, I will coordinate with Billy. And share with him my feelings about Kepler 10, and how you should remain as our captain."

Jacob's expression looked briefly hopeful, then the emotion shut down. Daisy wondered at that. Had Jacob learned that shutting down his emotions was the only way he could survive the fame of his father's name?

"Captain, uh, Jacob," called Lori from her left. "I'm pretty sure everyone on Navigation Deck will support you. Short of the chief. Who has no friends. Even the two ensigns who are his chief fix-it people do not care for his company." Like Quincy, she now became aware of being the center of attention. She flushed, her light brown skin darkening as her blue eyes looked down.

"Lori, thank you," Jacob said, his gaze moving from her to the other people at the table. "Quincy, thank you for that weapons input. Carlos, thank you for your help earlier in figuring out we can head for Kepler 10." His gray eyes now rested a moment on her. "Daisy, you took to being XO the way a young duck takes to water. Thank you!" He grinned suddenly. "Now, a surprise for you folks from me. As I shared with Lieutenant Branstead, I consider you folks to be my brain trust, besides being my friends. I need you all close by. So," he looked to Daisy, "Lieutenant Stewart, please move your things into the XO's quarters on Command Deck. Lori, Quincy and Carlos, I want you three to also move to Command Deck. Take up the empty ensign quarters. The personal items of the former residents should be delivered to Chief Warrant Officer Cheryl Zhang on Supplies Deck. Agreed?"

Her friends all agreed. Branstead looked surprised at the news Lori would be leaving her quarters on Science Deck. Daisy caught

Jacob's attention. "Acting captain, I'm happy to leave my space on Navigation Deck. Like some people, I have not enjoyed the company of chief Bannerjee. But . . . if we four are moving up here, well, *you* should occupy the captain's cabin. It's bigger than a standard ensign's quarters, and anyway, that will allow Kenji to find you the next time he has a meal to deliver!"

Jacob looked shocked, then he smiled big. "I accept the suggestion of my Executive Officer," he said, his tone bemused. He looked around, then fixed on Branstead. "Lieutenant, many thanks for coming, for your advice and for your support."

Branstead put down her can. She gave Jacob a relaxed smile. "Good beer. I'll let you know when the new cartoon video is ready. And I will work on alerting the other deck chiefs to the need for unity once we arrive at Kepler 10."

Her friend nodded slowly. "Looking forward to seeing the video. And yes, we do need all decks on board when we arrive at Kepler 10." Jacob looked her way. "Everyone, time to break up this meeting and get back to our posts on the Bridge."

Daisy stood up, but stepped back to put her shoulders against the wall of the large room. Lori, Carlos and Quincy passed her by as they followed Branstead out of the room and into the hallway. At the hiss of the slidedoor closing, Jacob looked to her, his thick eyebrows lifting. "Daisy?"

She stepped toward him, stopping a half meter back. Just on the edge of his personal space. She looked up a bit. Her friend was a few inches taller than she was.

"Jacob, we will be safe once we enter Alcubierre space-time, right?"

"Right." Puzzlement showed on his lightly tanned face.

"Well," she said, allowing a half smile to show. "The weekly Dance Night will happen at the end of the first day in Alcubierre flight. Jacob, will you go dancing with me?"

Surprise filled his face. His eyes opened wide. His two strong hands lifted halfway up. Then he froze all movement, only his eyes moving as they scanned her. Was he seeing all of her, for the first time? Was he seeing beyond her mixed-race appearance? Did he realize she liked him? Did he—

"Sure thing," Jacob said, a big grin coming over his face. "Took lessons in swing, square and other dance forms back in

Binghampton. Danced a bit at the senior prom there. Not much since. You may have to give me some guidance."

She grinned back. "Well, guiding a good guy into being a neat guy is something we women have lots of experience with. You show up at my slidedoor an hour before the dance starts and I'll be ready!"

Jacob nodded, his grin easing to a happy-looking smile. Not looking away, he reached down and grabbed his tablet from the top of the table. "Shall we head back to the Bridge?"

"Sure," she said, her heart beating faster as she turned and headed for the slidedoor. Already she was wondering how his arms would feel around her, how close he would allow himself to come, and how open in his emotions and feelings would he be? Clearly her young man had learned to assume a certain persona in the company of other adults. And before military superiors. But he had grown beyond that personal history, as she had seen in the last half day. Surely he would continue to grow, both as their commander and as someone she would enjoy spending time with.

CHAPTER TWELVE

Support Hunter Seven entered the Practice Chamber of Hunter One's large flying nest. As instinct told him to do, he skittered to one side as his five eyes took in the chamber's high ceiling, the white-yellow illumination strips that made the room feel like Nest, and the crowd of other Swarmers gathered atop stone perches to his left side. His sound membranes heard desultory rasping of limbs against their hard shells as a few Servants, Worker Leaders and some Fighter Leaders left the pheromone emission to Hunter One. Who rested above them on a stone perch that stuck out from what appeared to be a natural group of boulders. A Matron perched atop a boulder to one side, while the four other Support Hunters perched nearby, on top of a separate group of boulders. Each flying nest was represented here.

Elsewhere in the chamber were some of the green-barked trees of Nest, their purple leaves swaying in the artificial wind created by dead contrivances. A small blue pond lay at some distance. His foot pads felt the softness of green tendrils that covered the soil, with a scatter here and there of yellow flowers full of nectar. Clearly this chamber, like the similar one in his nest, was meant to provide food, drink and the sense of flying free under the sky light of home. It also served as a chamber where young Swarmers practiced their flight moves as they learned to fly in a group, like every cohort did on Nest. A strong scent flowed to him from Hunter One. It was a mix of signal, territorial and trail pheromones.

"The Challenger arrives!" his opponent scent cast. "Do you wish to die soon, or after pretending to attack many times?"

Insults always began any Challenge.

"Why is the Responder hiding atop a high perch? Do you need the support of Servants below you in order to feel powerful? Come to my level so we may converse, mandible to mandible."

Hunter One lifted his brown wings and fluttered them a bit, but stayed at his perch. "You guide your nest poorly. It suffered damage to one side during your failed attack on the large Soft Skin nest."

That response told him all Swarmers everywhere on the nest were perceiving their Challenge by way of both perception imagers and scent repeaters. It also told him Hunter One had need to reassure the Swarmers in his nest. As well he should.

"This nest suffered far greater damage! You lead our nests like a Swarmer who has sucked in too many sips from the Blurry Flower," he scent cast back in a mix of alarm and signal pheromones. "How else could we lose a six-group of nests to these miserable Soft Skins? Was the attack against the meeting site your thought, or the thoughts of a Fighter Leader elsewhere? The deadliness of that attack was lost in your later leadership of our nests!"

Hunter One's two black antennae rose up sharply. Clearly he did not like the suggestion he was of blurred vision and mind when he had led the two attacks against the Soft Skins. The nectar of the Blurry Flower on Nest was well-known as a producer of a confused mind and false eye visions. The Swarmer's mandibles opened to either side, then clacked together.

A scent of excitement came from many of the other Swarmers. Mixed among the pheromones was a scent of aggregation from Support Hunter Four, who perched with the other Support Hunters from the other three flying nests. That group included at least one Support Hunter who was known to be a cohort relative of Hunter One, and therefore bound to support him. The other two gave no scent of any reaction to the Challenge and Response pheromones cast by him and One. Clearly they awaited the result of this Challenge battle.

"I claimed leadership of this colonizing flight in the cold dark spaces above Nest," One scent cast in a massive flow of territorial pheromones. "We found a good new land nest for our larvae. Each flying nest has deposited Pods on the new land. Each nest contributed Servants, Worker Leaders and Workers to raise the new Swarmers. That is the success of the Swarm!" He paused, then a scent of frustration came forth. "Then arrived the strange Soft Skins, who did not become incoherent and weak of mind from the loss of their leaders. On Nest, we control such Soft Skins. Such must be the case here, in this new sky light home for Swarmers. Therefore I led our attack! We destroyed one Soft Skin nest and badly damaged three other nests. Even now they flee from us!"

Seven moved on his footpads to be near a cluster of green bark trees. He leaned back, then whipped his wings strongly, rising up like a particle disruption seed newly launched.

"Responder! Meet me in open air the way our ancestors once battled each other!"

Hunter One seemed startled by his quick rise to a level equal with him. "Challenger, now you die!"

Pheromones of signal, alarm, excitement and trail now filled the air between him and One. He canted his flight to one side, then back to the opposite side, repeating the ancestral flight pattern known to every Swarmer. One did the same, matching his movements with an ease that belied the slight age fading of his hard shell colors.

First attack was always up to the Challenger. Seven lifted up higher, his wing beats blurring, then he bent forward and dropped toward the red and black stripes of One's back.

Empty air met his attack.

Footpads kicked at his belly as One flew upside down below him, his tail stinger already lifting to pierce Seven's abdomen. The bottom of the abdomen was the softest spot on any Swarmer's exoskeleton. Aside from the head, which was nearly impossible to reach.

Seven twisted to the left, dropped lower than One, then beat his wings fast to rise up toward the back of his enemy. With a twist in mid-air he shifted his flight form so his stinger was aimed at the head and antennae of Hunter One.

"Youthful arrogance does not win a Challenge!" scent cast One as the creature turned over and lifted his stinger upward toward Seven's stinger.

A twist of his body barely allowed Seven to avoid impaling his abdomen on One's stinger. Beating his wings into a blur, he rose up sharply, then dove down toward the exposed thorax of One.

"Taste your death!" he scent cast harshly.

One shifted sideways, avoided Seven's downward plunge, then swept low, wings nearly touching Seven's wings as they fell side by side toward the green covered soil below.

"You prolong your death. Turn over and present your—"

Seven twisted to the right, turning his abdomen up, then flew sideways to be just under the abdomen of One. But instead of feeling the satisfying thrust of his stinger and the pumping of venom into his enemy, he felt only the sudden impact of One's thorax and abdomen against his. Their stingers clashed against each other, unable to reach a soft spot. One's foot pads gripped his hard shell. Seven did the same in return. He opened his mandibles and reached for the narrow nerve cord that connected One's head to his thorax.

One did the same.

Their mandibles met in a loud clacking.

"Surrender!" scent cast One in a strong flow of releaser pheromones. "You are below me. You are defeated."

A fast beat of his wings to one side reversed their positions, with Seven atop One even as his opponent's wing beats pushed him up against Seven's abdomen.

Seven beat his wings harder, but was unable to counter the strong counter wing beat of One.

They hovered in mid-air, mandibles biting each other's lower head, neither achieving a death bite due to the hardness of each other's hard shell.

"You surrender!" Seven scent cast in an equally strong blast of releaser pheromones. "You are below me!"

They reversed positions in the air seven more times, hurling scent insults even as they gripped each other tight and their stingers tried and tried to find a soft spot on the tail of each other.

"Swarmers stop fighting!" came a primer pheromone from the Matron below. "Stop biting! Let go. Move to separate perches!"

Shock filled Seven.

Never before had a Matron interfered with a Challenge fight. While a flying nest's Matron was the reason for any Swarmer cohort to found a new nest, to defend an existing nest, or to fly out to other sky lights to spread the larvae of the Swarm, they were also the final authority on any nest. For they laid the eggs that became larvae who became the new generation of Swarmers. All Hunters were male. Neither he nor One could give forth new eggs. Only the Matron could do that. Which was why a Matron resided in the Flight Chamber of every flying nest. They were reputed to be wise in the ways of the Swarm. Must he give up this Challenge?

"Separate!" came an incredibly strong primer pheromone.

Primer pheromones are the scents that force an egg to become a larva. They cause more than a change in behavior. They cause a change in emotions, feelings and even the inner gut of a Swarmer.

When emitted as strongly as now, there was nothing Seven or One could do but obey.

Seven stopped his stinger striking. He let go of his foot pad hold on One. He felt One do the same, at almost the same moment. They separated, their wings beating rapidly, their eye clusters fixed on each other, their antennae lifted stiffly high. Each gasped for air through the pumping of their spiracles. Each hovered above the green tendriled soil below.

"Go to separate perches!"

With a shudder, Seven slowed his wing beat, dropped lower and then flew swiftly to an empty perch among the group of other Support Hunters. His friend Four made room for him, then put his left wing over the back of Seven. It was meant to comfort. It shocked Seven as much as the sight of One lowering down onto his high perch. More shock came.

The large, heavy form of the Matron now beat her brown wings strongly, lifting her large mass up from her solitary perch atop a boulder. She rose up, slowly, to a height equal to that of One. A blast of signal, releaser, territorial and trail pheromones flowed from her, flowed outward to envelop the three groups of Swarmers.

"Hunters! Our colony flight is half the size it was when we left Nest," she scent cast. "We have but six nests still flying. Most nests have need of repairs to their outer shells. Most seriously, we cannot afford to lose the talent and battle energy of any Hunter!" She paused, her hovering flight an amazement to Seven, who had never seen a Matron take flight. "This Challenge has become a blocked fight. Neither Challenger nor Responder prevailed. Each Hunter is as strong as the other Hunter. Which told me we Swarmers must preserve both Hunters!" Her five eyes glistened with wetness. Her mid-air hover changed as she swung about to look directly at Seven and the other Support Hunters, over to the gathering of Servants, Workers and Fighter Leaders, then up to One. "Hunter One, I command you to work with Support Hunter Seven, and with all our still living Support Hunters. Find a means of defeating these Soft Skins! Let us follow them wherever they fly in the cold dark sky! Let us battle them again when our nests are repaired. We must know more about these Soft Skins. Where did they come from? Are there more who would arrive at our new colony sky light? What can we Swarmers do to discourage the Soft Skins from ever again visiting any Swarmer sky light?"

"Your scent I will obey," One finally said, his stance atop his perch stiff and formal and not showing the exhaustion Seven now felt.

Seven lifted up his head and angled his antennae toward the hovering Matron. "Source of our lives, I will obey you. My flying nest will work with Hunter One and with our other nests to defeat these Soft Skins!"

The Matron lowered her flight slowly, finally touching down atop her boulder. "Defeating these new Soft Skins is just one task we face. Before we kill them all, we must learn the answers to my questions. Set your Servants to work learning from the behavior of these Soft Skins. The way any life behaves is the silent scent that tells other life what that life intends. Learn from these Soft Skins! Then consult with me and our other Matrons before making any attack!"

One beat his wings quickly but stayed on his roost. "Your scents carry wisdom. I will lead our six-group out to the edge of this sky light's magnetic field, then we will cast all eyes on the flight track the Soft Skins take to another sky light. We will follow them. At the new sky light there will be time for another attack flight!"

Seven breathed deep. He still lived. And the failure of his Challenge was made a non-event, thanks to the interference of the Matron. He would return in an air bubble to his nest and resume his leadership of that nest. He would cooperate with One in their pursuit of the Soft Skins. But somehow, someway, in the future he would replace Hunter One!

◆ ◆ ◆

Hunter One hid his shock at the Matron's interference behind the scent of cooperation and consent. This Matron was the highly fertile female he had chosen over two other Matrons with a higher status in the cohort. Now, she betrayed him! Or had she saved him? The fight with Seven had gone on longer than he had expected. The youth's strength in flight, his nimbleness and his persistence had been greater than One had expected. He'd taken his high perch with the expectation of diving down against the shocked Challenger and driving his stinger into the head of Seven. Instead, the youth had risen to meet him. In open air there are too many flight paths one can take. Just as in cold dark space there are angles of attack and retreat more numerous than on the ground.

Tiredness had filled him in the last two reversals of position in the air. If he had lost his grip on the abdomen of Seven, then the Challenger's tail stinger would have had a clear shot at his soft abdomen. The interference of the Matron had prevented his possible death. Which was something he could not tolerate. He had too many plans for using the successful colony planting to improve his caste rank among all Hunters, back on Nest. The loss of a six-group of flying nests to these miserable Soft Skins had dented the scent of success he had worked hard to build. Now, he had to defeat these Soft Skins, or lose his status back on Nest.

He beat his wings strongly, flew off his perch and followed his Servants, Fighter Leaders and Worker Leaders out into the tube that linked with his Flight Chamber. As he flew, he created an order of tasks to assign to his Servants. First among them was the repair of the deep hole in the nest's head that had caused the shut-down of vital energies from the front energy node. Second would come the replacement of hull plates so he could once again extend out the gravity plates that made the Pull Down device work. The issue of whether such work could be done in the cold dark space of this sky light was a dark dream that left his inner gut disturbed.

♦ ♦ ♦

An hour after the meeting with Branstead, Jacob sat in the admiral's high seat in the center of the Bridge, with Daisy in the XO seat to his left and O'Connor in the captain's seat to his right. Lori and Carlos sat in their rear observer seats. Ahead, all function posts were fully manned. The front wallscreen showed a mix of images. In the center was the true space image of the six wasp ships, as shown in the ship's electro-optical scope. To the right was a flat view of the situational holo which showed the positions of the battle group ships, wasp ships and the asteroid belt and comet belt of Kepler 22. To the left were a group of images that displayed repair robots hauling hull plates to the deep holes on the nose and belly of the *Lepanto*. Another group of robots were replacing adaptive optics lenses on the right outrigger pod and at three other side hull spots where lightning bolts had blasted the lenses into vapor. In front of his seat were four holos that repeated the wallscreen imagery. The central wallscreen image of the wasp ships now changed.

"Tactical, the wasp ship formation is changing. What is your analysis of their aim?" he called to O'Hara. Or Rosemary, as she had reminded him upon his return to the Bridge.

The Irish woman, still dressed in her vacsuit with helmet thrown back, like everyone on the Bridge and elsewhere on the ship, looked up, then back to him. Her eyebrows lifted. "Acting captain, it looks as if the five ships are moving out and away from the large wasp ship. Maybe they had a meeting." She looked back to her holo of the true space image, checked a sensor readout on her armrest, then fixed on him. "My sensors say the wasp ships are expanding their hexapod formation. Ahhh. They've stopped. Each ship is 2,143 kilometers distant from any other ship. Distance from one side of their hexapod to the other side is 12,430 kilometers." A beep drew her attention to her armrest sensor panel. "They're pulling back! They were at 20,000 klicks out from us on a parallel vector track. Now, they have increased their distance from us to 70, 90, now 97,120 klicks!"

Jacob felt relief that the enemy was pulling away, and frustration that they continued to follow his battle group. Were they following to confirm his departure? Were they aiming to attack right on the edge of the magnetosphere? Or perhaps were they planning to follow to Kepler 10?

"Acting captain!" called Oliver from Weapons. "My scope and sensor imagery says there are wasps on the hull of the giant wasp ship! And also on the hulls of two other wasp ships." The Brazilian paused, looked down at his armrest, then up at one of the holos in front of his post. "Uh, yup. Spectroscope reports intense ultraviolet and infrared spots where those wasps are located. Looks like they are doing hull repairs."

"Interesting. Tactical, Weapons, thank you for those reports." Jacob looked down at Daisy's tight curls of blue-black hair. His XO and future dance partner was studying the same images that the two function posts had highlighted. "XO, what is your assessment of the enemy actions?"

Her shoulders stiffened. "The wasp enemy appears to be doing hull repairs, fixing holes and punch throughs by our proton and CO_2 lasers. Their use of live people in vacsuits explains their pullback. They want to have time to pull people inside if we make a sudden attack on them. They would have ten or eleven minutes even if we changed our vector track and hit ten psol."

Jacob sat back in his seat, put elbows on the upper parts of each armrest, and folded hands over his gut. "XO, should we do the same? Here on the *Lepanto* and on the *Chesapeake, Hampton Roads, Philippines Sea* and the two frigates with hull damage?"

"Sir, yes sir, we should do the same."

He looked up. "Melody, open a neutrino video comlink with every ship in the battle group. Transmit all imagery on the front wallscreen."

"Link established," the AI said, her tone now sounding almost sleepy. Weird.

"*Chesapeake, Hampton Roads, Philippines Sea, Ofira* and *Marianas*, please observe the changed position of the enemy wasp ships. Note there are live wasps active on the outer hulls of three wasp ships. Clearly they are repairing hull damage." He paused, knowing his words and image were also going to every deck on his ship, thanks to the constant All Ship vidcom repeat of every Bridge action that he had ordered at the beginning of the conflict. "I suggest each acting captain consider if their own repairs could be accelerated by using Spacers in EVA, rather than relying only upon repair robots. Here on the *Lepanto* we will be sending out vacsuited Spacers to directly guide the repair robots. And to hit spots too tight for the bots. Respond."

The black face of Swanson appeared in Jacob's comlink holo. The stocky woman wore a clear vacsuit over her NWU woodland camos. "Acting captain and leader of the battle group, do we maintain Alert Combat Ready status?"

"We do," Jacob said quickly.

She blinked dark brown eyes. "Exactly so. Yes, we will send out vacsuited Spacers to work on our hull damage. The *Chesapeake's* nose railgun and topside plasma battery were knocked out as we shielded the frigates. We are still combat operational. But yes, I would like to repair our hull damage. Sending people out onto the hull during Alcubierre transit is not a gamble I'm willing to take."

Jacob understood her point. The academy instructors had emphasized how early experiments using chimps in vacsuits had resulted in mentally disturbed chimps upon their return to the interior of the transiting starship. Putting humans on the hull during Alcubierre transit was strongly discouraged.

"Agreed. Transit EVA should not be attempted. Proceed with your repairs," he said.

"Proceeding with EVA repairs. *Chesapeake* out."

Her image disappeared. Replacing it was the youthful face of Joy Jefferson. The woman's straw blond hair was tied in a ponytail. She eyed Jacob. "Heard the chat with *Chesapeake*. Yes, we need to repair one of our two tail laser nodes. Got knocked out in the last exchange. We are still combat operational. Our single repair robot is overloaded. Sending out Spacers is ideal. With your permission, proceeding to deploy Spacers."

Jacob liked the no-nonsense manner of the young woman, who was just five years out from her own academy graduation. Her climb up the ranks to be a lieutenant on a destroyer had impressed Admiral Johanson. Or so said the admiral's personnel files. Those files said she was single, the only child of a sea-going Navy couple and had reported two fellow ensigns for sexual harassment when they had groped her while both served on another starship. The ensigns had been assigned shore duty and Jefferson's superior had promoted her off his ship and onto the *Philippines Sea*. In the three years since she had received only Superior and Outstanding ratings from the now dead XO of her ship.

"Acting Captain Jefferson, you have my permission to conduct live EVA repairs on the *Philippines Sea*," Jacob said. "Stay alert to the enemy formation. Any sign the wasp ships are moving closer and I will order all EVA personnel inside, here on the *Lepanto* and on all battle group ships."

"Understood," she said, looking aside to something on her Bridge. She looked back. "Acting captain, proceeding with EVA repairs. *Philippines Sea* out."

Her image was replaced by the bulldog face of Wilcox. The man fixed blue eyes on Jacob. "Group leader, yes, we need to repair the left side proton laser and our belly plasma battery. The *Hampton Roads* is still combat operational, but we will hit harder with these areas fixed up."

"Acting Captain Wilcox, you heard my earlier comments. Same goes for you and your ship and people. Keep alert. Proceed with repairs."

The mostly bald man nodded. "Understood. *Hampton Roads* out."

He had similar conversations with Lieutenant JG Metz on the *Marianas* and Chief Warrant Officer Mansour on the *Ofira*. Both were happy to put Spacers out on their hulls to do work their single robots were slow to do. Jacob looked ahead, saw no change in the wasp ship formation, then looked up.

"Melody, connect me with Supplies Deck chief Cheryl Zhang."

"Connecting over All Ship vidcom."

The face of the Chinese-American woman who ran their Supplies Deck appeared in a holo to Jacob's left. Like everyone else she wore NWU woodland camos under her vacsuit. She seemed to be in what might be the control center for her deck, given the multiple wallscreens, blinking lights and hurried movements of three assistants who crossed behind her.

"Acting Captain Renselaer, good to hear from you," she said, her voice low but musical. "How can I assist you?"

Jacob smiled the best he knew how to smile. "Chief Warrant Officer Zhang, it is good to finally see you in person. My regrets for not visiting earlier. We've been busy up here."

Zhang's pale lips lifted to one side in a half grin. "So I and all my Spacers have noticed. Your transmittal of everything over the All Ship vidcom has been informative. And positive in the effects on my personnel."

His heart beat eased at the sign of one more deck chief who seemed friendly to his command status. "Thank you. The wasp enemy has retreated further from the battle group and has put out their people on the hulls of three damaged ships. I've given five of our ships permission to do the same, to help their repair robots. Or do work the robot is not doing on the smaller ships." He paused. "I've been watching the work of the five repair robots you sent out to weld hull plates over the big holes in our nose and belly. Your teleoperators are doing a fine job. However, I think repairs would go faster if we put out Spacers on the hull. Do you agree?"

Zhang's smooth-skinned face grew a big smile. "Would it! Yes! We've got to replace one of our hull sensor arrays and that is not a job for a robot. Plus, Spacers can work faster inside the deep holes in the hull than robots. I'll send out twenty of my people to the nose and belly holes, and two out to replace the sensor array. Uh, sir."

Jacob smiled back. "Excellent. Proceed with Spacers doing repairs in addition to your teleoperated robots. While we have 28 hours before we reach the magnetosphere, I would like the hull breaches to be sealed up well before we arrive there. Can that happen?"

She frowned. A few lines on her face betrayed her late 40s age. She looked up. "Yes, it can happen. While we cannot pour two meters of molten hull metal into the breaches, we can put in new hull plates, new interior structural beams and make sure the inner hull surface is water-tight. Give me fifteen hours and we should be vacuum tight on the exterior."

"Very good," Jacob said. He knew nothing about metal welding in microgravity, but he did know it was dangerous work thanks to some of Newton's laws. Still, there were plenty of Spacers trained in deck repairs in Supplies Deck, and the personnel file on Zhang said she was a wizard at getting stuff done on time, or earlier. He had been amazed to see the admiral use the word 'wizard' in the man's notations in her personnel file. But he was willing to believe it. "Chief Zhang, you have your fifteen hours. If you need support from another deck, call me. If you and your people need meals brought down to you, contact Spacer Kenji Watanabe in the Mess Hall. He's a friend of mine. He'll take good care of you."

Zhang's black eyebrows lifted, then her lips grew into a pleased smile. "Glad to hear that. My assistants are watching the wasp ship formation. If it changes, I will call in my people. Until that happens, I'm sending 22 of them outside. Anything else?"

"Nope," Jacob said. "Proceed with the repairs as you see fit."

The woman nodded. "Proceeding. Supplies Deck out."

Her holo image disappeared. Leaving him at the center of the Bridge. Daisy was busy checking deck status and Weapons Deck needs. O'Connor was tablet talking quietly with two of his Marines, who were also pilots of two of their four Darts. Ahead, the function post people were all busy. Behind him, Lori and Carlos watched and were ready to assist him with matters of Science and Navigation. Well, he could not put it off any longer.

"Communications, send a neutrino contact signal out to Lieutenant Commander Mehta of the *Salamis*."

Andrew Osashi's shoulder stiffened. Then the older man leaned forward, tapped his control pillar and then looked back. His dark brown eyes fixed on Jacob. "Acting captain, signal sent. Incoming response going up on the wallscreen. Or do you prefer it just to your comlink holo?"

Jacob gave the man a relaxed look. Clearly the warrant officer felt tense at the contact with the rebel ship captain. "Put him up on the wallscreen, in addition to my holo. Let this go out over the All Ship."

"As you order," Osashi said softly.

The dark-skinned, black-haired, Hindu-looking figure of Chatur Mehta now filled Jacob's comlink holo. And also the front wallscreen in an inset icon that left other imagery intact. Beside Mehta sat the Asian woman, a Vietnamese-American he recalled from scanning Mehta's personnel file. She was his XO and the person who had warned him of the Star Navy rule that required any Star Navy ship to offer aid to another ship under attack. Her expression was neutral. His was irritated.

"Mehta here. What do you want Renselaer?"

Insolence became the man. Briefly Jacob wondered if he was related to Aarhant Bannerjee, another man insulted by the rise of an ensign to authority over him.

"Acting captain and Lieutenant Commander Mehta, thank you for your return to the battle group and the fire support from the *Salamis*," he said calmly, reaching for the even temper his father had insisted he have even as the old man listed Jacob's faults. "Your ship's assistance helped us drive off the wasp enemy."

Mehta's tense face relaxed a bit as he heard Jacob's compliment. "Thank you, acting captain of the *Lepanto*. The *Salamis* is proceeding outward with the rest of the battle group. My ship stands ready to further defend against any new wasp attack."

Jacob chalked up one to his father's fanatical lessons. "I see that. Please continue your ship's vector track. As you have heard from my contacts with other ship captains, I am aiming to take the battle group out to the magnetosphere, then transit to Kepler 10. Where I will make a report to the captain of the Star Navy base." He paused, licked his lips and told himself the man could not hurt him. Defy him, yes. Treat Jacob as if he were a school geek, yes. But the man could not defy the reality of their current situation. "Will you accompany the battle group to Kepler 10?"

"Yes!" Mehta said loudly. His XO winced as if the sound hurt her ears. "That was where I was headed when the wasps attacked your ship and the battle group. In conformance with Star Navy regulations, I reversed course and rendered combat aid. What do you want now?"

Jacob was not about to ask the man if he accepted Jacob's command authority. He knew the answer to that question. The man's continued reference to the battle group gave a sign of the best approach. "Acting Captain Mehta, I would ask that you stay with the battle group after our arrival at Kepler 10. Hold off on setting course for Earth until I contact the Star Navy base and learn their wishes. Also, we will remain in Alert Combat Ready status upon arrival since the wasp ships may follow us to Kepler 10. Can I have your cooperation?"

Mehta's lips curled in a sour look. His black eyes blinked. "I will hold off on heading to Earth until contact is made with the Star Navy base at Kepler 10. My ship will assist any other Star Navy ship that is attacked by these aliens. Satisfied!"

Jacob showed an easy smile. "Very satisfied. Your return to assist the battle group was commendable. I will so state to the Star Navy base captain. Your continued cooperation in group defense is appreciated. *Lepanto* out."

"*Salamis* out!"

Silence filled the Bridge as Jacob's encounter with the rebel ship captain ended.

Below him, O'Connor looked up. The man's gray eyes fixed on Jacob. His thin lips curved up in a small smile. "Nicely done, acting captain. Putting him in the position of having to defend the battle group, in compliance with Star Navy regs, was exactly right. Neither of you got into personal issues." The man reached up and ran stubby fingers through his white crewcut hair. His expression sobered. "More importantly, lives depend on the cooperation of you, Mehta and every other acting captain in the battle group. Let's hope our hull repairs continue without incident and that we arrive at the magnetosphere without another wasp attack."

Jacob breathed deep. The pragmatic manner of O'Connor told him once more he had done the right thing in inviting the man up to serve as his combat advisor. Now, would the next 28 hours be calm, peaceful and devoid of laser beams and lightning bolts? He hoped so. He was tired. While the Awake pills taken by him, Daisy and everyone else on the Battlestar kept them awake and alert, the fatigue of not sleeping built up in the body. Already his muscles felt sore. Already his back hurt. Already he wanted to sleep.

"Communications, is the All Ship vidcom still active?"

"Acting captain, it is," Osashi said, his voice sounding almost eager in his response.

Well, at least all of his Bridge crew were loyal to him. "All personnel, maintain Alert Combat Ready status. However, the enemy has retreated to a distance of a hundred thousand kilometers. The enemy shows no sign of a renewed attack. Enemy parallels our course outward." He paused, licked his lips and wished he had a bottle of spring water. "Therefore, all deck chiefs are advised to allow half of their personnel to take a sleep and food break of no more than ten hours. Upon their return, allow the other half a similar break. When we approach the magnetosphere boundary, make sure all personnel are awake and at combat posts."

Cheers came over the vidcom holo as regular folks reacted to good news.

"Yes!" cried Rosemary from up front, lifting up her pale white arms and stretching. "Damn, but I'm sore. Acting captain, can I be in the first break group?"

He smiled. Her Tactical position had been front and center ever since he'd arrived on the Bridge. "Yes, Chief Petty Officer O'Hara, you may take a ten hour break. As may your colleagues at Power, Gravity, Navigation and Communications. Everyone else, stay here and suffer."

Laughter filled the Bridge.

Briefly, for a few moments, Jacob was ready to join the laughter. Then the ghosts of seventy-one dead came to him from the flaming atoms of the *Britain*. The hairs rose up on the back of his neck. A chill ran down both arms. The tips of his fingers tingled. The discomfort he felt vanished as memories flooded in. Joining them were family memories. The image of his dead mother stayed in the forefront of his mind over the following hours.

CHAPTER THIRTEEN

Jacob looked over the quarters that had belonged to Captain Miglotti. He saw there was a modest relaxation room with one wall providing high density holo imagery of a place in the Italian Alps. Birds flew in the living color holo. A red fox moved along a shallow ravine. In the distance tromped a small herd of white sheep, moving along at the nipping of a black and white collie dog. Distant whistles said the dog's master was somewhere out of sight.

The wall holo fit Miglotti's Italian heritage. He may have grown up in Cleveland, but Italy was his first and enduring love. Looking to the left he saw a dark wood cello instrument, man high, that the captain must have loved playing if he used part of his shipboard weight limit to bring it onboard. Between Jacob and the two side walls were a small couch on the left, a tall disk case on the right that held antique DVDs and in the middle lay a Persian-style rug that covered the gray metal of the room's floor. Looking beyond he saw the far end of the room held a Food Alcove with fridge, sink and microwave. A pull-out counter allowed for the making of fresh foods, versus the Nutrition Paks that were the emergency stocks on Supplies Deck. He pulled off his vacsuit and helmet and tossed them into a corner of the relaxation room.

Walking ahead, his left shoulder supporting the small weight of the green duffle that held his personal clothing and mementoes, he saw an opening on the left. The open archway led to a bedroom with a real, normal waterbed, that no doubt was bolted to the room's floor. Above the twin size bed, affixed to the gray metal wall, was an actual oil painting. It showed some famous woman opera singer. Or he assumed she was famous. Otherwise why have a picture of her? On the right was the outline of a clothing cubicle. The left side of the rectangular room had a glass slidedoor. When he slid it into the wall he saw the bathroom space. It held a sink, a suction-based toilet and a shower alcove. A reflective metal mirror filled the wall above the sink. Turning away, he went into the bedroom, sat on the end of the bed and looked out through the archway to the relaxation room beyond. He noticed a rectangular outline in that room's far wall. It must be the fold-down work desk, since he saw no such item in the bedroom. With a start he realized music had just come on. A woman singing some kind of opera swept down from the ceiling of the bedroom. There was no sign of family pictures anywhere. Well, he could fix that.

Minutes later he had Miglotti's clothes piled on the front room's couch, the DVDs stuffed alongside the clothes, with the oil painting on top. Shaving and tooth cleaning items from the bathroom lay next to the painting. The cello now lay against the side of the couch. He walked over to the work desk site, touched the upper right corner of the outline and stepped back as the flat metal of the desk folded out. Just like in his ensign's quarters. A flat padded seat came out below the desk, emerging from a slot in the wall below the desk. It protruded out just enough for someone to sit on it and do stuff atop the work desk. Grabbing his duffle he pulled out his two flat pictures and the holo cube, put them on the empty shelves that were inset into the desk's wall, laid his tablet on the work desk, and put hands on his hips as he stared at his Mom's image and the barn and horse image. They were the images that had floated through his mind as he watched Bridge crew leave for their ten hour food break and sleep escape.

Movement drew his eyes down to where his hands rested on top of his dress blue pants. His fingers were shaking. Both hands could not stay still. He took a deep breath, closed his eyes and focused on the memory of the old barn at his former home. The green trees behind it and the sweet smell of yellow hay had always helped him relax after one of his father's verbal lashings. Two minutes later he opened his eyes and looked down. Unmoving were his fingers. Good. His quarters were the one place he could allow his anxiety over being in command of 321 people, and the leader of eight other starships, to become visible. Still, the shakes bothered him. In the past he'd been shaky or hyper-nerved only when dealing with his father. He got up, turned around and walked to the bedroom, then into the bathroom. He touched an icon on the wall above the sink. A tray slid out. His shaving and tooth cleaning items lay there. Beside them were several pill packets.

Should he take an anti-anxiety pill? That was way better than a meth pile. He was already too nerved up from the shock of being in command, the bigger shock of space combat, and the final shock of the deaths of the people on the *Britain*. A third packet drew his attention. It held pot pills, commercial grade. He opened two packets, filled the plastic cup with water and downed a pot pill and an anxiety pill. Turning away, he sat on the bed. Then he lay down. The opera singer music flowed through the room. Closing his eyes, Jacob told himself he could handle the shocks. He could handle the stress. He could handle the politics that came with being a commander. But could he handle his yearning to be close to Daisy?

♦ ♦ ♦

Daisy watched from her XO seat as Lieutenant Branstead walked onto the Bridge and handed a small memory block to Jacob. Like her and everyone else, she wore her vacsuit with helmet pushed back. She looked up as she gave the block to Jacob.

"Acting captain, here's the cartoon video you asked for. Sorry it took so long, but my people argued over just how simple to make the imagery," she said.

"Thank you," Jacob said, taking the block from her. He inspected it, then looked back to the Science Deck chief. "Do you wish to remain here while I transmit it to the aliens?"

"Yes," Branstead said, giving a nod to O'Connor and Daisy. She waved over to Willard at the Science post. "I'll join your people in one of the rear observation seats."

"Very good," Jacob said, his expression neutral even though his voice sounded pleased. He inserted the block into a slot on his seat's left armrest, then looked up. "Melody, transmit the contents of the memory block I just installed on my seat to the six enemy ships. Use the frequency that the enemy used upon our arrival at the fourth planet. Repeat the transmission five times."

"Understood. Frequency selected. First transmission going out. Video runs for approximately one point seven minutes," the AI said, her tone almost relaxed. "Do you wish the video displayed on the wallscreen?"

"I do," Jacob said. "Please display any incoming enemy response alongside the video. And resume neutrino transmission of all events on this Bridge, including the video, to the other ships in the battle group. Also transmit Bridge events over the All Ship vidcom."

"Neutrino link to other ships established. All Ship vidcom transmission resumed. Acting Captain Renselaer, are all humans as redundant in their language as you are?"

Daisy felt surprise at the personal tone of the AI's words. While the depth of algorithms in the AI allowed it to well imitate human emotions, behaviors and language, she had never heard it act as if it cared what it did, or what any human did. Was this AI developing a true self-awareness?

Jacob's image in her Bridge holo looked startled, then he smiled. "Some humans do chatter redundantly. Others do not."

"Does one gender speak more redundantly than another gender?" the AI asked, her tone sounding almost human-normal.

Jacob chuckled. "That question must go unanswered in the interests of Bridge harmony!"

Daisy joined the soft laughter that came from Rosemary, Maggie, Louise, Cassandra, Akira, Branstead and Lori. But her duties drew her attention. She focused on the situational holo that showed the six wasp ships holding position at nearly 100,000 kilometers out, along with their nine ships and the asteroid belt they had passed some hours back. They had five hours to go until they reached the local Kuiper belt of comets and the system's magnetosphere. The repairs to battle group ships and to the wasp ships had ended some hours ago. Since then, there had been no sign of aggressive behavior by the wasps. But that could change at any moment.

"Incoming wasp signal!" called Andrew at Communications.

♦ ♦ ♦

Hunter One had just returned to his bench in the Flight Chamber of his nest when the Servant responsible for monitoring external perception signals let loose a flurry of alarm pheromones.

"Hunter! The largest Soft Skin nest sends us an imagery signal similar to the one we sent them when they arrived above the world of Warmth! Shall I display it?"

"Yes!" he said with a strong mix of releaser, trail and territorial pheromones. "Let us see what scent these creatures now attempt."

The largest perception imager, which filled the chamber's wall in front of the main group of Servants, lost its image of dark cold space and was filled with a kind of land map image. Simple outlines depicted his people, his nests and the flying nests of the Soft Skins with outlines of Soft Skins. A series of outline images first showed things as they were. The six Swarmer ships moved along the same flight path as the nine Soft Skin ships. They moved well beyond the four worlds brightened by the central sky light. Then the imagery changed. The new imagery showed his six Swarmer nests curving about and flying back to Warmth. The next image showed his nests landing on Warmth. A further image showed small versions of Swarmers gathered around images of full size Swarmers. The final image showed the nine Soft Skin ships moving out to the far edge of the local sky light, then disappearing. But a series of small dots made a flight track that moved outward. The wall imager went blank, then the imagery signal began to repeat.

He put all five eyes on the older male Servant who studied aberrant social behavior. "Servant! How do you understand the message of these images?"

The faded yellow of the Servant's hard shell was bright under the chamber's white lighting. Two major and three small eyes looked his way. Two black antennae dipped toward him, signaling his acceptance of Hunter's dominance. His upper appendages rasped his shell even as a complex flood of pheromones came from the Servant.

"The Soft Skins show they understand we have settled the world of Warmth with our larvae and helpers. They suggest our six-group should return to Warmth, there to land and be made welcome by our colonists." The Servant breathed deep through his spiracles. His position on his bench shifted. The creature's head and thorax lowered in further acceptance of Hunter's dominance. "The nine Soft Skin nests propose they fly out to the edge of the sky light's magnetic field, there to disappear in some far distance."

"Will the Soft Skins return?" he scent cast a strong signal pheromone.

The compound lenses of the Servant's two major eyes seemed bright under the chamber's light. "Unknown. What the Soft Skins do after they leave this sky light is not shown. They might return. They might never return."

Hunter knew what he would do in the place of the Soft Skins. It was what any Swarmer cohort would do when engaged in a nearly equal sky battle with another cohort. He shifted his gaze to the young female who had led the efforts to restore the front energy unit so power could be delivered to his nest's front ring of stinger tubes.

"Stinger Servant, how do you scent this flight imagery?"

"It is an image of deception," she scent cast in a mix of aggregation, alarm and signal pheromones. "Leader, these Soft Skins wish us to return to Warmth, then to leave our flying nests. When we leave our nests, those nests will be vulnerable to a new attack from these invaders! While they say they will leave, nothing prevents them from hopping to the far side of this sky light's boundary, there to reappear behind the sky light. We might not see their return until too late!"

The maneuver was one he had not considered. He kept it in mind for a future encounter with the Soft Skins. But now, he must reply to this imagery. And he must make a reply that would satisfy the Support Hunters on the other five nests. And also please the Matron who rested behind him. Her scent was one of intense curiosity. Well, he could deal with these Soft Skins.

"Speaker To All, prepare a reply image signal. Use parts of this imagery. Show the Soft Skin nests turning around and flying to Warmth. Show our six nests englobing the Soft Skin nests. Upon arrival at Warmth, show the Soft Skins leaving their nests and landing on Warmth," he scent cast, then drew in several quick breaths. "The Soft Skins will then become food for our new larvae as we sting them into paralysis!"

Excitement pheromones came now from all the Servants in the Flight Chamber. Those pheromones, along with his strong aggregation pheromone, would quickly flow out to the other nests. The Support Hunters would recognize his proposal as a classic Swarmer cohort response to an invading cohort. Come and die for us so we may feed our larvae! No Swarmer cohort that was defending a nest would ever allow an invading cohort to escape. They might return stronger than the defending Swarmer cohort. Best to englobe and sting to death any invading cohort before the cohort could call in allies. So had spoken the long history of the Swarm on Nest. It was the reason his two six-groups of flying nests were fitted with three rings of stingers. No Swarmer group setting out to build a new colony nest ever traveled anywhere without their most deadly Fighters and Fighter Leaders!

"Response signal will go out as you command," replied Speaker To All in a strong mix of aggregation, trail and territory pheromones.

Hunter One settled back on his bench. He would not attack the Soft Skins, since they might surrender of their own choice. If they did not surrender, but continued out to the edge of the magnetic field, he and his allies would follow this invading cohort to another sky light. Perhaps the new sky light would have worlds about it suitable for Swarmer colonization. If a Soft Skin nest world lay at the new sky light, so much the better. More Soft Skins meant more opportunities for capturing live food while his Servants studied their means of talking about themselves. For where one group of Soft Skins flew and nested, other Soft Skin groups were soon to visit. He and his people would be ready for such a future visit!

◆ ◆ ◆

Jacob watched the wasp reply play out on the front wallscreen. It was not an agreement to what they had proposed. It was something else. He looked back over his shoulder to where Branstead sat next to Lori and Carlos. The Aussie woman's high-cheeked face was scrunched up as she watched the reply cartoon video.

"Lieutenant Branstead, will you come up here?"

The woman released her seat straps, stood up and came to stand in front of him. She stood beside O'Connor. Who was resting his chin on his right fist as he thought about the wasp reply. Daisy was busy with her situational holo and the imagery of the wasp ships. Plus she was sending text messages to people on other decks. No doubt confirming everyone was on duty and at battle stations as part of the ship's continuing Alert Combat Ready status.

"What is your pleasure, acting captain?" Branstead said, her hands behind her back as she stood at parade rest.

"What do you make of this signal that tells us to head back to planet four, allow our ships to be surrounded, then for all of us to head down to the surface of planet four?"

She frowned. Then her gaze fixed on him. "I don't trust it. Why should we put our ships and our people at risk? These are the aliens who killed our senior officers. Now, they invite us all to come down to the planet? They could launch another plasma lightning strike, then take over our orbiting ships at the same time." She paused, licked her lips, glanced back to the wallscreen, then back to him. "While I admit we may have made an error in coming into the system after getting the mysterious signal from the wasp satellite, we did not know the wasps were claiming this system for their colony. They only sent down colonists after attacking our officers. They could do it again."

Jacob thought the woman had put into good wordage his own thoughts. "Agreed. The battle group will continue out to the magnetosphere and head for Kepler 10. Should we make any reply?"

She nodded sharply. "Yes. Resend our new cartoon video. Resend it five times just to be sure every wasp ship perceives it. We are leaving this system. They can have it. Maybe they won't follow us."

Jacob nodded, then looked to the man next to her. "Chief Warrant Officer O'Connor, what are your thoughts?"

The man waved dismissively at the front wallscreen image. "Like the Science chief said, I don't trust it. Resend our recent video. But these wasps have set a pattern of attacking us even as we retreat from their system. They will continue to attack us. Either just before we leave, or in Kepler 10. I am certain they will follow us there."

He felt his fingers tingle. Combat might be impending. Or it might not happen until Kepler 10. Now he better understood his classes on managing stress in groups of people. He'd thought it silly at the time. Now, he understood the training was aimed at helping Star Navy crews cope with extended uncertainty amidst a deadly situation.

"I agree," Jacob said. "Engines, move us up to eleven percent of lightspeed. Power, increase fusion reactor energy flows. Tactical and Weapons, be alert for sudden moves by the enemy." He paused, looked around, then his situational holo reminded him of the rest of his duty. "Melody, is the neutrino link to the other ships still active?"

"It is," she said in a husky feminine tone. "Do you not recall that I have always advised you of any change to the last orders you give me?"

What was it with the AI? "All ships, speed up to eleven percent of lightspeed. Maintain Alert Combat Ready status. Be alert to any change in wasp enemy ship behaviors. Confirm back to me your compliance."

"Speeding up," came the words and face of Swanson from *Chesapeake*.

"Stoking our reactors. Accelerating. Maintaining status," said Wilcox from the *Hampton Roads*, sounding a bit touchy and grumpy.

Well, Jacob knew *he* felt touchy, grumpy and full of nerves. The other ships responded similarly, the images of their captains appearing as small icons across the top of the front wallscreen. The images disappeared shortly after they appeared to acknowledge his orders. Even Mehta of *Salamis* responded briefly.

"XO, do you detect any change in wasp ship formation?"

"None," Daisy said quickly.

"I do!" called Rosemary from Tactical. "Just this moment all six wasp ships increased their speed to eleven percent. Looks like they do not wish to be left behind."

"Tactical, thank you."

Jacob now saw that change in his own situational holo. His own copy of Daisy's ship cross-section holo showed their isotope fuel reserves were at 81 percent full. Well, once they all hit eleven psol, they would shut off the fusion pulse main thrusters on each ship. Momentum would carry them through the cometary belt and out to the magnetosphere. Course every ship would reactivate their main thrusters in order to make the final vector lineup for Kepler 10. Once that was done, he would have Louise of Navigation establish a neutrino comlink so every ship activated their Alcubierre stardrives at the same moment. Doing it that way meant all nine ships should emerge at the outer edge of Kepler 10 at the same time.

Now, all he had to do was sit in place for five more hours. And be patient. Mentally he cursed patience.

♦ ♦ ♦

Hunter One watched as, long wing beats after the Soft Skin repeat of their first map signal, the Soft Skin flying nests neared the edge of the local sky light's magnetic field. It was time.

"Speaker To All Servant, advise our five allied nests to move outward," he said in a flow of alarm and trail pheromones. "Warn them of the need to make visual and radiation perception records of the direction and angle the Soft Skin nests take before they enter the alternate dimension."

"Scent casting your words and scents, my leader," the young male replied with a strong dose of aggregation and territorial pheromones.

He liked the youth's emphasis on loyalty and protection of their nests. Now for the other vital Servant. "Flight Servant, work your panel to record the exact direction and angle of the fleeing Soft Skins."

"Your wishes are my life," scent cast the male at that post.

Hunter One went scent silent, content to watch the behavior of the Soft Skins. He doubted the outward movement of his fellow nests would cause any violent action by these defiers of the natural order. Still, he stayed alert.

♦ ♦ ♦

"Captain!" called Rosemary. "The wasp ships are changing position. They are moving outward. But they are not coming closer to us."

Daisy saw what the Tactical chief reported. Her own situational holo was finely detailed. Its depiction of all solid objects in the Kepler 22 system was so real she sometimes felt she could reach out and take hold of a wasp ship. Or push their own ship faster forward. She looked aside to the ship cross-section holo. All decks of the *Lepanto* were sealed against pressure loss and all weapons stations were occupied. Including the right front outrigger pod laser node that Quincy operated. Hopefully there would be no sneak attack just before they went Alcubierre.

"I see it," came the deep voice of Jacob from behind her. "Navigation, any sign of a course vector change by the wasps?"

"None," Louise said hurriedly.

To Daisy's right, Richard gripped his armrests, though his face looked calm and relaxed.

She felt reassured to see that even an old combat veteran could become tense as the moment of truth neared.

"Science, what is your take on the wasp ship movements?" called Jacob.

She looked to the right end of the front row of function stations. Willard might be portly, but she had never observed him be less than alert at his station. The man tapped his control pillar, then spoke.

"Acting captain, I believe the wasp ships are preparing to triangulate on our vector track for Kepler 10," Willard said thoughtfully. "The outward movement of their six ships will allow them to increase the triangulation angle for their visual and sensor records of our vector track. They will know our course vector to within a stellar second."

"Well, we expected that. Navigation, compute our vector track for Kepler 10. Once you have the exact angle and direction, transmit the settings to the other battle group ships."

"Acting captain, computing our track," the red-haired woman said.

Daisy watched as Louise tapped her control pillar, transmitted by neutrino comlink the course vector, then called to Jacob. "Acting captain, I am ready to transmit the Alcubierre space-time stardrive activation signal."

"Good," Jacob said. "Engines, activate the Alcubierre stardrive. Prepare to initiate space-time modulus creation."

"Activating," called Akira. "Ready to initiate."

"Navigation, cross-link your post to Engines. Maintain the neutrino comlink signal."

"My post is cross-linked," Louise said. "Comlink signal active."

"Engines, all ships, initiate Alcubierre stardrive transition."

Daisy watched as the front wallscreen went from true space active to a sudden wash of gray.

That was it. There was no vibration, no howl of engines, nothing. The Alcubierre stardrive was a solid state microelectronic wonder combined with a gravity generator that warped space ahead of them into a smaller zone, while expanding the space-time to their rear. The expanding space pushed the *Lepanto* and the other eight ships of the battle group out into deep space at a velocity beyond imagining. She just knew that they moved now at 25 light years per day.

"We're on our way. All ships, change ship status to Alert Alcubierre Transition. You have permission to move ship weapons to standby status," Jacob said.

Responses came in by way of the neutrino comlink that allowed all battle group ships to speak instantly no matter the distance between them, or the fact they were now moving faster than lightspeed. The neutrino comlink signals traveled through an alternate dimension, she recalled from her academy classes. She let out a sigh.

"Acting captain, can we all please get the hell out of these stinky vacsuits!"

Jacob's laugh was the first honest laugh she had heard from him in many hours.

"All personnel on the *Lepanto*, you are free to remove vacsuits. Verify weapons moved to standby. Mess Hall, prepare for a rush. All deck chiefs, set a priority list for your staff to take relief breaks, eat a meal and get some rest," Jacob said. "Ship is now back to routine shifts."

She smiled. Now she was free to think about just which dress of hers would be exactly perfect for the Dance Night rendezvous with Jacob!

◆ ◆ ◆

Hunter One watched as the nine Soft Skin ships disappeared into the alternate dimension that allowed swift travel among the sky lights that filled the flight space of cold darkness. He focused all his eyes on the Servant who monitored radiations from the outside.

"Servant," he scent cast to that Swarmer. "Do you and your fellow Servants on the other flying nests have the exact flight angle and direction of the fleeing Soft Skins?"

"I do," the Servant replied in a strong flow of aggregation and trail pheromones. "It is being shared with the Servant who handles our propulsive devices."

Hunter did not object to the initiative shown by the Servant. It was the logical action after his earlier commands. He looked to the elder female who monitored events in external space.

"Servant, what does this new flight track tell us about the Soft Skins? What sky light do they fly to?"

The female fluttered her wings, then lifted her antennae stiffly. "Hunter One, the new flight track aims at many sky lights. However, a yellow sky light very similar to the one about which Warmth now wings lies not far from us. Other yellow sky lights glow on this flight track, but further away."

He had expected that news. "How long a flight is it to the nearest yellow sky light?"

"A journey of three sleep cycles," she said in a flow of aggregation, signal and trail pheromones. "If this is a colony sky light of the Soft Skins, then we know the Soft Skins are very close to Warmth."

So it seemed. Strengthening his pheromone flow so the other flying nests would scent his determination to pursue, he rasped his hard shell and spoke. "Propulsive device Servant, prepare the alternate dimension device. Let us follow these Soft Skins to their new nest. Surely we will then attack and kill every Soft Skin hiding from us!"

The flows of excitement pheromones reached a peak. Hunter One soaked in those scents and knew he still led the Swarm.

CHAPTER FOURTEEN

Aarhant Bannerjee sat in his private quarters on Navigation Deck, running through his mind the options before him. The young whelp had been lucky. The wasp aliens had not again attacked the battle group. Did the luck of the youth's father even reach out to affect aliens? He did not understand how the young whelp had been able to make the right action choices when faced with unpredictable and violent aliens, even as junior officers on other ships figured out how to fly and fight their ships. The loss of the frigate *Britain* was sad, but Aarhant had expected much greater losses. Now, they were headed for Kepler 10. At least it had a Star Navy base that orbited the fourth planet of the system. A Command level captain was in charge of the base, according to his check of routine Star Navy assignments for colonial star systems. Surely the captain at the base would recognize his right to command the Battlestar!

"Lieutenant Commander Bannerjee, there is an incoming neutrino signal from the *Salamis*. Its captain responds to your earlier signal to him," the mouthy AI said, her tone a melody he did not care for.

At last! He'd put in the private signal call not long after they entered Alcubierre. It was two hours later and only now had Mehta seen fit to respond. He took a deep breath and worked to school the expression on his face. Unlike many on the Battlestar he did not have a beard that could hide his facial expressions. There was no way he was going to antagonize Mehta.

"Put through his vidcom signal to this room's wallscreen."

"Linking signal to your wallscreen," the AI murmured tunefully.

The flat screen that covered part of one wall of his relaxation room now filled with the long black hair, dark brown skin and brooding eyes of Chatur Mehta. The man was not on his ship's Bridge. Instead, he appeared to be in his own captain's quarters, judging by the spaciousness of the relaxation room where he now sat on a red leather seat.

"Bannerjee, I'm responding to your call. Only now could I leave the Bridge to my XO. What do you want?"

Aarhant restrained his first impulse. Which was to tell the man to speak more respectfully to him. That he could not do. Mehta was a lieutenant commander just like him. Equal ranks meant careful conversation.

"To be blunt, I should be commanding the *Lepanto*," he said, deciding to credit the man for a basic awareness of staffing on the Battlestar. "You may know I now command the Navigation Deck. I am the senior surviving officer on this ship. I plan to make my case for taking command shortly after we arrive in Kepler 10." He paused, breathed deep and made sure to show no sign of nervousness. "What are your thoughts? Would you accept me as the commander of the battle group once I gain command of the Battlestar?"

Mehta pursed his lips sourly. "Did you see and hear my comments to Renselaer, before the aliens attacked? That I felt it my duty to leave and warn Earth Command?"

"I did. The young whelp continues to defy Command tradition by feeding all our decks a continuous vidcom of his chatter with other ship captains and with his Bridge people."

Mehta lifted a thick black eyebrow. "So I am aware. It is a primary reason why I turned back to help fight off the wasp aliens. Star Navy regulations required that I do so, as perhaps you heard. Once we arrive at Kepler 10, I had planned to leave for Earth before the aliens arrive."

"You think they will follow us to Kepler 10?" Aarhant said, his heart beating too fast. "That seems improbable to me."

Mehta squinted. "It is in keeping with their actions to date. They attacked our meeting site. They attacked the battle group twice. They paralleled our course out to Kepler 22's magnetosphere. They are competent star travelers. I am certain they will follow us, once they confirm the presence of a nearby G-type star on our outbound track."

The man's statement made his plans more complicated. "If the aliens follow us, this Battlestar needs the experience of a senior ranking officer. Myself. Will you support me?"

The man blinked black eyes. "If the Star Navy base captain puts you in command of the Battlestar and of the battle group, yes, I will accept that change of command."

Aarhant detected a distinct lack of enthusiasm in the man's deep voice. "Will you signal the base captain on my behalf? Will you support my assumption of command of the Battlestar?"

"No," Mehta said, reaching to one side to grab a bottle of what looked like spring water. "Your ship is your issue, not mine. Unlike some at Earth Command, I do not care for politics. Nor do I care for it in the battle group when we are in a state of armed combat." He took a sip from the bottle. "While early on I doubted Renselaer's right to command the Battlestar, he has done better with it and with the battle group than some senior officers I know." The clean-shaven man let his words linger, causing Aarhant to wonder if the last comment was aimed at him. "I will comply with any order given by the Star Navy base captain. If the aliens arrive and attack us, or the colony on the fourth planet, I will do my duty and lead the *Salamis* in fighting the aggressors. Beyond that, I will not play at musical chairs."

The reference to an ancient American past-time game shocked Aarhant. He had thought Mehta was a loyal follower of ancient Hindu culture. The castes of India had worked well to lead the people of Earth's second largest population. Now, this man was refusing to endorse him and his argument for following tradition on the *Lepanto*. One potential ally lost. Perhaps there would be others.

"Captain Mehta, I thank you for this conversation. It has clarified my thinking on these issues. Good day."

The black eyes of Mehta scanned him, his face neutral. "You are welcome. Good day."

Mehta's image vanished. The wallscreen returned to the three dee depiction of Nepal and the Himalayan Mountains that were the ancestral home of the Bannerjee clan.

He sat in his own black leather seat, drumming his fingers on the arms of the overstuffed seat. First, Swanson had refused him. Now, Mehta had done the same. Who else could he bring to his side in the two and a half days that remained before they arrived at Kepler 10? The Marine leader was out. He had spent hours on the Bridge, assisting the whelp. Were there other deck chiefs who might support him? Time to find out.

◆ ◆ ◆

Jacob stood in front of the gray metal slidedoor that gave access to Daisy's quarters. The rooms had been the place where Commander Anderson once lived. They were the same layout as in his captain's quarters, based on his recollection from visiting the man in company with Admiral Johanson. Now, *she* lived there. Did she feel the ghost of the dead man? He shrugged and focused on her. When he'd first met Daisy on the orbital shipyard, high above the blue oceans and white clouds of Earth, he'd liked her looks and her manner. Just shy of six feet, she was almost as tall as Jacob. Her oval face was framed by a thick halo of blue-black curls. Her brown eyes were lively, constantly looking here and there during the holo cube shoot setup.

Afterwards, she had treated him like any other ensign. That had made him pay closer attention to her. She was nice-looking, even if her full breasts were hidden by the formal jacket, white blouse and pantsuit that was required clothing for all Star Navy women. Her dark brown skin was a lovely mix of her Anglo father and Black mother. Tall, trim and lively, that was her physical manner. Later on that day he'd joined her, Carlos, Quincy, Kenji, Lori and other freshly graduated ensigns in drinking pale ale beers at a saloon. The place, though orbiting 400 kilometers high, was done up in an imitation Wild West motif, with swinging wooden half doors, a long wooden bar, racy paintings on the wall behind the bar and with images of famous Star Navy captains and commanders adorning the metal walls. The saloon's owner walked through the bolted down tables, holding his Russian wolfhound on a metal chain. Lori had loved the animal. Jacob had been uneasy at first, then had enjoyed petting the animal's well-formed head. Daisy had been boisterously loud as she played Rock, Paper and Scissors with some guys at the table. None of them were able to outguess her. That was her mental manner and her natural persona. Smart, lively, boisterous and willing to hang with anyone so long as they didn't bore her, Daisy had struck him as someone well worth knowing.

He could not put it off any longer. He spoke.

"Acting Captain Renselaer requests admission to the quarters of Executive Officer Stewart," he said firmly, putting his hands behind his back in parade rest mode. It was a silly stance considering they flew in a bubble of space-time that traveled faster than the speed of light. But it was the best he could do.

"Door, admit Acting Captain Renselaer," came Daisy's warm mezzo-soprano voice.

The door moved sideways into the wall. Standing in the middle of her relaxation room was Daisy. He couldn't help himself. He gave her a whistle.

"You look beautiful!"

She smiled big, then turned around slowly, letting him see the back of the green Spring dress filled with flower images. The dress hung from her right shoulder, with a slanting neckline that went down and under her left arm. The bodice clung tightly from her waist up. The lower folds of the dress flared out from her hips, stopping just at her knees. She wore pale green hose that ended in black leather loafers. He noted that her two silver-bar lieutenant rank was clipped to her right shoulder. He had insisted on the field promotion since he'd appointed her to the job of Executive Officer. XOs were almost always lieutenants or higher in rank.

While Dance Night dress rules emphasized casual, civilian wear, it was required that all officers, CPOs and CWOs, and Spacers wear their rank or rating insignia on some part of their clothing. That was in case of an emergency while in space. Knowing he would be the center of attention for more than a hundred *Lepanto* crew, he'd chosen to wear his Service Dress Blue coat, white shirt, four-in-hand necktie and pants, with four gold stripes sewn onto the end of each coat sleeve, while similar boards adorned each shoulder. His captain's eagle was on his upper left chest, with the single ribbon of the *Lepanto's* current mission Operation StarFight. He didn't like the white combo hat, but it was part of the standard uniform. At least it was not a Full Dress Navy Blue uniform that required white gloves and a sword hanging on one hip!

Daisy stopped and faced him. A happy smile had replaced the grin. "You look good too! You ready to go dancing?"

He turned and held out his left arm. "Yes! May I escort you to the Dance Night?"

"For sure," she said, her voice warm and friendly. She walked up, put her right arm through the loop of his elbow and they both headed for the closed slidedoor. "Door, open."

They stepped out into the hallway of the Command Deck. A hiss made them look toward the end of the hallway. Carlos stepped out, looked left and saw them.

"Wow! What a couple. I'm jealous," Carlos said loudly.

"Thank you, Carlos," Daisy said.

He and Daisy walked toward their friend. A second hiss sounded and beyond his friend there emerged Lori, wearing a beautiful Russian peasant's dress that made her look like someone stepping out of a French dress salon. She turned, looked their way and smiled easily. Her pale brown face held Slavic cheekbones that framed wonderfully attractive blue eyes. Or so Jacob had thought until he spent time with Daisy.

"Hey!" his dance partner called, jerking on his left arm. "That's enough attention paid to the other belle of the ball!"

He and Carlos both laughed. Then his friend from East LA, wearing a dress blue outfit like Jacob's, turned and walked toward Lori, holding out his left arm. "May I escort the other beautiful belle of the ball?"

"*Da*," she said, her Russian spoken in what Lori had informed him was the Novgorod dialect of standard Russian. "Did you bring the Stolichnaya Red Label vodka?"

Carlos laughed. "Yes, my sweet. It's hidden inside this hideous formal jacket!"

As Jacob and Daisy joined the couple, he felt happy that the two hetero folks had found each other. He had spent plenty of time playing chess with Carlos and sharing news about their very different hometowns. The man's ability with algorithms and knowledge of stellar navigation had astounded Jacob. His friend had only once mentioned Jacob's father the famous admiral, then they'd fallen to talking about the different breeds of horses and which were most fun to ride. He looked back along the hallway but did not see either Kenji or Quincy. While both Spacers had been surprised by his orders to move to the place where officers lived on Command Deck, they had complied. It pleased Jacob. They might be a laser gunner's mate and a line cook, but they were his friends. And they were part of the brain trust he relied on to keep him stable in his unique situation. As he, Daisy, Carlos and Lori stopped in front of the between decks grav lift, he guessed they must have gone early to the Dance Night room on Habitation Deck.

A big slidedoor opened. He followed his friends into the gray metal box. Knowing what was expected, he spoke. "Melody, deliver us to Habitation Deck."

"Moving your compartment," the AI replied as it told the metal box's gravity plates to reduce their repulsion so they dropped down a level to Habitation Deck.

As they dropped slowly, Daisy's bare hand moved down to hold his hand. It felt nice. And the smell of her lavender perfume filled him with desire. Mentally shaking himself, he sought refuge in a memory of the ship's layout of decks. There were actually seven levels or decks. The central deck was a combination of Command in the front half of the *Lepanto,* with the Engines section taking up the rear half. Below Command were Habitation, Science and Supplies decks. Above Command were Life Support, Navigation and Weapons. The grav lift box stopped moving. The large slidedoor opened. They walked out into the main hallway of Habitation, saw clusters of people on their left all heading toward the Exercise Chamber that doubled once a week as Dance Night hangout, and followed after the other singles, couples and groups. As he walked, he hoped the crews on the other ships of the battle group were enjoying their own Dance Nights. When you mixed up both genders, multiple sex orientations, and different ranks and ratings inside a big metal tube for a long time, opportunities for relaxation and escape from the normal rigidity of military service became vital. Daisy squeezed his hand.

"Jacob, what are you thinking?"

An easy question. He told her. "Do you think the other crews are having fun?"

"Are *we*?" she said, turning her smiling face to him. Her black eyebrows lifted.

"Most definitely!" he said, pulling her a bit closer as they followed after their friends and other people making their way through a wide opening.

The Dance Hall resembled an old style high school gymnasium, in that its floor was fake wood parquet, with bench seating along the four walls of the long rectangle that made up the chamber. Overhead, real drop lights hung from the high ceiling, their yellow glow filling every corner of the room. On the left side, up against the wall, were three long tables filled with food platters, soft and hard drinks and tasty sweets from twenty nations. On the right side were the alcoves that gave admission to the restrooms. In front of them, standing on an elevated platform set against the far wall, was a band of violins, drums, electric guitars, a few cellos, some brass horn players and two flute players. Live music that resembled Country Western came from them.

Carlos looked his way. "Jacob, you gonna join that band? I recall you saying you had once played a coronet."

He shook his head. "Never! The only music I know is what I had to study in high school or at the academy. But I do like live music. And dancing." Jacob turned to face Daisy. "May I have this dance?"

"Oh yes!" She smiled easily, her eyes bright. Daisy moved closer to him, put her right arm out to hold his left hand, then laid her left arm over his shoulder.

It all felt very very good. And she smelled delightful. He gave thanks the music was slow and suitable to a waltz type step. He drew her sideways. Daisy matched every step he took. Keeping his attention on her lovely face, he pulled her closer. "You like this?"

"Very much so." She moved closer and laid her chin on his right shoulder. "You dance better than most guys I've met."

Putting aside an immediate wonderment about how many young men she had dated and danced with, Jacob looked outward and enjoyed the movement of other couples as they moved to the rhythm of the band.

He saw Quincy dancing with a slightly shorter man close to his age. They made a nice gay couple. Looking past them, he caught sight of Kenji dancing with a Korean gal from Science that his friend knew from visiting with Lori during the long Alcubierre flight out to Kepler 22. Like most of the 321 people on the *Lepanto*, they were hetero. Beyond them he caught sight of red-haired Louise dancing with swarthy Oliver. Her file said she was married. Oliver was standard hetero and single. It seemed they were enjoying each other's company. As he and Daisy circled through the middle of the dance floor, he caught sight of Maggie dancing with Akira. Their files said both were lesbians. Some of the best instructors at the academy had been tough as nails lesbians. He hoped they found time to develop a relationship. Or continue one that may have started earlier. Another swing about and he caught sight of Alicia Swanson dancing with Leonard Schwartz, the chief of Habitation Deck. Elsewhere the other deck chiefs talked, danced or drank. Drinking was what Richard O'Connor was doing, now wearing white Marine formal dress, as he talked with the four fellow Marines who were pilots of the *Lepanto's* four Darts.

"Jacob, why are you ignoring me?"

He started, then looked down to Daisy's face. Which had a look of concern. Lies would not do. Not with her. "I'm really attracted to you. I really like you. You were the first person in the shipyard to treat me normal, rather than the son of a world-famous admiral. And it's been a long time since I felt this close with any woman."

Her eyebrows lifted. Her expression changed to one of empathy. "You don't like feeling vulnerable, do you?"

Jacob took in a sharp breath. Then told himself Daisy was as smart as he, more talented in some areas and came from Chicago. There was likely nothing she did not know when it came to relationships among people. Including being raised by a single mom after her father divorced that mom.

"No, I don't. My father told me to hide all evidence of weakness if I was to grow up and be a commander of men. And women. When my mom died, it got worse. Think of being on guard duty 24 hours a day."

She grimaced. Her soft lips opened a bit. "Sounds goddess awful." Daisy pulled back a little, looked him over, then resumed being close, her breasts pressing against his chest. "Well, you are now off duty! So enjoy yourself. And pay attention to me, rather than being on the watch for everyone else!"

He chuckled and pulled her closer. "A wonder you are!"

The band music changed to a foxtrot and they separated, except for brief hand grips as they danced in parallel form, their legs moving in synchrony with the music.

As Daisy moved, her green flowery dress swirled and swirled, making the curve of her hips visible and her stockinged legs nicely viewable. His arousal was strong enough that he briefly worried about the next time they would be close. Then he dismissed it. No one in the room had sought him out to solve a problem. No one had laughed and called him a fake captain who was just an ensign. And no one spoke of the *Britain* and its ghosts. He told himself to put aside that memory and to treat Daisy as she deserved.

"Now you're hopping!" she said happily.

They danced and danced. They got drinks and sweet snacks. She allowed him to feed her a tortolino and he allowed her to stuff a blueberry muffin into his mouth. They stayed with drinking beer, in the interest of remaining vertical. It went on like that, her smiling, him laughing now and then, until the music stopped. He had not realized it was midnight until the overhead lights dimmed and the baritone at the bandstand announced the end of Dance Night. Daisy took his left arm and guided him toward the exit, which was crowded with dozens of other late revelers.

"Jacob, this was fun! You're fun."

He smiled, marveled at how earlier she had pulled him close and kissed him, and now hugged his arm close to her side. "You're more than fun. You inspire me. Never knew I could do a samba!"

She laughed as they went down the hallway of the Habitation Deck, other couples and groups ahead of and behind them. "Well, your foxtrot was pretty decent." She paused as they stopped before the grav lift, sharing the space with four other couples, none of whom he knew and all of whom were not the slightest bit interested in the fact the ship's captain stood among them. Daisy looked up to him, her warm brown eyes fixing on him. "You wanna have a drink in my place? Got a nice *pinot noir* bottle that my mom gave me as a graduation present."

Would this invite lead to something more? Did he want more? Silly questions the mind poses. "Sure! Would love to taste your red wine. And hear about your mom the super scientist!"

She laughed, followed him into the grav lift, then laid her head against his left shoulder as the metal box rose slowly. "She really is a wonder. Got me my first flying lessons. Stood by on the runway when I soloed. And took a backseat ride with me in the jet trainer that I qualified on. Plus she taught me to play chess early on."

Jacob had heard some of these details during their flight out to Kepler 22. It was clear that Daisy's mom was both her role model for achievement and the sole family link she had. "I am very very glad she got you those piloting lessons. Otherwise, we might not have met each other since you were originally assigned to Navigation Deck."

She squeezed his arm, then walked close to him as they stepped out onto the hallway of Command Deck. The grav lift's door hissed shut behind them. No one else was present in the hallway. She turned and looked up to him.

"Kiss me."

Bending down a bit and pulling her closer, he kissed Daisy Stewart with all his heart, all his hopes and all his wishes that they would survive the future. Being the master of a Battlestar starship was fine, but except for the crazy AI Melody, there was no emotional return in doing his duty. Being with Daisy was so much better than sitting atop a seat in the middle of the Bridge and being at target center for all the worries, problems and crises that came with being a ship's captain.

"Let's have some of that wine," he whispered to her as his lips separated from hers.

Her face showed caring and kindness and . . . was that love? Perhaps too soon for that. But Daisy was showing him a side of her that was beyond special. She was inviting him into her heart.

"Wine sounds good. Along with other nice things. Follow me," she said, turning and pulling him along after her as they headed for her quarters.

Jacob followed willingly.

CHAPTER FIFTEEN

Daisy watched the holos in front of her XO seat, waiting for the front wallscreen's color to change from gray to black filled with white sparkles, and maybe the yellow dot of Kepler 10's star. That should happen in eleven minutes, according to the time clock notation in the corner of her situational holo. Her ship cross-section holo showed everyone at their combat duty posts, ready to fight the second after their arrival if needed. She had listened to Jacob's comment earlier, on the neutrino link with the group's other ships and captains, as her friend said there was a possibility the wasp alien stardrive might get them to Kepler 10 before they arrived. Willard at Science kept quiet, but she knew the man did not believe that was possible. More likely, according to Lieutenant Branstead, was an arrival of the wasps some hours, or even a day after their arrival. Branstead, or Alicia as Daisy now thought of her, had shared this with Jacob during an all deck chiefs video conference. Alicia was convinced it would take the wasps some hours to convert their triangulation readings into an exact vector track. The wasps would easily see, early on, that the nearest G-type yellow star was Kepler 10. But they would have to discuss whether the *Lepanto* was headed there, or to another G-type star further along that vector track. Behind her the slidedoor that gave access to the Bridge hissed open.

"Lieutenant on the Bridge," called out Willard, looking beyond Daisy.

She turned in her seat. It was Alicia, wearing her woodland camo outfit. That was what everyone on the Bridge now wore, except for Jacob, who was dressed formally in his dress blues. The woman stood in the open doorway, her amber eyes looking to Jacob, her right hand lifted to her brow in a salute.

"Permission to enter the Bridge requested," she said tightly.

Daisy's holo that showed an overhead view of the Bridge had Jacob turn in his seat, stand up and salute her back. "Permission to enter granted. What brings you here, Lieutenant Branstead?"

The stocky Aussie marched quickly to the room's center, her expression thoughtful. She stopped in front of Daisy and looked up.

"Acting captain, I wish to be present here when the *Lepanto* exits Alcubierre space-time. Our emergence will be quickly detected by the base. Someone there will contact the ship. I wish to be present to lend my support to your report to the captain in charge of the base."

Daisy's feeling of worry eased. She knew Alicia supported Jacob as the ship's new captain. The woman had made that clear during the discussion in the admiral's conference room. Was something else going on? Now, anxiety filled her as she hoped the woman held good news for the man she had come to care for deeply.

Her holo showed Jacob sitting down and locking his straps. He looked down. "Your assistance and the assistance of Science Deck are always welcome. We have nine minutes. Is there anything you wish to share with me before we emerge?"

Alicia's high-cheeked face grew a small smile. "There is. My discussions with every deck chief has resulted in them all agreeing with me that you should continue as the captain of the *Lepanto*. Only Lieutenant Commander Bannerjee declined to join our consensus view."

In the holo, Jacob nodded. "And you wish to convey that news to the base captain?"

"I do."

"Thank you." Jacob sat back in his seat. He looked ahead. "Communications, open an All Ship vidcom line to the rest of the ship. Melody, establish a neutrino comlink with the other ships in the battle group."

"All Ship comlink activated," said Andrew from where he sat near the middle of the front row of function posts.

"Neutrino comlink established," the AI said, her tone now sounding distracted to Daisy. What was it with this AI's algorithms?

"All personnel, all ships, move your ship status to Alert Combat Ready. Put on your vacsuits, though the helmets may be left unsealed," Jacob said in that command voice she was coming to appreciate. "Battle group captains, prepare your ships for enemy fire. It is possible the wasp aliens arrived here before us. As for the Star Navy base contact, I will speak to it on behalf of the battle group. Acknowledge."

The lights went to blinking red as the speakers gave out a high-pitched siren, Acknowledgments came from every ship captain, including Mehta on the *Salamis*. She wondered just how loyal the man might be to Jacob. During the Alcubierre transit the man had responded to every signal from the *Lepanto*, and he had participated in Jacob's all captains conference call to discuss ship repairs, fuel levels and recycling functions.

"All captains, upon emergence we will assume formation Alpha Hammerhead."

Brief acknowledgements followed.

Daisy's mind filled with an academy lesson on the formations that were official Star Navy combat arrangements. Hammerhead meant the battle group would form up in a series of lines, one after the other. The Battlestar, flanked by the two cruisers, would form the hammerhead. The three destroyers would form the middle line. The three frigates would bring up the rear as the third and last line. The last two lines would be tilted to give those ships a clear field of fire. It was a formation aimed at presenting maximum forward firepower. To her, it made sense due to the fact they would exit Alcubierre spacetime with their nose aimed at the yellow sun of Kepler 10. The other battle group ships would materialize to either side of the *Lepanto*, since that was their formation upon departure from Kepler 22.

Reaching down to the side of her seat, she grabbed the folded up vacsuit and flexible helmet, released her seat straps and donned her vacsuit. To her right Richard was doing the same. Willard had handed Alicia a vacsuit and the woman was donning hers. Behind them Carlos and Lori were putting on their vacsuits. Up front, everyone at the function stations was also donning a vacsuit. Soon enough they were all seated again and strapped in. She briefly wished the straps were not standard regs, but then her memory provided an academy video of a pig being smashed against the side wall of a spaceship as the ship's inertial damper lost power during a sharp sideways thrust change. Inertial dampers rarely failed. And grav lifts almost never failed. But that history did not prevent the Star Navy from installing seat straps and adding access ramps to connect each ship deck in case grav lifts failed to operate. There were even old-style fire extinguishers bolted to hallway walls, despite the modern fire suppression systems built into each spaceship. She liked that kind of redundancy.

"Lieutenant, please occupy the seat I had installed beside CWO O'Connor," Jacob said calmly. "You should be able to participate in my discussion with the base from that seat."

"Thank you," Alicia said and moved to sit in the seat.

Daisy had wondered why a new seat had been added to their central cluster when she'd arrived on the Bridge four hours earlier. Now she knew. But how had Jacob known Alicia would want to be present on the Bridge?

"XO, what is the status of our decks?" Jacob said.

Feeling her nerves drain away as normal routine took hold, she answered him. "Acting captain, all decks are secure. All pressure hatches are sealed. All deck control centers are occupied by deck chiefs and assistants. There are three crew residents in the Med Hall. All other personnel are awake, on duty and prepared to perform."

"Good. Weapons, what is the status of our weapon stations?"

Ahead of her, Oliver looked to his holo. "The antimatter cannon has a full four shots in its magfield reservoir. All front and back CO_2 lasers on both outrigger pods are energized and ready to fire. The proton lasers at spine, belly and both flanks are operational. The belly and spine plasma batteries are functional, though the belly unit may not hold up to sustained output," he said, the excitement in his voice clear to Daisy. "All railgun launchers have full Smart Rock loads, and the eight stern silos are filled with missiles. Half of the missiles carry x-ray laser thermonukes while the other half carry multiple independently targeted and mobile thermonuke warheads set for three megaton yields. Sir."

"Thank you," Jacob said calmly. She could not believe how relaxed he sounded while hearing they possessed enough weaponry to destroy a small planet. "Engines, Power, Navigation, Gravity, Life Support, Communications, Science and Tactical, report your status."

She sat and listened to the reports from the chief petty officers and chief warrant officers who operated the Bridge function posts.

"Two minutes," called Louise from her nav post.

Daisy sat up straighter in her seat, all too aware that every action and every word by everyone on the Bridge was being recorded by the AI, and live transmitted to the other ships and to folks on the other decks. She had early on appreciated Jacob's decision to provide live vidcom imagery of everything that happened on the Bridge. Later he had explained it was his way of building confidence in the *Lepanto's* crew while also keeping them informed, rather than guessing and worrying. The crew had lost the senior officers they had served with for four years. That loss would unsettle any crew. Jacob's move to command the Battlestar was surely a surprise to most crew. It had surprised her, and she was his friend. A member of the small group of people who he felt at ease with. Well, that open sharing policy was now about to get a new airing, this time with the captain in charge of the Star Navy base.

"Twelve seconds," Louise said.

She looked ahead at the gray wallscreen and hoped the captain would be reasonable. After all, they were survivors of Earth's first encounter with aliens, an encounter that had quickly turned deadly. This captain, the base, the colonists and Earth needed to know what had happened. And hopefully, support Jacob as the *Lepanto's* continuing captain.

"Transition completed."

♦ ♦ ♦

Aarhant sat in his control center for Navigation Deck and watched the wallscreen that repeated every image from the Bridge. This openness policy of the whelp allowed him to see and hear everything that happened. And to make his own record of any mistake Renselaer made. He laid his right hand on his seat's armrest, feeling the neutrino comlink activation stud. It was Star Navy regs for every deck's control center to have neutrino communications independent of the Bridge neutrino comlink. The reg was there in case a part of the ship was disabled or lost power. He had used the comlink to talk to Mehta. Which had not helped his cause. His contacts with other deck chiefs had been rebuffed, thanks to Branstead's active lobbying of the chiefs to support Renselaer. What blindness!

Well, he was ready to send his own signal to the captain in charge of the base. Whomever the man might be, surely he would listen to a lieutenant commander calling from a combat-damaged starship!

The wallscreen image that showed the view from the rear of the Bridge now showed the people as they put on their vacsuits. Something he had ordered his people to do ten minutes earlier. More waiting followed. Then the front wallscreen on the Bridge lost its gray portrayal of Alcubierre space-time.

At last!

♦ ♦ ♦

Jacob blinked as the wallscreen went from gray to deep black. The white streak of the Milky Way stretched over one corner of the image, while the yellow star of Kepler 10 was centered in the middle of the screen. Hundreds of white, red, yellow and blue dots filled the space between the two. His holo with the cross-section of the *Lepanto's* decks showed Green normal. The right front holo with its true space image repeated what the front screen showed. The upper left holo held multiple sensor images that reflected multi-spectral input from the ship's sensor arrays. The left side holo was the situational holo that showed an overhead plan view of the star system, its seven planets, and their nine ships at their arrival point in the cometary belt of Kepler 10. Two AU inward was planet seven, a Pluto clone with several small moons. The sight of the other eight ships showing Green normal status was a relief.

"All ships, eject Smart Rocks on sideways vectors," he said, recalling his plan to leave an intelligent minefield for the enemy. "Let's leave the wasps a bothersome calling card!"

The destroyers and cruisers acknowledged his order. As did Oliver at Weapons.

"Incoming neutrino comlink from the Star Navy base," called out Andrew from Communications.

He sat more upright and looked straight ahead. "Display signal on the front wallscreen."

The image of an Asian male ensign wearing his Service Khaki uniform now appeared to the left of the yellow star. He sat at a table in a room filled with flatscreens, radar and lidar arrays and three control panels. He sat before one of them. The man looked surprised.

"Battlestar *Lepanto*, your arrival and that of your battle group is a surprise," the man said with a Minnesota accent. "We thought you were at Kepler 22 and headed further out to find more colony stars." The man looked aside, then frowned. "My neutrino emissions screen reports only nine ships in your group. You left Earth with ten ships. And where is Captain Miglotti? Are you a deck officer filling in for him and his XO?"

"I am Acting Captain Jacob Renselaer," he said quickly. "Captain Miglotti, Executive Officer Anderson and Rear Admiral Johanson are all dead. Killed by wasp-like aliens who proposed a

First Contact meeting on the fourth planet of Kepler 22. We lost a frigate in two space battles with the aliens. Get your captain now! The alien enemy could arrive at any time!"

Shock filled the man's face. "Uh, why, damn!" He looked down and tapped something. "Captain O'Sullivan, report to the Com room now! Immediately! Emergency!"

"Heading your way, Mikoto, and it damn well better be an emergency!"

Jacob thought the captain's voice had a hint of Irish to it. Which meant he could hail from Ireland, or from the northeast of America, perhaps Boston. Whatever. He tapped a control patch on his right armrest.

"Ensign Mikoto, I'm sending you a four minute video of the site where our senior officers for this ship, and our other ships, were all killed. Set it up to display once your captain arrives."

The slim man blinked black eyes, then looked relieved to have something to do. "Got your transmission. Setting it up on our side wall display. Uh, did this come from someone at the meeting?"

"No! No one was left alive. It's a Cloud Skimmer image."

Before the base comlink man could say more, in rushed the tall form of a Navy captain. He was Anglo, had some gray streaks in his short hair and wore brown Service Khakis that looked rumpled. Had the man been in his quarters, resting? He looked at Jacob.

"Who are you? And what are doing on the Bridge of the *Lepanto*?"

Jacob repeated what he had told the com ensign. "Captain, when we arrived at Kepler 22 we were contacted by aliens. They sent a vid signal proposing a meeting on planet four. Captain Miglotti, XO Anderson and Rear Admiral Johanson went down to the meeting site. So did the captains and XOs of the battle group's ships. They died there." He waved a hand. "The video on your wall shows what was left of the meeting site. A smoking pit with their shuttles half melted by a lightning like weapon strike by these wasp aliens," he said quickly as the man's brown eyes looked at Jacob, down to Daisy, then over to Richard and Alicia, then back to him. "I was the sole remaining ensign on Command Deck. I was personal assistant to the admiral. When my XO Lieutenant Stewart contacted me about the loss of tablet communications with our officers, I came to the Bridge to find out what had happened. Since it appeared hostile action might have caused the loss of communications, I ordered the ship's AI to allow the launch of a Cloud Skimmer. That required a change in the ship's status. By luck I was aware of the ship status change code. I entered it and took the admiral's seat, hoping to see the signal loss was due to a simple thunderstorm. As you can see from the short video I've transmitted, it was not."

The man had turned away while Jacob spoke and was watching the video on a screen out of view of the com imagery. He took a deep breath, looked down at a tablet he held in his hands, then looked back to Jacob. His expression was intense. "It's clear the battle group officers died at that location. My tablet lists all personnel on the *Lepanto*. You are listed as an ensign freshly graduated from the academy. How the *hell* did you come to be in command?"

"Necessity," Jacob said quickly, staring at the man as the memory of the *Britain's* ghosts filled a part of his mind. "Someone had to act to find out what had happened. There were no other Command Deck officers present in the ship. I acted. After our skimmer got to the site, the alien ships left geosync and came our way in what appeared to be an attack formation. I ordered the other ships to locate their ship status change code. Acting captains came into control of those ships." He tapped the transmit button once more. "I'm sending you a list of the acting captains for every ship in the battle group. With their help, we repelled the first attack from the enemy, destroying three enemy ships. As we moved away from the planet, heading for the magnetosphere, we were attacked again. We lost the frigate *Britain*. The enemy lost three more ships. Since then, the enemy followed us out to the system's edge. I ordered the group to make vector for Kepler 10 as I did not want the wasp aliens to know the vector direction to Earth. Your system and your base were closest to Kepler 22."

O'Sullivan frowned. "Why didn't you ask the aliens to stop? Or ask why the officers were killed? Surely no intelligent species attacks for zero reason."

Below him Alicia stood up. "Captain O'Sullivan, I am Lieutenant Alicia Branstead, chief of Science Deck. I can answer that question. The aliens are wasp-like people. My assistants believe they communicate by pheromones. Our radio and lidar broadcasts to them failed to gain a reply. The only true communication we've had from them were a series of cartoon videos that they initiated in order to get our people down to planet four. Jacob?"

He tapped the send patch. "I'm transmitting our cartoon videos now."

O'Sullivan looked aside again. He squinted. Then looked back. "So they told your officers to meet them. Then you sent a video suggesting they go back to planet four while the battle group went outward. They replied with this last video cartoon that told you to meet them on the planet. You didn't. Lieutenant Branstead, why are you not sitting in the *Lepanto's* command seat?"

"Because I believe former Ensign Renselaer is the best person to be in command of the *Lepanto* and of our battle group," she said quickly. "He had the foresight to change the ship status code. He had the initiative to send the Cloud Skimmer to give us facts. He ordered the group into a battle formation that withstood the aliens' first attack. He figured out a way for the *Lepanto* to escape from the black hole weapon of the aliens." She paused. "And he ordered the *Lepanto* and the two cruisers to move to block deadly enemy beam fire on our frigates. Without his combat judgment in both battles, we would have lost half the battle group. As it is, the aliens lost six ships to our single ship loss. For your information, every deck chief on the *Lepanto* except for one now supports Mr. Renselaer continuing as acting captain of our ship and as leader of the battle group."

The com ensign, who was seated as O'Sullivan stood over him, spoke. "There is an incoming neutrino signal from a Lieutenant Commander Bannerjee, chief of the *Lepanto's* Navigation Deck. Sir, do you wish to view it?"

"Bannerjee is the only deck chief who did not support Mr. Renselaer retaining ship command," Alicia said quickly.

O'Sullivan grew thoughtful. "Renselaer, Branstead, hold a moment while I hear what this officer has to say."

Jacob watched and watched and felt the hairs on his neck and arms rise up. Was this going to be the end of his first command? What he had done had never before been done. The base captain moved back into view, his expression neutral.

"Mr. Renselaer, Lieutenant Commander Bannerjee says he is the senior surviving officer on the *Lepanto*, of which only two others are present. Lieutenant Branstead and Lieutenant JG Yamamoto. Why should you remain in command?"

Below him Richard stood up. "Captain O'Sullivan, I am Chief Warrant Officer Richard O'Connor, in charge of our Marine boarding team and assault Darts. Don't you recognize me, son?"

O'Sullivan looked startled, then thoughtful. "I do, now. You were my hand-to-hand combat instructor at the academy, far too many years ago. Richard, what is your role in this melee of crises?"

Below Jacob the Marine leader stood stiff and formal. "I am adding my endorsement to the retention of Acting Captain Renselaer to remain in command of the *Lepanto* and of this battle group. He has acted with daring, with deadliness and with concern for the survival of all members of this battle group. Billy, he's faced the elephant. And he's still in one piece. Ignore Bannerjee. Keep Renselaer. He's a chip off the block of his father."

Jacob wondered what Billy O'Sullivan would now do. It was a surprise to learn that Richard knew this captain in charge of an out of the way colony outpost. Alicia's support was a known. Richard's support was a welcome surprise. Whatever happened next, he could accept knowing that two people far more experienced than he had stood by him.

O'Sullivan bit his lower lip. "What of the other acting ship captains? Do they support him? And are you saying I should accept these field promotions for the battle group ships?"

Richard chuckled. "You've had tough assignments before. You ran the occupying force on Callisto, after the rebellion. Then you volunteered for the Star Navy base on our first star colony. Now, here you are in charge of our farthest out colony." The Marine paused, then lifted a hand and pointed a finger at O'Sullivan. "You are a Command officer. You have the rank to regularize this situation. And son, we need to get this sorted out before those yellow flying fuckers arrive here! They are deadly and the colony below your base has 70,000 plus folks in it."

O'Sullivan straightened his posture. Decision shown in his face. "Acting Captain Renselaer, I knew your father. I respected his actions in the Callisto Conflict. I never served under him. Nor would I make a decision just because you are his son," the man said, his tone thoughtful and measured. "But I did serve under Chief Warrant Officer 5 Richard O'Connor. I do not need to hear from the other ship captains. If Richard supports you, and most of your deck chiefs support you, then that's that." The man reached down and tapped a spot on the com panel. The ensign sitting below him looked surprised. "Today, September 10, 2091, at 14:02 Earth time, I hereby endorse the field promotion of Ensign Jacob Renselaer to be Captain of the Battlestar *Lepanto*. I also endorse his continued command of the battle group that is engaged in mission Operation StarFight." He paused and met Jacob's gaze directly. "Captain Renselaer, what do we need to do to protect this colony?"

Jacob felt relief. Then a sense of urgency. "We need to alert Earth to the threat from these aliens, to the fact of their existence and to the battle group's need for a supporting force here at Kepler 10. To do that I propose sending our frigate *Ofira* off to Earth now, before the aliens arrive and can track her vector line. Do you have a better plan?"

O'Sullivan blinked. "Now I see why Richard is sitting there on your Bridge, next to your new XO and to Lieutenant Branstead. You are not afraid to ask for help from those with more knowledge than you possess." He paused. "I support the sending of a frigate to Earth. I would send our base frigate *Aldertag*, but it would take 50 hours for her to reach the system's magnetosphere. You are already there. Your frigate can leave now, before the enemy arrives. Do as you propose. I will send the *Aldertag* out to you to join your formation. Its captain is Joan Sunderland. She has combat experience."

"Captain, thank you," Jacob said. "I will send off the *Ofira* now. Then our battle group will head inward. If we are lucky, we can join with *Aldertag* and set up a defense for the colony." A thought hit him. "You may wish to alert the civilians to head for shelters, if they have any. These aliens have mobile atomic bombs, but no thermonukes. Still, their plasma lightning weapon zapped the meeting site pretty badly. A few atomics hitting the colony towns and port city could be disastrous."

O'Sullivan's face became grim. "Will do. You do your best to hold them off. The *Aldertag* should join you within twenty hours or so, perhaps out by planet six. Our small gas giant. Good luck."

"The same to you," Jacob said, his mind swirling with options, plans and hopes.

"Jacob," called Daisy from below. "You can do this. We can do this. And we outnumber them nine to six. Believe in our people."

Jacob did believe in everyone on the *Lepanto* and on the other ships. The issue was not that. The issue for him was whether new ghosts would join those of the *Britain*.

CHAPTER SIXTEEN

Daisy felt relief as the conversation with O'Sullivan ended. Jacob was still the captain. She was still his XO. And their togetherness would have time to grow. Maybe. Who knew what would happen when the wasp ships showed up? Would they attack the battle group? Would they attack the colony world? Or would they see the occupied system and leave, figuring there was no point in further combat? She shook her head. Her academy training told her to put aside the personal and focus intently on the professional. Her duty. Their ship. The enemy.

"Captain Mansour, respond," Jacob said.

The front wallscreen shimmered. In the place where O'Sullivan's image had been there now appeared a new image. It was the face and shoulders of Lieutenant Arman Mansour, formerly the chief of Supplies Deck on the *Ofira*. Now its acting captain since he had been the one to force open the dead captain's safe and locate the ship status change code. The man's brown face and hawk-like eyes fixed on them.

"Mansour reporting, Captain Renselaer. Congratulations and when do you want my ship to leave for Earth?"

"Very soon," Jacob said. Behind her she heard him tapping on his seat. "I'm sending you a complete vidcom record of everything that happened in Kepler 22, including our battles, the aliens at the meeting site, everything recorded by any of us. Take that record to Earth. Share it with Earth Command." Jacob paused. She heard him take a deep breath. "And tell them I request combat assistance. Holding Kepler 10 is our duty, but if more wasp ships arrive than the six that followed us, we will need more fighting ships to keep possession of our colony on planet four."

Mansour's black eyebrows lifted. Then he nodded. "Understood. The record has been received. Anything I can help you with before I leave?"

"No," Jacob said. "Your ship was outstanding in its targeting of enemy ships and in our formation maneuvers. But the *Ofira* is vulnerable to concentrated enemy beams. You will serve the battle group best by getting to Earth and getting Earth Command to send us some support. Reverse course and make your Alcubierre transition as soon as you can."

Mansour gave them a thumbs-up. "Reversing course. We will go Alcubierre within twelve minutes. *Ofira* out."

The Bridge was quiet. After the encounter with O'Sullivan, the actions of Alicia and Richard, and Jacob's words now to dispatch the *Ofira*, she wondered if everyone else felt as tense as she did. What new surprise might show up?

"All battle group ships, head for planet four," Jacob said calmly. "Navigation, set a vector track for planet four. Engines, move us up to one tenth of lightspeed. Let's get the hell away from this barren space!"

"Vector set."

"Firing our three main thrusters."

Daisy watched as Louise and Akira did their jobs well and quickly. Her situational holo showed that the other ships had moved into the Alpha Hammerhead formation during Jacob's talk with the Star Navy captain. They began to speed up even as the icon that was the *Lepanto* swung its nose slightly and then accelerated. She felt nothing, thanks to the inertial damper field that covered the ship. But her heart beat too fast, a chill ran down her back and her breathing quickened.

They were headed for the fourth of seven planets, an Earth-like world. She recalled the system's layout from her study of it during the transit. Planet one was a super-Mercury clone that was tidally locked to the star. It orbited the star in less than a day. Planet two was a super-Venus world, with a mass of 15 Earths and a width nearly three times that of her home world. It orbited in 45 days. She recalled that the large amount of water on that world was supposed to be in a state called 'hot ice' phases. Whatever that meant. Both the inner planets were too big, too hot and with too high a gravity for humans. Planet three, though, orbited just inside the star's liquid water zone at one-half AU. It was a Mars size rocky world with plenty of air, a few seas, lots of jungles and a half-gee gravity. Humans could live there, though it had a high oxy level in the air. Better was planet four, an Earth clone with green forests, large oceans, tall mountains and a gravity of nine-tenths gee. It orbited at seven-tenths AU out from the yellow star that was somewhat cooler than Sol. Beyond four was planet five, another Mars size world that had a thinner atmosphere, some lakes, some green zones and not much else. It lay at 1.1 AU, at the outer edge of the star's water zone. Planet six was a Uranus-like small gas giant lying at five AU out, while planet seven was a Pluto-like ice ball of frozen nitrogen and methane at 19 AU. Beyond those worlds, at 35 AU, began a Kuiper Belt zone of comets that reached out to the system's magnetosphere boundary at 45 AU. Which made their transit inward a 52 hour journey. If they didn't have to stop and fight off invading wasp ships!

"All personnel," called Jacob. "The ship remains at Alert Combat Ready. However, deck chiefs may release ten percent of their crews for relief breaks, some food, whatever they can do in an hour. Rotate breaks among your staff. Captain out."

"Captain," called Andrew from Communications. "I have an incoming signal from Lieutenant Jefferson of the *Philippines Sea*. Will you accept it?"

"Of course," Jacob said quickly. "Put the signal up on the wallscreen and continue to share what happens here with everyone on the ship by way of our All Ship vidcom."

"Signal goes up. Vidcom continues active."

Daisy looked ahead. The middle of the front wallscreen suddenly filled with the youthful face of Joy Jefferson, a trim blond Daisy only knew from the all captains conference call during Alcubierre transit, and from brief contacts during the battles. The woman sat in the captain's seat on the Bridge of her destroyer. Next to her in the XO seat sat a middle-aged man who resembled the Navajo men she had seen during a visit to their reservation. His face brought up memories. It had been winter break time and she had joined a tour group of other cadets. The round hogans occupied by traditional Navajos had been interesting, while their side trip to visit the mesas where the Hopi people lived in multi-story pueblos had been even more fascinating. She'd learned a bit of Southwest history from the perspective of its original inhabitants, seen a ritual Hopi dance from a distance, and now here was a Navajo in space. Clearly he was an academy graduate like her.

"Captain Renselaer, my ship is in the middle of this formation," Jefferson said, her voice sounding tense. "If the enemy appears behind us, that will leave the frigates exposed. I request permission to move the *Philippines Sea* to Tail End Charlie position.

My CO_2 lasers on our stern can discourage any close approach by the wasps."

Why was Jefferson seeking a change in the formation? Daisy thought the Hammerhead formation made sense. And their ship arrangement could shift rearward in a matter of minutes. So having a destroyer at the rear did not make sense.

Jacob chuckled. "Lieutenant, I've read your file. You like to pursue the enemy and cook their butts. That is a good attitude in my book. Sure, move back to provide cover to the frigates. Though I think *St. Mihiel* and *Marianas* might dispute who among you is the deadliest!"

Jefferson smiled, then shook her head, which caused her ponytail to swing back and forth. She might be encased in her vacsuit, but Daisy had the impression the woman was ready to jump out of it and bite the butt off of anyone who got in her way. If her crew was as battle hungry as she was, perhaps it would be very good to have her on their tail.

"And I've read the public record on you, your father and your time at the academy," the woman said, amusement filling her face. "Did you really put a cactus pad under the saddle of the horse your father was going to ride during Binghampton's Pioneer Days?"

Daisy bit her lip to keep from laughing. The image was just too precious.

"No truth to that rumor whatsoever!" Jacob said quickly. But he sounded amused. "My father was in ready reserve retirement at the time. I save such surprises for active duty officers."

Everyone on the Bridge laughed or chuckled or snorted. Including Daisy.

Jefferson smiled. "I will remember that. Be warned, I always check any seat I choose to occupy. *Philippines Sea* out."

Her image disappeared from the wallscreen. None of the other battle group captains showed up. She missed Rebecca Swanson on the *Chesapeake*. She was a no-nonsense woman like Daisy's mom and ran her heavy cruiser with a stern grip. Or so she had heard from some of the old hands on the *Lepanto*. The woman had kept her cruiser in the thick of the two battles, accepting damage as readily as Jacob accepted it. If the wasps really did come to Kepler 10, she was glad Swanson was going to be one of the strong ship leaders that Jacob could rely on. She switched her attention to the situational holo. On it a new ship icon appeared, heading outward from planet four. Time to do her XO work.

"Captain, the *Aldertag* is heading our way," she said quickly before Rosemary or someone else could speak.

"So I see," Jacob said. "Do you wish to take an hour off?"

Daisy doubted the wasps would appear in the next hour. "Yes. Can I bring you a snack from the Mess Hall?" She turned around and looked up to the young man who was now her lover.

He smiled, then gave her a wink. "Sure. Bring me a sandwich and ice tea. I feel comfortable up here. Time for the rest of the Bridge crew to get some break time."

She smiled back. "Heard and understood. I'll be back sooner than an hour with your snack and drink."

Daisy unsnapped her seat straps, stood up and headed for the rear exit door. She waved at Lori and Carlos, who had been sharing a tablet and looking at something. The two smiled at her and waved back. She kept on going, out the slidedoor, then down the silent empty hallway. The empty hall reminded her of the other night when she had invited Jacob into her quarters for a glass of red wine. They had quickly moved beyond sharing drinks and smiles and kisses. Soon they were naked atop her bed. She cherished the memory of Jacob's caresses, his soft kissing, his taking the time for her to match his arousal. Joining together several times over the next hour had been wonderful. Waking up beside him the next morning had been just as good. She could even forgive him for the time he took to carefully shave and make a production out of combing his hair. Better to have a man who liked to be clean and spiffy rather than a man who left a mess behind, expecting the woman to clean up. Jacob was not that way. And she had found he could cook a decent breakfast *al fresco*. That had been a talent he'd learned from his mom, he'd told her. Now, she wished the woman was still alive so she could meet her. But she wasn't. However, Daisy's mom was alive. And whenever they returned to Earth, the battle group would likely pass by Pluto. She looked forward to introducing Jacob to her mom.

♦ ♦ ♦

Hunter One observed the forward perception imager as its depiction changed from gray to the black of cold dark space. A yellow sky light filled the middle of the imager, while more distant sky lights blazed with colors across the range of light that Swarmers could see. He didn't care that some sky lights were only visible at the dark red end of viewing. Which he could not see. There were plenty of white-yellow sky lights, the kind of sky light around which his world of Nest now flew. While Swarmers could survive on the world of Warmth, which was cooler than Nest, the presence of a yellow sky light limited the growth of their green bark trees. The purple leaves of those trees were stunted compared to the originals on Nest. Still, it was their tenth colony world. The Swarm had expanded its life zone. He focused his three small eyes on the details in another imager.

"Alarm!" scent cast the elder female Servant in charge of monitoring external space. "The Soft Skin flying nests are here! Eight of them take flight. They wing toward the fourth world."

The female's scent was filled with trail, territorial and aggregation pheromones, clearly signaling her desire for the Swarm to pursue and kill the fleeing Soft Skins. Soon enough that would happen. He noticed something about the fourth world. "Servant, are those propulsion emissions coming from just above the fourth world? And also from the surface of the world?"

"You see clearly, my leader," she scent cast with a hint of embarrassment. "The radiative emissions are similar to what our propulsive device and our energy nodes emit. That is either a flying nest above that world, or a nest in permanent flight, like those above Nest," she said. She fluttered her brown wings. "The presence of such emissions on the land of the world suggest there is a Soft Skin colony on that world."

Hunter understood that. But his view of another imager that gave details on each of the seven worlds that flew about the yellow sky light caused him puzzlement. "Servant for aberrant behaviors, our tools say the fourth world has a pull down strength twice that of Nest. Why would any Soft Skin live there?"

The old male emitted a complex mix of trail, territorial and releaser pheromones, tinged with excitement pheromone. "Hunter One, perhaps these Soft Skins come from a world with such a heavy pull down. If so, that explains why they did not fly down to Warmth. It has not the right pull down for their lives. Have you studied the other life on Nest and how each lifeform requires a certain set of life boundaries to thrive? Perhaps—"

"Enough!" Hunter yelled in a harsh flow of alarm and command pheromones. "I am no fool. The lifeforms of Nest are well known to me. Including the tree-climbing Soft Skins that live in the depths of our forests. These Soft Skins prefer yellow sky lights. They live on a world with twice our pull down strength. It matters not. We will—"

"Leader!" cried the Servant who studied distant sky lights. "Look at the third world! Our imager reveals it. It resembles Nest! Its pull down is what we now live with and its air is high in metabolizing gases and low in waste air," the Servant said with a rush of excitement, trail, territorial and releaser pheromones. "There are no radiative emissions from it. The Soft Skins do not live on it. It could be our eleventh colony world!"

Hunter saw that. The tools affixed to the hard shell of his flying nest were diverse and complex. They sensed all sorts of emissions. They could tell the mix of gases that filled a world's air, the type of water on its surface and whether anything artificial was present on a world. His Servants used those tools to build an image of the outer world. His work was to lead a Swarm to a new nesting place, claim it, defend it and send down Pods filled with small ones to grow and thrive on the new world. World number three did indeed resemble Nest. Its discovery alone justified his decision to follow the Soft Skins. Its emptiness called to him. It gave added reason to pursue the Soft Skin flying nests, destroy them and then remove the Soft Skins on world four so no one could harm their younglings.

"Servant for propulsive devices, push us after the fleeing Soft Skins," he scent cast to the older male. "Speaker To All, direct our other nests to follow in six-group form. Flight Servant, send out the scent path which we must follow to reach these Soft Skin nests!"

Mixed flows of aggregation, trail, territorial and alarm pheromones flowed through the Flight Chamber. And thence outward to the nests flown by his Support Hunters. They would obey. All Swarmers would obey now that a world like Nest had been discovered. Removing pests like the Soft Skins was a task they had done often on Nest, and on other colony worlds. While the web of life might be hurt on world four by the killing of these Soft Skins, he must make certain the web of life on world three stayed intact. It was vital for that web to survive so their offspring would have plentiful food to feed on as they grew to mature Swarmers. While artificial foods were present in each flying nest, no Swarmer enjoyed them. Natural foods were vital for the health of young Swarmers. He would see that the next load of colonizing nests had plenty to eat on world three.

"Hunter One," scent cast the Matron from behind him. "Remember my judgment from the Challenge? You and your fellow Hunters must find answers before you eliminate all Soft Skins. Where do they come from? Are there more who might come to this sky light? Do they have more colonies like ours? Set your aberrant behaviors Servant to the study of these questions," she said in a mix of trail, territorial and aggregation pheromones, making clear her demand was for the benefit of all Swarmers.

"Servant of aberrations, do you have answers for the Matron?" he scent cast.

The older male lowered his antennae in a sign of regret. "I do not have those answers. I know only what we have observed, and what we can perceive in the trail images they sent to us," he said in a mix of releaser and stay away pheromones. "These large Soft Skins come in both male and female variations. They are comfortable living in a pull down field twice that of Nest. They have at least one colony, which lies in this sky light system. Their stinger tools are the equal of our own. They have other tools that send messages which we do not understand. And they do not know how to talk by way of pheromones."

Hunter One briefly wondered how any intelligent sky traveling lifeform could not talk by way of pheromones. All lifeforms on Nest spoke in pheromones, whether a few like the tiny Soft Skins that dug holes in the land, or in many like the tree-climbing Soft Skins that always sought to steal any possession of a Swarmer. What other means of speaking could exist? The image of world three pushed such thoughts out of his attention. Here was a new colony world ideal for Swarmers. Here was a land nest of Soft Skins. The land nest must be removed, or else the Soft Skins would steal food and resources and artificial nests from their new Swarmer colony. While all their larval Pods had gone down to the world of Warmth, more colony Pods would arrive in other Swarmer nests, once he brought word of this sweet-smelling world to his cohort and to the Matrons of Nest. There would be a happy flood of Swarmer flying nests traveling out to this sky light. Now, he must complete what he had begun on the world of

Warmth. The final removal of all Soft Skins from the domain of Swarmers must now proceed.

♦ ♦ ♦

"Captain! The wasp ships have arrived," called Daisy from below.

Jacob looked to his situational holo. It did indeed show the red icons of six ships now appearing at the edge of Kepler 10's magnetosphere. It was 20 hours since they had arrived. Which meant his ships were in the middle of the system, not yet arrived at the system's outermost ice ball world. The frigate *Aldertag* was still heading their way. He looked ahead.

"Navigation, what is the speed of the wasp ships?"

Louise looked back to him, her expression concerned. "They are up to one-tenth lightspeed. Our speed inward," she said.

Which meant that the battle group would arrive at the fourth planet colony just as the wasps reached the outermost world of the system. That world lay at 19 AU out from the star. The wasps were now 45 AU out. Should they orbit the ice world and wait for the wasps? Or should they prepare for a fight closer to the colony world?

"Chief Warrant Officer O'Connor, what is your opinion about the best location to battle these wasps?"

The Marine looked up from his seat. So did Daisy and Branstead, both looking curious.

"Captain, I suggest we fight them out near the moon of the fourth world, which the locals call Valhalla." He shrugged. "What can I say, most of the colonists hail from Minnesota and are of Scandinavian heritage."

"Why?" Jacob probed.

The man's gray eyes fixed on him. "To reduce the chances for a wasp ship to do a swing around attack on Valhalla. If we battle out by planet six or seven, part of the wasp fleet could swing around our battle group and head inward. They could hit the colony with nukes and their plasma lightning bombs." He gestured at the front wallscreen which now showed Valhalla and its moon. "The local moon is just 300,000 klicks away from Valhalla. If we battle them at the midway point between the moon and the planet, our ships could move sideways just as quickly as the wasps could. And therefore intercept any wasp ship on a missile launch trajectory."

Jacob mentally played with angles and trajectories based on Archimedes' triangle. He saw what the Marine was saying. "So, being closer to Valhalla makes it harder for the wasps to swing off to a side vector track that would let them bypass our ships?"

"Exactly," O'Connor said.

He looked again at the situational holo that showed ships, moons and the system's seven worlds. The battle group's inward trajectory would take them by the seventh world as they headed for Valhalla. Worlds one, two, three and five were scattered around the star, on different orbital tracks. Though planet three was just twenty degrees ahead of Valhalla. He looked to Willard.

"Science, why would the wasps attack Valhalla? To date they've come after us. Why attack the planet?"

Willard tapped his control pillar. A new image went up on the wallscreen. He pointed. "Because of that world. Planet three is similar in size and vegetation to the fourth world of Kepler 22. Most vitally, its gravity is just a half gee. Like at Kepler 22. Its atmosphere is 30 percent oxygen, with more CO_2 than is normal for Earth. That means planet three is jungle hot, humid, with plenty of oxy. It is the kind of planet these wasps may have evolved on." Willard paused, then looked his way. "Captain, the wasps may attack our people on Valhalla because they see a perfect wasp colony world in *this* system. They attacked us when we came close to their new colony world. Why shouldn't they do the same here? And add the colony into the mix so this system would not have anyone in it to be a threat to their colonists?"

Jacob did not like what Willard was saying. It made too much sense. He looked back to where two of his friends were seated. "Ensign Antonova, Ensign Mendoza, come up here."

His friends arrived. They saluted him. He saluted them back. Were they happy together, he briefly wondered. They had spent more time together during the rest breaks as the battle group moved in system. Putting that aside, he focused on Lori.

"Ensign Antonova, you had some early insights into the wasp people when we discovered the meeting site attack. What can we do to discourage them from attacking our people?"

She looked over to Branstead, her deck chief. The woman's tanned face showed a quick smile, followed by a nod. Lori looked back to him.

"Captain, I suggest we create a new cartoon video. This one should show an image of Valhalla with a circle of people around it. Remember the old images of Earth from early this century? During the global warming crisis?" She caught her breath. "Let us create a cartoon that shows humans standing on the surface of Valhalla, then show our nine ships lined up in space above them, to signal we are protecting these people. Next, the cartoon can show the incoming six wasp ships stopping, then turning around and departing. It's a way of telling the wasps we are defending the world of Valhalla."

Jacob liked that idea. He looked to Carlos. "Ensign Mendoza, do you agree with chief O'Connor's reasoning for fighting close to Valhalla, rather than far away?"

He pursed his lips and grew thoughtful. Then he nodded. "I do. Fighting further out does indeed give the wasps better room to maneuver around us. Fighting closer in, say at 200,000 klicks out from Valhalla, lets us spread our ships out and thereby have a broader field of fire. Course, Rosemary and Oliver could say this better than I can."

Jacob doubted that. The man was not only a world-class chess player, he was able to compose algorithms in his head that set out an ideal navigation vector track. They would need his talents amid the mixed gravity fields of Valhalla and its moon. He looked to Alicia.

"Lieutenant Branstead, can your people create such a cartoon? And do it before the wasps arrive near Valhalla?"

"We can," Alicia said. "Can we do anything else to assist you?"

"Yes," Jacob said, thinking ahead to the future. "You and Ensign Antonova both made the point these wasp aliens likely communicate by way of pheromones. So. Can we figure out how to send a radio signal that causes pheromone emissions at the other end?" A memory hit him hard. "Maybe that was what the wasp satellite was trying to do when we first arrived. But we rely on voice modulation and images to communicate. The wasps may not. Can it be done?"

"We can try," Alicia said, her expression doubtful. "But we lack one of their signaling devices. So we do not know how they use radio waves to evoke a smell at the receiving end. I'll get my best linguists working on it."

"Good. Finish the cartoon before the wasps get to four." Jacob looked up. "AI Melody, open a neutrino comlink with the captain of the ship *Aldertag*."

"You wish to speak redundantly to more humans?" the AI said, its tone . . . he could swear it sounded amused. "Neutrino comlink established. Image projected."

The front wallscreen now grew a new inset image. It showed a pale-skinned, older woman who might be hitting 50. Or more. Jacob could not tell. Her face was smooth and showed no wrinkles. Only the creases around her eyes, and the gray streaks in her blond hair betrayed the fact she was older than most ship captains in the battle group. Her pale blue eyes looked at him.

"Captain Renselaer, good to hear from you. I am Captain Joan Sunderland. To my left is my XO, Oscar Abimbola of Nigeria. We are heading your way as fast as we can."

Jacob looked down at the screen in his right armrest, saw the personnel data on Sunderland, and smiled. "So you hail from Minnesota, Captain Sunderland?"

The woman smiled briefly. "I do. It was one reason Earth Command dispatched me here. My Scandinavian heritage matches the backgrounds of most of the settlers."

Jacob noticed the tall, middle-aged black man who sat to Sunderland's left was attentive and watchful. Good. That was what a good XO should be like. He nodded. "So tell me how the colonists are living on Valhalla. How many population concentrations? Towns, villages and so forth."

Her expression grew serious. "You wonder how many might be killed by orbital bombardment. The 71,233 colonists are mostly dispersed in rural homesteads in the northern temperate zone of the largest continent. They farm, they cut timber, they trade among themselves. There are seven small villages of a few thousand people." She paused and looked down at her own armrest screen, then looked up. "The single urban area big enough to be called a city is Stockholm. It has the only landing pad big enough for a spaceship. Shuttles can land in the backcountry of course. Anyway, Stockholm has 12,000 or so people living in it. Do you expect the wasp aliens to attack the colony?"

"Thank you for that information. And yes, I do expect them to *try* to attack Valhalla." It meant at least half the colonists lived in dispersed areas that would not be subject to nuke bombs. Or the lightning plasma bombs. He tapped a stud on his armrest. "Captain Sunderland, I'm transmitting to you the full record of our battles with the wasp aliens, their ships, their weapons fire, all of it that we encountered. Study it. See the formations we used. And in particular, be aware that the wasp energy beams have a greater range than our ship-mounted lasers."

She frowned. "That is a bother. My XO and I will study this record along with our Tactical and Weapons people. Thank you for the data."

Jacob waved. "Just doing what needs to be done. Now for part two. Stop your acceleration out to us. Hold position out by planet seven. Our battle group will join you there," he said calmly, hoping the woman could tell from his tone that this was a considered choice. "For your information, I have decided to mount a defense of Valhalla by taking position between its moon and the planet, at 200,000 klicks out. There are strong tactical reasons for fighting close to the planet. I look forward to the *Aldertag* joining our group in the next few hours."

The woman bit her lip. "So do we, Captain Renselaer. It sounds like we have a deadly enemy coming our way."

"You do. But this battle group will fight, overcome and lose lives if need be in order to defend the colonists of Valhalla. You have my word on that."

She nodded, her expression deeply serious. "Thank you. *Aldertag* out."

The image disappeared.

Jacob sat back in his seat, running through his mind all the tactical maneuvers that were possible with a battle group of three frigates, three destroyers, two cruisers and a Battlestar. No one bothered him. No one spoke to him. Perhaps they were all thinking ahead to the coming battle. He knew he was.

CHAPTER SEVENTEEN

Hunter One watched the new imagery transmitted from the Soft Skins. This one said the obvious. There were Soft Skins on world four, the Soft Skin flying nests would protect them, and they wished the Swarm to leave the system. He could not help but release a humor pheromone. Which made its way to the Matron and the twelve Servants in the Flight Chamber. How could such intelligent Soft Skins be so lacking in basic survival understanding?

"Leader," called the Servant for aberrant social behaviors. "Do we send a reply?"

It seemed pointless. Still, the senior Hunters and Matrons on Nest would expect him to do his best to rid this system of Soft Skin pests before he killed them all. On Nest, some hard shell and soft shell pests had needed only to see the colors of a Swarmer to send them fleeing. Others had fled upon seeing a few die from stinger thrusts. A few required mandible bites. He would give these blind, unhearing Soft Skins a chance to flee.

"Yes. Reply with an image map that tells them to remove the Soft Skins on world four and for all to leave this group of worlds," he scent cast in a strong flow of signal and territorial pheromones. "Use parts of their image signal if that is worthwhile."

"Proceeding on creation of the map reply," the older male replied. "It will be ready in 900 wing beats."

"Hunter," called the Matron in a strong flow of sex and aggregation pheromones. "Have your Servants elsewhere on this nest determined how these Soft Skins speak among themselves? It is clear they do, in view of how jointly they move in biting us."

"They have not," he scent cast, adding a releaser pheromone to put an end to the issue. They were nearing world four and the clustered Soft Skin sky nests. "We will enter sky battle shortly. If any Soft Skins remain, such as on the surface of world four, my Servants will capture them, sting them into compliance and inform you of their results."

"Perhaps that is the best sky map for us," she scent cast softly.

He knew it was. "Speaker To All, scent cast to the other Support Hunters that we attack soon! Tell them to focus their sky bolts and sky light beams on the target I choose. We will kill these flying nests one by one!"

♦ ♦ ♦

Jacob saw the six wasp ships as they swung round the white bulk of Valhalla's moon. It had been an hour since the wasps had replied to Branstead's video with an image sequence that said all humans and all human ships must leave the Kepler 10 system. That was not going to happen. He looked ahead. Everyone was at their function post. He looked down. Daisy, Richard and Alicia were all seated and strapped in. Behind them were Carlos and Lori. Jacob looked aside at his seat's situational holo. The battle group was arranged in a ball of ships with the *Lepanto* at the center. It was a formation that said nothing about their defense and attack plans. Now, with the enemy just 90,000 kilometers away and approaching at 12,000 kilometers per minute, it was time to change things.

"All ships, go to Alert Hostile Enemy status. Weapons go Hot. Kills authorized. Move into Alpha Vortex formation!"

In the holo, the green ship icons of the group moved back, leaving the *Lepanto*, the *Chesapeake* and the *Hampton Roads* at the forefront, arranged in a triangular formation. The *Lepanto* held top slot, with the two cruisers moving down and out to 120 degree angles relevant to his ship. That made their front group a perfect triangle. Behind them the destroyers moved back 500 kilometers and assumed the same triangle formation, but tilted so their firing angle ahead would not hit the rears of the first row of ships. The three frigates moved back a further 500 klicks, and rotated their triangle formation so their front lasers had a clear field of fire. The Vortex formation resembled a long tube with ships arranged in a spiral. The Battlestar and the two cruisers covered the group's flanks due to having proton lasers on their sides, and on top and bottom for the *Lepanto*. The destroyers had proton lasers at their fronts, with tail CO_2 lasers. And the frigates had CO_2 lasers at their nose and tail. Every ship carried thermonuke-loaded missiles.

Acknowledgments came from every captain. Their images formed a row of faces along the top of the front wallscreen. The face of Joy Jefferson on the *Philippines Sea* looked happy. The woman knew she would be able to hit hard at the alien enemy. And wanted to hit hard! He smiled.

"Captain," called Richard from below. "Can my people man their Darts? We may need them for boarding a damaged enemy ship. I recall you saying we wished to capture some wasps and some of their signaling equipment."

He had indeed said that during the all ships video conference during the Alcubierre transit. "Chief O'Connor, order your men to their Darts. No one launches until I say so."

"Understood!" The man tapped quickly on his armrest, speaking hurriedly into the private comlink reserved for the Marines.

Jacob's holo cross-section of the *Lepanto* and its decks now showed four red spots lighting up near the rear Engines part of the hull. The Darts would launch out of a single missile silo, one after the other, before turning and aiming for the target ship.

"Captain," called Rosemary. "The wasp ships are spreading out. They are keeping their hexagon formation but are putting lots of room between each ship. Looks like they aim to envelop us."

Briefly he wondered why the wasps always tried to englobe his ships. Was this cultural or biological or the function of a rigid command structure? No matter. He was not bound by any rigid rule other than the prime rule—attack and defeat the enemy!

"All ships, move out at 9,000 klicks per minute," he said, relying on the continuous neutrino comlink to carry his words, just as they carried back the images of each ship captain.

Acknowledgments came. In his holo, the tubular grouping of nine starships moved forward toward the incoming ring of wasp ships. He hoped the wasp ships came within range of his antimatter cannon, but that was unlikely. Just as it was a certainty he would not allow any battle group ship to get within the range of the black hole weapon of the wasp aliens.

It was time to pick a target. "All ships, cross-link your Weapons stations. Maintain weapons fire on the single wasp ship we hit first. Let's see how quickly we can burn through that damned hull metal!"

"All stations are ready to fire," Oliver said from Weapons.

"Enemy has slowed to 9,000 kilometers per minute," called Louise from Navigation. "They are still in ring formation."

Jacob watched the distance counter get smaller as the two groups of ships moved toward each other. Fifteen thousand, fourteen, thirteen, twelve . . .

"Incoming enemy lasers!" called Oliver.

"All ships, go to jinking and jiggling," Jacob said firmly, avoiding the temptation to yell. Every ship captain knew how to use their attitude thrusters to push their ship off of a direct line of sight track so as to frustrate enemy gunners.

One green laser beam hit the nose of the *Lepanto*.

"Beam energy deflected by our adaptive optics lenses," called Joaquin from Life Support.

Now it began. "Weapons, all ships, fire your lasers at the wasp ship W3 at 140 degrees declination!"

Two green beams from the *Lepanto* were joined by two beams from each cruiser and beams from the destroyers and frigates. That made for twelve green laser beams striking the upper hull of the wasp ship he had selected.

"Hits!" cried Rosemary. "Spectroscope and electro-optics show water and air release. Punch through!"

Jacob focused on the telescopically enlarged image of the log-shaped alien ship whose icon showed W3. Its front ring of laser and lightning tubes were firing back. Like his fleet, the counterfire from the wasps was focusing on the frigate *Aldertag*. Sunderland and her people were at risk of ship destruction.

"*Chesapeake*! Move to block those beams hitting the *Aldertag*. All ships, continue firing on the wasp ship!"

His distance counter gave a separation of 7,213 kilometers. His ships and the wasp ships had slowed again to 900 kilometers per minute, allowing for better targeting on both sides. Yellow lightning bolts and green laser beams streamed against his ships while their own green laser beams and the destroyers' proton beams concentrated on a single ship. Time to mix things up.

"All ships, go to target rotation! Weapons, move your beams to wasp ship W4 at 160 degrees!"

"Firing," Oliver called. "Other ships joining my fire."

"Rotate to the next wasp ship once a minute," Jacob called to the Brazilian who had shown himself to be a maestro of energy beams. "Skip the giant wasp ship. Its hull is too thick to warrant gas laser attack. Rotate!"

As the wasp ships changed their laser and lightning bolt fire from the sheltered *Aldertag* to the front of the *Chesapeake*, Jacob knew it was time to go to the next step in his plan.

"*Chesapeake* and *Hampton Roads*, turn to present your flank to the enemy. Fire your proton lasers at the first wasp ship we hit. Let's see if we can blow W3 in half!" He looked to the right. "Navigation, swing us so we can add our right flank proton laser to this mix. Three proton beams, plus proton lasers from the destroyers and CO_2 lasers from the frigates, might just get us a kill!"

In the holo the green ship icons of his battle fleet changed orientation even as they stayed in Vortex formation. The counter hit 5,000 kilometers.

A star blossomed.

"One hostile splashed!" yelled Jefferson from the *Philippines Sea*.

"Captain!" yelled Rosemary. "The *Chesapeake* has a punch through on their right flank side. They are rotating to present their left flank to incoming fire. Their left side proton laser will begin firing shortly."

The black face of Rebecca looked to him from the wallscreen. "Fleet captain, we got hit deep. Our right side proton laser node is gone. Fifteen crew with it. We are continuing to fire on the enemy."

He knew that. Jacob could see that every battle group ship was firing either proton or CO_2 lasers at the wasps in a rotating target scheme. It had seemed like a good idea earlier.

"Swanson, fall back behind the *Lepanto*. *Hampton Roads*, move forward with us to block what beams you can. Fire your side proton laser at that wasp ship getting hit by our lasers. Do it now!"

"Moving," Swanson said.

"Coming up to join you," said Wilcox, his blue eyes blazing with fierce determination.

"Captain!" called Daisy. "We got a leaker. One wasp ship is moving out. It's aiming for Valhalla!"

Damn.

On the wallscreen, Joy Jefferson let out a screech. "I'm after him! You bastard! Let me burn your tail!"

No other ships left the Vortex formation. But Jacob could tell there was a desire to help the *Philippines Sea*.

"All ships, maintain formation! Captain Jefferson, you have my permission to pursue that wasp ship. Stop him by any means necessary! Do not let him get close enough to launch nukes at the planet!"

She didn't acknowledge. Instead, she told her Engines person to increase speed toward planet four.

It was time.

"All ships, go to Alpha Wheel formation. We are seven against their four." He looked ahead. "Weapons, activate the antimatter cannon."

"Activating," Oliver said. "But no enemy is within range."

"I know. We can still fire." He tracked the enemy ships arrangement and saw what he needed to see. "Navigation, shift our nose to aim at the giant wasp ship. But lead it by a twenty degree angle. Weapons, you ready to fire yet?"

"Ready."

"Fire!" yelled Jacob.

A black beam of negative antimatter shot out from the nose of the *Lepanto*. It streaked toward the spot in space where the giant wasp ship should be, in a few moments.

"Captain, the AM beam will lose coherence at 4,000 klicks," called Alicia.

"I know. But the antimatter will still be present on that target vector. Yes, it will be a cloud. And no, it cannot kill that ship when so dispersed. But I bet that wasp ship won't like what it does to their outer hull!"

"Yes!" cried Oliver as he understood Jacob's reasoning.

"We're hit bad!" yelled Metz from the *Marianas*. "Lost all thruster power. Still able to fire lasers and our plasma battery."

Jacob saw the telltale stream of water and air spewing out from the midbody of the frigate.

In the Wheel formation there was no chance for another ship to get between the frigate and incoming beams. Which it was now receiving from all four wasp ships.

A second star flared.

"Shit!" yelled Richard.

Deep frustration hit Jacob. They had killed a wasp ship and the wasps had killed one of their frigates.

"Fleet captain!" called Sunderland. "We are taking the beams now! What is your command?"

He made the decision he knew had to be made.

"All frigates, withdraw beyond enemy laser range! Go to max acceleration to get away. The rest of us can handle the enemy."

"Moving out at one percent, five, nine, ten psol," called Captain Lorenz from the *St. Mihiel*.

"We're also moving beyond the enemy beams," called Sunderland from the *Aldertag*.

His mind's eye filled with images. The destroyer *Philippines Sea* was curving off to one side in pursuit of the wasp ship that was trying to get close to Valhalla. Two frigates were now beyond enemy firing range. With one ship dead and three out of engagement range, that left him five ships against the four of the wasps. His eyes caught the names beside each icon. *Lepanto, Chesapeake, Hampton Roads, Salamis* and *Tsushima Strait*.

"All ships, concentrate your beams on the giant ship! Let's kill that big mother!"

♦ ♦ ♦

Hunter Seven felt pleasure at the perception image of a Soft Skin flying nest dying in a ball of sky light fire. Now, it was time for his nest to do the vital job of extinguishing Soft Skins from the land of world four. He shared Hunter One's conviction that world three must be made safe for a future colony of Swarmers. Their lives on Nest had proven that safety lay in killing or chasing off all intruders, all lifeforms that sought to live in the home range of Swarmers. That must now happen here.

"Stinger Servant, are we within flight range for our particle disruption seeds to land on the world below?" he scent cast.

"Not yet," the Servant replied, lowering his antennae in a show of regret that mixed with pheromones of aggregation as he spoke of his loyalty to Seven.

Frustration filled Seven. A Soft Skin nest even now closed on his nest. It fired red heavy sky light beams that hit near the propulsive part of his nest. Even though his Servant who guided the nest through dark space now moved the nest from side to side, in the classic flight formation of all Swarmers, still, the enemy hit more often than he missed.

"Leader!" scent cast the Servant in charge of propulsive devices. "One propulsive unit is dead! We now move at half our flight speed."

More frustration filled Seven's inner gut. His nest had but two propulsive devices to send them winging through cold dark space. Losing one meant a loss of flight ability.

"Stinger Servant! Fire our tail sky bolts at that creature! Bite him to death!"

"Biting!" the Servant scent cast strongly. "But our beams do not harm!"

Seven looked to the imager that showed the circle of world four. They were not far from its upper air zone. If they were to attack, now was the moment.

"Stinger Servant, fire a swarm of particle disruption seeds! Fire our Storm Bringer globes! Some will surely get through!"

♦ ♦ ♦

Hunter One felt no pleasure at the death of the Soft Skin flying nest. His Swarm had lost one of their own nests. Other nests were being badly damaged by the concentrated beams of the disgusting Soft Skins. While one Soft Skin nest pursued after Seven's nest, two other nests now flew off and out of range of his stingers. That left him with four nests against five Soft Skin nests. And those nests were coming directly at his dispersed nests, matching their ring to his ring.

"Alarm!" scent cast the male Servant who monitored external radiations. "Black beam particles are impacting on us! Two of our outer tool groups are dead."

"Our hard shell!" yelled One in a harsh flow of pheromones. "Is it intact?"

"It is," the Servant replied. "But the place where the heavy sky light beams cut deep into us is now being struck again by sky light beams. The outer hard shell piece we put in place is now gone!"

He could not allow his nest to lose its forward energy node. That would disable the Pull Down device. Hunter One looked again at the image of the Soft Skin nests. All five were concentrating their sky light beams on his nest. So. Leader against leader. He wished to kill whomever led the Soft Skins on the largest nest. But he had a duty which all Hunters had to first obey.

"Flight Servant, swing up!" he scent cast in a mix of alarm, signal and anger pheromones. "Take us away from this world! Move us to the outer magnetic boundary. We must return to Nest and advise other Hunters and Matrons of the existence of this new colony world!"

"Swinging up," scent cast the Servant.

He looked to another Swarmer. "Speaker To All, toss scent to the three nests flying with us that they are to join our journey outward. Tell them we will head first for Warmth to avoid giving the Soft Skins any scent of the direction to our home of Nest. Speak now!"

"Sending your scent outward," the Servant replied.

"We are moving to the edge of the range at which we can bite," called the Stinger Servant.

One ignored the obvious. There was one more task to accomplish before they took flight for Warmth, the presence of other Swarmers and the welcome they would receive on Nest, once he brought forth the news of a new colony world. Their loss of a six-group of nests plus one would be nothing when the colony news spread through Nest.

"Speaker To All, link my scent to that of Support Hunter Seven."

"Scent linked," the Servant said in a strong signal pheromone.

On a side imager there appeared the black and red striped head of Hunter Seven. He who had thought to challenge his leadership of the colonizing Swarm. The young male had one last duty to perform. Perhaps he would survive it.

"Support Hunter Seven, have you attacked the Soft Skin colony world?"

"I have," he replied in a mix of signal, trail and frustration pheromones. "A Soft Skin pursues us. It has killed one of our propulsive units."

Even better. "Then you cannot follow us out to the magnetic boundary as we head for Warmth, to later share the news of the new colony world with other Swarmers on Nest." Seven's five black eyes glistened in the white-yellow light of his Flight Chamber. "Take yourself and your nest out to the far reaches of this world assemblage.

Hide among the balls of ice. Keep watch on what the Soft Skins do here, after we leave. We will return with many more nests to claim world three for our people!"

The black antennae of Seven drooped. It was clear he understood he was a sacrifice to be made in order to distract the Soft Skins from following One's nest group.

"This nest moves outward," Seven said in a mix of primer, releaser and trail pheromones. There was no scent of aggregation in his reply. "My Servants, my Workers, my Fighters and my Matron will keep a high flight watch on the Soft Skins. Signal us when you return."

"I am a Hunter. You have my cohort promise that you will be signaled upon our return here to claim world three for the Swarm!"

"My wings grow tired. Until you return."

Seven's image vanished. On the imager that showed the nests of his people and of the Soft Skins, the nest of Seven now curved downward, in the opposite direction from the flight path One now followed with his three Support Hunters. As a Hunter, he felt pride that another Hunter now chose to lead the Soft Skin pests away from the other nests of the Swarm. Of course, every Swarmer nest had stingers in its tail, just like every living Swarmer. Surely Seven would fire on any pursuer. He might even survive to find refuge among the ice balls that flew about the outer edge of this world group.

"Propulsive Servant, move our wing speed to maximum. Let us leave this pest-filled place."

"Moving us to maximum wing speed," the Servant replied.

One settled down on his bench and contemplated just how he would present the fact of the loss of another flying nest to the Swarmers now working to colonize Warmth. They would be a practice audience. When he and his three allied nests then flew to Nest, he would have the perfect scent and pheromone flow to make clear what had happened with the Soft Skins was not a defeat, but a fortunate discovery of a new colony world.

♦ ♦ ♦

"Captain! The wasps are fleeing!" cried Daisy.

Jacob saw that incredible news in his situational holo. The giant wasp ship and its three allies were swinging up and away from the planetary ecliptic, clearly heading for the magnetosphere boundary. The wasp exit speed was now one percent of lightspeed and rapidly increasing. What was even more positive was the movement of the solo wasp ship that had launched nuke warheads at Valhalla. It was diving down, below the ecliptic, similarly aiming for the boundary.

"Tactical, what of the warheads launched by the wasp ship?" he called to Rosemary. "Are any entering the atmosphere?"

"A few are," she said. "Captain Jefferson's sharpshooters killed 31 with her proton laser. The proton lasers on the Star Navy base took out 14 more. Five are now entering the atmosphere. Two are going down faster, while three seem to be globular in shape. They are trailing behind the group of two."

Anger and frustration filled him. "What will they hit? Any sign they are guided?"

"No, they are not showing guidance ability," Rosemary replied, her voice catching. "They appear to be in freefall reentry mode. The two falling faster will hit the dense forest on the northern continent. The three falling slower will hit close to Stockholm." She looked back to him, her green eyes looking wet. "Does anyone on Valhalla have a fighter jet? A ground laser? Smart missiles?"

He didn't know. But someone else did know. "Andrew, link me up with O'Sullivan at the base. Quickly!"

"Sending a neutrino signal," the man replied swiftly.

"Fleet captain!" called Joy Jefferson from her image icon at the top of the wallscreen. "We're diving down after those warheads! We'll do our best to kill them!"

"Acknowledged!" he said quickly. "Do your best." Jacob wished he and the other ships were closer but they were on an outward track toward the local moon. The planet lay behind them.

"Captain?" called O'Sullivan. "Our moving neutrino tracker shows the wasp ships are going away. What's happening?"

He told the man about the five incoming warheads.

"Damn! I thought our proton lasers killed the last stragglers," he said. He lifted his helmeted head and fixed on Jacob. "We have no ground weaponry of any sort. No smart missiles. No lasers. Earth Command thought outfitting this base with six proton lasers would suffice for incoming asteroids, comets or a pirate raider."

"We got one!" cried Jefferson. "One of the heavies is dead."

O'Sullivan heard that. Jacob looked to Rosemary. "Tactical, what about the one heavy and the three lighter ones. Have they impacted?"

She shook her head, then spoke over her helmet comlink. "Not yet. The heavy will hit in four seconds. The three lighter ones in 30. The lighter ones will strike the western outskirts of Stockholm. Homes and businesses are there, from what I can see in our scope."

He looked up at the wallscreen. The ship's electro-optical scope was tightly focused on the part of Valhalla that was the warhead target. Green forest filled the top half of the image, with a grassy plain on the lower left and the silver sparkle of buildings and housing and factories over by the eastern seacoast.

A yellow flame blossomed among the trees.

"Anyone in the strike zone?"

"No, captain," Oliver said. "Warhead yield is atomic, about 50 kilotons. Thank God it was not a thermonuke!"

Jacob knew that. Still, the fallout rain from a 50 kiloton atomic blast would spread over dozens of miles of forest. But it would not reach any of the villages that lay west and south of Stockholm.

Three yellow lights that resembled lightning bolts now spread over the western edge of Stockholm. Black clouds formed.

"Those were plasma lightning globes!" Oliver yelled.

Jacob gave brief thanks to the Goddess that they had not been atomics. If they had, half of Stockholm would have been vaporized. As it was, a few city blocks were likely molten soil, with everyone in those blocks gone up into vapor. Hopefully most city residents were hiding in bunkers or out in the countryside, thanks to his earlier warning.

O'Sullivan looked down at a display in the com room, then up. His face was stricken. "Word from Stockholm landing pad. Their western Salonika neighborhood was hit. Three city blocks gone, in a spread out footprint. Storms are forming above the city. Their responders are heading out to help survivors."

Jacob slumped in his seat. Seventy-one ghosts from the *Marianas* now joined the ghosts from the *Britain* and the several hundred people who had died in the lightning plasma strikes. Telling himself that most of Valhalla was untouched and that most colonists were alive and healthy did nothing for him.

A hand touched him. Daisy.

"Jacob, you did your best. We all did our best. As did Captain Jefferson. She risked her ship by diving into the atmosphere at high velocity." Daisy's face held deep caring. "She's out safe. The frigates are safe. Our other ships are intact. We fought them off, Jacob. We beat the wasps!"

Had they? What would the four surviving wasp ships do? Would they head home and bring back dozens more ships to attack Valhalla? Or would they avoid any human ship? And what of the single wasp ship that was headed outward. Would it depart too? Or would they have to go hunting for it in the system's Kuiper Belt of comets?

He didn't know. So he fell back on routine he'd learned at the academy.

"All ships, change status to Alert Combat Ready. Make repairs to your ships. Stay alert for a return by the wasp ships." He ignored the blinking red lights and sirens. A useful thought hit him. "Daisy, uh, damn. Can you take your LCA down to Stockholm and help them evac the wounded to their hospital? Or up here to our Med Hall on the *Lepanto*?"

"I can," she said, her expression moving from sorrow to determination. "When do I go?"

"Now."

"Fleet captain," called Swanson from the *Chesapeake*. "I will send our LCA down to help. With your approval."

"Same for me," growled Wilcox from the *Hampton Roads*. "We're not that far away. Can we send our LCA down to help?"

"Yes and yes," Jacob replied. "Captains, thank you for helping me find a way to help the people we are pledged to protect."

Both captains gave a nod and turned to their XOs to get things going.

Below him, Richard looked up. His gray eyes fixed on Jacob. "Welcome to the side of combat that none of us like to see. Or feel. It won't go away. But . . . you saved a lot of lives. And most of the battle group is intact. To me, that counts for a victory."

Jacob hoped that was true. He didn't know if it was, this being his first experience with real combat. He just knew that he had gained more ghosts to populate his dreams and nightmares.

"You also have me," Daisy said, standing up.

Had he spoken that aloud?

The faces of his Bridge crew told him he had.

"Thank you, XO. And thank you, everyone on the Bridge, for fighting our first interstellar battle. Let us hope it will be our last such encounter."

People nodded. A few smiled. Richard shook his head and sat down. Alicia gave him a thumbs-up and an encouraging smile. Daisy gripped his hand, or rather the glove of his vacsuit. She gave him a smile.

"The future will be better," she said.

He hoped so. Jacob hoped to the ends of the universe that bloody combat and dead ships and particles of flesh that had once been people would not populate his future. But this was what he had signed up for, when he joined the Star Navy. He had to prepare for more such bloodiness in any future he might have. At least that future would include Daisy.

"It surely will be better," he said, showing her the smile he always gave his mother.

Together they held hands on the Bridge of the Battlestar *Lepanto*, together in thoughts, together in sadness, united in love and determination.

THE END

ABOUT THE AUTHOR

T. Jackson King (Tom) is a professional archaeologist, journalist and retired Hippie. He learned early on to question authority and find answers for himself, thanks to reading lots of science fiction. He also worked at a radiocarbon dating laboratory at UC Riverside and UCLA. Tom attended college in Paris and Tokyo. He is a graduate of UCLA (M.A. 1976, archaeology) and the University of Tennessee (B.Sc. 1971, journalism). He has worked as an archaeologist in the American Southwest and has traveled widely in Europe, Russia, Japan, Canada, Mexico and the USA. Other jobs have included short order cook, hotel clerk, legal assistant, telephone order taker, investigative reporter and newspaper editor. He also survived the warped speech-talk of local politicians and escaped with his hide intact. Tom writes hard science fiction, anthropological scifi, dark fantasy/horror and contemporary fantasy/magic realism. Tom's novels are **DEFEAT THE ALIENS** (2016), **FIGHT THE ALIENS** (2016), **FIRST CONTACT** (2015), **ESCAPE FROM ALIENS** (2015), **ALIENS VS. HUMANS** (2015), **FREEDOM VS. ALIENS** (2015), **HUMANS VS. ALIENS** (2015), **GENECODE ILLEGAL** (2014), **EARTH VS. ALIENS** (2014), **ALIEN ASSASSIN** (2014), **THE MEMORY SINGER** (2014), **ANARCHATE VIGILANTE** (2014), **GALACTIC VIGILANTE** (2013), **NEBULA VIGILANTE** (2013), **SPEAKER TO ALIENS** (2013), **GALACTIC AVATAR** (2013), **STELLAR ASSASSIN** (2013), **STAR VIGILANTE** (2012), **THE GAEAN ENCHANTMENT** (2012), **LITTLE BROTHER'S WORLD** (2010), **ANCESTOR'S WORLD** (1996, with A.C. Crispin), and **RETREAD SHOP** (1988, 2012). His short stories appeared in **JUDGMENT DAY AND OTHER DREAMS** (2009). His poetry appeared in **MOTHER EARTH'S STRETCH MARKS** (2009). Tom lives in Santa Fe, New Mexico, USA with his wife Sue. More information on Tom's writings can be found at www.tjacksonking.com/.

PRAISE FOR T. JACKSON KING'S BOOKS

EARTH VS. ALIENS

"This story is the best space opera I've read in many years. The author knows his Mammalian Behavior. If we're lucky it'll become a movie soon. Many of the ideas are BRAND NEW and I loved the adaptability of people in the story line. AWESOME!!"—**Phil W. King,** *Amazon*

"It's good space opera. I liked the story and wanted to know what happened next. The characters are interesting and culturally diverse. The underlying theme is that humans are part of nature and nature is red of tooth and claw. Therefore, humans are naturally violent, which fortunately makes them a match for the predators from space."—**Frank C. Hemingway,** *Amazon*

STAR VIGILANTE

"For a fast-paced adventure with cool tech, choose *Star Vigilante*. This is the story of three outsiders. Can three outsiders bond together to save Eliana's planet from eco-destruction at the hands of a ruthless mining enterprise?" –**Bonnie Gordon,** *Los Alamos Daily Post*

STELLAR ASSASSIN
"T. Jackson King's *Stellar Assassin* is an ambitious science fiction epic that sings! Filled with totally alien lifeforms, one lonely human, an archaeologist named Al Lancaster must find his way through trade guilds, political maneuvering and indentured servitude, while trying to reconcile his new career as an assassin with his deeply-held belief in the teachings of Buddha. . . This is a huge, colorful, complicated world with complex characters, outstanding dialogue, believable motivations, wonderful high-tech battle sequences and, on occasion, a real heart-stringer . . . This is an almost perfectly edited novel as well, which is a bonus. This is a wonderful novel, written by a wonderful author . . .Bravo! Five Stars!" –**Linell Jeppsen,** *Amazon*

LITTLE BROTHER'S WORLD

"If you're sensing a whiff of Andre Norton or Robert A. Heinlein, you're not mistaken . . . The influence is certainly there, but *Little Brother's World* is no mere imitation of *Star Man's Son* or *Citizen of the Galaxy*. Rather, it takes the sensibility of those sorts of books and makes of it something fresh and new. T. Jackson King is doing his part to further the great conversation of science fiction; it'll be interesting to see where he goes next."–**Don Sakers,** *Analog*

"When I'm turning a friend on to a good writer I've just discovered, I'll often say something like, "Give him ten pages and you'll never be able to put him down." Once in a long while, I'll say, "Give him five pages." It took T. Jackson King exactly *one sentence* to set his hook so deep in me that I finished **LITTLE BROTHER'S WORLD** in a single sitting, and I'll be thinking about that vivid world for a long time to come. The last writer I can recall with the courage to make a protagonist out of someone as profoundly Different as Little Brother was James Tiptree Jr., with her remarkable debut novel **UP THE WALLS OF THE WORLD**. I think Mr. King has met that challenge even more successfully. His own writing DNA borrows genes from writers as diverse as Tiptree, Heinlein, Norton, Zelazny, Sturgeon, Pohl, and Doctorow, and splices them together very effectively." – **Spider Robinson, Hugo, Nebula and Campbell Award winner**

"*Little Brother's World* is a sci-fi novel where Genetic Engineering exists. . . It contains enough details and enough thrills to make the book buyers/readers grab it and settle in for an afternoon read. The book is well-written and had a well-defined plot . . . I never found a boring part in the story. It was fast-paced and kept me entertained all throughout. The characters are fascinating and likeable too. This book made me realize about a possible outcome, when finally science and technology wins over traditional ones. . . All in all, *Little Brother's World* is another sci-fi novel from T. Jackson King that is both exciting, thrilling and fun. Full of suspense, adventure, romance, secrets, conspiracies, this book would take you in a roller-coaster ride." –**Abby Flores,** *Bookshelf Confessions*

THE MEMORY SINGER

"A coming of age story reminiscent of Robert A. Heinlein or Alexei

Panshin. Jax [the main character] is a fun character, and her world is compelling. The social patterns of Ship life are fascinating, and the Alish'Tak [the main alien species] are sufficiently alien to make for a fairly complex book. Very enjoyable."—**Don Sakers,** *Analog Science Fiction*

"Author T. Jackson King brings his polished writing style, his knowledge of science fiction 'hardware,' and his believable aliens to his latest novel *The Memory Singer*. But all this is merely backdrop to the adventures of Jax Cochrane, a smart, rebellious teen who wants more from life than the confines of a generational starship. There are worlds of humans and aliens out there. When headstrong Jax decides that it's time to discover and explore them, nothing can hold back this defiant teen. You'll want to accompany this young woman . . in this fine coming-of-age story."—**Jean Kilczer,** *Amazon*

RETREAD SHOP

"Engaging alien characters, a likable protagonist, and a vividly realized world make King's first sf novel a good purchase for sf collections."–*Library Journal*

"A very pleasant tour through the author's inventive mind, and an above average story as well."–*Science Fiction Chronicle*

"Fun, with lots of outrageously weird aliens."—*Locus*

"The writing is sharp, the plotting tight, and the twists ingenious. It would be worth reading, if only for the beautiful delineations of alien races working with and against one another against the background of an interstellar marketplace. The story carries you . . . with a verve and vigor that bodes well for future stories by this author. Recommended."–*Science Fiction Review*

"For weird aliens, and I do mean weird, choose **Retread Shop**. The story takes place on a galactic trading base, where hundreds of species try to gain the upper hand for themselves and for their group. Sixteen year-old billy is the sole human on the Retread Shop, stranded when his parents and their shipmates perished. What really makes the ride fun are the aliens Billy teams up with, including two who are plants. It's herbivores vs. carnivores, herd species vs. loners, mammals vs. insects and so on. The wild variety of physical types is only matched by the extensive array of cultures, which makes for a very entertaining read." –**Bonnie Gordon,** *Los Alamos Daily Post*

"Similar in feel to Roger Zelazny's Alien Speedway series is ***Retread Shop*** by T. Jackson King. It's an orphan-human-in-alien-society-makes-good story. Well-written and entertaining, it could be read either as a Young Adult or as straight SF with equal enjoyment." – **Chuq Von Rospach,** *OtherRealms 22*

"If you liked Stephen Goldin's Jade Darcy books duo, and Julie Czerneda's Clan trilogy, then you will probably like ***Retread Shop*** since it too has multiple aliens, an eatery, and an infinity of odd events that range from riots, to conspiracy, to exploring new worlds and to alien eating habits . . . It's a fun reader's ride and thoroughly entertaining. And, sigh, I wish that the author would write more books set in this background." –**Lyn McConchie, co-author of the** ***Beastmaster*** **series**

HUMANS VS. ALIENS

"Another great book from this author. This series has great characters and story is wall to wall excitement. Look forward to next book."— **William R. Thomas,** *Amazon*

"Humans are once again aggressive and blood thirsty to defend the Earth. Pace is quick and action is plentiful. Some unexpected plot twists, but you always know the home team is the best."—**C. Cook,** *Amazon*

ANCESTOR'S WORLD

"T. Jackson King is a professional archaeologist and he uses that to great advantage in *Ancestor's World*. I was just as fascinated by the details of the archaeology procedures as I was by the unfolding of the plot . . . What follows is a tightly plotted, suspenseful novel."– *Absolute Magnitude*

"The latest in the StarBridge series from King, a former Rogue Valley resident now living and writing in Arizona, follows the action on planet Na-Dina, where the tombs of 46 dynasties have lain undisturbed for 6,000 years until a human archaeologist and a galactic gumshoe show up. Set your phasers for fun."–*Medford Mail Tribune*

ALIEN ASSASSIN
"The Assassin series is required reading in adventure, excitement and daring. The galactic vistas, the advanced alien technologies and the action make all the Assassin books a guarantee of a good read. Please keep them coming!"—**C. B. Symons,** *Amazon*

"KING STRIKES AGAIN! Yes, T. Jackson King gives us yet again a great space adventure. I loved the drama and adventure in this book. There is treachery in this one too which heightens the suspense. Being the only human isn't easy, but Al pulls it off. Loved the Dino babies and how they are being developed into an important part of the family of assassins. All of the fun takes place right here and we are not left hanging off the cliff. Write on T.J."—**K. McClell,** *Amazon*

THE GAEAN ENCHANTMENT
"For magic, a quest and a new battle around every corner, go with *The Gaean Enchantment*. In this novel, Earth has entered a new phase as it cycles through the universe. In this phase, some kinds of "magic" work, but tech is rapidly ceasing to function. In the world of this book, incantation and sympathetic magic function through connection to spirit figures who might be described as gods." – **Bonnie Gordon,** *Los Alamos Daily Post*

"In *The Gaean Enchantment* the main character, Thomas, back from Vietnam and with all the PTSD that many soldiers have—nightmares, blackouts—finds his truth through the finding of his totem animal, the buffalo Black Mane. He teaches Thomas that violence and killing must always be done as a last resort, and that the energies of his soul are more powerful than any arsenal . . . Don't miss this amazing novel of magic and soul transformation, deep love, and Artemis, goddess of the hunt and protector of women."–**Catherine Herbison-Wiget,** *Amazon*

JUDGMENT DAY AND OTHER DREAMS

"King is a prolific writer with an old-time approach–he tells straight-ahead stories and asks the big questions. No topic is off limits and he writes with an explorer's zest for uncovering the unknown. He takes readers right into the world of each story, so each rustle of a tree, each whisper of the wind, blows softly against your inner ear."–**Scott Turick,** *Daytona Beach News-Journal*

"Congratulations on the long overdue story collection, Tom! What I find most terrific is your range of topics and styles. You have always been an explorer."–**David Brin, Nebula and Hugo winner**

"I'm thoroughly loving [the stories]; the prose is the kind that makes me stop and savor it – roll phrases over my tongue – delicious. I loved the way you conjure up a whole world or civilization so economically."–**Sheila Finch, SF author**

"*Judgment Day and Other Dreams* . . . would make a valued addition to any science fiction or fantasy library. There is a satisfying and engrossing attention to detail within the varied stories . . . The common thread among all works is the intimate human element at the heart of each piece. King's prose displays a mastery over these myriad subjects without alienating the uninitiated, thus providing the reader with a smooth, coherent, and altogether enjoyable experience . . . King is able to initiate the reader naturally through plot and precise prose, as if being eased into a warm bath . . . There is a dedicated unity amongst some of the entries in this anthology that begs to be explored in longer formats. And the works which stand apart are just as notable and exemplify King's grasp of human emotions and interactions. This collection displays the qualities of fine writing backed by a knowledgeable hand and a vivid imagination . . . If *Judgment Day and Other Dreams* is anything to go by, T. Jackson King should be a household name." –**John Sulyok,** *Tangent Online*

Printed in Great Britain
by Amazon